# MIKE CAVALLARO's

# NICO BRAVO

## ⚡ AND THE ⚡
## HOUND OF HADES

:01

First Second

NEW YORK

First Second

Copyright © 2019 by Mike Cavallaro

Published by First Second
First Second is an imprint of Roaring Brook Press, a division
of Holtzbrinck Publishing Holdings Limited Partnership
175 Fifth Avenue, New York, NY 10010
All rights reserved

Don't miss your next favorite book from First Second! For the latest updates
go to firstsecondnewsletter.com and sign up for our enewsletter.

Library of Congress Control Number: 2018938076

Paperback ISBN: 978-1-62672-751-9
Hardcover ISBN: 978-1-250-19698-9

Our books may be purchased in bulk for promotional, educational, or business use.
Please contact your local bookseller or the Macmillan Corporate and Premium Sales Department at
(800) 221-7945 ext. 5442 or by email at MacmillanSpecialMarkets@macmillan.com.

First edition, 2019
Edited by Mark Siegel and Steve Behling
Book design by Rob Steen
Color by Gabrielle Gomez and Mike Cavallaro
Printed in China by 1010 Printing International Limited, North Point, Hong Kong

Written in fits and starts on whatever was handy, including scraps of paper, notepads, smartphones,
and laptops. The artwork was drawn digitally in Clip Studio on a MacBook Pro and a Cintiq 13HD,
lettered using Adobe Illustrator, and colored in Photoshop.

Paperback: 10 9 8 7 6 5 4 3 2 1
Hardcover: 10 9 8 7 6 5 4 3 2 1

*TO BART*

# PART 1:
# ROUND,
# LIKE A CUBE.

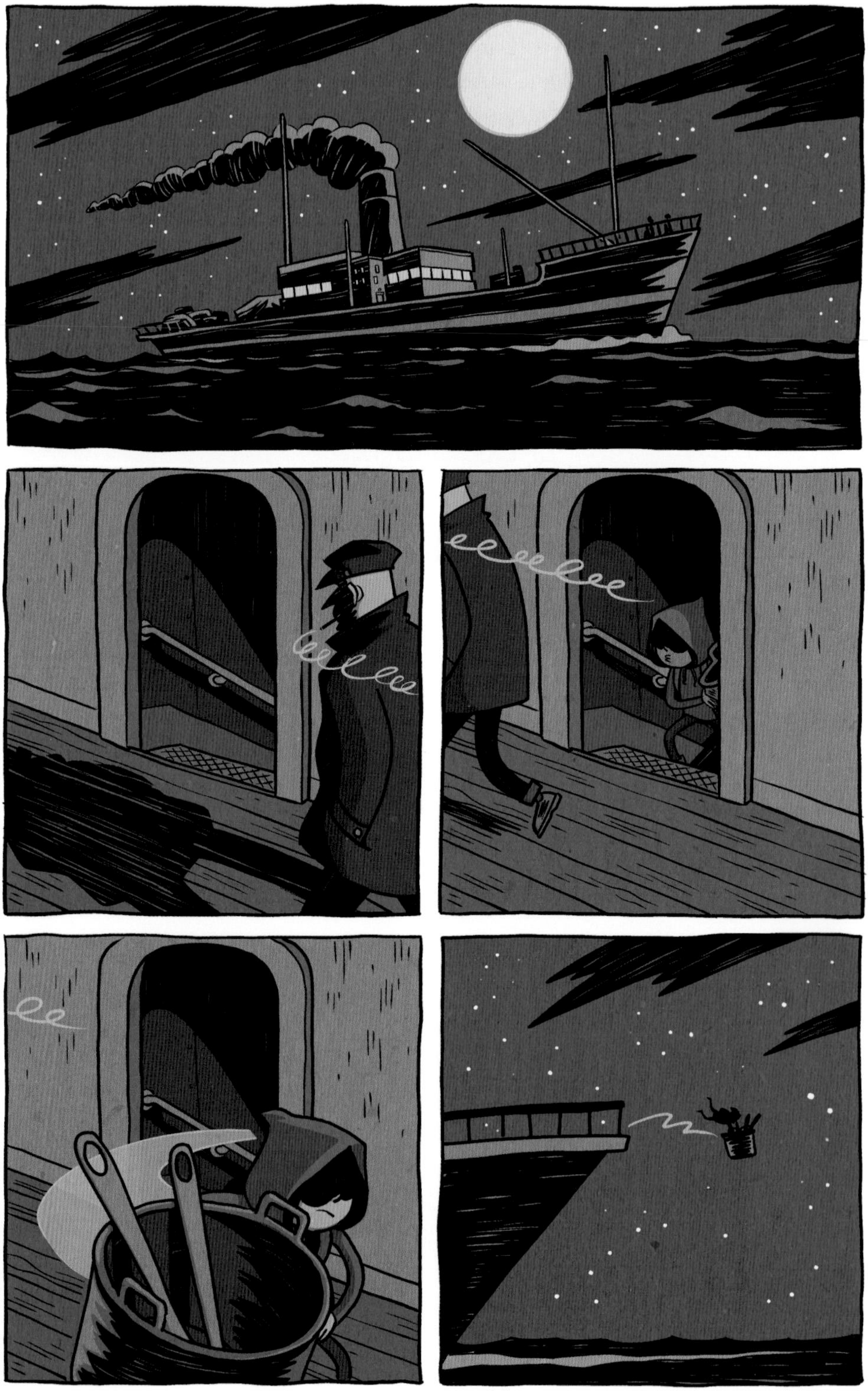

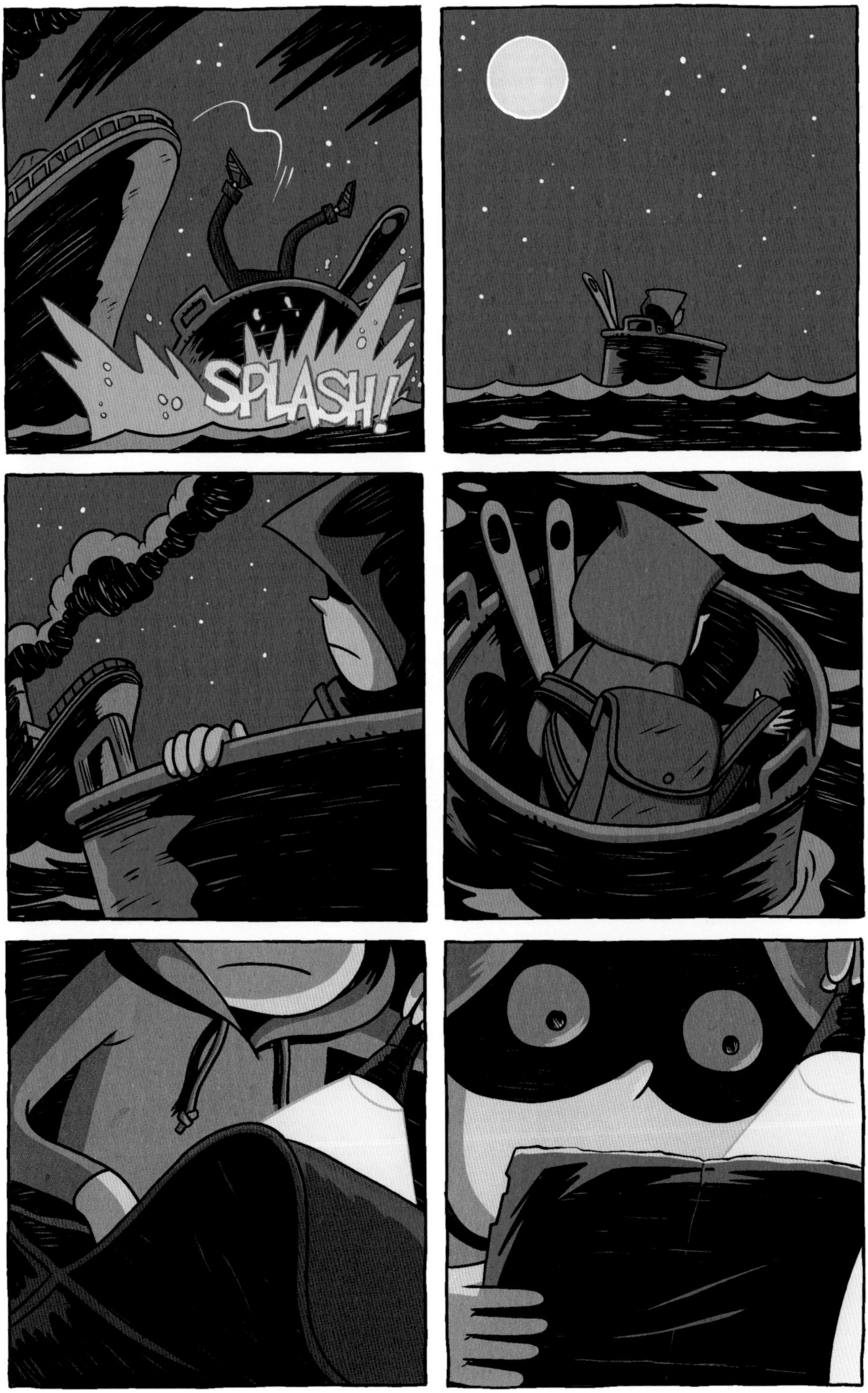
SPLASH!

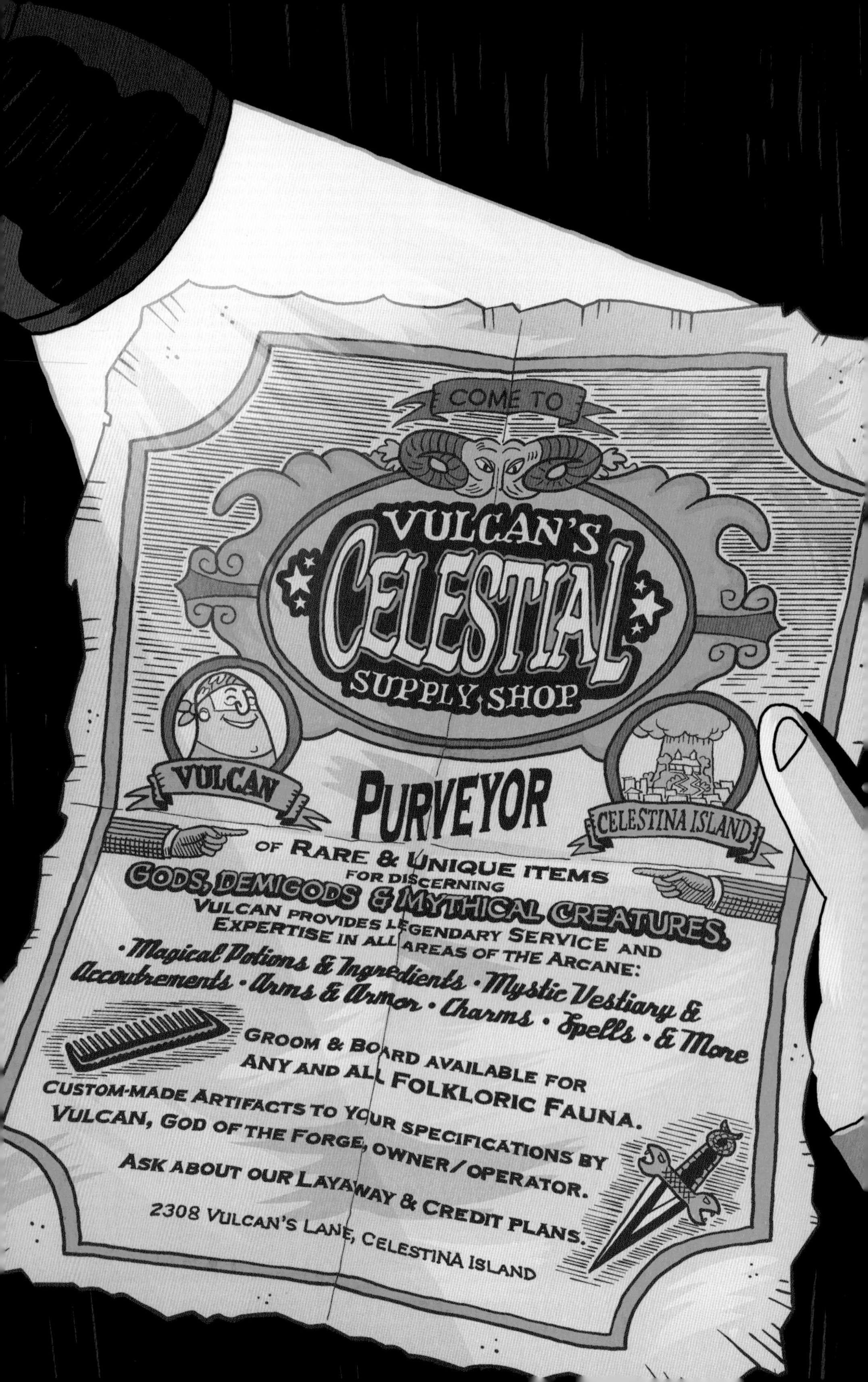
COME TO
VULCAN'S
CELESTIAL
SUPPLY SHOP
VULCAN
CELESTINA ISLAND
PURVEYOR
OF RARE & UNIQUE ITEMS
FOR DISCERNING
GODS, DEMIGODS & MYTHICAL CREATURES.
VULCAN PROVIDES LEGENDARY SERVICE AND
EXPERTISE IN ALL AREAS OF THE ARCANE:
• Magical Potions & Ingredients • Mystic Vestiary & Accoutrements • Arms & Armor • Charms • Spells • & More
GROOM & BOARD AVAILABLE FOR
ANY AND ALL FOLKLORIC FAUNA.
CUSTOM-MADE ARTIFACTS TO YOUR SPECIFICATIONS BY
VULCAN, GOD OF THE FORGE, OWNER/OPERATOR.
ASK ABOUT OUR LAYAWAY & CREDIT PLANS.
2308 VULCAN'S LANE, CELESTINA ISLAND

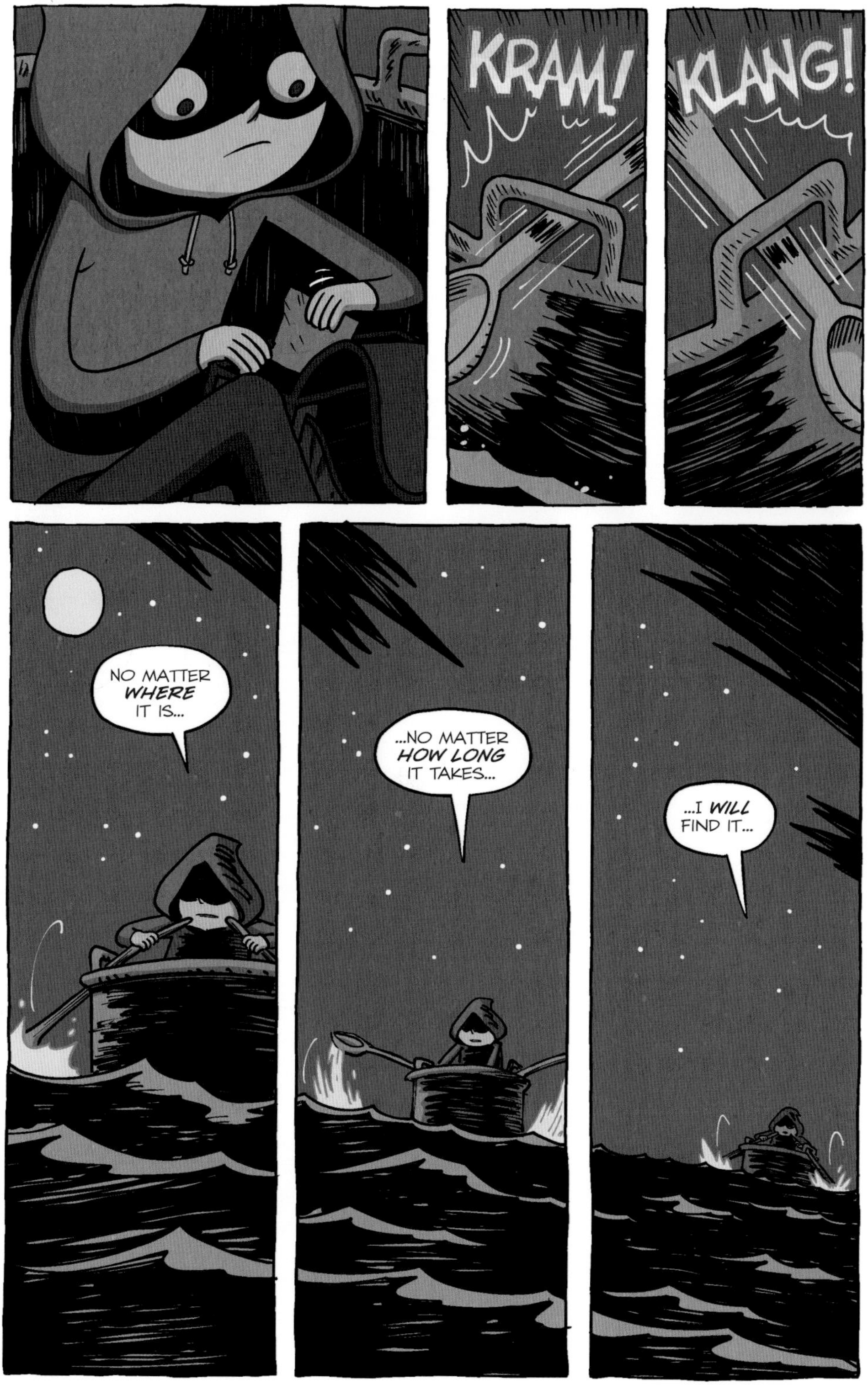
KRAM!
KLANG!
NO MATTER *WHERE* IT IS...
...NO MATTER *HOW LONG* IT TAKES...
...I *WILL* FIND IT...

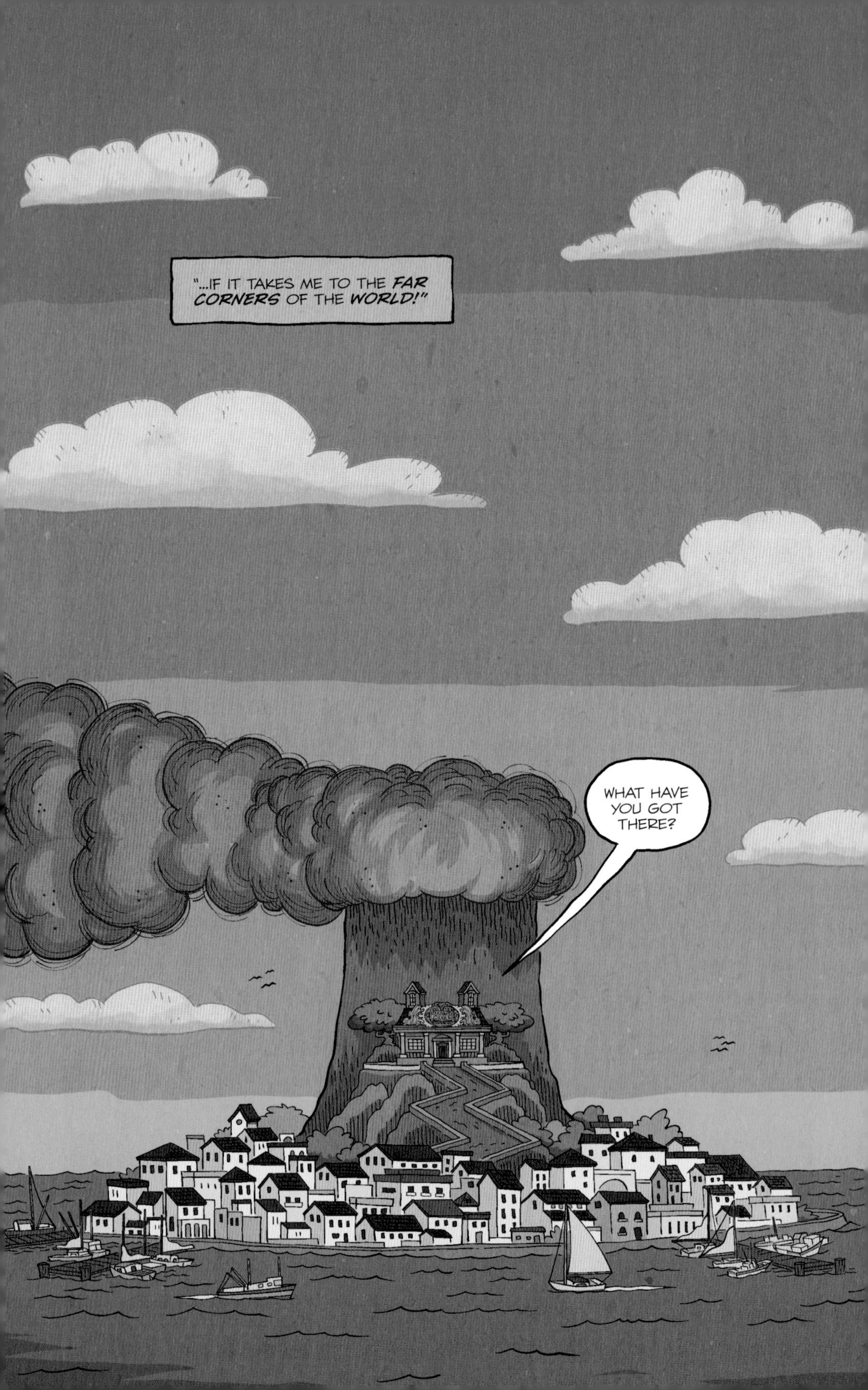
"...IF IT TAKES ME TO THE *FAR CORNERS* OF THE *WORLD!*"
WHAT HAVE YOU GOT THERE?

THE FAR CORNERS OF THE WORLD
WHAT'S THAT SUPPOSED TO MEAN, ANYWAY?
THE WORLD'S ROUND, YOU KNOW...
OF COURSE IT'S ROUND, BUCK...
...THE CORNERS ARE INVISIBLE...
...SEE?
Asgard
Olympus
YEAH?
YEAH. ACCORDING TO THIS, THERE'S EIGHT CORNERS AND WE LIVE RIGHT IN THE MIDDLE OF ONE...
Celestine Island
AND PEOPLE SAY I'M CRAZY...

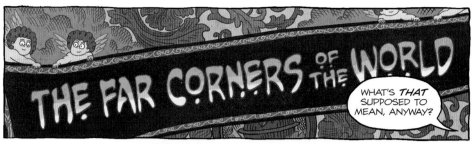

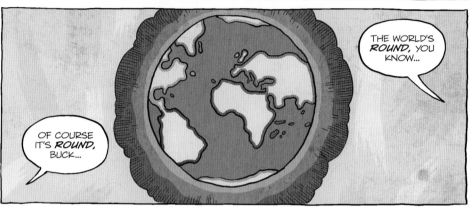

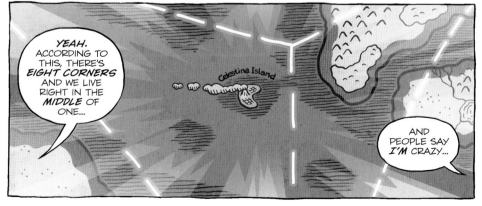

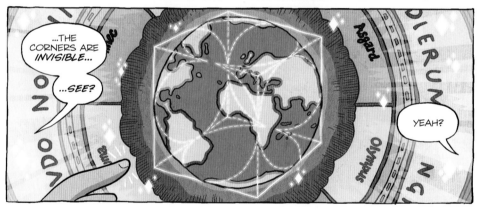

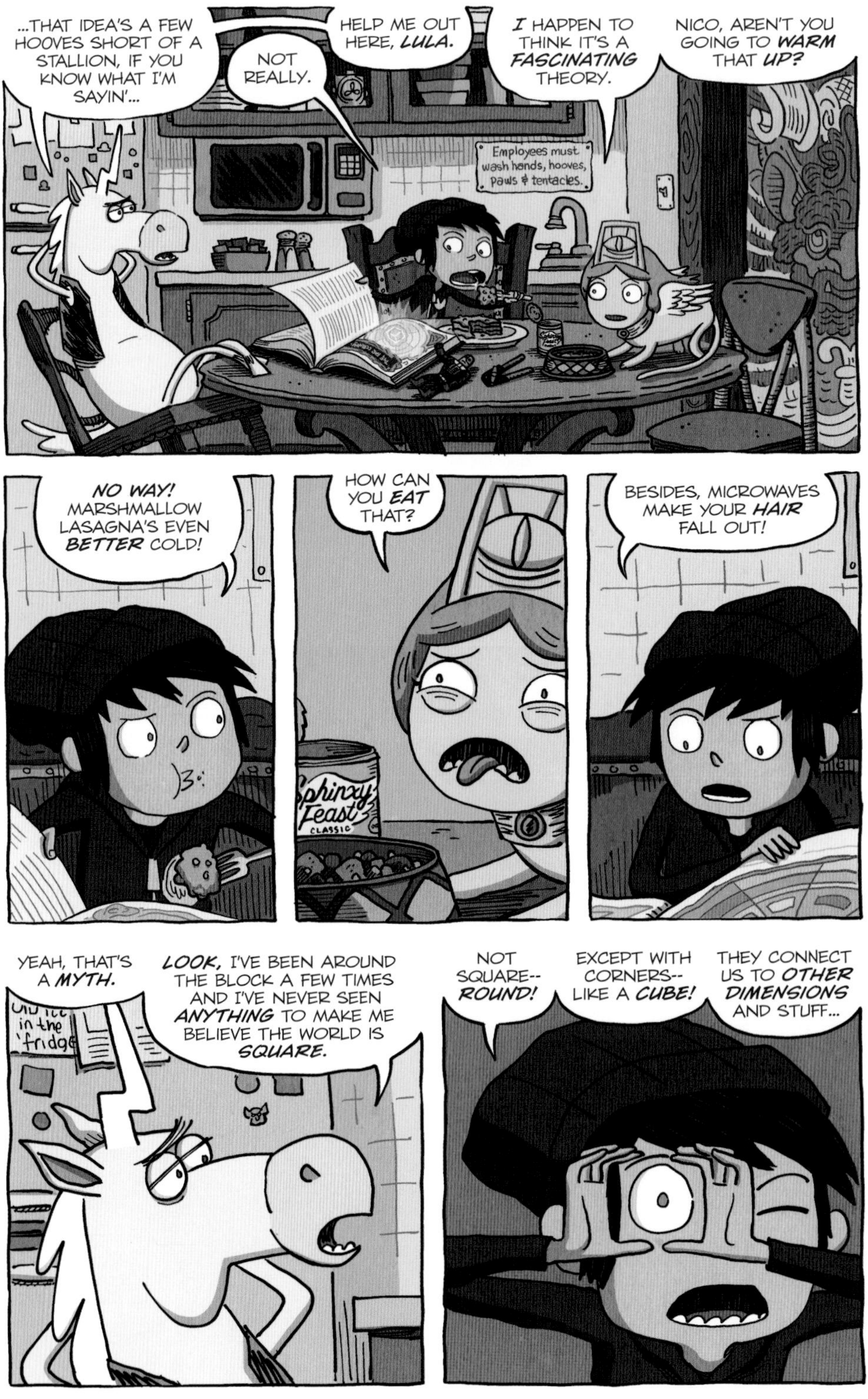
...THAT IDEA'S A FEW HOOVES SHORT OF A STALLION, IF YOU KNOW WHAT I'M SAYIN'...
NOT REALLY.
HELP ME OUT HERE, LULA.
I HAPPEN TO THINK IT'S A FASCINATING THEORY.
NICO, AREN'T YOU GOING TO WARM THAT UP?
Employees must wash hands, hooves, paws & tentacles.
NO WAY! MARSHMALLOW LASAGNA'S EVEN BETTER COLD!
HOW CAN YOU EAT THAT?
Sphinxy Feast CLASSIC
BESIDES, MICROWAVES MAKE YOUR HAIR FALL OUT!
YEAH, THAT'S A MYTH.
LOOK, I'VE BEEN AROUND THE BLOCK A FEW TIMES AND I'VE NEVER SEEN ANYTHING TO MAKE ME BELIEVE THE WORLD IS SQUARE.
in the fridge
NOT SQUARE-- ROUND!
EXCEPT WITH CORNERS-- LIKE A CUBE!
THEY CONNECT US TO OTHER DIMENSIONS AND STUFF...

DIMENSIONS AREN'T STUCK ONTO *INVISIBLE CORNERS*...

...THEY'RE SORTA *KNIT* TOGETHER-- LIKE A *SCARF.*

WHO KNITTED THEM?

WHERE DID THE YARN COME FROM?

*I DON'T KNOW!*

Employe wash hands, hoov, paws & tentacles.

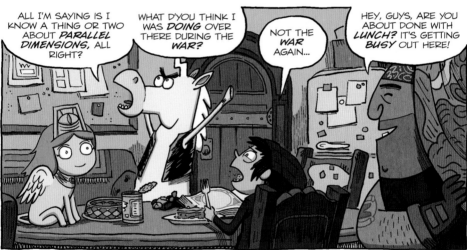

ALL I'M SAYING IS I KNOW A THING OR TWO ABOUT *PARALLEL DIMENSIONS*, ALL RIGHT?

WHAT D'YOU THINK I WAS *DOING* OVER THERE DURING THE *WAR?*

NOT THE *WAR* AGAIN...

HEY, GUYS, ARE YOU ABOUT DONE WITH *LUNCH?* IT'S GETTING *BUSY* OUT HERE!

COMING, *BOSS!*

MAYBE WE SHOULD ASK *VULCAN* ABOUT IT. I FOUND AT LEAST HALF OF IT IMPOSSIBLE TO UNDERSTAND.

*SAME HERE.* DID YOU GET TO THE PART ABOUT *SHAMAYIM TRANSMUTATUM* AND THE *RETROGRADE MOTION OF THE SPHERES?* IT MAKES MY HEAD HURT.

*YEAH*--AND WHY DO SMELLS *SMELL,* AND WHERE DO *SOCKS* GO WHEN YOU LOSE THEM?

LOOK, IF YOU DON'T WANT TO LISTEN TO ME, HAVE IT *YOUR* WAY...

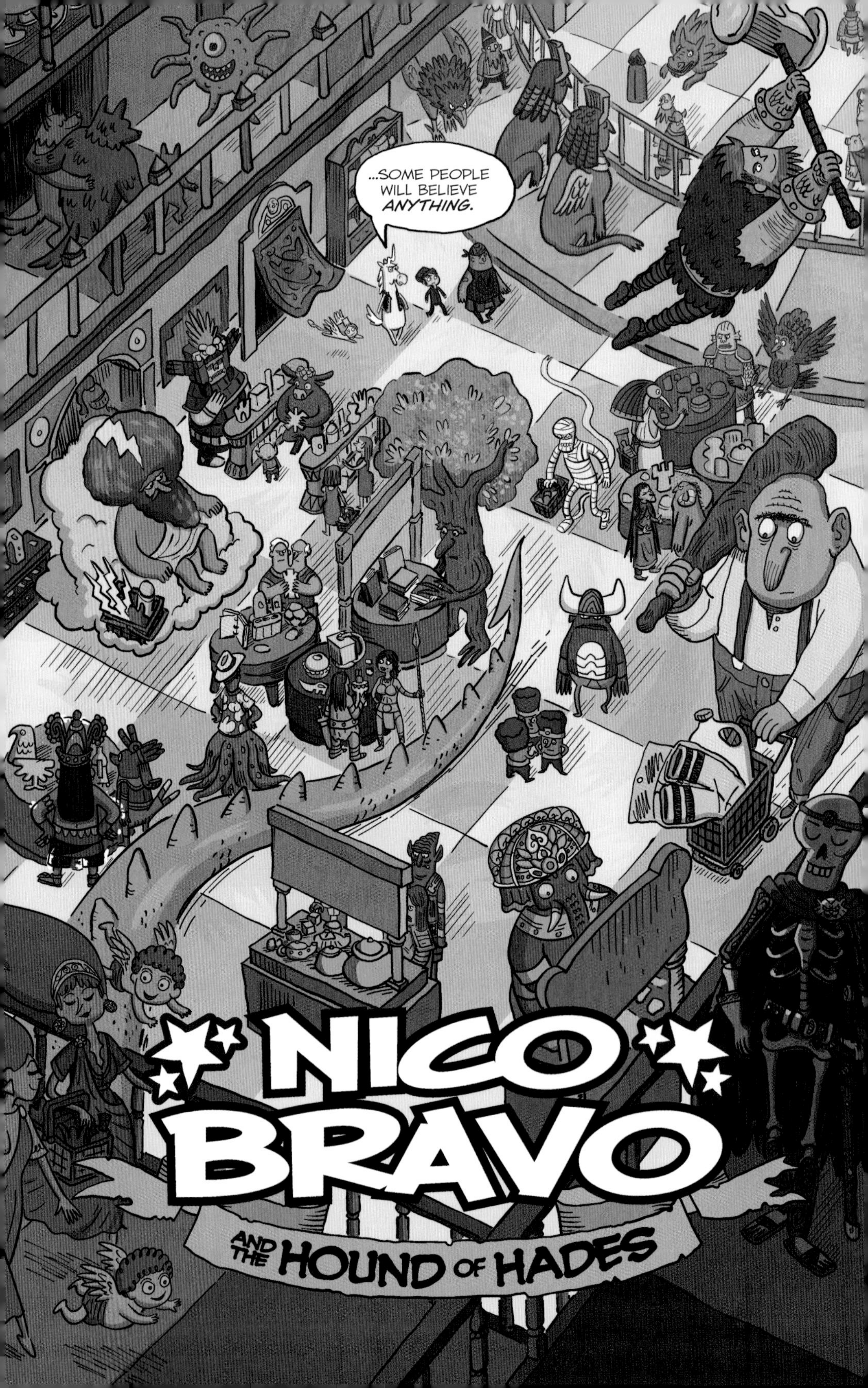
...SOME PEOPLE WILL BELIEVE *ANYTHING.*
NICO BRAVO
AND THE HOUND OF HADES

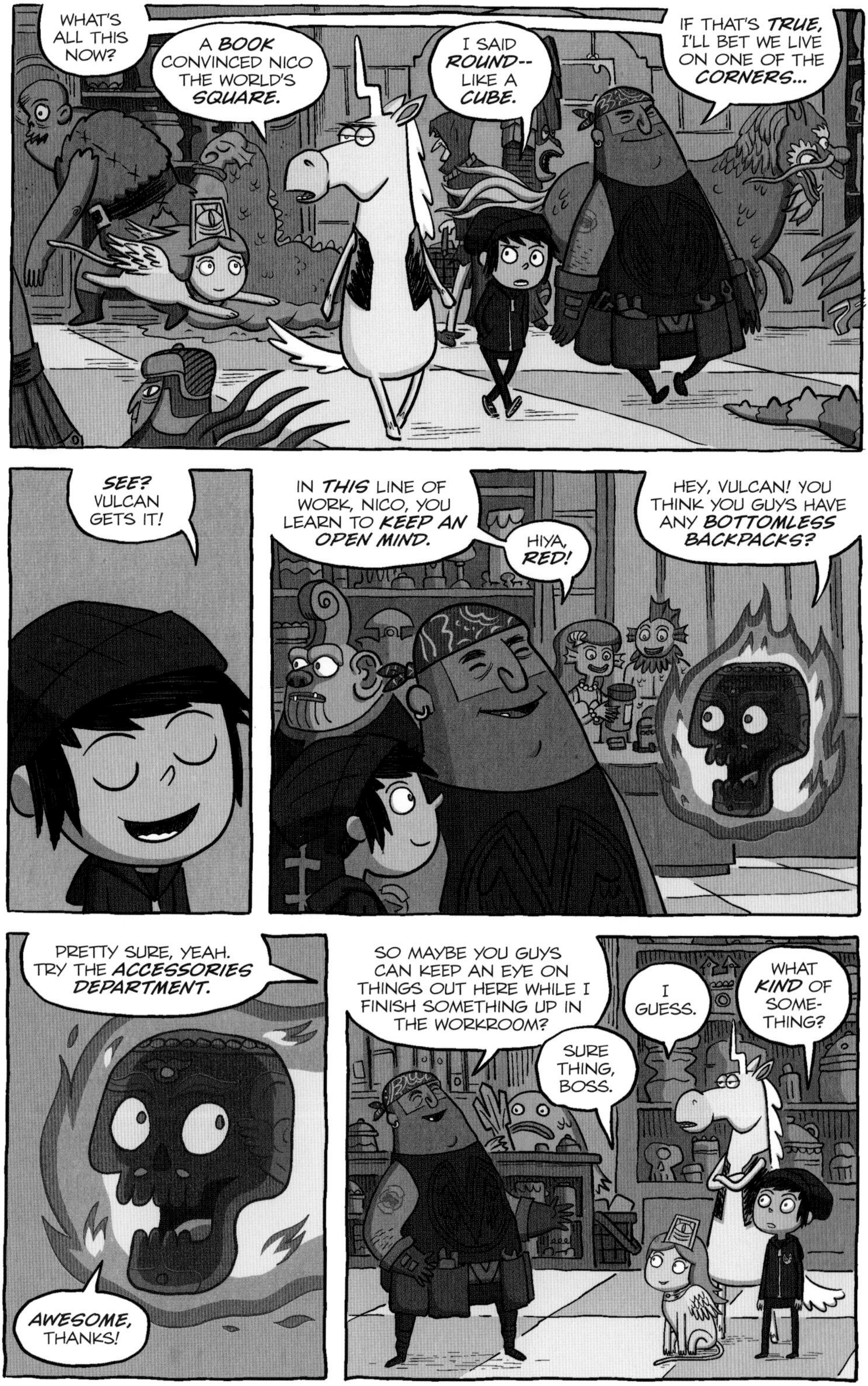
WHAT'S ALL THIS NOW?
A BOOK CONVINCED NICO THE WORLD'S SQUARE.
I SAID ROUND-- LIKE A CUBE.
IF THAT'S TRUE, I'LL BET WE LIVE ON ONE OF THE CORNERS...
SEE? VULCAN GETS IT!
IN THIS LINE OF WORK, NICO, YOU LEARN TO KEEP AN OPEN MIND.
HIYA, RED!
HEY, VULCAN! YOU THINK YOU GUYS HAVE ANY BOTTOMLESS BACKPACKS?
PRETTY SURE, YEAH. TRY THE ACCESSORIES DEPARTMENT.
AWESOME, THANKS!
SO MAYBE YOU GUYS CAN KEEP AN EYE ON THINGS OUT HERE WHILE I FINISH SOMETHING UP IN THE WORKROOM?
SURE THING, BOSS.
I GUESS.
WHAT KIND OF SOME-THING?

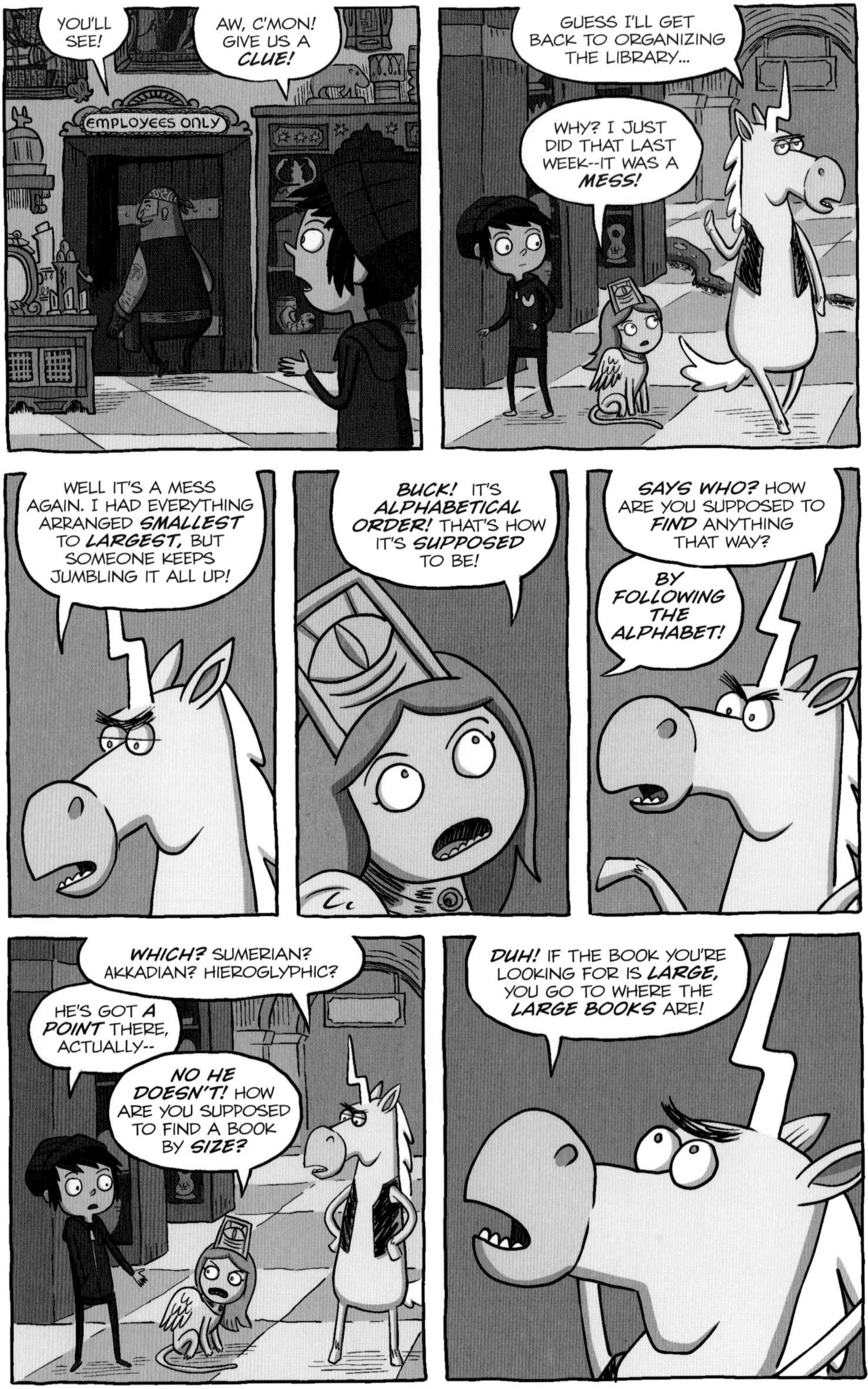
YOU'LL SEE!
AW, C'MON! GIVE US A CLUE!
EMPLOYEES ONLY
GUESS I'LL GET BACK TO ORGANIZING THE LIBRARY...
WHY? I JUST DID THAT LAST WEEK--IT WAS A MESS!
WELL IT'S A MESS AGAIN. I HAD EVERYTHING ARRANGED SMALLEST TO LARGEST, BUT SOMEONE KEEPS JUMBLING IT ALL UP!
BUCK! IT'S ALPHABETICAL ORDER! THAT'S HOW IT'S SUPPOSED TO BE!
SAYS WHO? HOW ARE YOU SUPPOSED TO FIND ANYTHING THAT WAY?
BY FOLLOWING THE ALPHABET!
WHICH? SUMERIAN? AKKADIAN? HIEROGLYPHIC?
HE'S GOT A POINT THERE, ACTUALLY--
NO HE DOESN'T! HOW ARE YOU SUPPOSED TO FIND A BOOK BY SIZE?
DUH! IF THE BOOK YOU'RE LOOKING FOR IS LARGE, YOU GO TO WHERE THE LARGE BOOKS ARE!

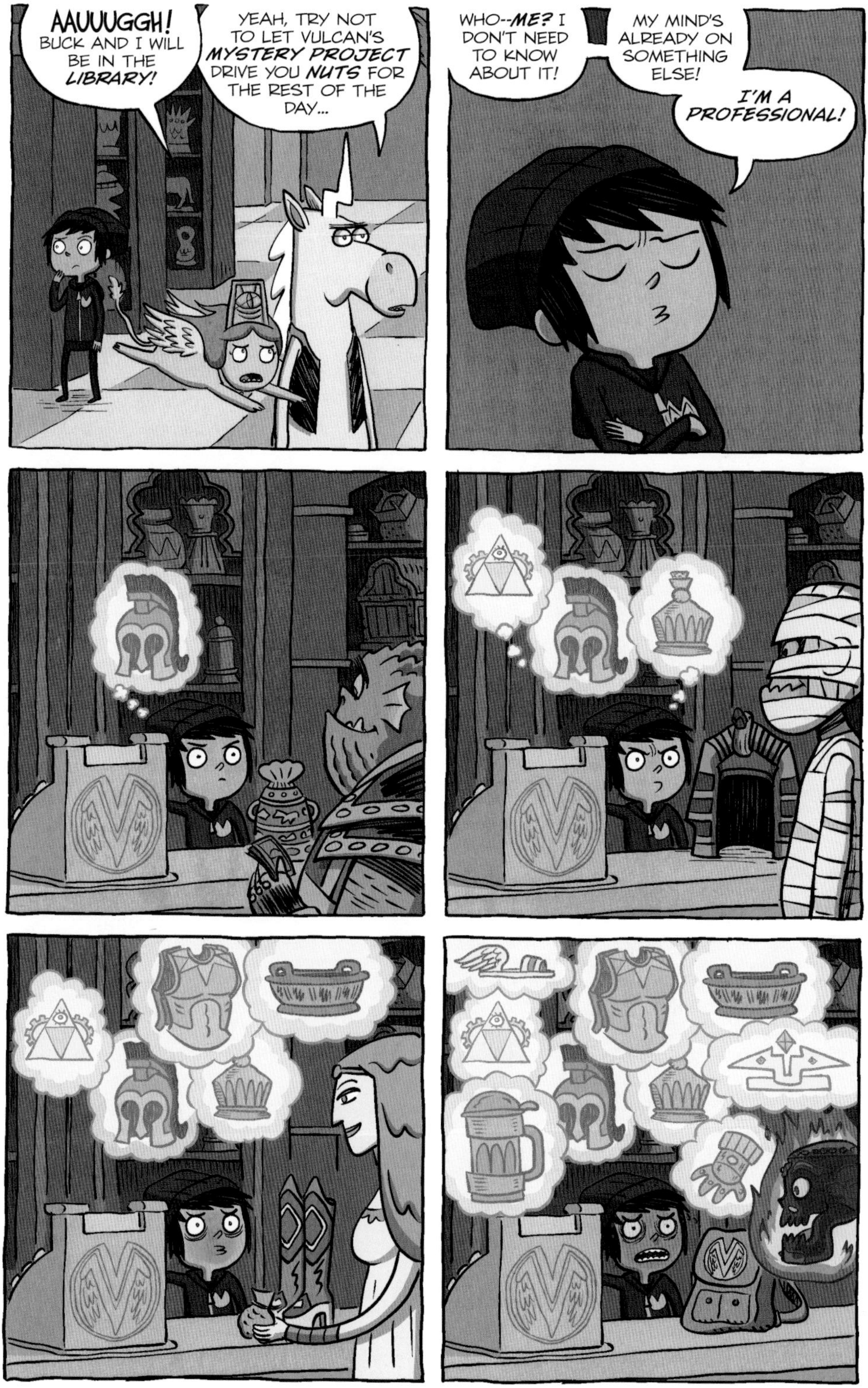
AAUUUGGH! BUCK AND I WILL BE IN THE LIBRARY!
YEAH, TRY NOT TO LET VULCAN'S MYSTERY PROJECT DRIVE YOU NUTS FOR THE REST OF THE DAY...
WHO--ME? I DON'T NEED TO KNOW ABOUT IT!
MY MIND'S ALREADY ON SOMETHING ELSE!
I'M A PROFESSIONAL!

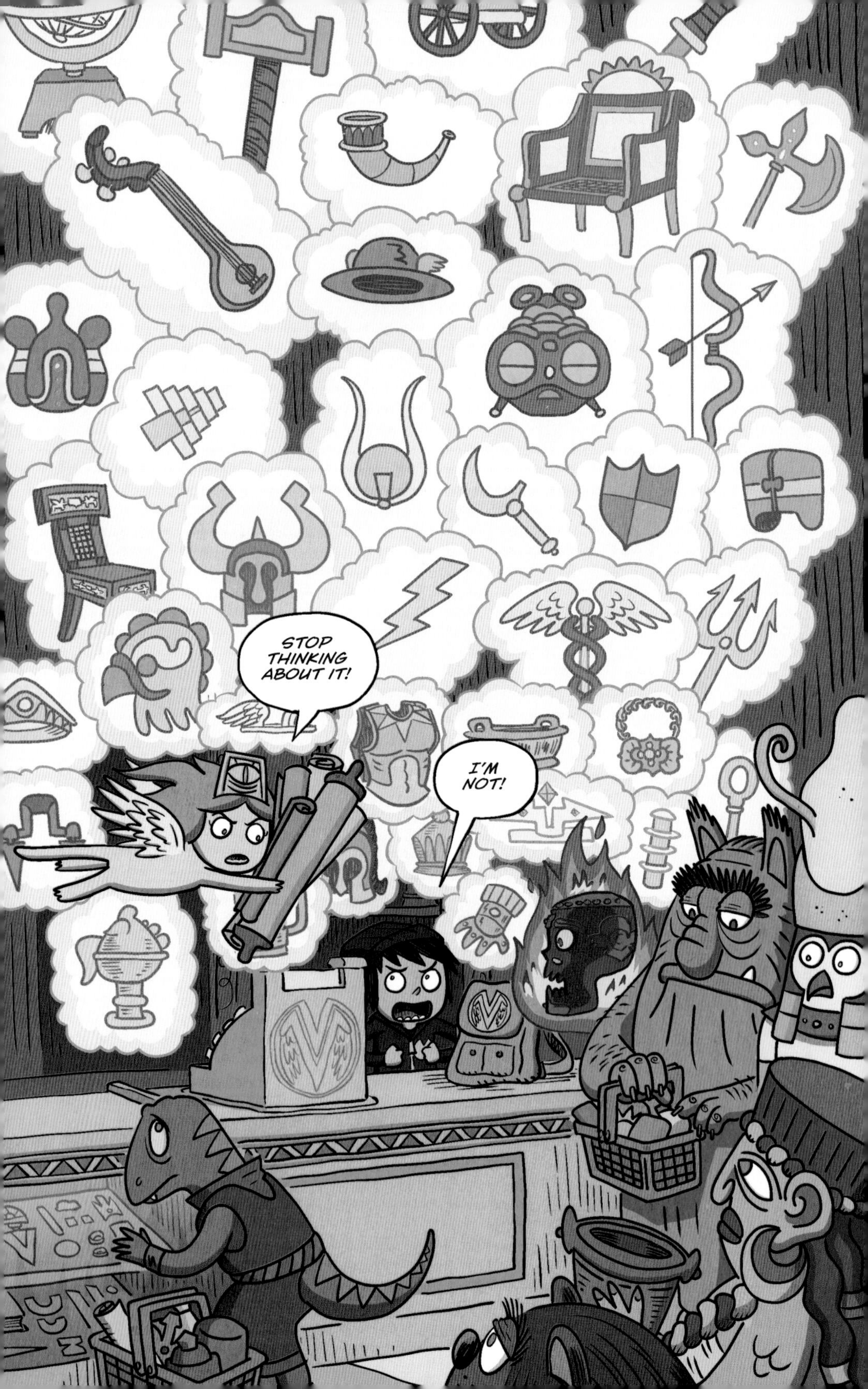
STOP THINKING ABOUT IT!
I'M NOT!

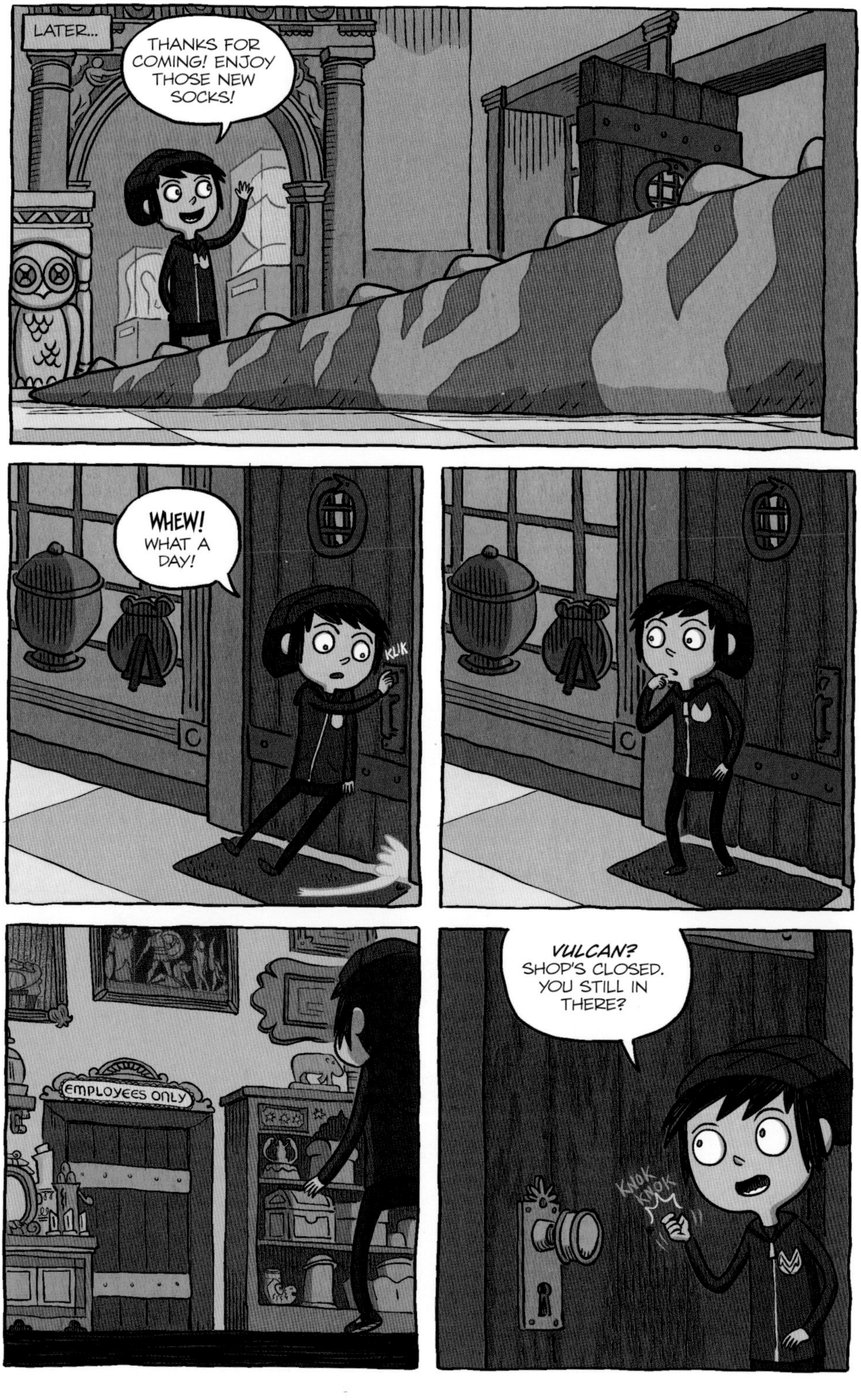
LATER...
THANKS FOR COMING! ENJOY THOSE NEW SOCKS!
WHEW! WHAT A DAY!
KLIK
EMPLOYEES ONLY
VULCAN? SHOP'S CLOSED. YOU STILL IN THERE?
KNOK KNOK

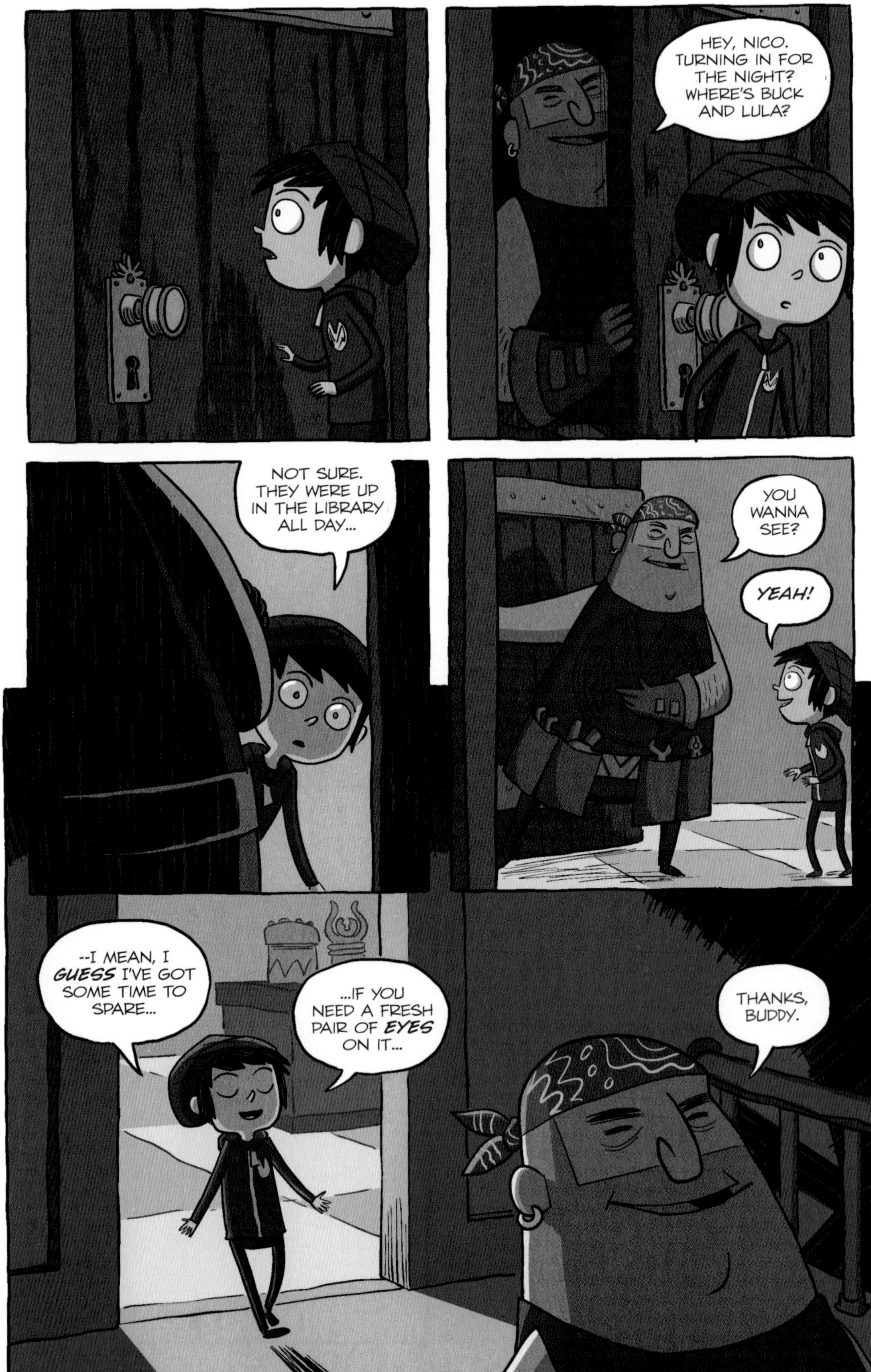
HEY, NICO. TURNING IN FOR THE NIGHT? WHERE'S BUCK AND LULA?
NOT SURE. THEY WERE UP IN THE LIBRARY ALL DAY...
YOU WANNA SEE?
YEAH!
--I MEAN, I GUESS I'VE GOT SOME TIME TO SPARE...
...IF YOU NEED A FRESH PAIR OF EYES ON IT...
THANKS, BUDDY.

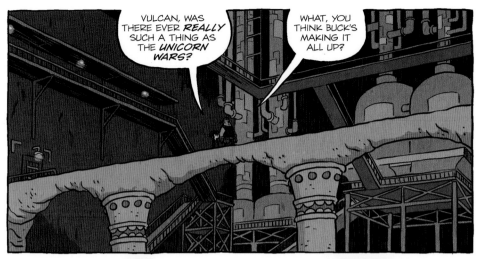

VULCAN, WAS THERE EVER *REALLY* SUCH A THING AS THE *UNICORN WARS?*

WHAT, YOU THINK BUCK'S MAKING IT ALL UP?

WELL, IT'S JUST THAT *OTHER* WARS HAVE BOOKS AND MOVIES AND STUFF ABOUT THEM, BUT ONLY *BUCK* EVER MENTIONS THIS ONE.

OKAY, BUT HOW MANY OTHER *UNICORNS* DO YOU KNOW?

HMM. *NONE*, I GUESS. WHY IS THAT?

MAYBE YOU SHOULD ASK BUCK.

MAYBE.

MAYBE IT DOESN'T MATTER.

MAYBE BUCK IS JUST *BUCK.*

GREAT GULA'S GHOSTS!

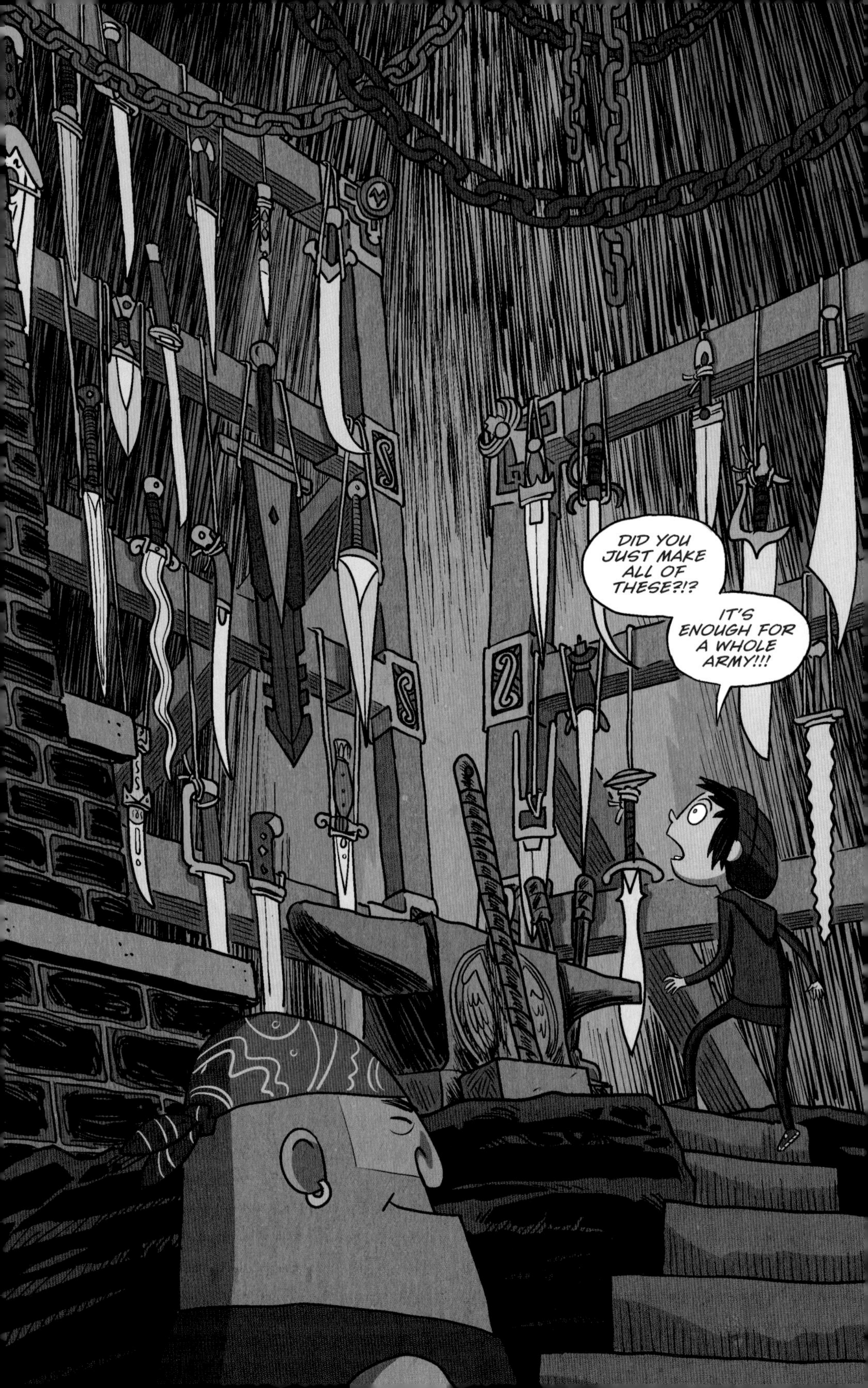
DID YOU JUST MAKE ALL OF THESE?!?
IT'S ENOUGH FOR A WHOLE ARMY!!!

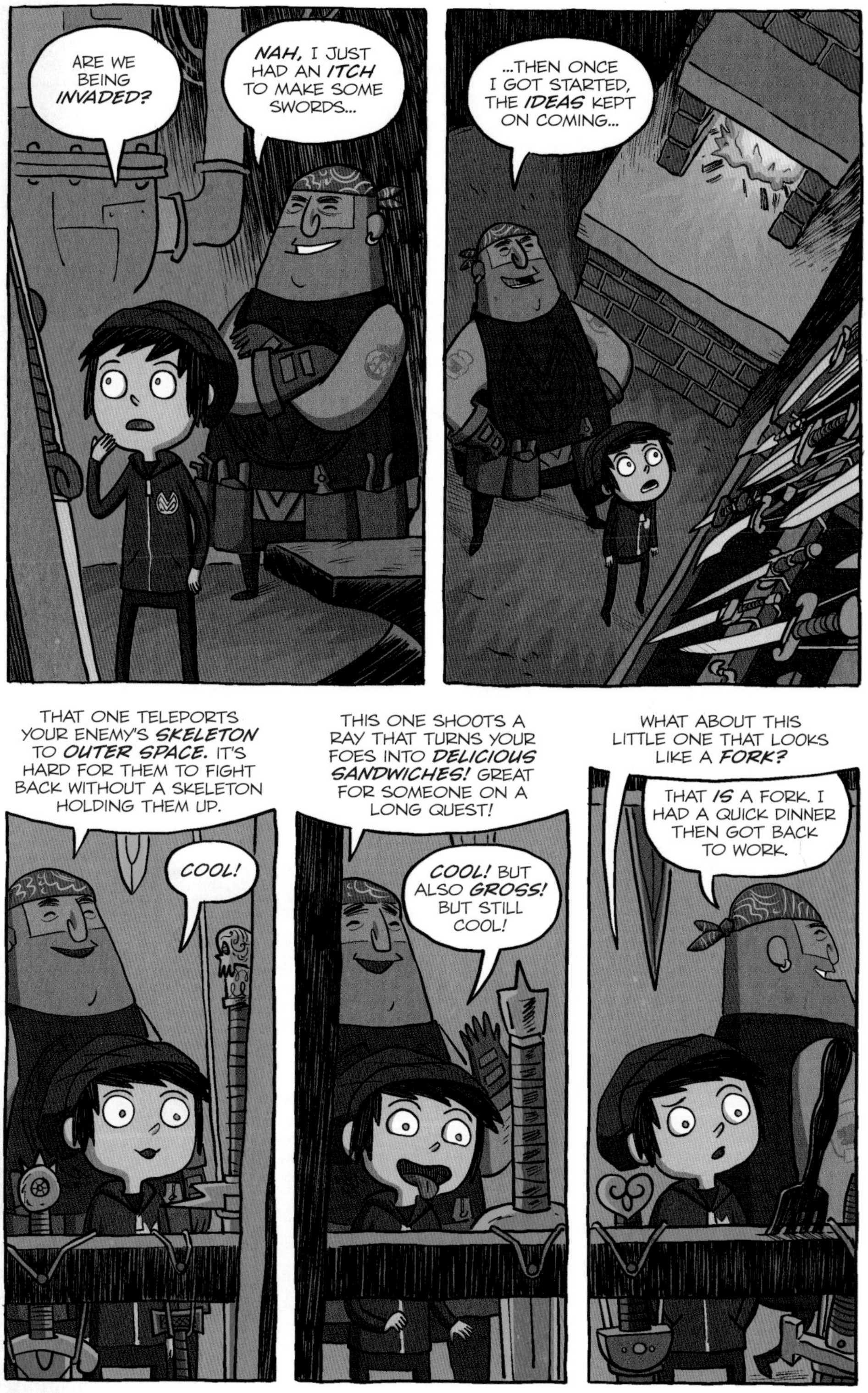
ARE WE BEING INVADED?
NAH, I JUST HAD AN ITCH TO MAKE SOME SWORDS...
...THEN ONCE I GOT STARTED, THE IDEAS KEPT ON COMING...
THAT ONE TELEPORTS YOUR ENEMY'S SKELETON TO OUTER SPACE. IT'S HARD FOR THEM TO FIGHT BACK WITHOUT A SKELETON HOLDING THEM UP.
COOL!
THIS ONE SHOOTS A RAY THAT TURNS YOUR FOES INTO DELICIOUS SANDWICHES! GREAT FOR SOMEONE ON A LONG QUEST!
COOL! BUT ALSO GROSS! BUT STILL COOL!
WHAT ABOUT THIS LITTLE ONE THAT LOOKS LIKE A FORK?
THAT IS A FORK. I HAD A QUICK DINNER THEN GOT BACK TO WORK.

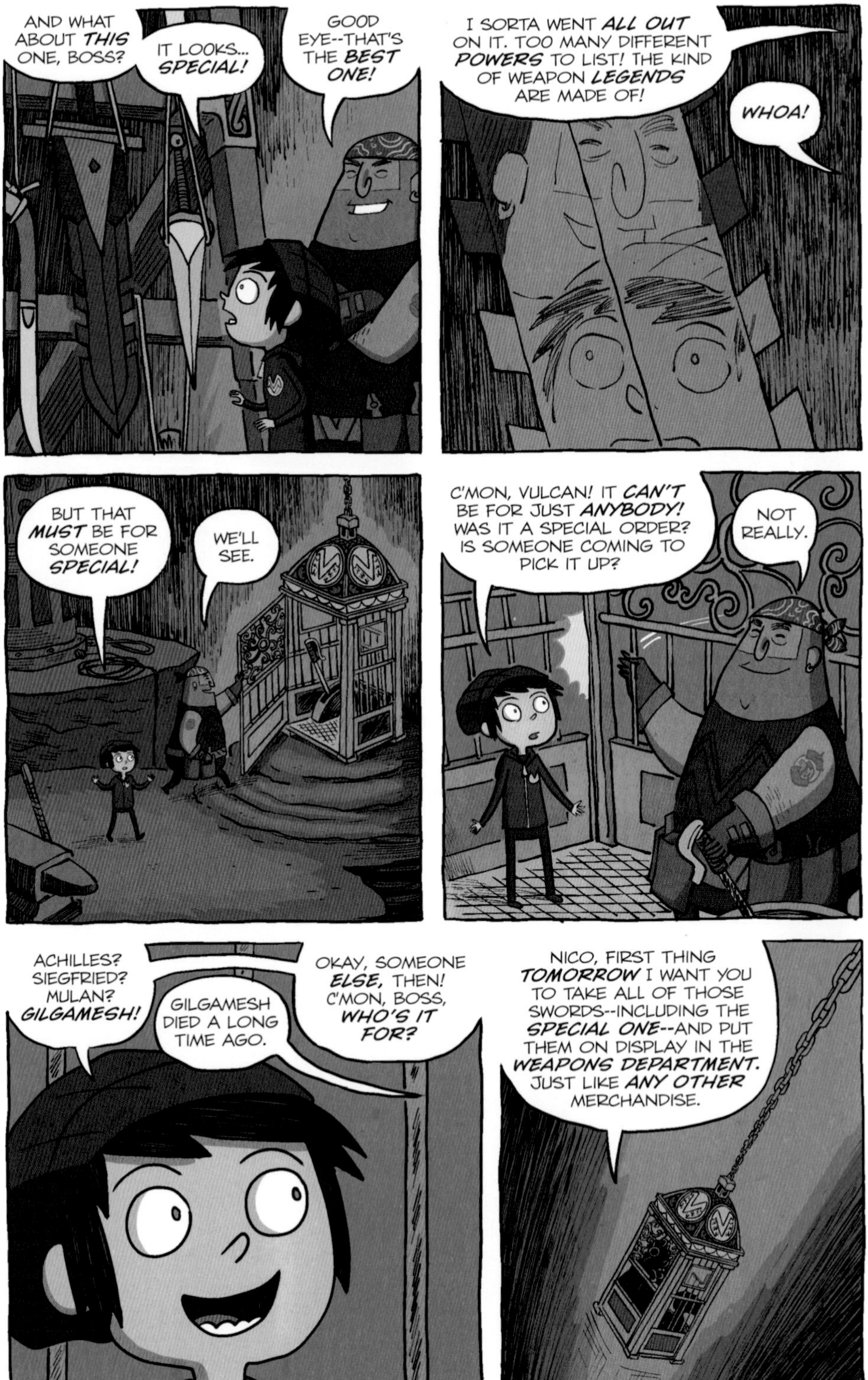
AND WHAT ABOUT *THIS* ONE, BOSS?
IT LOOKS... *SPECIAL!*
GOOD EYE--THAT'S THE *BEST ONE!*
I SORTA WENT *ALL OUT* ON IT. TOO MANY DIFFERENT *POWERS* TO LIST! THE KIND OF WEAPON *LEGENDS* ARE MADE OF!
*WHOA!*
BUT THAT *MUST* BE FOR SOMEONE *SPECIAL!*
WE'LL SEE.
C'MON, VULCAN! IT *CAN'T* BE FOR JUST *ANYBODY!* WAS IT A SPECIAL ORDER? IS SOMEONE COMING TO PICK IT UP?
NOT REALLY.
ACHILLES? SIEGFRIED? MULAN? *GILGAMESH!*
GILGAMESH DIED A LONG TIME AGO.
OKAY, SOMEONE *ELSE,* THEN! C'MON, BOSS, *WHO'S IT FOR?*
NICO, FIRST THING *TOMORROW* I WANT YOU TO TAKE ALL OF THOSE SWORDS--INCLUDING THE *SPECIAL ONE*--AND PUT THEM ON DISPLAY IN THE *WEAPONS DEPARTMENT.* JUST LIKE *ANY OTHER* MERCHANDISE.

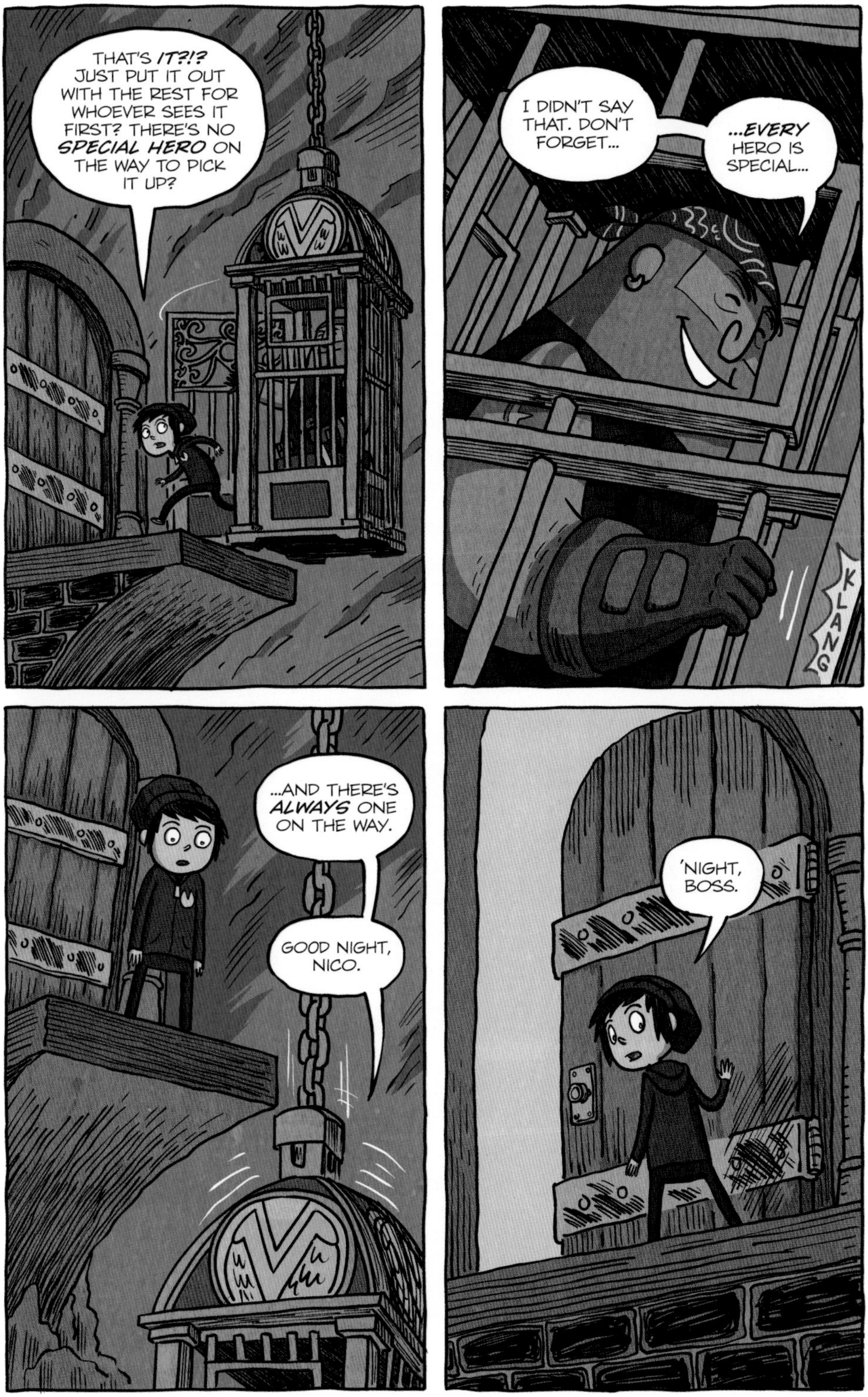
THAT'S *IT?!?* JUST PUT IT OUT WITH THE REST FOR WHOEVER SEES IT FIRST? THERE'S NO ***SPECIAL HERO*** ON THE WAY TO PICK IT UP?
I DIDN'T SAY THAT. DON'T FORGET...
***...EVERY*** HERO IS SPECIAL...
KLANG
...AND THERE'S ***ALWAYS*** ONE ON THE WAY.
GOOD NIGHT, NICO.
'NIGHT, BOSS.

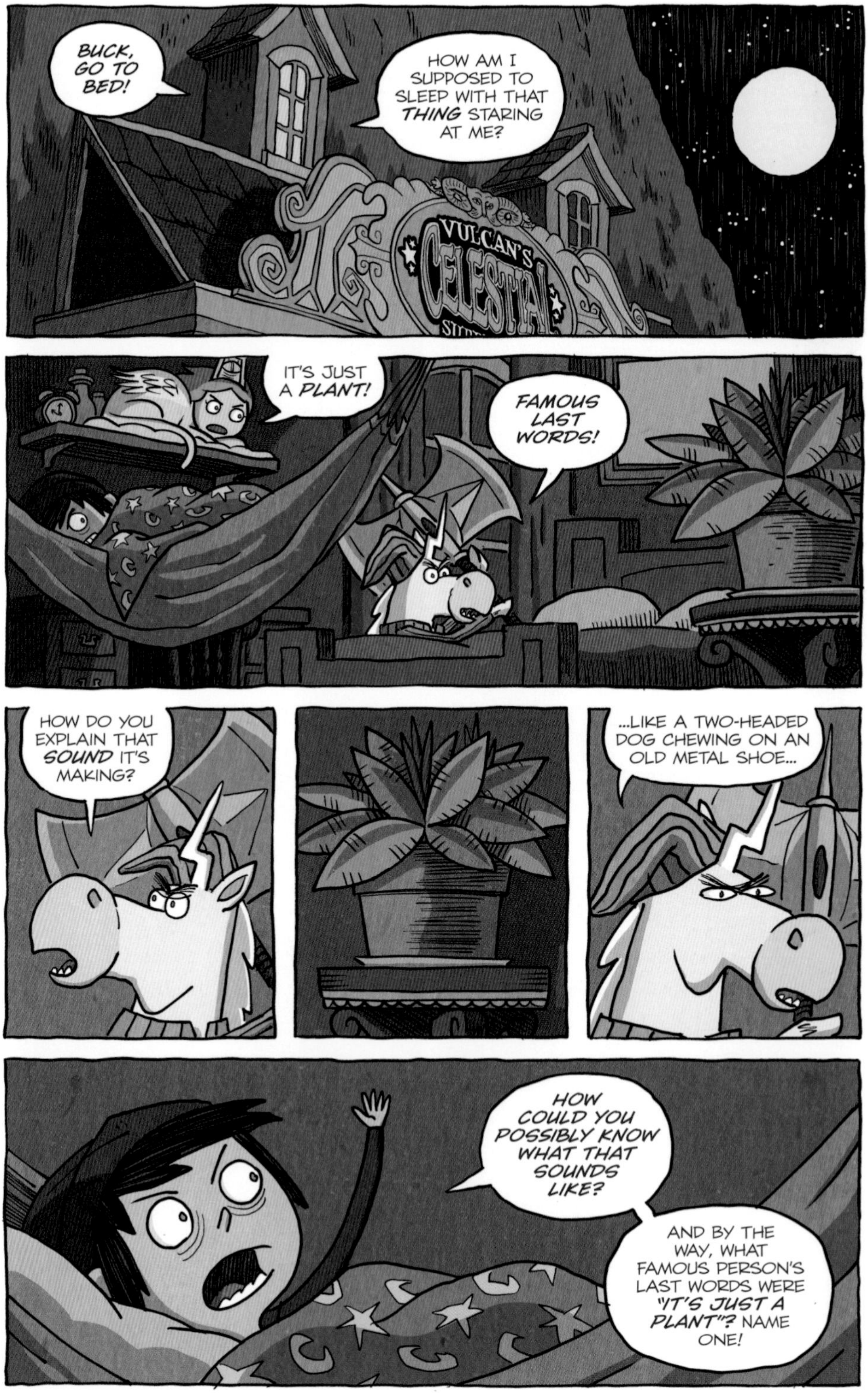
BUCK, GO TO BED!
HOW AM I SUPPOSED TO SLEEP WITH THAT *THING* STARING AT ME?
VULCAN'S CELESTIAL
IT'S JUST A *PLANT!*
*FAMOUS LAST WORDS!*
HOW DO YOU EXPLAIN THAT *SOUND* IT'S MAKING?
...LIKE A TWO-HEADED DOG CHEWING ON AN OLD METAL SHOE...
*HOW COULD YOU POSSIBLY KNOW WHAT THAT SOUNDS LIKE?*
AND BY THE WAY, WHAT FAMOUS PERSON'S LAST WORDS WERE *"IT'S JUST A PLANT"?* NAME ONE!

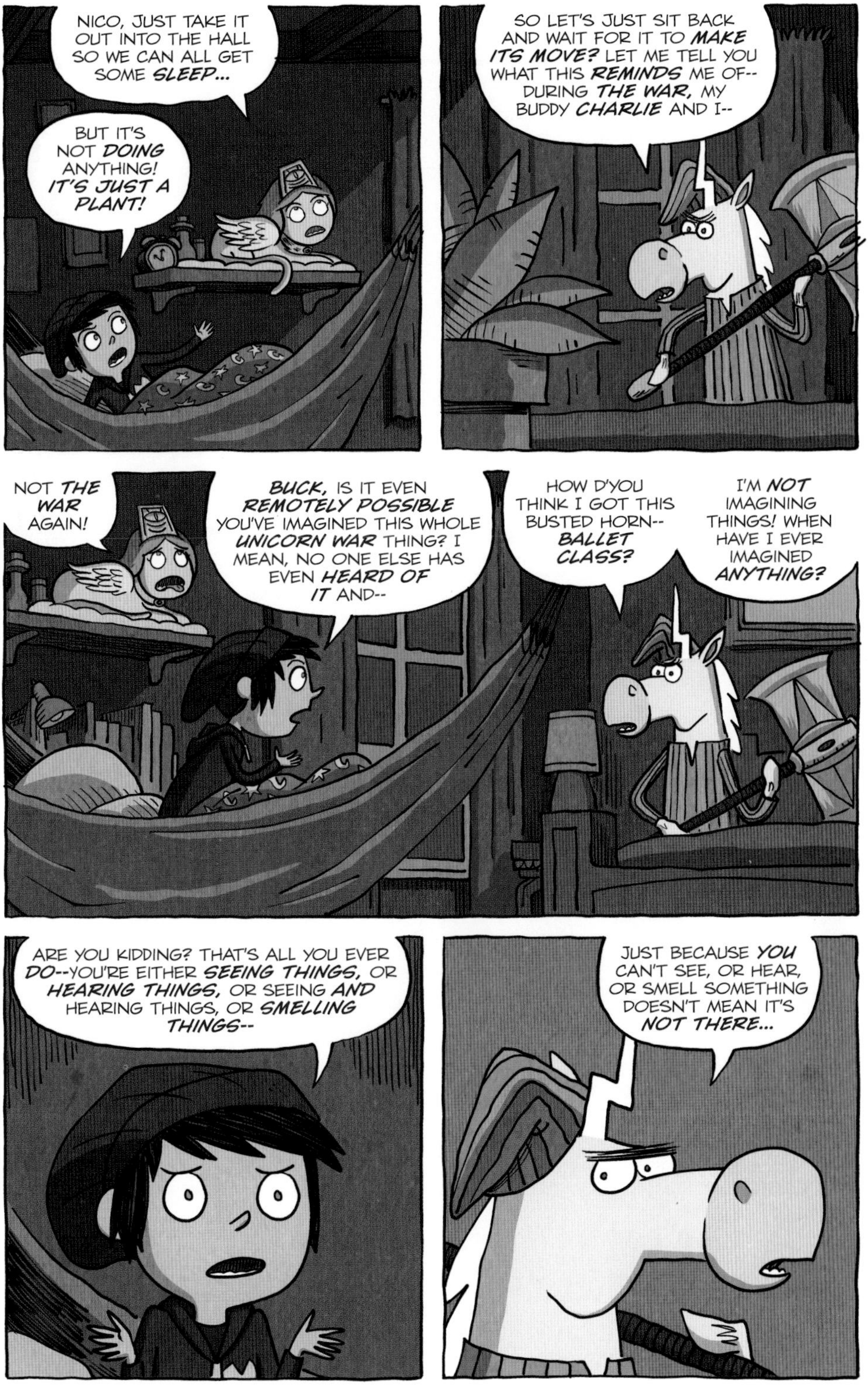
NICO, JUST TAKE IT OUT INTO THE HALL SO WE CAN ALL GET SOME SLEEP...
BUT IT'S NOT DOING ANYTHING! IT'S JUST A PLANT!
SO LET'S JUST SIT BACK AND WAIT FOR IT TO MAKE ITS MOVE? LET ME TELL YOU WHAT THIS REMINDS ME OF-- DURING THE WAR, MY BUDDY CHARLIE AND I--
NOT THE WAR AGAIN!
BUCK, IS IT EVEN REMOTELY POSSIBLE YOU'VE IMAGINED THIS WHOLE UNICORN WAR THING? I MEAN, NO ONE ELSE HAS EVEN HEARD OF IT AND--
HOW D'YOU THINK I GOT THIS BUSTED HORN-- BALLET CLASS?
I'M NOT IMAGINING THINGS! WHEN HAVE I EVER IMAGINED ANYTHING?
ARE YOU KIDDING? THAT'S ALL YOU EVER DO--YOU'RE EITHER SEEING THINGS, OR HEARING THINGS, OR SEEING AND HEARING THINGS, OR SMELLING THINGS--
JUST BECAUSE YOU CAN'T SEE, OR HEAR, OR SMELL SOMETHING DOESN'T MEAN IT'S NOT THERE...

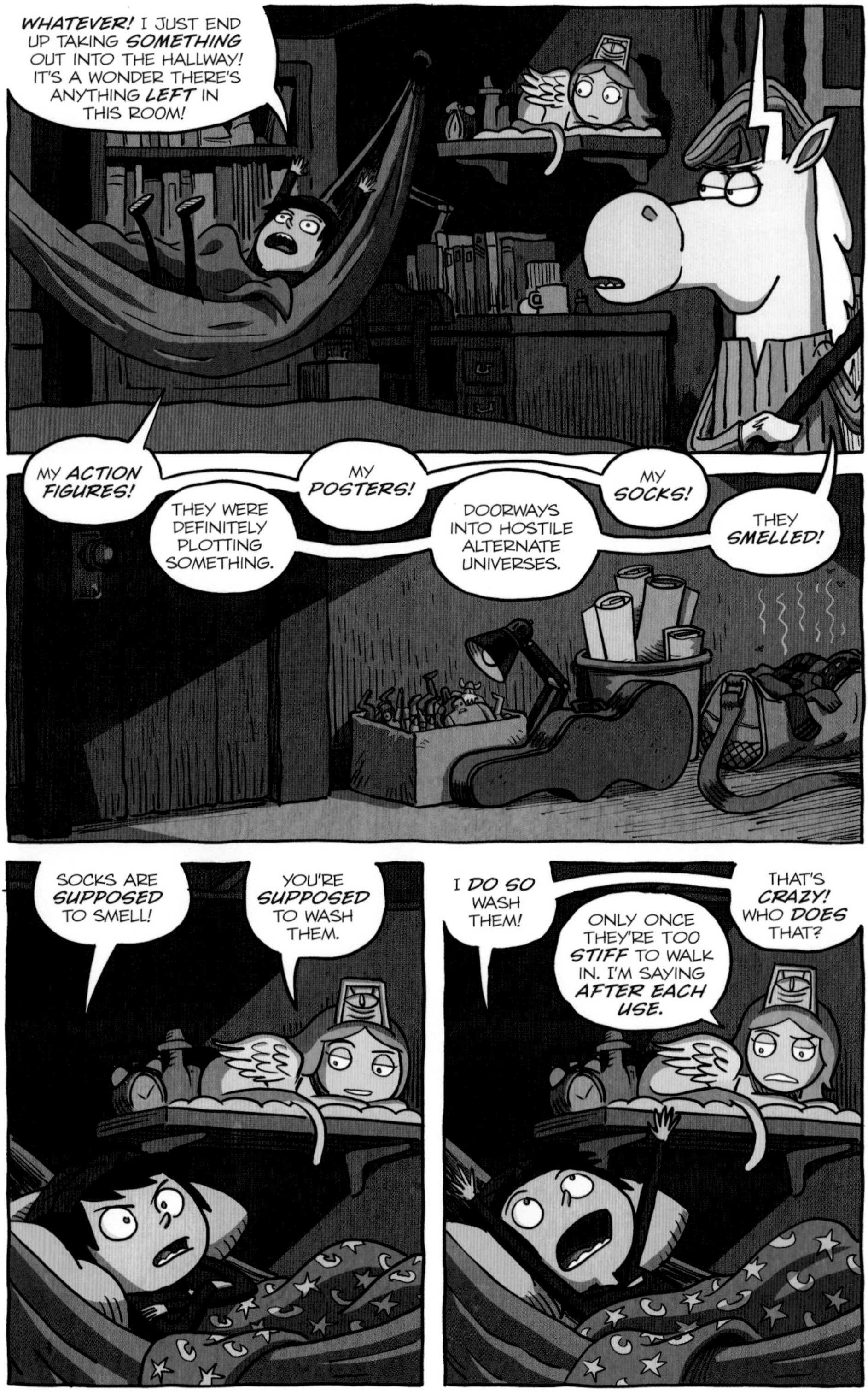
WHATEVER! I JUST END UP TAKING SOMETHING OUT INTO THE HALLWAY! IT'S A WONDER THERE'S ANYTHING LEFT IN THIS ROOM!
MY ACTION FIGURES!
THEY WERE DEFINITELY PLOTTING SOMETHING.
MY POSTERS!
DOORWAYS INTO HOSTILE ALTERNATE UNIVERSES.
MY SOCKS!
THEY SMELLED!
SOCKS ARE SUPPOSED TO SMELL!
YOU'RE SUPPOSED TO WASH THEM.
I DO SO WASH THEM!
ONLY ONCE THEY'RE TOO STIFF TO WALK IN. I'M SAYING AFTER EACH USE.
THAT'S CRAZY! WHO DOES THAT?

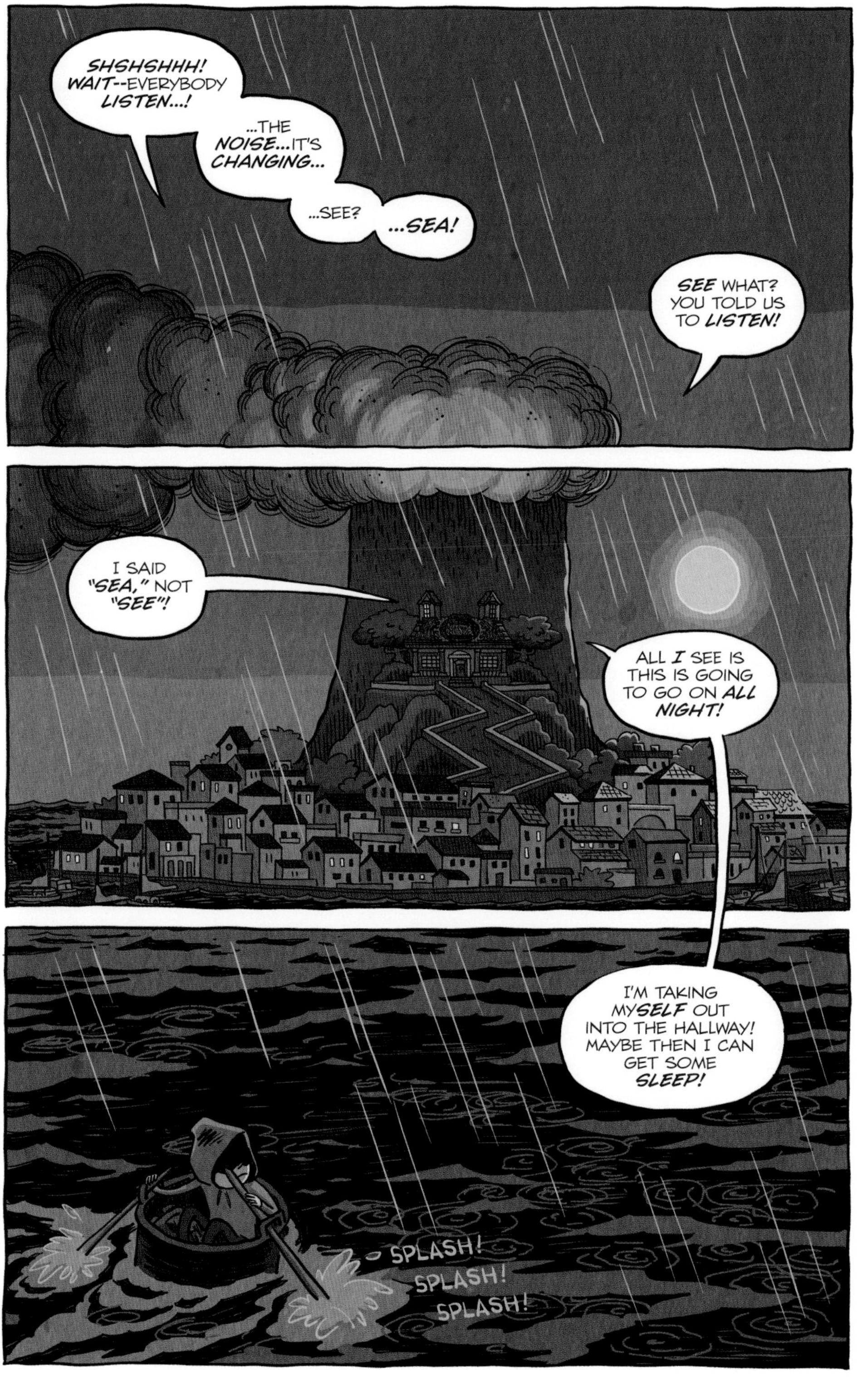
SHSHSHHH! WAIT--EVERYBODY LISTEN...!
...THE NOISE...IT'S CHANGING...
...SEE?
...SEA!
SEE WHAT? YOU TOLD US TO LISTEN!
I SAID "SEA," NOT "SEE"!
ALL I SEE IS THIS IS GOING TO GO ON ALL NIGHT!
I'M TAKING MYSELF OUT INTO THE HALLWAY! MAYBE THEN I CAN GET SOME SLEEP!
SPLASH!
SPLASH!
SPLASH!

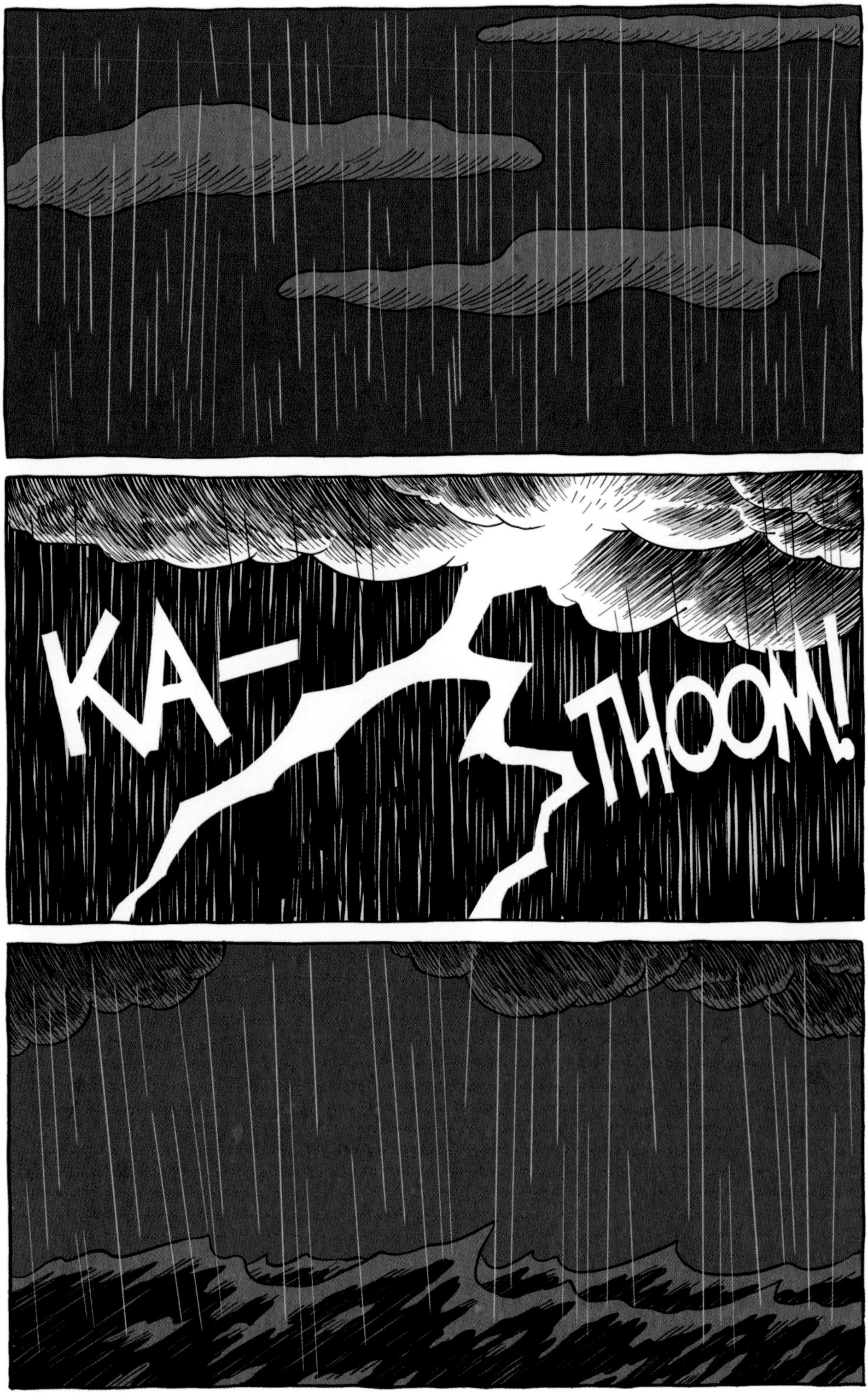
KA-
THOOM!

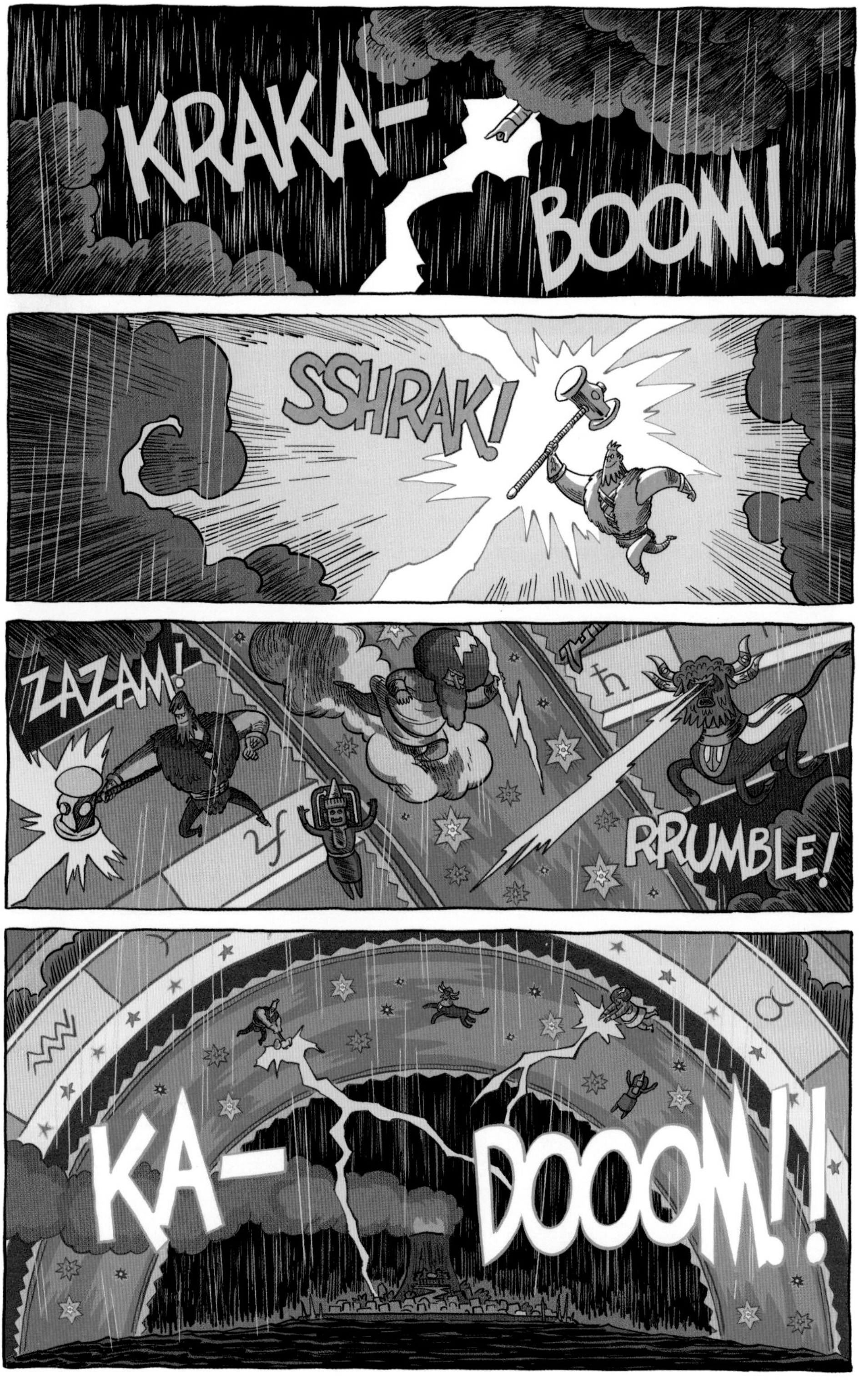
KRAKA-
BOOM!
SSHRAK!
ZAZAM!
RRUMBLE!
KA-
DOOOM!!

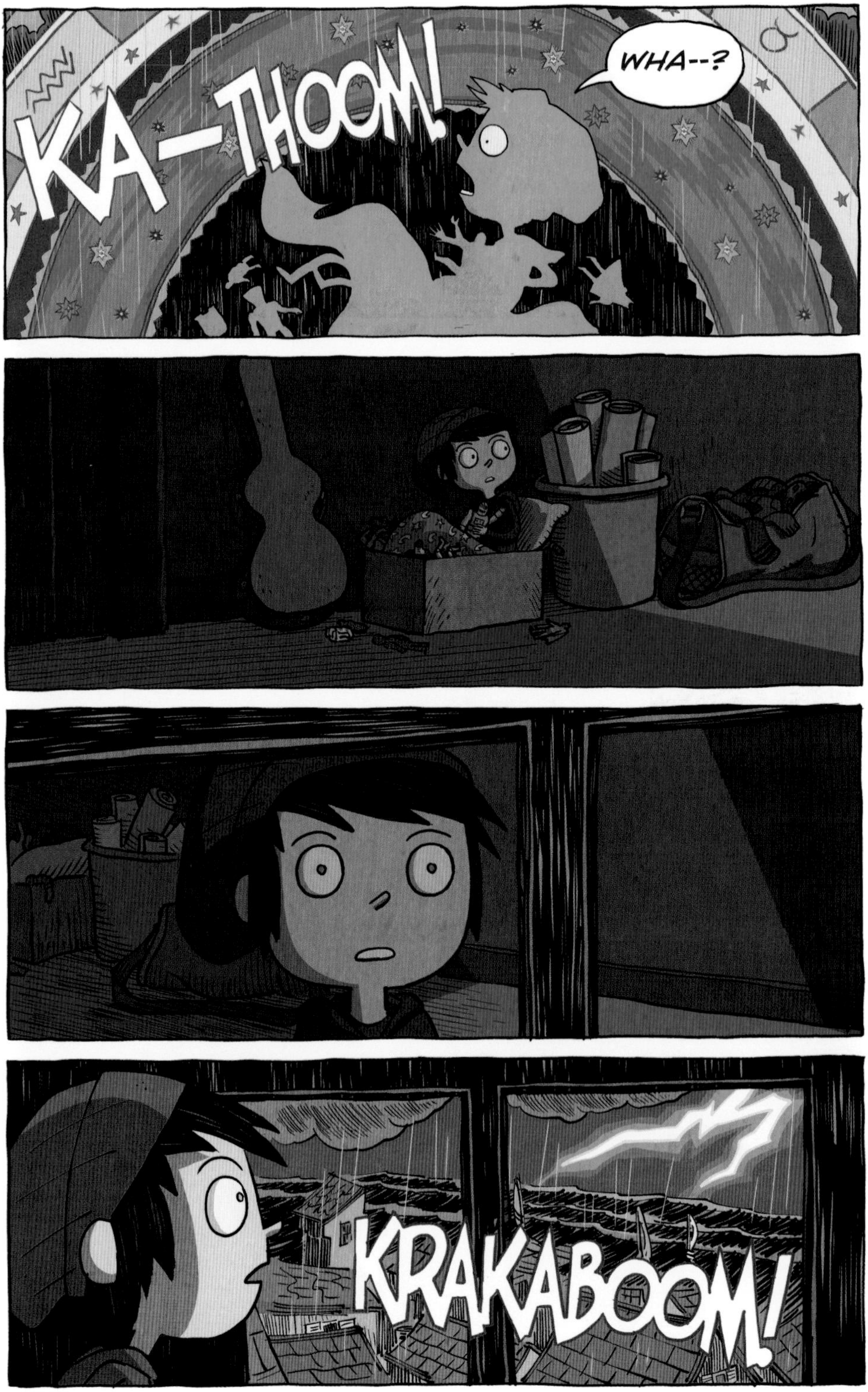
KA-THOOM!
WHA--?
KRAKABOOM!

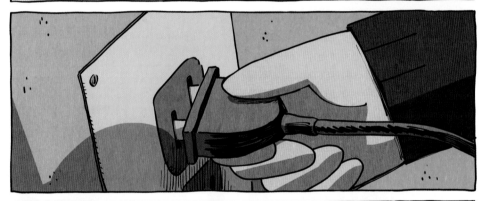

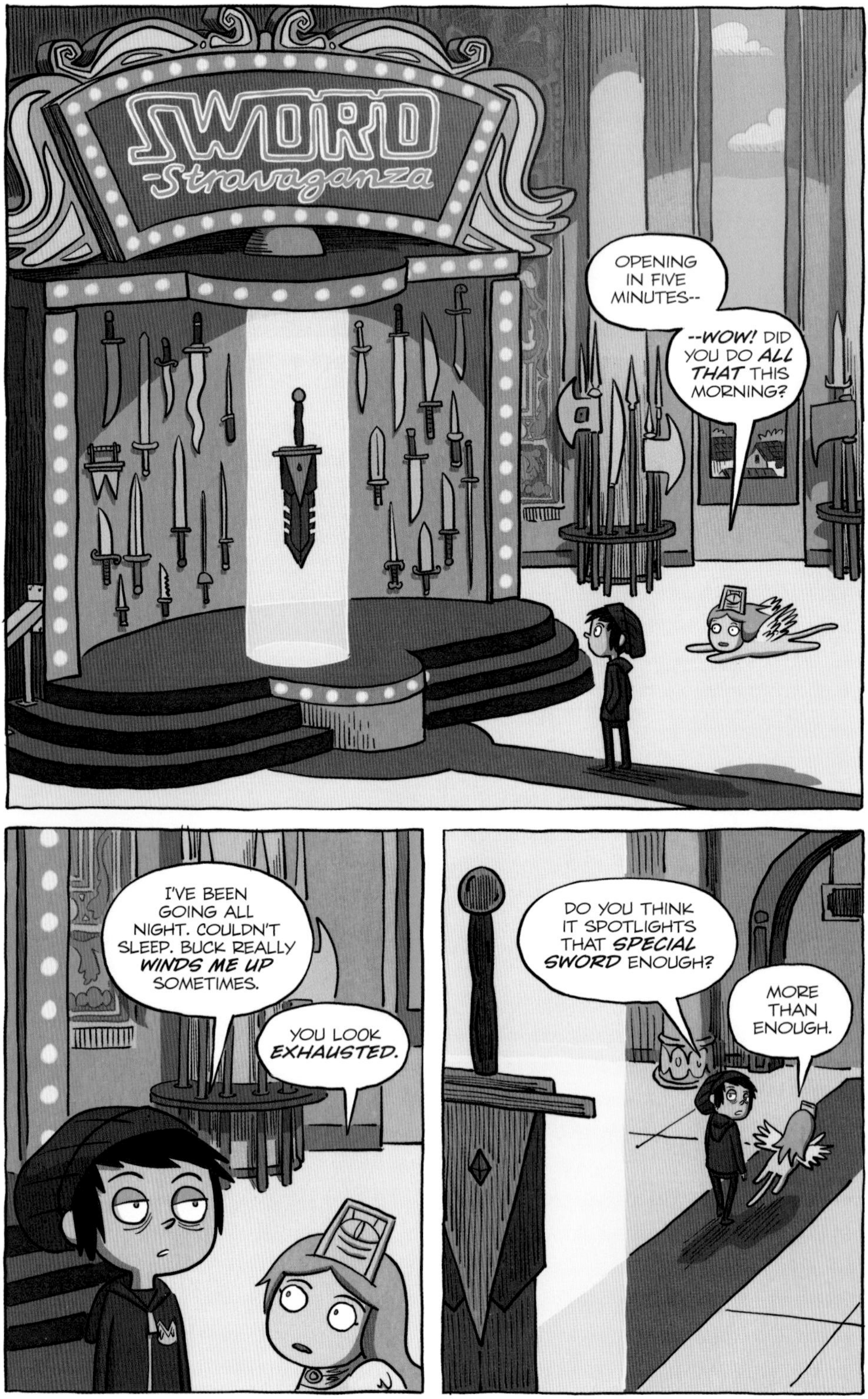
SWORD
-Stravaganza
OPENING IN FIVE MINUTES--
--**WOW!** DID YOU DO **ALL THAT** THIS MORNING?
I'VE BEEN GOING ALL NIGHT. COULDN'T SLEEP. BUCK REALLY **WINDS ME UP** SOMETIMES.
YOU LOOK **EXHAUSTED.**
DO YOU THINK IT SPOTLIGHTS THAT **SPECIAL SWORD** ENOUGH?
MORE THAN ENOUGH.

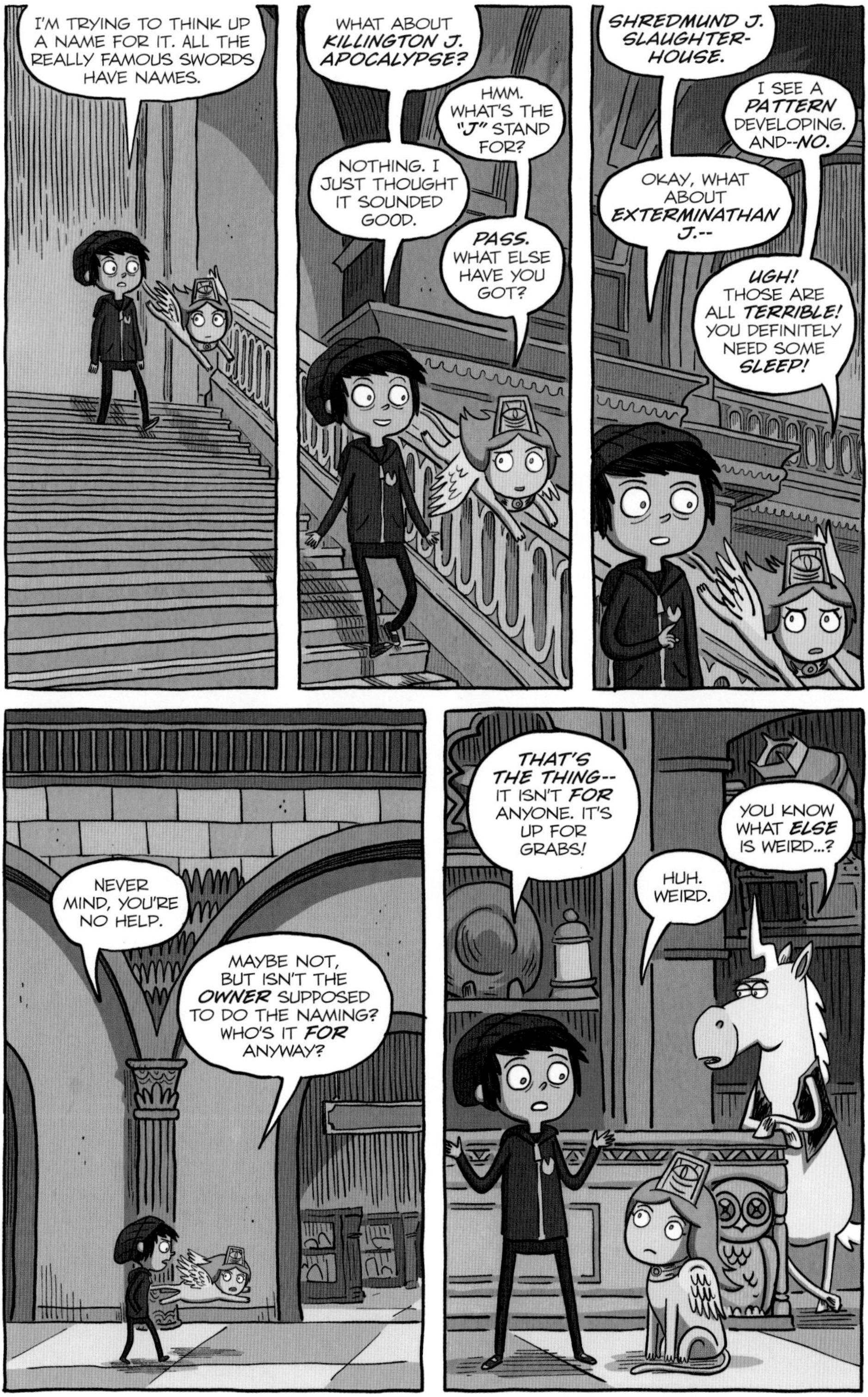
I'M TRYING TO THINK UP A NAME FOR IT. ALL THE REALLY FAMOUS SWORDS HAVE NAMES.
WHAT ABOUT **KILLINGTON J. APOCALYPSE?**
HMM. WHAT'S THE "J" STAND FOR?
NOTHING. I JUST THOUGHT IT SOUNDED GOOD.
**PASS.** WHAT ELSE HAVE YOU GOT?
**SHREDMUND J. SLAUGHTER-HOUSE.**
I SEE A **PATTERN** DEVELOPING. AND--**NO.**
OKAY, WHAT ABOUT **EXTERMINATHAN J.--**
**UGH!** THOSE ARE ALL **TERRIBLE!** YOU DEFINITELY NEED SOME **SLEEP!**
NEVER MIND, YOU'RE NO HELP.
MAYBE NOT, BUT ISN'T THE **OWNER** SUPPOSED TO DO THE NAMING? WHO'S IT **FOR** ANYWAY?
**THAT'S THE THING--** IT ISN'T **FOR** ANYONE. IT'S UP FOR GRABS!
HUH. WEIRD.
YOU KNOW WHAT **ELSE** IS WEIRD...?

...SOME SKETCHY-LOOKING CHARACTER IN A HOOD'S BEEN CREEPING AROUND THE FRONT DOOR ALL MORNING--

SLAM!

FINALLY! I THOUGHT YOU'D *NEVER* OPEN!

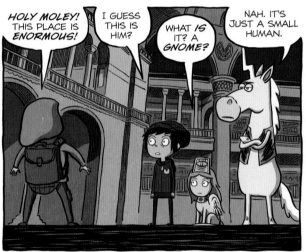

HOLY MOLEY! THIS PLACE IS *ENORMOUS!*

I GUESS THIS IS HIM?

WHAT *IS* IT? A *GNOME?*

NAH. IT'S JUST A SMALL HUMAN.

WELL *THAT'S* OUT OF THE ORDINARY! WELCOME TO *VULCAN'S CELESTIAL SUPPLY SHOP!* LET US KNOW IF YOU NEED ANY *HELP.*

I'VE GOT A *LIST.*

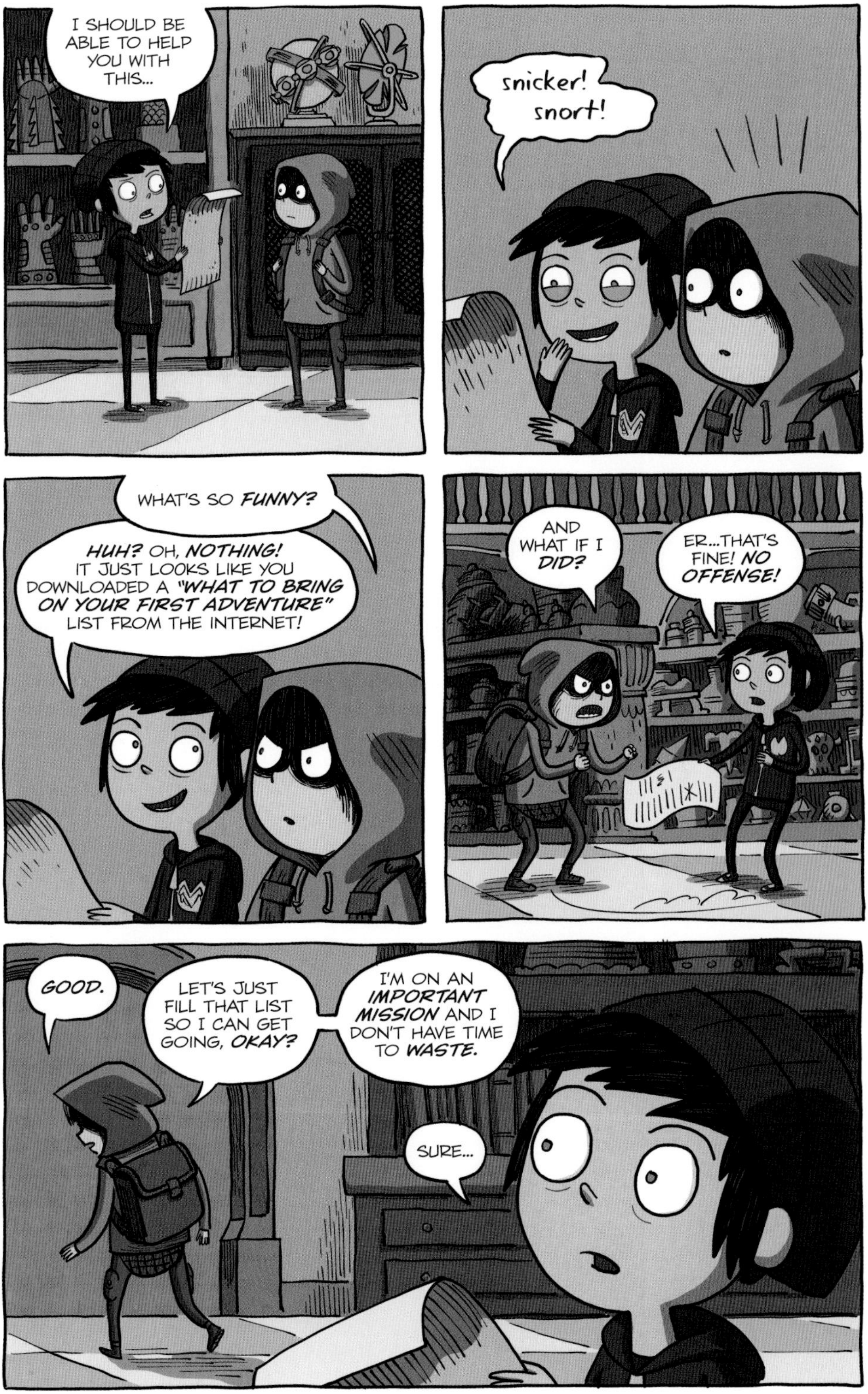

I SHOULD BE ABLE TO HELP YOU WITH THIS...
snicker! snort!
WHAT'S SO *FUNNY?*
***HUH?*** OH, ***NOTHING!*** IT JUST LOOKS LIKE YOU DOWNLOADED A ***"WHAT TO BRING ON YOUR FIRST ADVENTURE"*** LIST FROM THE INTERNET!
AND WHAT IF I *DID?*
ER...THAT'S FINE! ***NO OFFENSE!***
*GOOD.*
LET'S JUST FILL THAT LIST SO I CAN GET GOING, *OKAY?*
I'M ON AN *IMPORTANT MISSION* AND I DON'T HAVE TIME TO *WASTE.*
SURE...

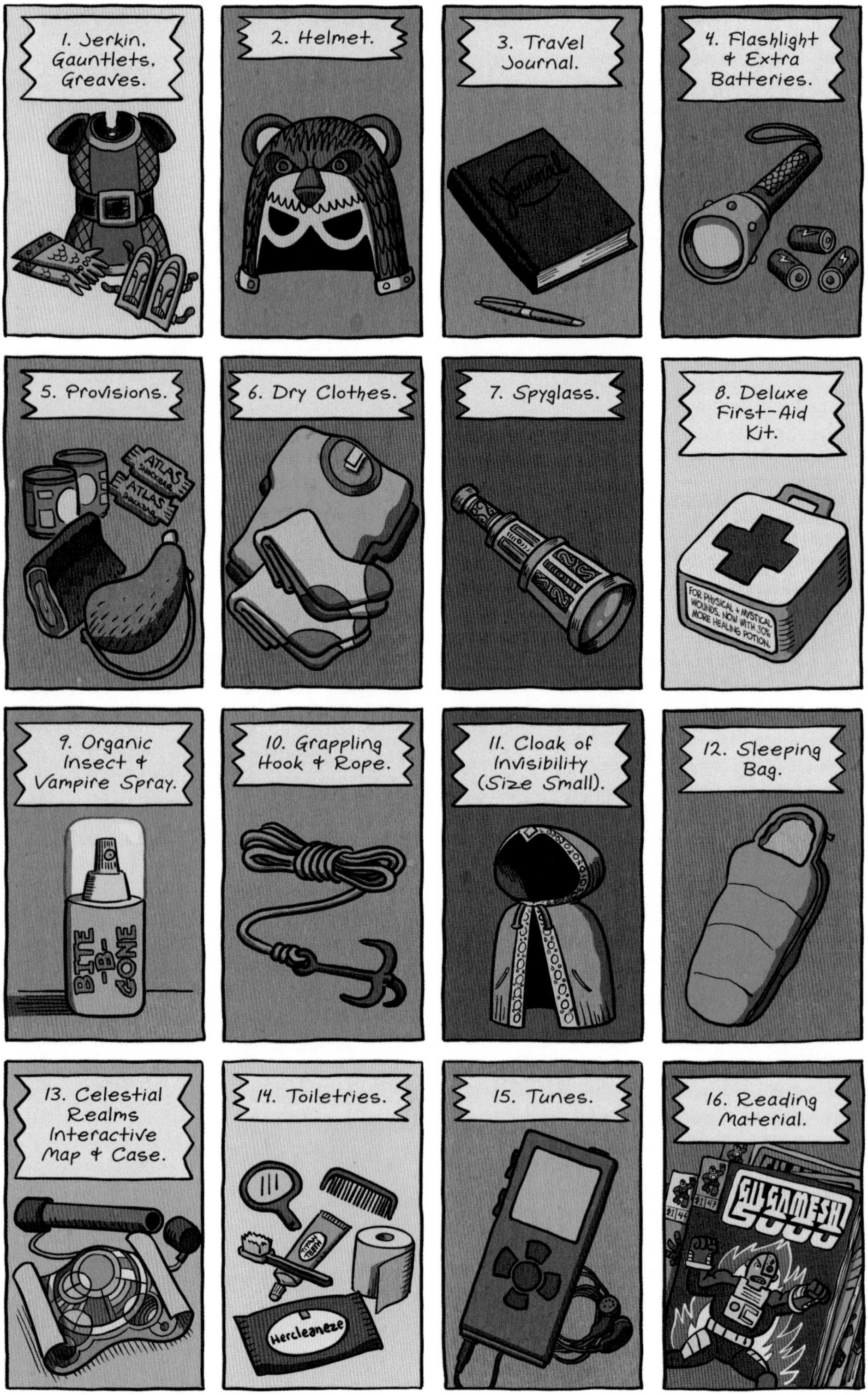
1. Jerkin. Gauntlets. Greaves.
2. Helmet.
3. Travel Journal.
Journal
4. Flashlight + Extra Batteries.
5. Provisions.
ATLAS SNACKBAR
ATLAS SNACKBAR
6. Dry Clothes.
7. Spyglass.
8. Deluxe First-Aid Kit.
FOR PHYSICAL + MYSTICAL WOUNDS. NOW WITH 30% MORE HEALING POTION.
9. Organic Insect + Vampire Spray.
BITE -B- GONE
10. Grappling Hook + Rope.
11. Cloak of Invisibility (Size Small).
12. Sleeping Bag.
13. Celestial Realms Interactive Map + Case.
14. Toiletries.
Hercleaneze
15. Tunes.
16. Reading Material.
GILGAMESH 5000

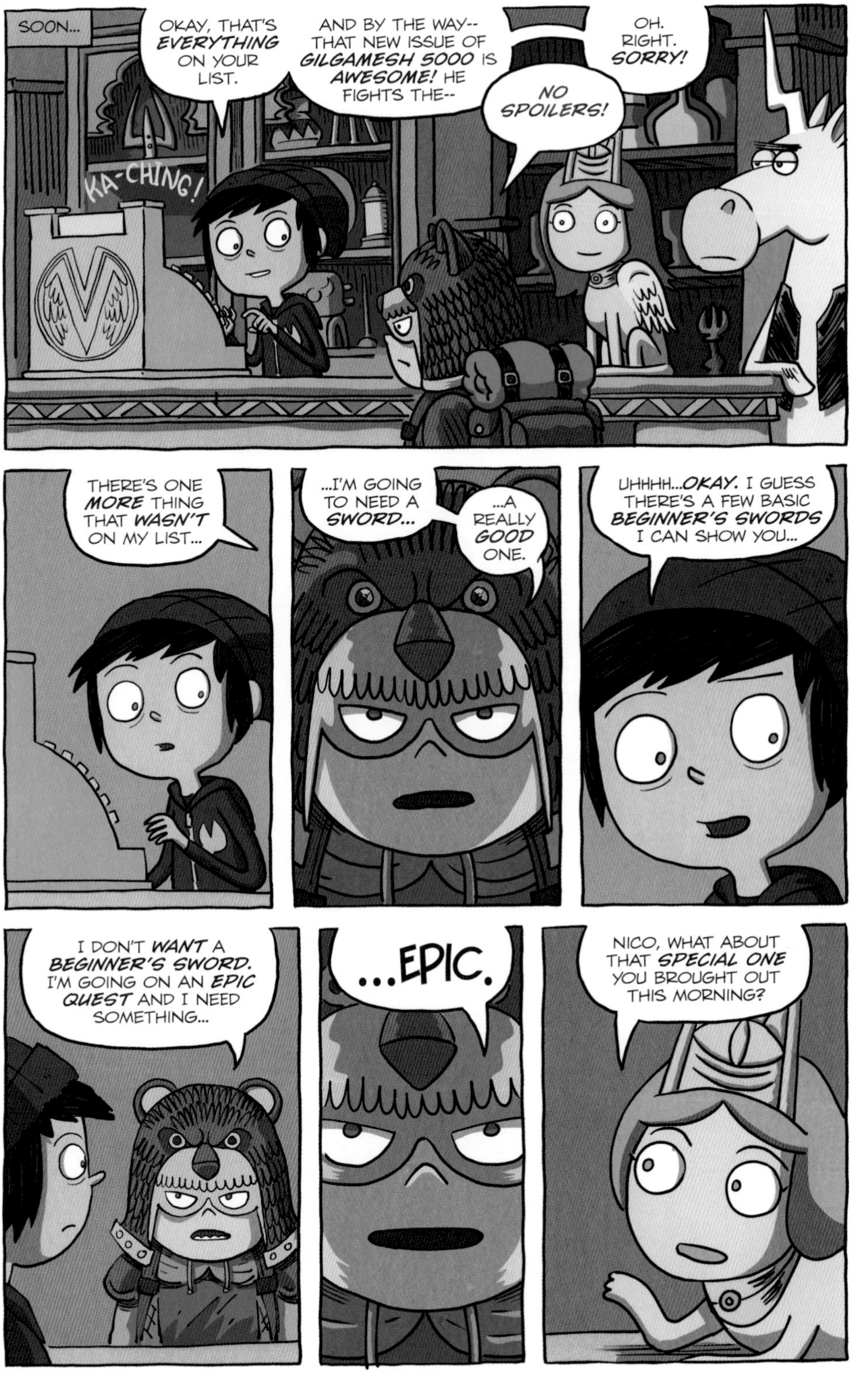
SOON...
OKAY, THAT'S **EVERYTHING** ON YOUR LIST.
KA-CHING!
AND BY THE WAY--THAT NEW ISSUE OF **GILGAMESH 5000** IS **AWESOME!** HE FIGHTS THE--
**NO SPOILERS!**
OH. RIGHT. **SORRY!**
THERE'S ONE **MORE** THING THAT **WASN'T** ON MY LIST...
...I'M GOING TO NEED A **SWORD...**
...A REALLY **GOOD** ONE.
UHHHH...**OKAY.** I GUESS THERE'S A FEW BASIC **BEGINNER'S SWORDS** I CAN SHOW YOU...
I DON'T **WANT** A **BEGINNER'S SWORD.** I'M GOING ON AN **EPIC QUEST** AND I NEED SOMETHING...
...EPIC.
NICO, WHAT ABOUT THAT **SPECIAL ONE** YOU BROUGHT OUT THIS MORNING?

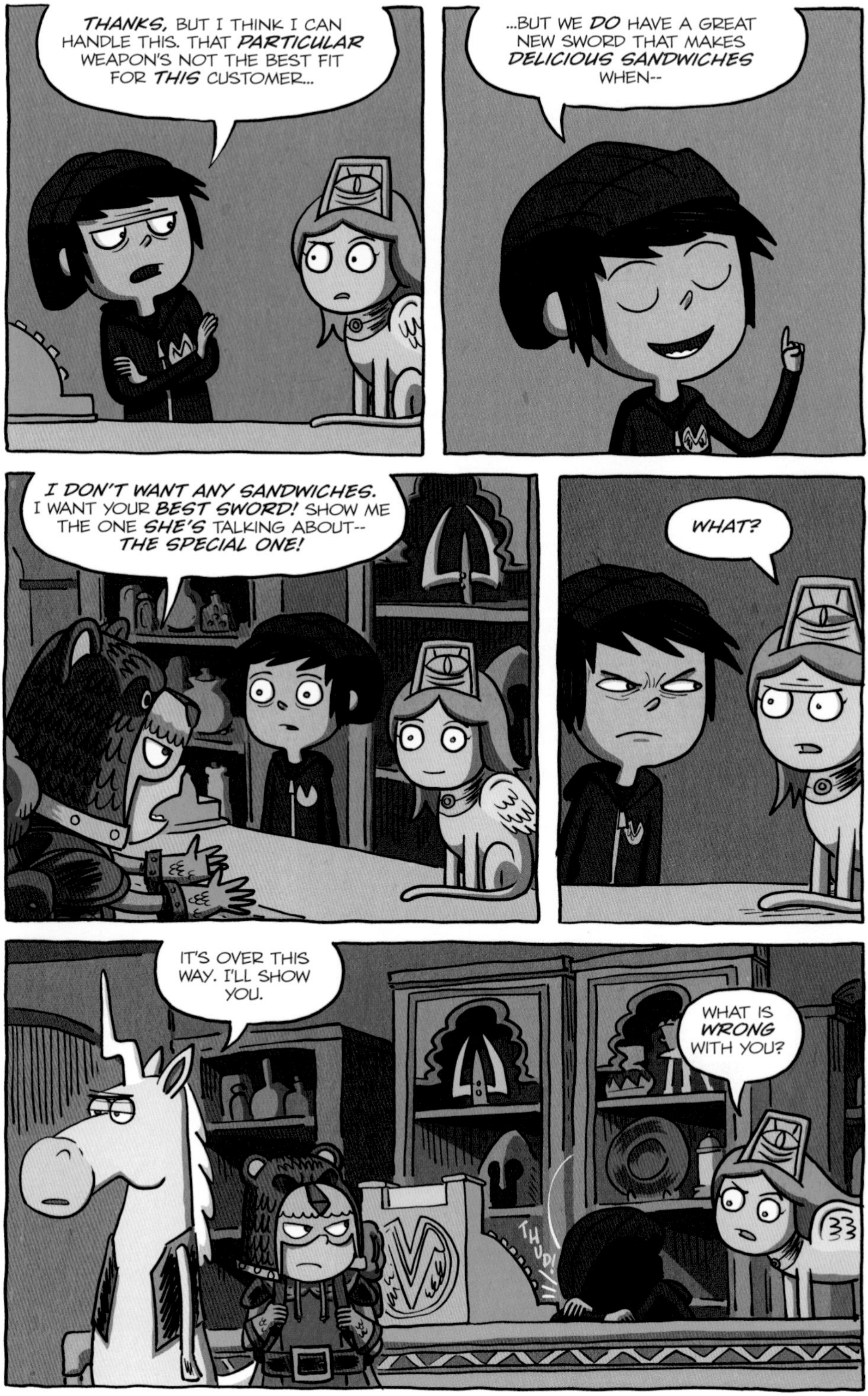
THANKS, BUT I THINK I CAN HANDLE THIS. THAT PARTICULAR WEAPON'S NOT THE BEST FIT FOR THIS CUSTOMER...
...BUT WE DO HAVE A GREAT NEW SWORD THAT MAKES DELICIOUS SANDWICHES WHEN--
I DON'T WANT ANY SANDWICHES. I WANT YOUR BEST SWORD! SHOW ME THE ONE SHE'S TALKING ABOUT-- THE SPECIAL ONE!
WHAT?
IT'S OVER THIS WAY. I'LL SHOW YOU.
WHAT IS WRONG WITH YOU?
THUD!

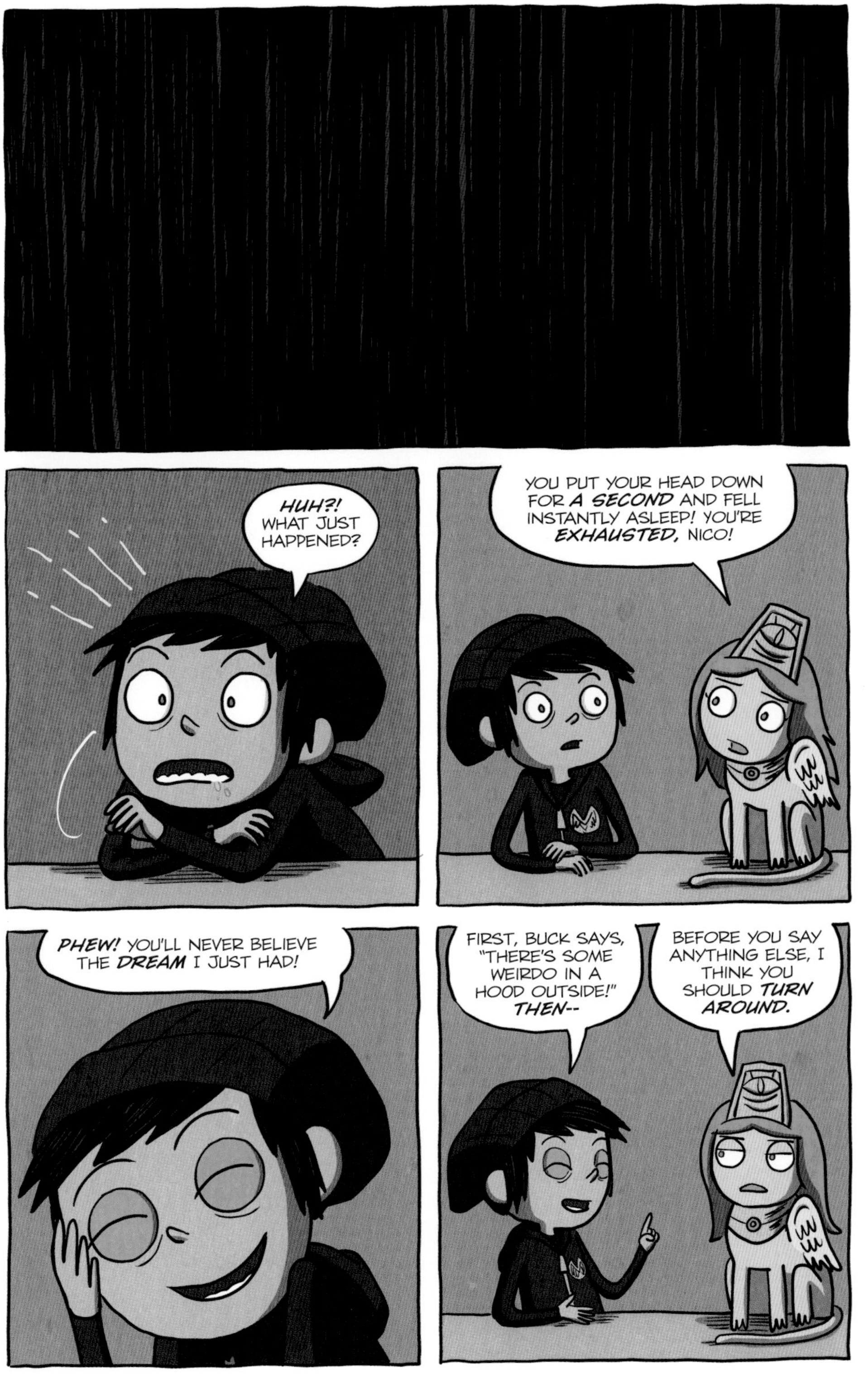
HUH?! WHAT JUST HAPPENED?
YOU PUT YOUR HEAD DOWN FOR A SECOND AND FELL INSTANTLY ASLEEP! YOU'RE EXHAUSTED, NICO!
PHEW! YOU'LL NEVER BELIEVE THE DREAM I JUST HAD!
FIRST, BUCK SAYS, "THERE'S SOME WEIRDO IN A HOOD OUTSIDE!" THEN--
BEFORE YOU SAY ANYTHING ELSE, I THINK YOU SHOULD TURN AROUND.

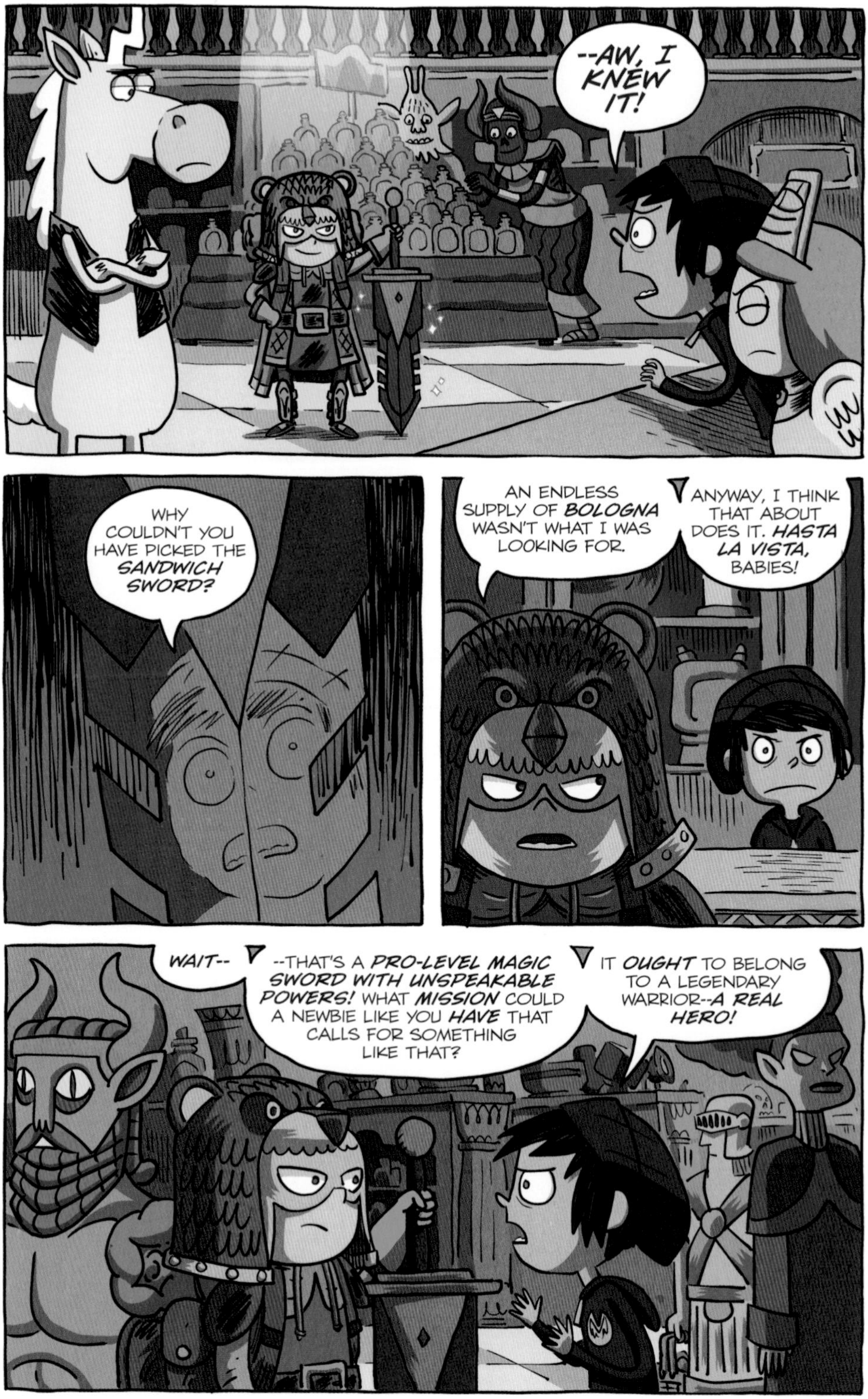
--AW, I KNEW IT!
WHY COULDN'T YOU HAVE PICKED THE SANDWICH SWORD?
AN ENDLESS SUPPLY OF BOLOGNA WASN'T WHAT I WAS LOOKING FOR.
ANYWAY, I THINK THAT ABOUT DOES IT. HASTA LA VISTA, BABIES!
WAIT--
--THAT'S A PRO-LEVEL MAGIC SWORD WITH UNSPEAKABLE POWERS! WHAT MISSION COULD A NEWBIE LIKE YOU HAVE THAT CALLS FOR SOMETHING LIKE THAT?
IT OUGHT TO BELONG TO A LEGENDARY WARRIOR--A REAL HERO!

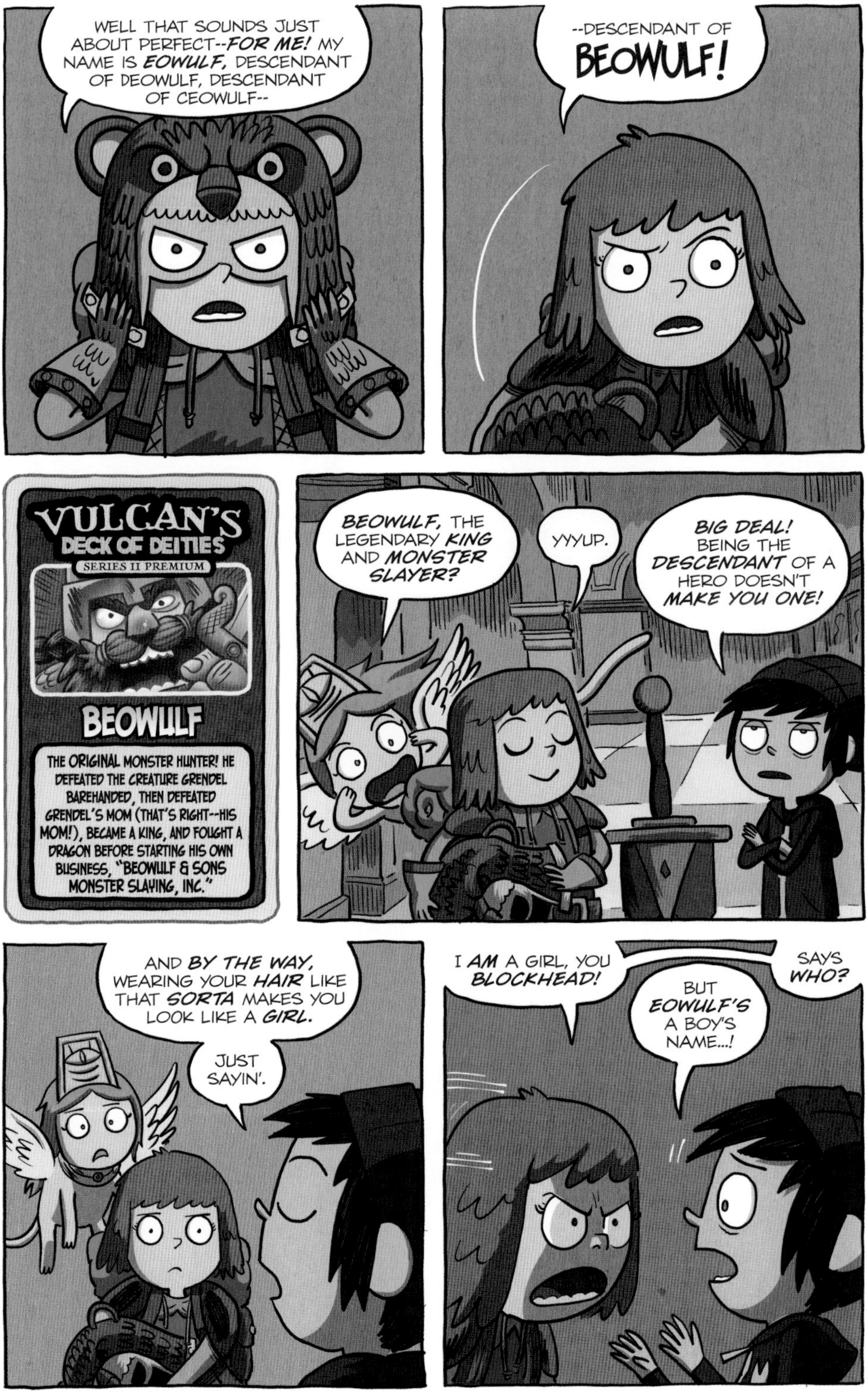
WELL THAT SOUNDS JUST ABOUT PERFECT--FOR ME! MY NAME IS EOWULF, DESCENDANT OF DEOWULF, DESCENDANT OF CEOWULF--
--DESCENDANT OF BEOWULF!
VULCAN'S DECK OF DEITIES
SERIES II PREMIUM
BEOWULF
THE ORIGINAL MONSTER HUNTER! HE DEFEATED THE CREATURE GRENDEL BAREHANDED, THEN DEFEATED GRENDEL'S MOM (THAT'S RIGHT--HIS MOM!), BECAME A KING, AND FOUGHT A DRAGON BEFORE STARTING HIS OWN BUSINESS, "BEOWULF & SONS MONSTER SLAYING, INC."
BEOWULF, THE LEGENDARY KING AND MONSTER SLAYER?
YYYUP.
BIG DEAL! BEING THE DESCENDANT OF A HERO DOESN'T MAKE YOU ONE!
AND BY THE WAY, WEARING YOUR HAIR LIKE THAT SORTA MAKES YOU LOOK LIKE A GIRL.
JUST SAYIN'.
BUT EOWULF'S A BOY'S NAME...!
I AM A GIRL, YOU BLOCKHEAD!
SAYS WHO?

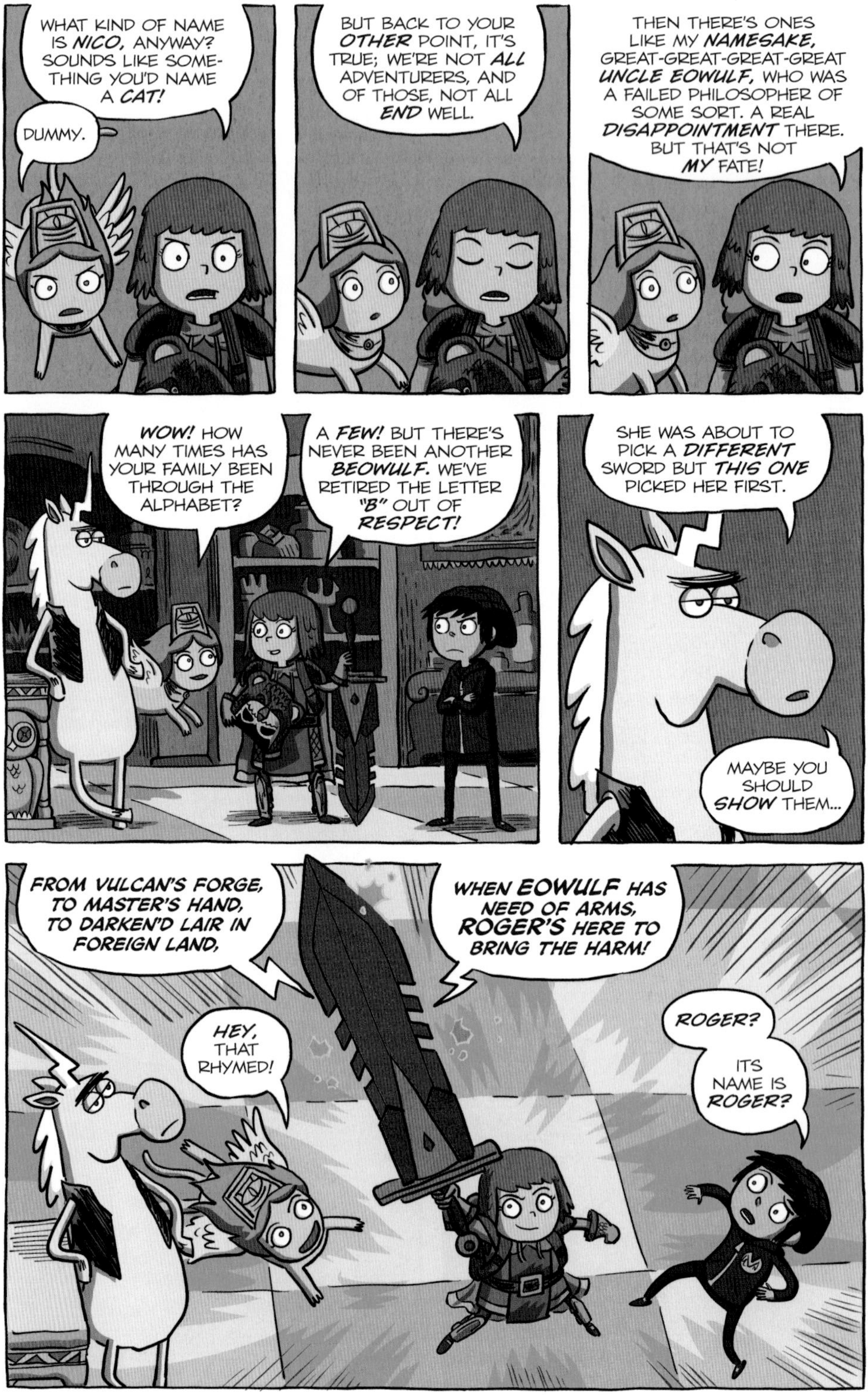
WHAT KIND OF NAME IS NICO, ANYWAY? SOUNDS LIKE SOMETHING YOU'D NAME A CAT!
DUMMY.
BUT BACK TO YOUR OTHER POINT, IT'S TRUE; WE'RE NOT ALL ADVENTURERS, AND OF THOSE, NOT ALL END WELL.
THEN THERE'S ONES LIKE MY NAMESAKE, GREAT-GREAT-GREAT-GREAT UNCLE EOWULF, WHO WAS A FAILED PHILOSOPHER OF SOME SORT. A REAL DISAPPOINTMENT THERE. BUT THAT'S NOT MY FATE!
WOW! HOW MANY TIMES HAS YOUR FAMILY BEEN THROUGH THE ALPHABET?
A FEW! BUT THERE'S NEVER BEEN ANOTHER BEOWULF. WE'VE RETIRED THE LETTER "B" OUT OF RESPECT!
SHE WAS ABOUT TO PICK A DIFFERENT SWORD BUT THIS ONE PICKED HER FIRST.
MAYBE YOU SHOULD SHOW THEM...
FROM VULCAN'S FORGE, TO MASTER'S HAND, TO DARKEN'D LAIR IN FOREIGN LAND,
WHEN EOWULF HAS NEED OF ARMS, ROGER'S HERE TO BRING THE HARM!
HEY, THAT RHYMED!
ROGER?
ITS NAME IS ROGER?

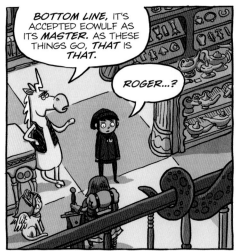

BOTTOM LINE, IT'S ACCEPTED EOWULF AS ITS MASTER. AS THESE THINGS GO, THAT IS THAT.

ROGER...?

SO AS I WAS SAYING, THANKS FOR ALL THE STUFF...

...SEE YOU IN THE EPIC BALLADS!

MAGIC ONE SIZE FITS ALL™ SCABBARD, SOLD SEPARATELY.

WHAT IS THIS MISSION OF YOURS, ANYWAY?

I'M JOINING THE FAMILY BUSINESS, OF COURSE...

...MONSTER SLAYING!

WHICH MONSTERS?

I MEAN, SOME OF OUR BEST CUSTOMERS ARE TECHNICALLY MONSTERS.

YEAH, I NOTICED. (I'D DEFINITELY SLAY SOME OF THEM...) BUT I NEED TO MAKE A NAME FOR MYSELF, SO I'M STARTING BIG--

--CERBERUS! THE LEGENDARY, TERRIFYING, THREE-HEADED HOUND OF HADES, LORD OF THE UNDERWORLD!

YOU'RE JOKING.

I'M NOT.

HOLD ON--CERBERUS ISN'T A TERRIFYING MONSTER. WE GROOM HIM AND STUFF ALL THE TIME.

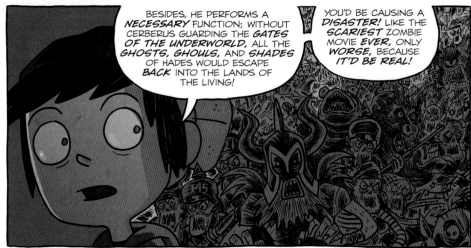

BESIDES, HE PERFORMS A NECESSARY FUNCTION; WITHOUT CERBERUS GUARDING THE GATES OF THE UNDERWORLD, ALL THE GHOSTS, GHOULS, AND SHADES OF HADES WOULD ESCAPE BACK INTO THE LANDS OF THE LIVING!

YOU'D BE CAUSING A DISASTER! LIKE THE SCARIEST ZOMBIE MOVIE EVER, ONLY WORSE, BECAUSE IT'D BE REAL!

42

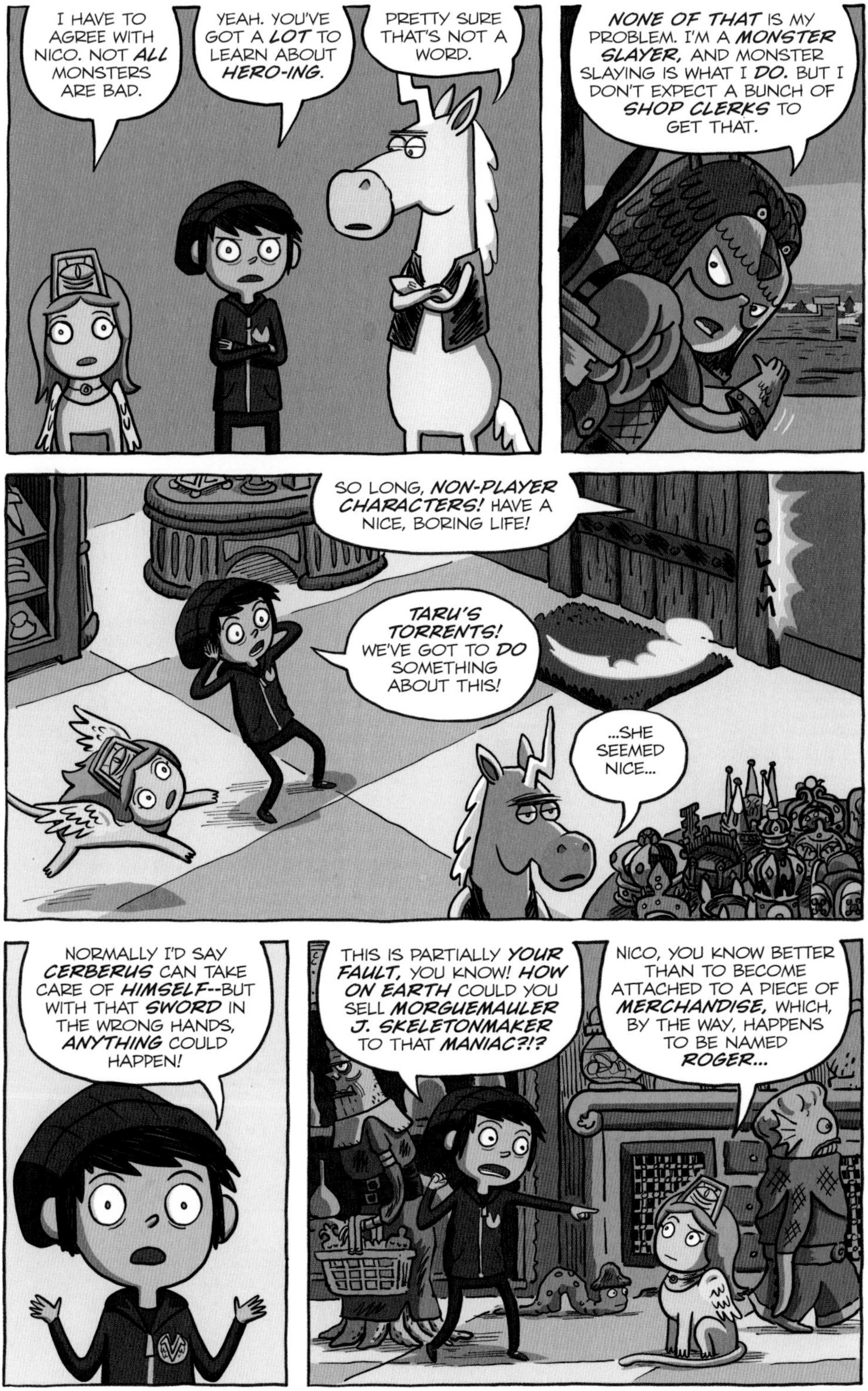
I HAVE TO AGREE WITH NICO. NOT ALL MONSTERS ARE BAD.
YEAH. YOU'VE GOT A LOT TO LEARN ABOUT HERO-ING.
PRETTY SURE THAT'S NOT A WORD.
NONE OF THAT IS MY PROBLEM. I'M A MONSTER SLAYER, AND MONSTER SLAYING IS WHAT I DO. BUT I DON'T EXPECT A BUNCH OF SHOP CLERKS TO GET THAT.
SO LONG, NON-PLAYER CHARACTERS! HAVE A NICE, BORING LIFE!
SLAM
TARU'S TORRENTS! WE'VE GOT TO DO SOMETHING ABOUT THIS!
...SHE SEEMED NICE...
NORMALLY I'D SAY CERBERUS CAN TAKE CARE OF HIMSELF--BUT WITH THAT SWORD IN THE WRONG HANDS, ANYTHING COULD HAPPEN!
THIS IS PARTIALLY YOUR FAULT, YOU KNOW! HOW ON EARTH COULD YOU SELL MORGUEMAULER J. SKELETONMAKER TO THAT MANIAC?!?
NICO, YOU KNOW BETTER THAN TO BECOME ATTACHED TO A PIECE OF MERCHANDISE, WHICH, BY THE WAY, HAPPENS TO BE NAMED ROGER...

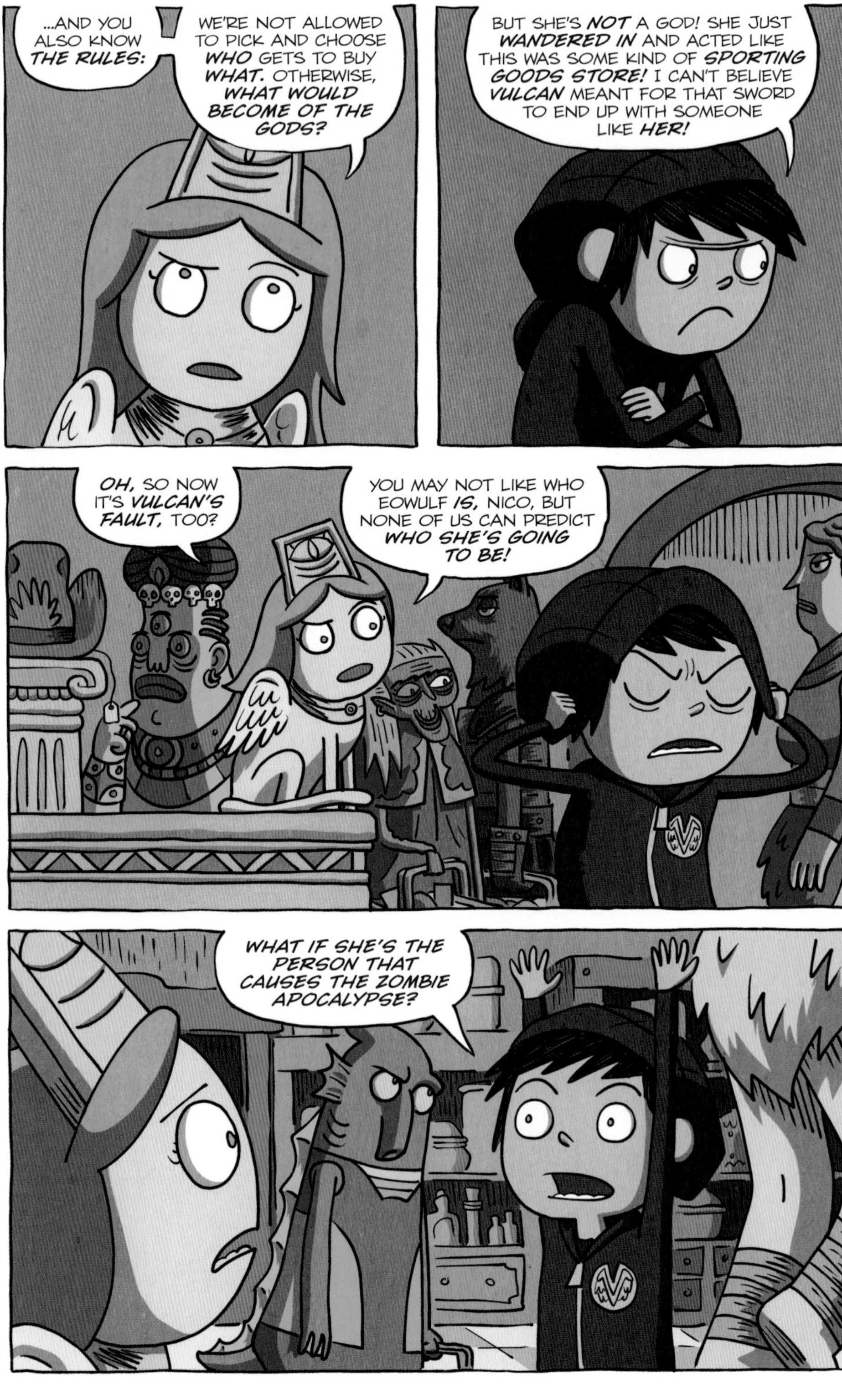
...AND YOU ALSO KNOW *THE RULES:*
WE'RE NOT ALLOWED TO PICK AND CHOOSE *WHO* GETS TO BUY *WHAT.* OTHERWISE, *WHAT WOULD BECOME OF THE GODS?*
BUT SHE'S *NOT* A GOD! SHE JUST *WANDERED IN* AND ACTED LIKE THIS WAS SOME KIND OF *SPORTING GOODS STORE!* I CAN'T BELIEVE *VULCAN* MEANT FOR THAT SWORD TO END UP WITH SOMEONE LIKE *HER!*
*OH,* SO NOW IT'S *VULCAN'S FAULT,* TOO?
YOU MAY NOT LIKE WHO EOWULF *IS,* NICO, BUT NONE OF US CAN PREDICT *WHO SHE'S GOING TO BE!*
*WHAT IF SHE'S THE PERSON THAT CAUSES THE ZOMBIE APOCALYPSE?*

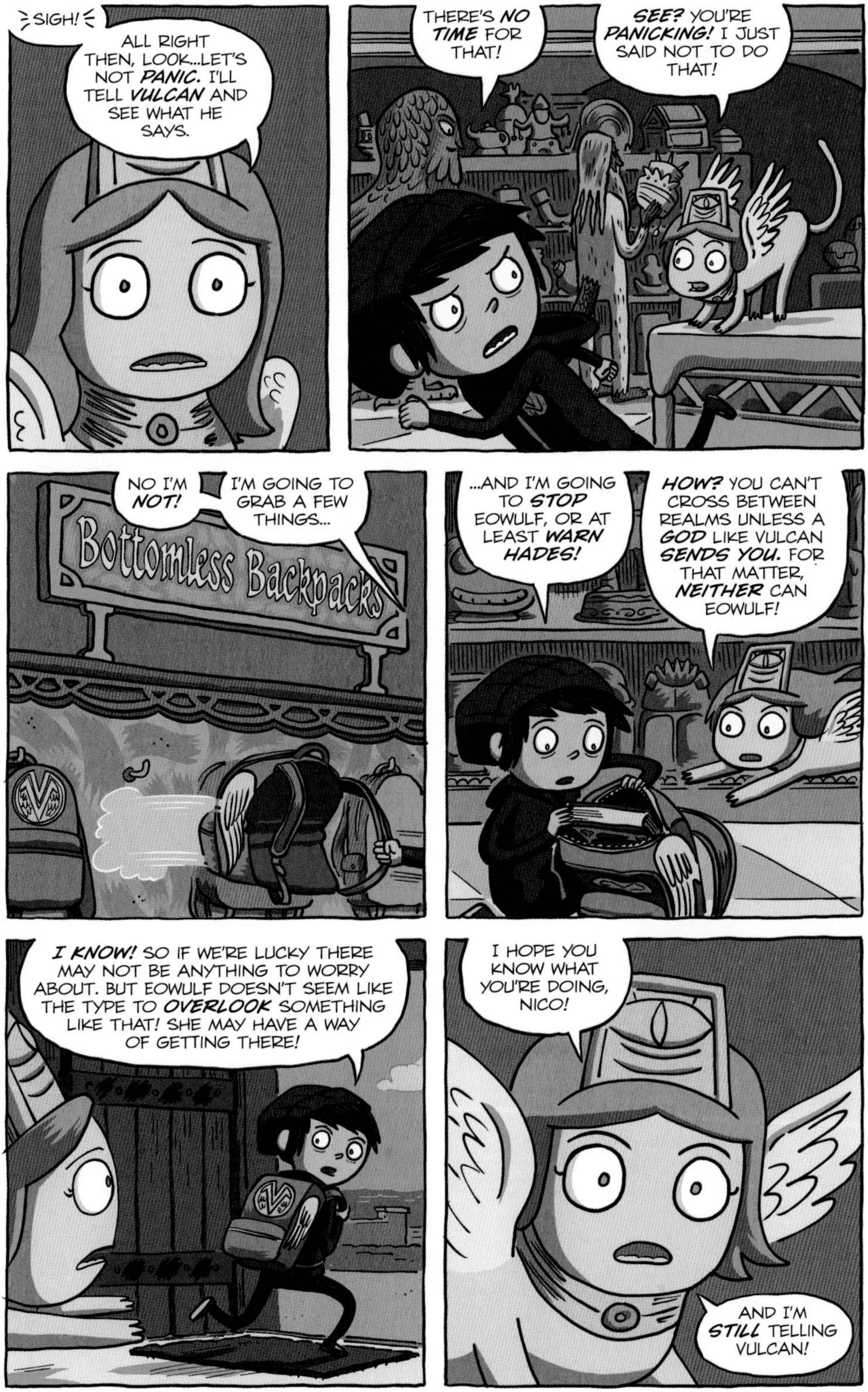
SIGH!
ALL RIGHT THEN, LOOK...LET'S NOT PANIC. I'LL TELL VULCAN AND SEE WHAT HE SAYS.
THERE'S NO TIME FOR THAT!
SEE? YOU'RE PANICKING! I JUST SAID NOT TO DO THAT!
NO I'M NOT!
I'M GOING TO GRAB A FEW THINGS...
Bottomless Backpacks
...AND I'M GOING TO STOP EOWULF, OR AT LEAST WARN HADES!
HOW? YOU CAN'T CROSS BETWEEN REALMS UNLESS A GOD LIKE VULCAN SENDS YOU. FOR THAT MATTER, NEITHER CAN EOWULF!
I KNOW! SO IF WE'RE LUCKY THERE MAY NOT BE ANYTHING TO WORRY ABOUT. BUT EOWULF DOESN'T SEEM LIKE THE TYPE TO OVERLOOK SOMETHING LIKE THAT! SHE MAY HAVE A WAY OF GETTING THERE!
I HOPE YOU KNOW WHAT YOU'RE DOING, NICO!
AND I'M STILL TELLING VULCAN!

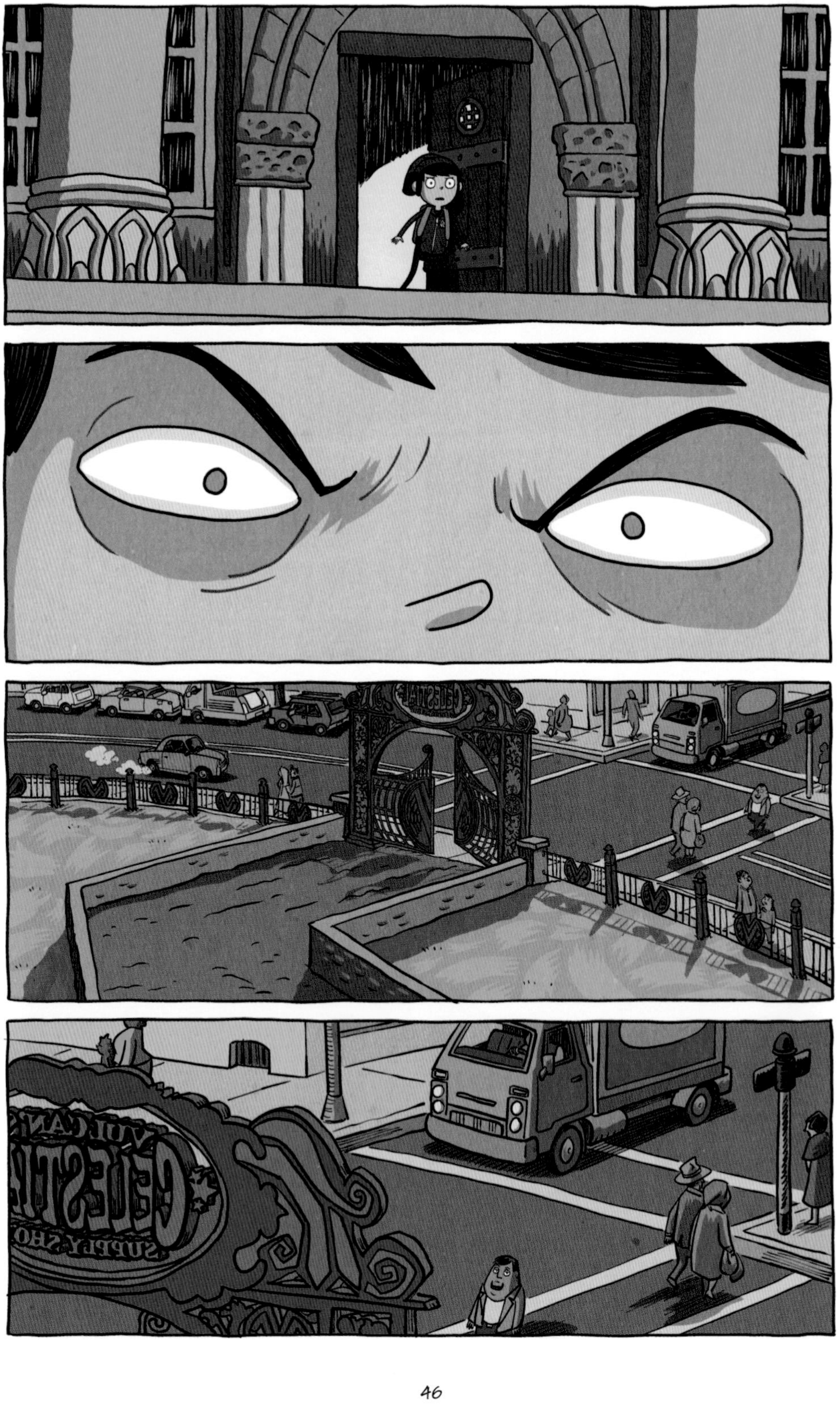

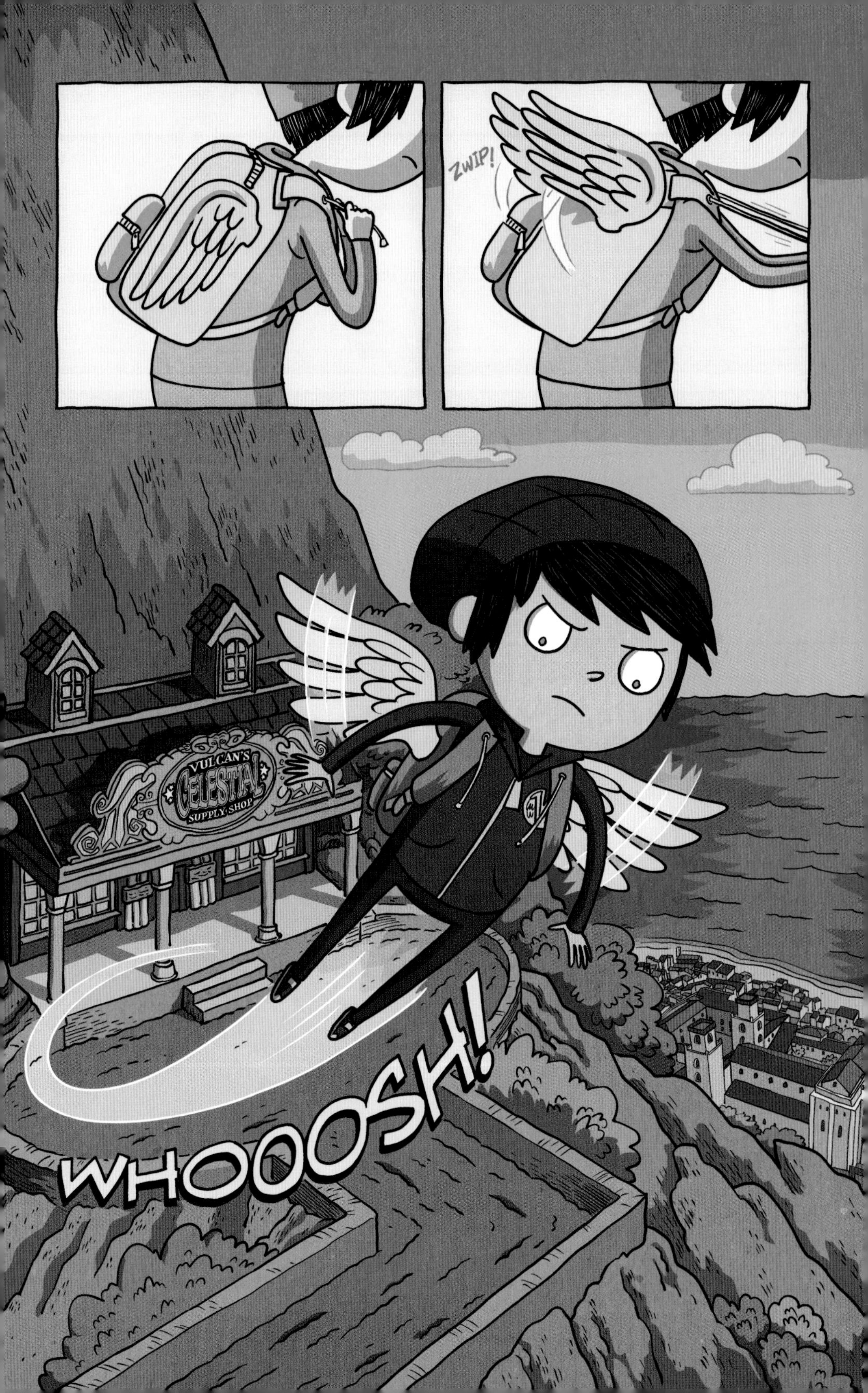
ZWIP!
VULCAN'S CELESTIAL SUPPLY SHOP
WHOOOOSH!

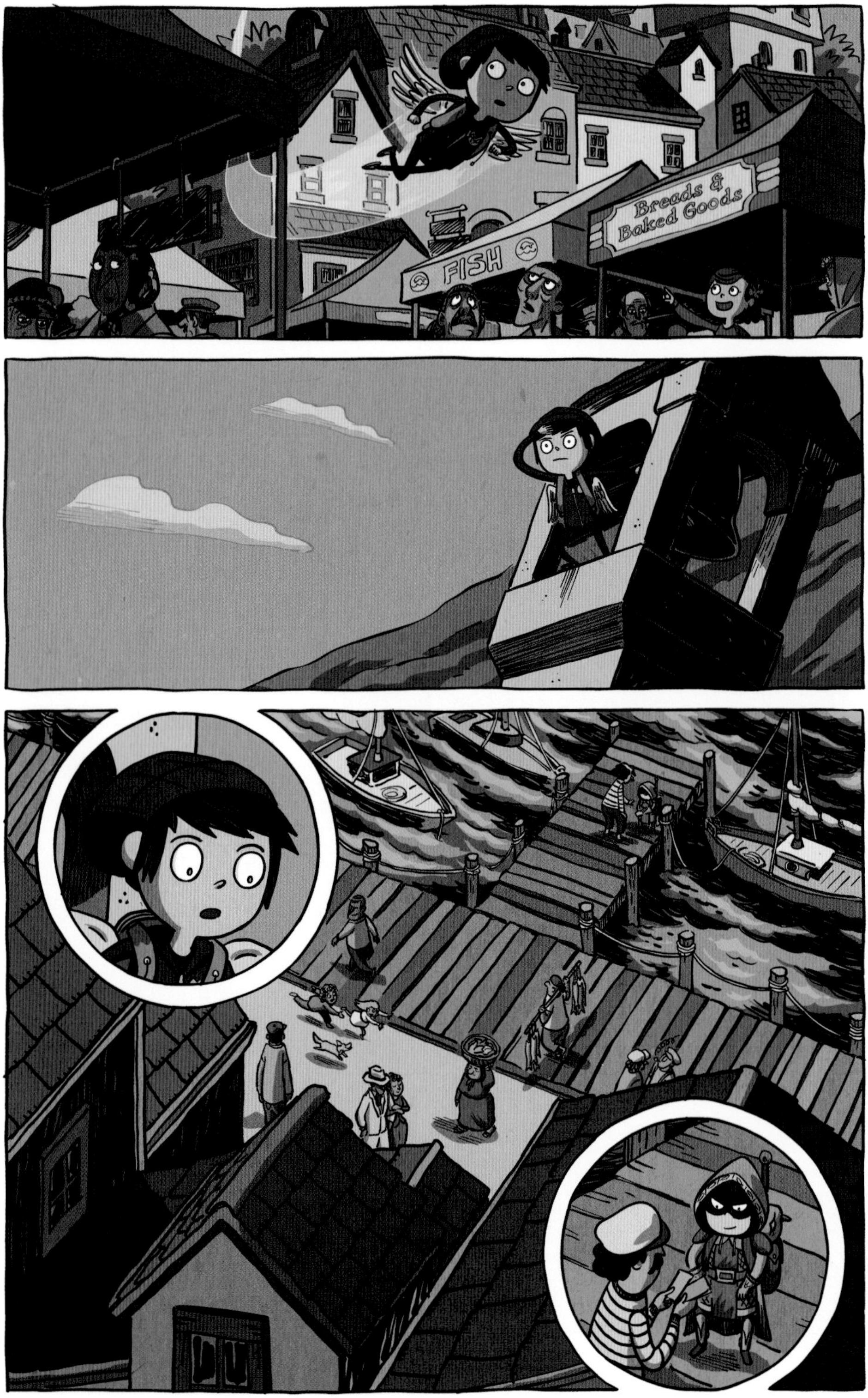
Breads & Baked Goods
FISH

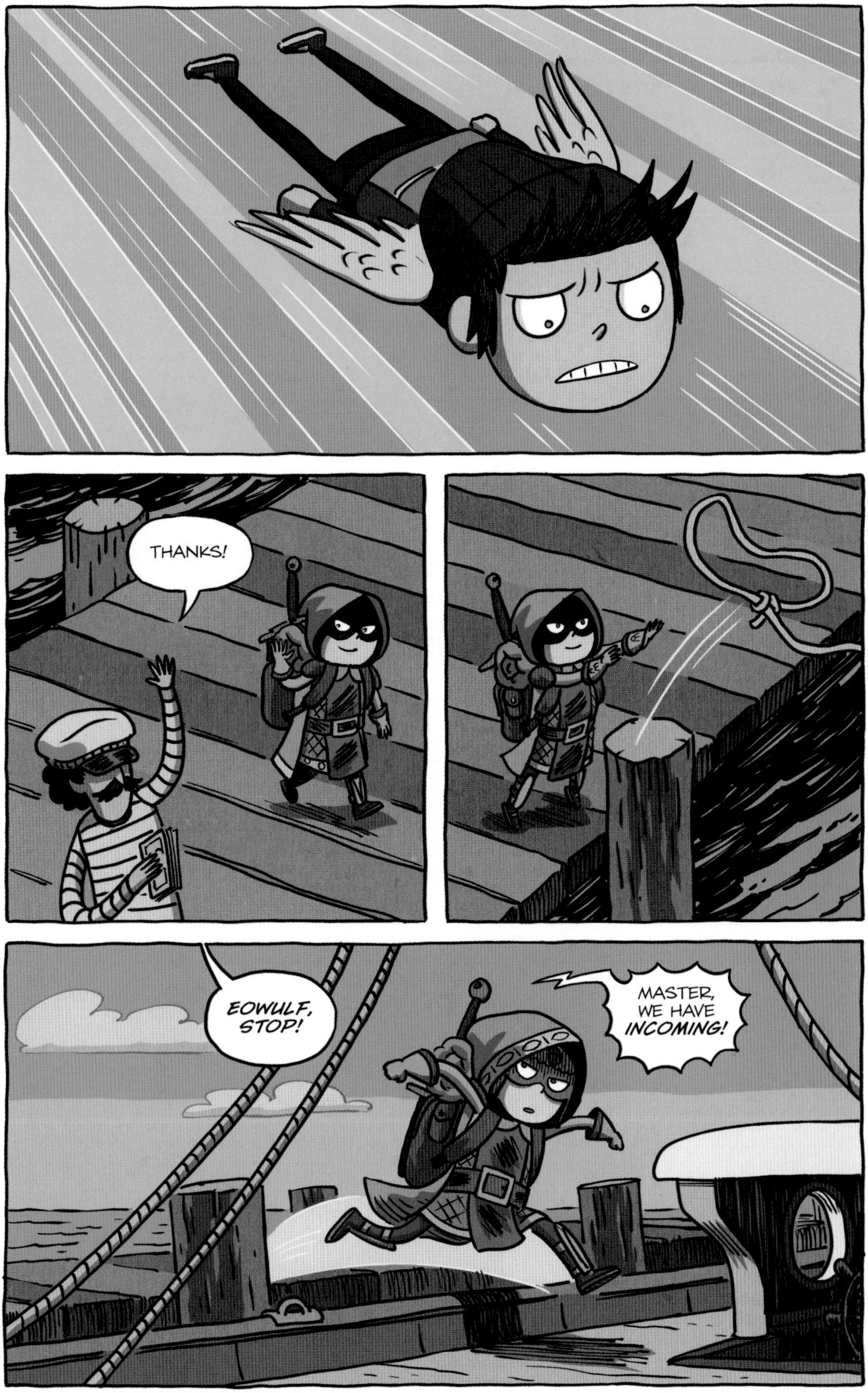
THANKS!
EOWULF, STOP!
MASTER, WE HAVE INCOMING!

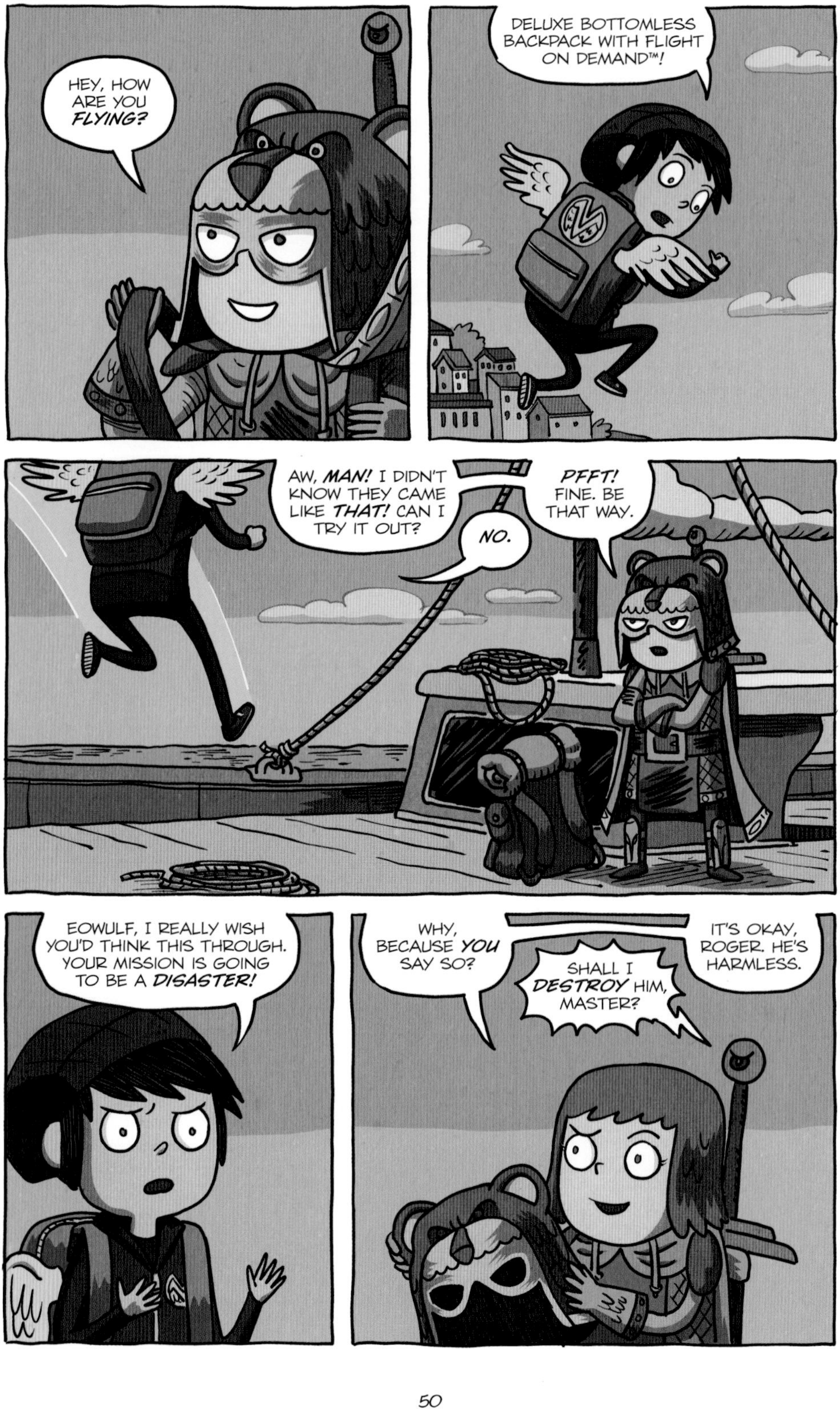
HEY, HOW ARE YOU FLYING?
DELUXE BOTTOMLESS BACKPACK WITH FLIGHT ON DEMAND™!
AW, MAN! I DIDN'T KNOW THEY CAME LIKE THAT! CAN I TRY IT OUT?
NO.
PFFT! FINE. BE THAT WAY.
EOWULF, I REALLY WISH YOU'D THINK THIS THROUGH. YOUR MISSION IS GOING TO BE A DISASTER!
WHY, BECAUSE YOU SAY SO?
SHALL I DESTROY HIM, MASTER?
IT'S OKAY, ROGER. HE'S HARMLESS.

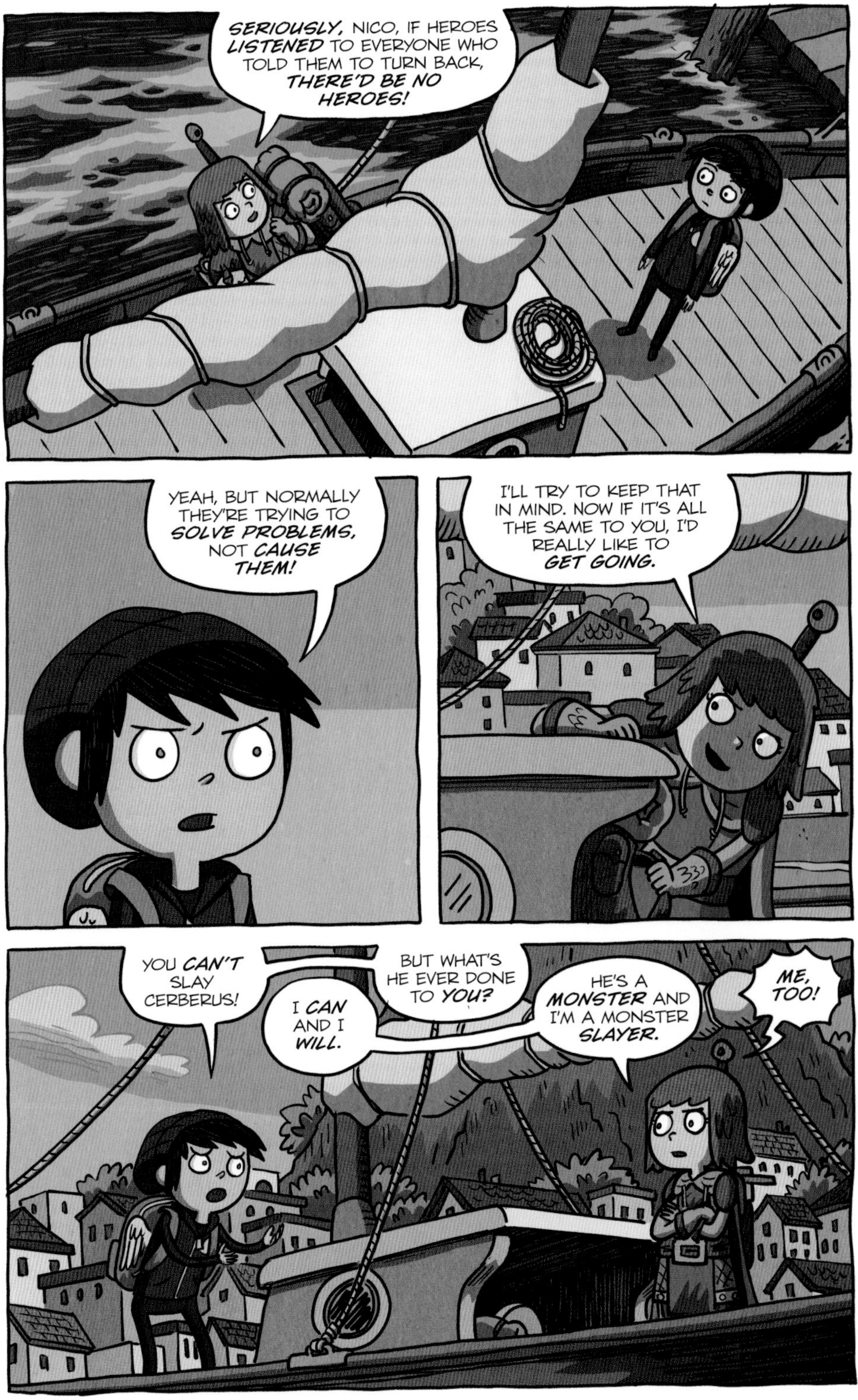
SERIOUSLY, NICO, IF HEROES LISTENED TO EVERYONE WHO TOLD THEM TO TURN BACK, THERE'D BE NO HEROES!
YEAH, BUT NORMALLY THEY'RE TRYING TO SOLVE PROBLEMS, NOT CAUSE THEM!
I'LL TRY TO KEEP THAT IN MIND. NOW IF IT'S ALL THE SAME TO YOU, I'D REALLY LIKE TO GET GOING.
YOU CAN'T SLAY CERBERUS!
I CAN AND I WILL.
BUT WHAT'S HE EVER DONE TO YOU?
HE'S A MONSTER AND I'M A MONSTER SLAYER.
ME, TOO!

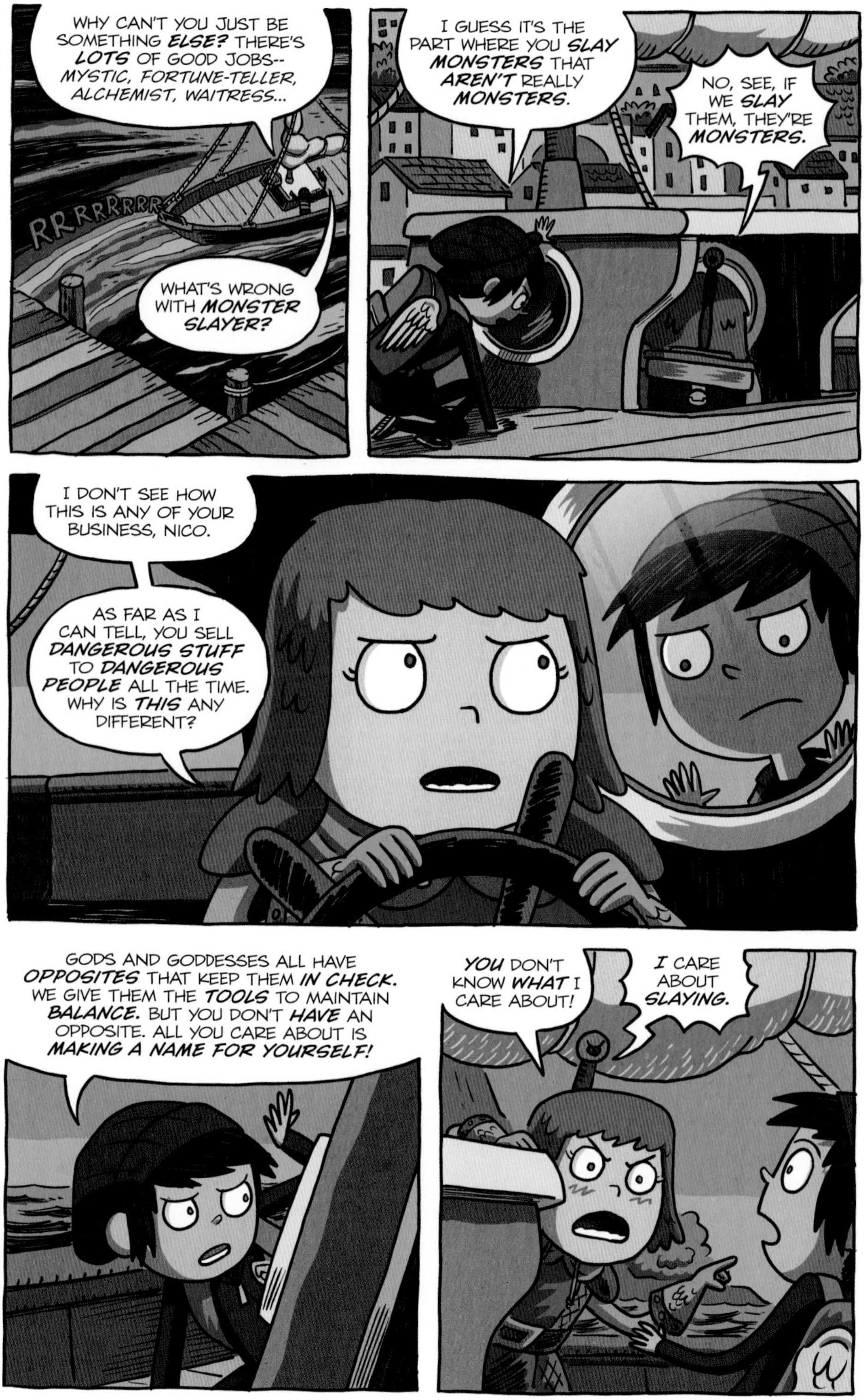
WHY CAN'T YOU JUST BE SOMETHING ELSE? THERE'S LOTS OF GOOD JOBS-- MYSTIC, FORTUNE-TELLER, ALCHEMIST, WAITRESS...
RRRRRRRR
WHAT'S WRONG WITH MONSTER SLAYER?
I GUESS IT'S THE PART WHERE YOU SLAY MONSTERS THAT AREN'T REALLY MONSTERS.
NO, SEE, IF WE SLAY THEM, THEY'RE MONSTERS.
I DON'T SEE HOW THIS IS ANY OF YOUR BUSINESS, NICO.
AS FAR AS I CAN TELL, YOU SELL DANGEROUS STUFF TO DANGEROUS PEOPLE ALL THE TIME. WHY IS THIS ANY DIFFERENT?
GODS AND GODDESSES ALL HAVE OPPOSITES THAT KEEP THEM IN CHECK. WE GIVE THEM THE TOOLS TO MAINTAIN BALANCE. BUT YOU DON'T HAVE AN OPPOSITE. ALL YOU CARE ABOUT IS MAKING A NAME FOR YOURSELF!
YOU DON'T KNOW WHAT I CARE ABOUT!
I CARE ABOUT SLAYING.

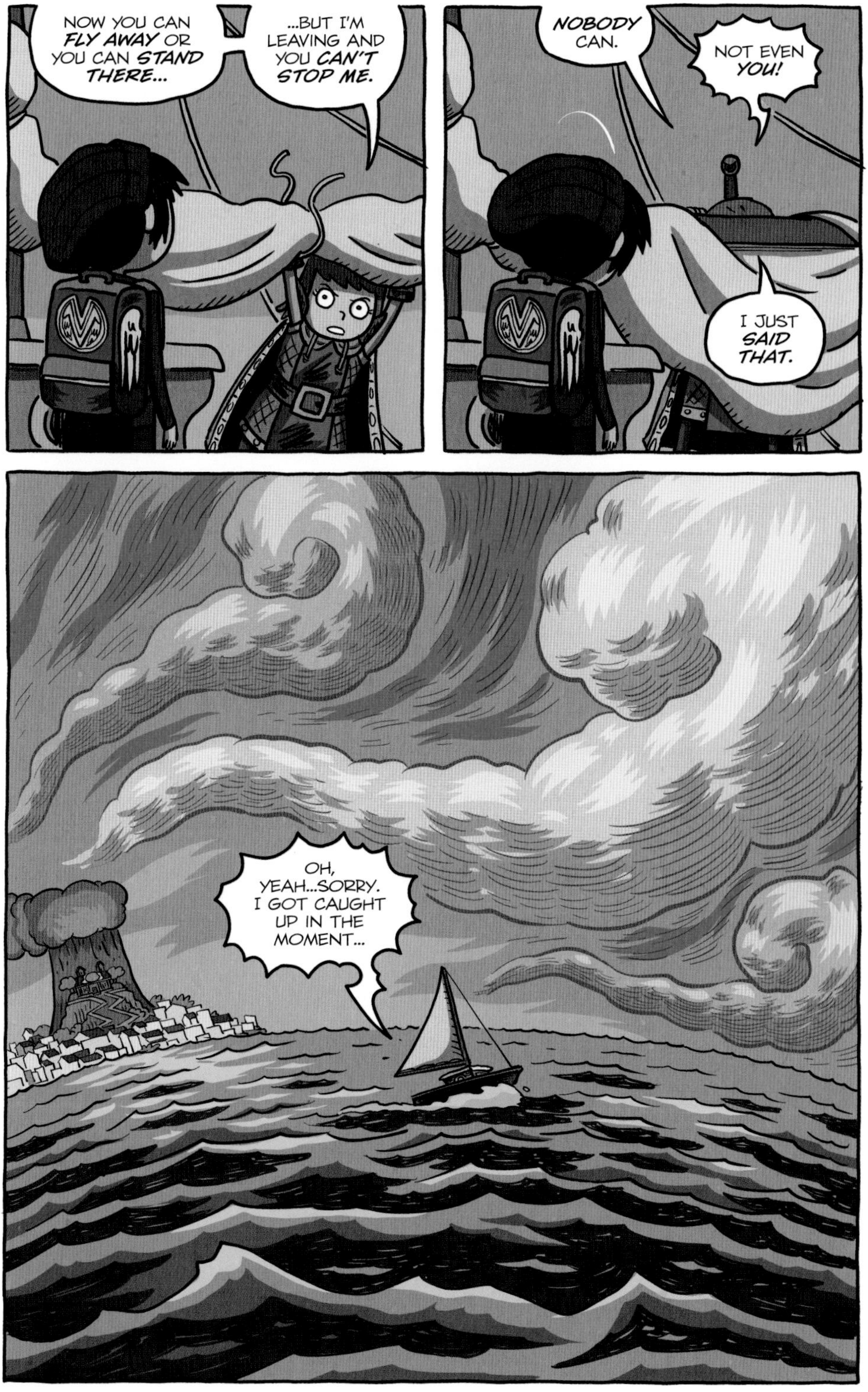
NOW YOU CAN FLY AWAY OR YOU CAN STAND THERE...
...BUT I'M LEAVING AND YOU CAN'T STOP ME.
NOBODY CAN.
NOT EVEN YOU!
I JUST SAID THAT.
OH, YEAH...SORRY. I GOT CAUGHT UP IN THE MOMENT...

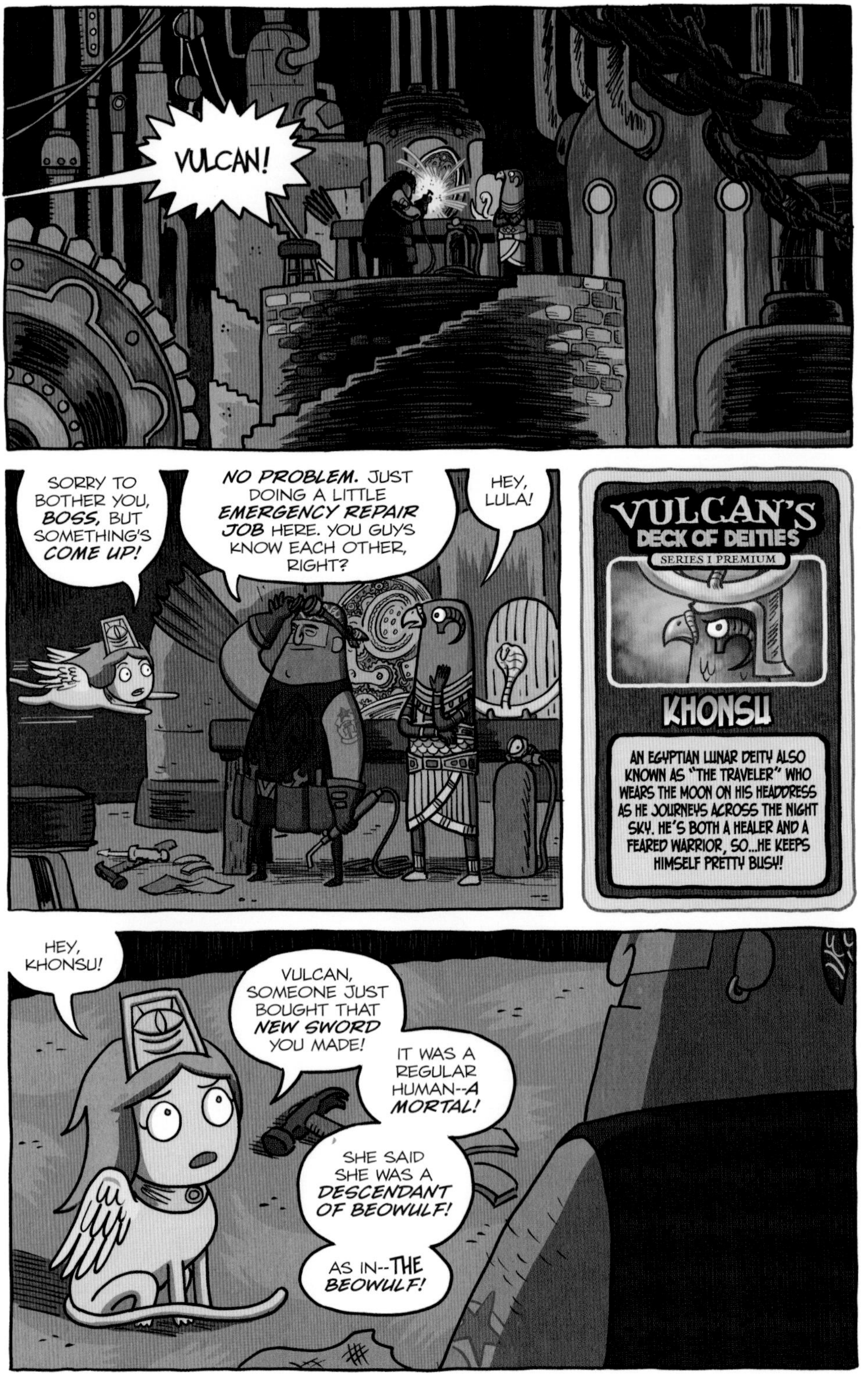
VULCAN!
SORRY TO BOTHER YOU, BOSS, BUT SOMETHING'S COME UP!
NO PROBLEM. JUST DOING A LITTLE EMERGENCY REPAIR JOB HERE. YOU GUYS KNOW EACH OTHER, RIGHT?
HEY, LULA!
VULCAN'S DECK OF DEITIES
SERIES I PREMIUM
KHONSU
AN EGYPTIAN LUNAR DEITY ALSO KNOWN AS "THE TRAVELER" WHO WEARS THE MOON ON HIS HEADDRESS AS HE JOURNEYS ACROSS THE NIGHT SKY. HE'S BOTH A HEALER AND A FEARED WARRIOR, SO...HE KEEPS HIMSELF PRETTY BUSY!
HEY, KHONSU!
VULCAN, SOMEONE JUST BOUGHT THAT NEW SWORD YOU MADE!
IT WAS A REGULAR HUMAN--A MORTAL!
SHE SAID SHE WAS A DESCENDANT OF BEOWULF!
AS IN--THE BEOWULF!

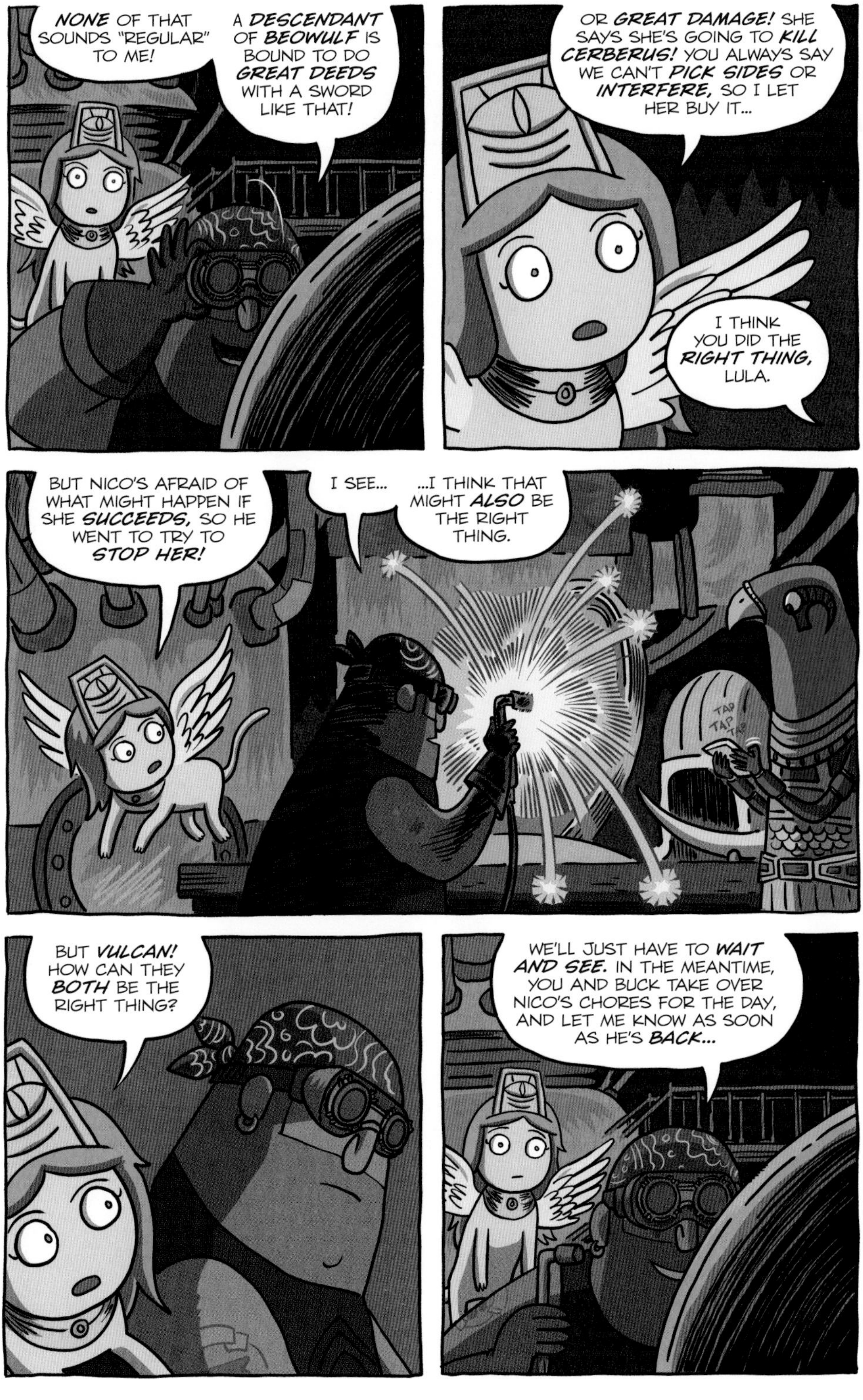
NONE OF THAT SOUNDS "REGULAR" TO ME!
A DESCENDANT OF BEOWULF IS BOUND TO DO GREAT DEEDS WITH A SWORD LIKE THAT!
OR GREAT DAMAGE! SHE SAYS SHE'S GOING TO KILL CERBERUS! YOU ALWAYS SAY WE CAN'T PICK SIDES OR INTERFERE, SO I LET HER BUY IT...
I THINK YOU DID THE RIGHT THING, LULA.
BUT NICO'S AFRAID OF WHAT MIGHT HAPPEN IF SHE SUCCEEDS, SO HE WENT TO TRY TO STOP HER!
I SEE...
...I THINK THAT MIGHT ALSO BE THE RIGHT THING.
TAP TAP TAP
BUT VULCAN! HOW CAN THEY BOTH BE THE RIGHT THING?
WE'LL JUST HAVE TO WAIT AND SEE. IN THE MEANTIME, YOU AND BUCK TAKE OVER NICO'S CHORES FOR THE DAY, AND LET ME KNOW AS SOON AS HE'S BACK...

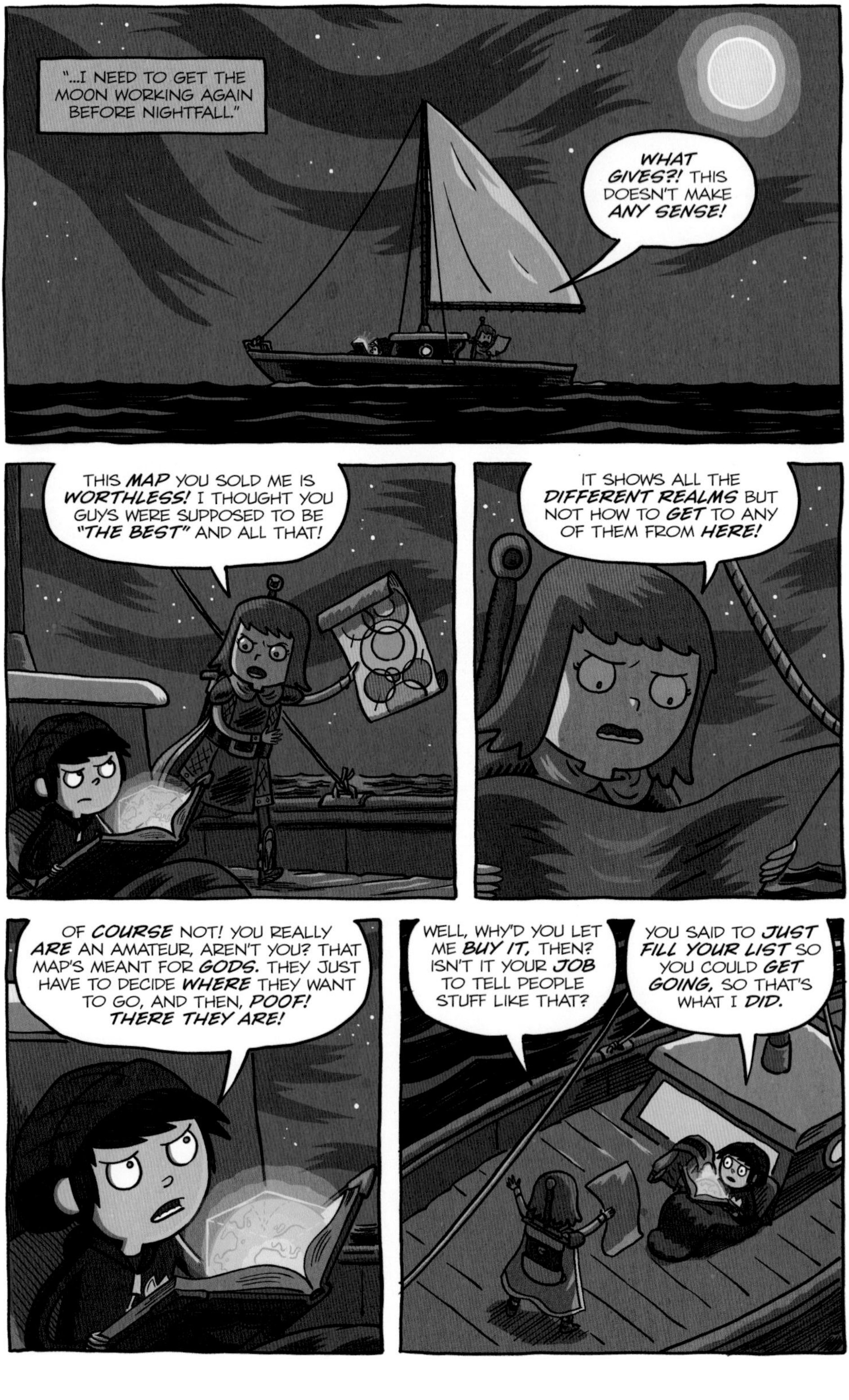
"...I NEED TO GET THE MOON WORKING AGAIN BEFORE NIGHTFALL."
WHAT GIVES?! THIS DOESN'T MAKE ANY SENSE!
THIS MAP YOU SOLD ME IS WORTHLESS! I THOUGHT YOU GUYS WERE SUPPOSED TO BE "THE BEST" AND ALL THAT!
IT SHOWS ALL THE DIFFERENT REALMS BUT NOT HOW TO GET TO ANY OF THEM FROM HERE!
OF COURSE NOT! YOU REALLY ARE AN AMATEUR, AREN'T YOU? THAT MAP'S MEANT FOR GODS. THEY JUST HAVE TO DECIDE WHERE THEY WANT TO GO, AND THEN, POOF! THERE THEY ARE!
WELL, WHY'D YOU LET ME BUY IT, THEN? ISN'T IT YOUR JOB TO TELL PEOPLE STUFF LIKE THAT?
YOU SAID TO JUST FILL YOUR LIST SO YOU COULD GET GOING, SO THAT'S WHAT I DID.

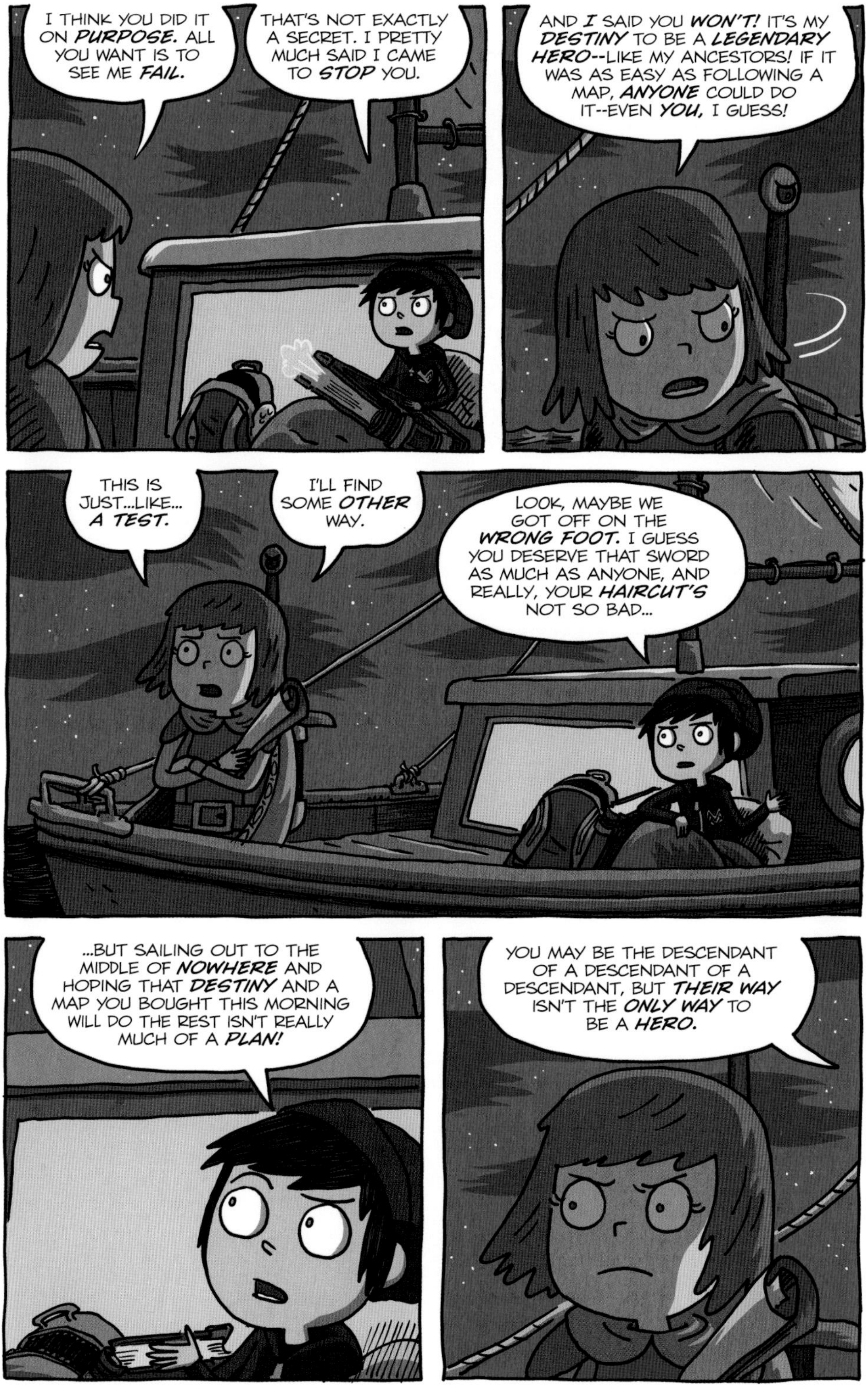
I THINK YOU DID IT ON PURPOSE. ALL YOU WANT IS TO SEE ME FAIL.
THAT'S NOT EXACTLY A SECRET. I PRETTY MUCH SAID I CAME TO STOP YOU.
AND I SAID YOU WON'T! IT'S MY DESTINY TO BE A LEGENDARY HERO--LIKE MY ANCESTORS! IF IT WAS AS EASY AS FOLLOWING A MAP, ANYONE COULD DO IT--EVEN YOU, I GUESS!
THIS IS JUST...LIKE... A TEST.
I'LL FIND SOME OTHER WAY.
LOOK, MAYBE WE GOT OFF ON THE WRONG FOOT. I GUESS YOU DESERVE THAT SWORD AS MUCH AS ANYONE, AND REALLY, YOUR HAIRCUT'S NOT SO BAD...
...BUT SAILING OUT TO THE MIDDLE OF NOWHERE AND HOPING THAT DESTINY AND A MAP YOU BOUGHT THIS MORNING WILL DO THE REST ISN'T REALLY MUCH OF A PLAN!
YOU MAY BE THE DESCENDANT OF A DESCENDANT OF A DESCENDANT, BUT THEIR WAY ISN'T THE ONLY WAY TO BE A HERO.

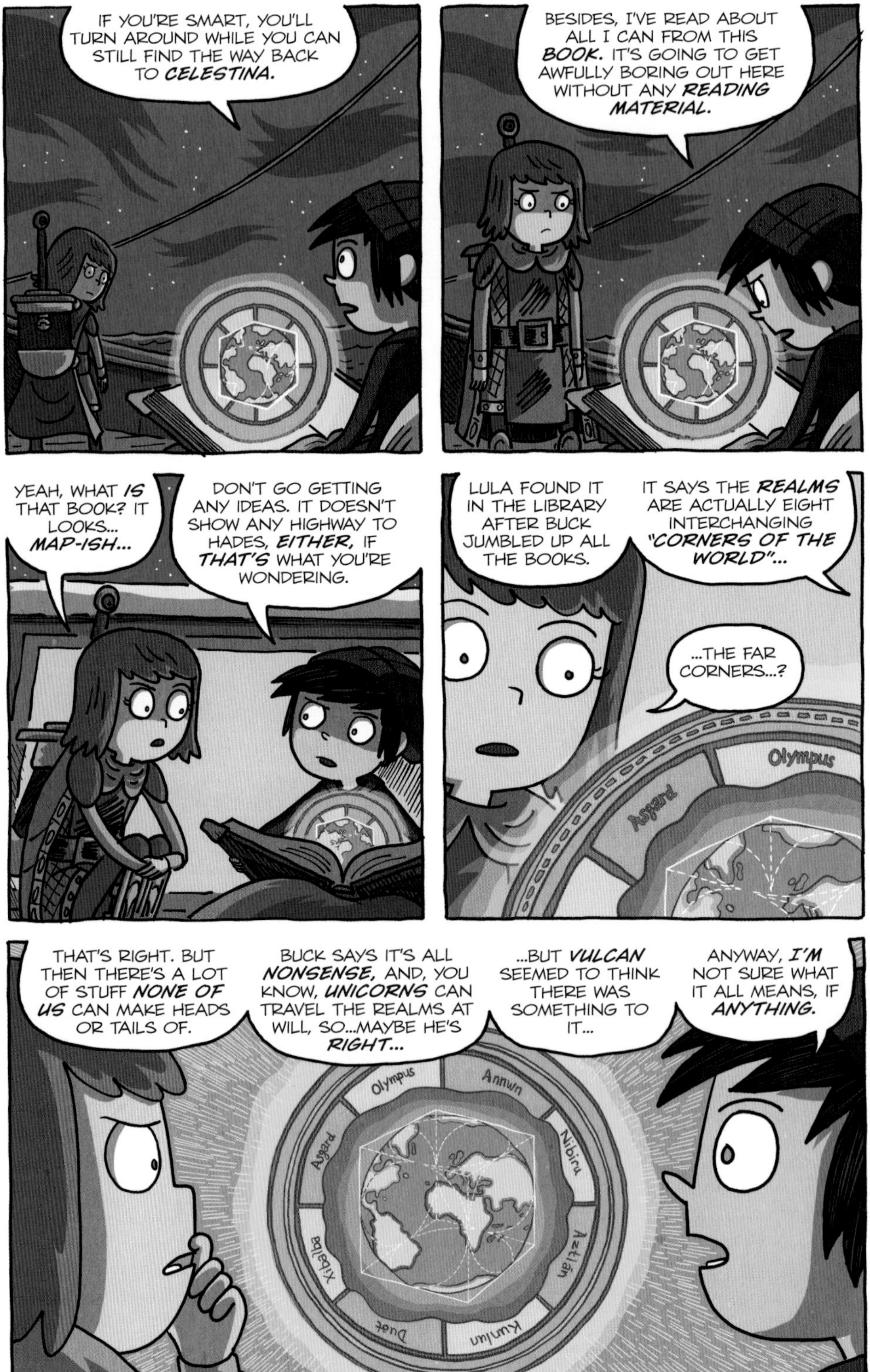
IF YOU'RE SMART, YOU'LL TURN AROUND WHILE YOU CAN STILL FIND THE WAY BACK TO CELESTINA.
BESIDES, I'VE READ ABOUT ALL I CAN FROM THIS BOOK. IT'S GOING TO GET AWFULLY BORING OUT HERE WITHOUT ANY READING MATERIAL.
YEAH, WHAT IS THAT BOOK? IT LOOKS... MAP-ISH...
DON'T GO GETTING ANY IDEAS. IT DOESN'T SHOW ANY HIGHWAY TO HADES, EITHER, IF THAT'S WHAT YOU'RE WONDERING.
LULA FOUND IT IN THE LIBRARY AFTER BUCK JUMBLED UP ALL THE BOOKS.
IT SAYS THE REALMS ARE ACTUALLY EIGHT INTERCHANGING "CORNERS OF THE WORLD"...
...THE FAR CORNERS...?
Olympus
Asgard
THAT'S RIGHT. BUT THEN THERE'S A LOT OF STUFF NONE OF US CAN MAKE HEADS OR TAILS OF.
BUCK SAYS IT'S ALL NONSENSE, AND, YOU KNOW, UNICORNS CAN TRAVEL THE REALMS AT WILL, SO...MAYBE HE'S RIGHT...
...BUT VULCAN SEEMED TO THINK THERE WAS SOMETHING TO IT...
ANYWAY, I'M NOT SURE WHAT IT ALL MEANS, IF ANYTHING.
Olympus
Annwn
Nibiru
Aztlán
Kunlun
Duat
Xibalba
Asgard

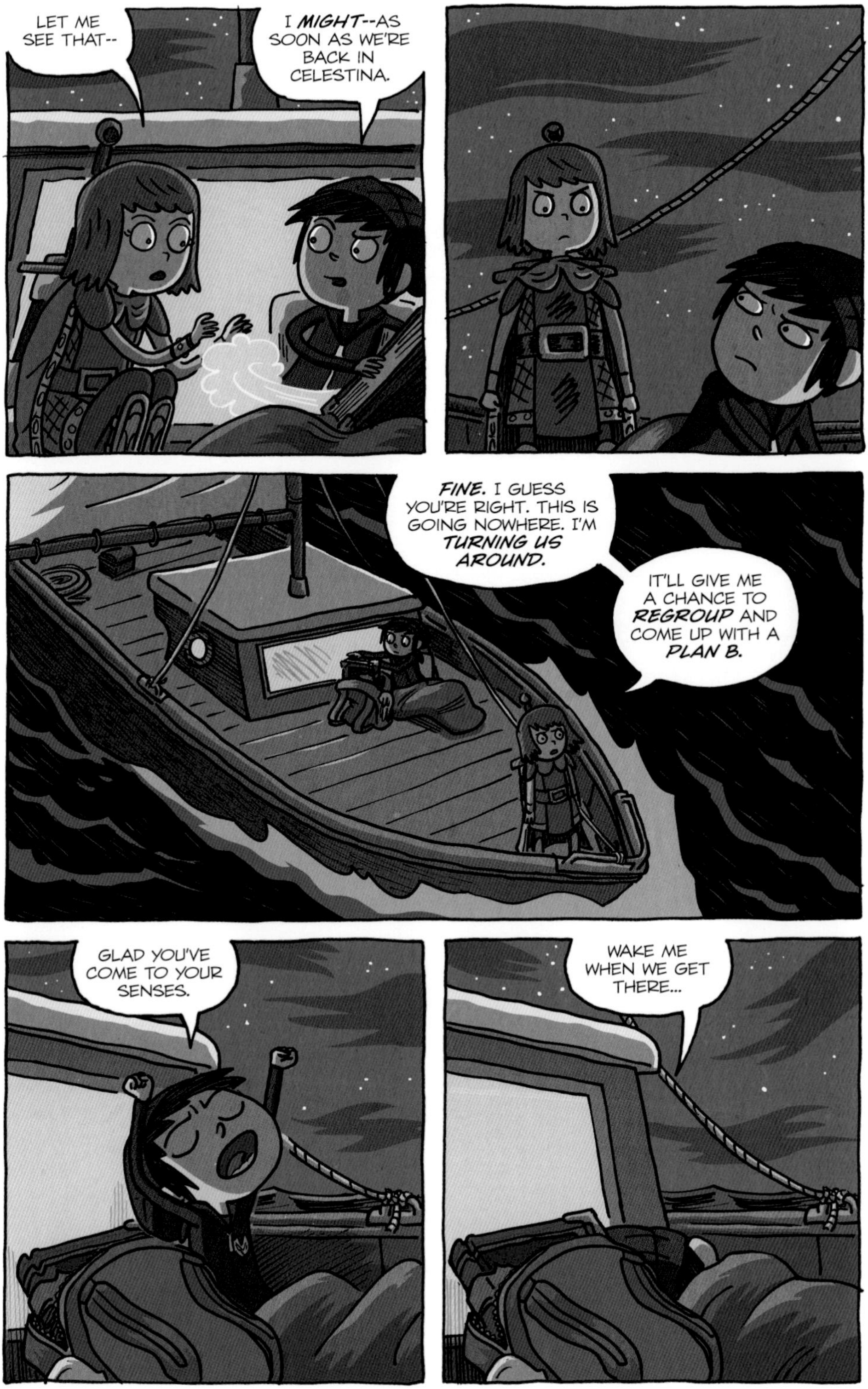
LET ME SEE THAT--
I MIGHT--AS SOON AS WE'RE BACK IN CELESTINA.
FINE. I GUESS YOU'RE RIGHT. THIS IS GOING NOWHERE. I'M TURNING US AROUND.
IT'LL GIVE ME A CHANCE TO REGROUP AND COME UP WITH A PLAN B.
GLAD YOU'VE COME TO YOUR SENSES.
WAKE ME WHEN WE GET THERE...

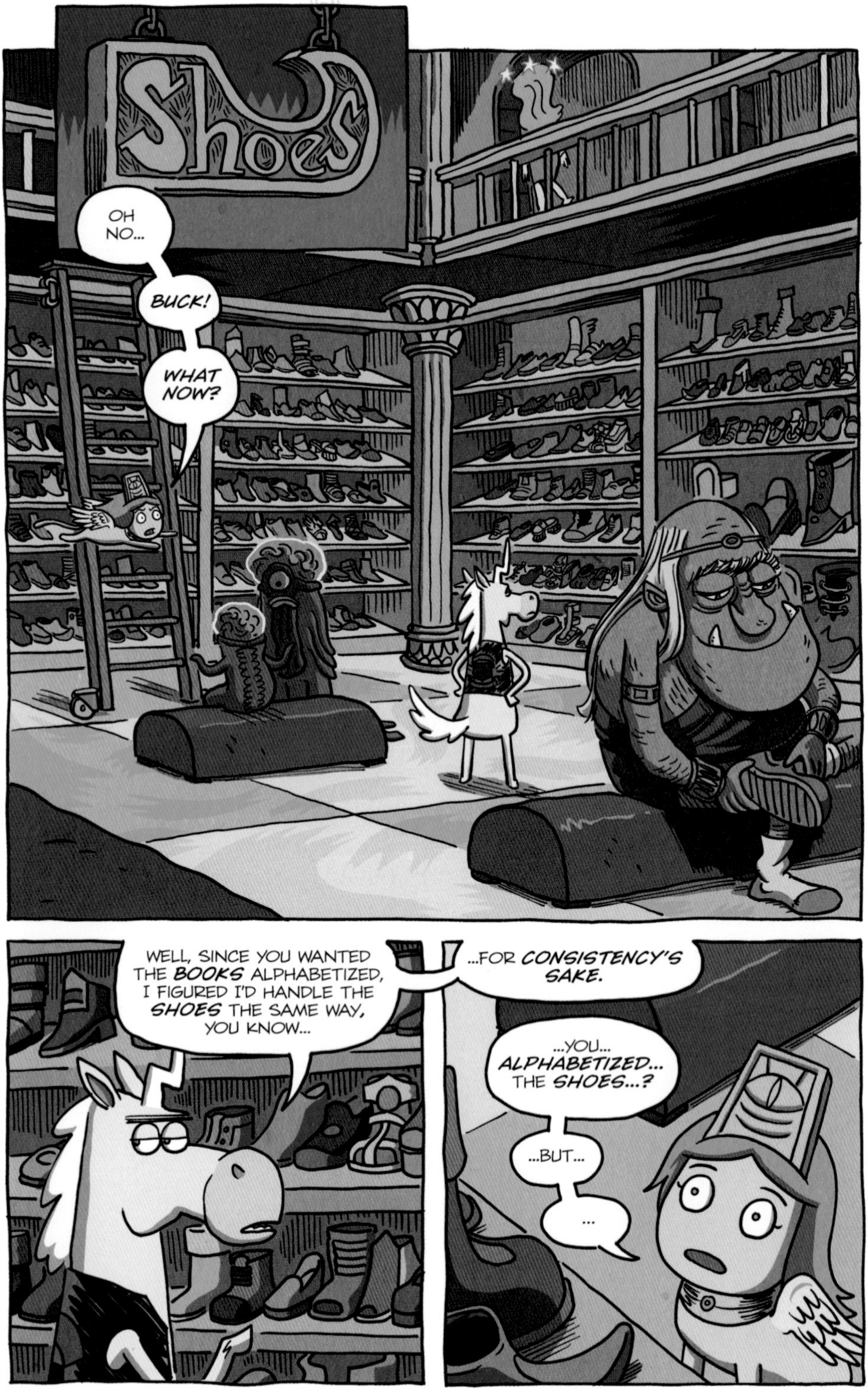
Shoes
OH NO...
BUCK!
WHAT NOW?
WELL, SINCE YOU WANTED THE BOOKS ALPHABETIZED, I FIGURED I'D HANDLE THE SHOES THE SAME WAY, YOU KNOW...
...FOR CONSISTENCY'S SAKE.
...YOU... ALPHABETIZED... THE SHOES...?
...BUT...
...

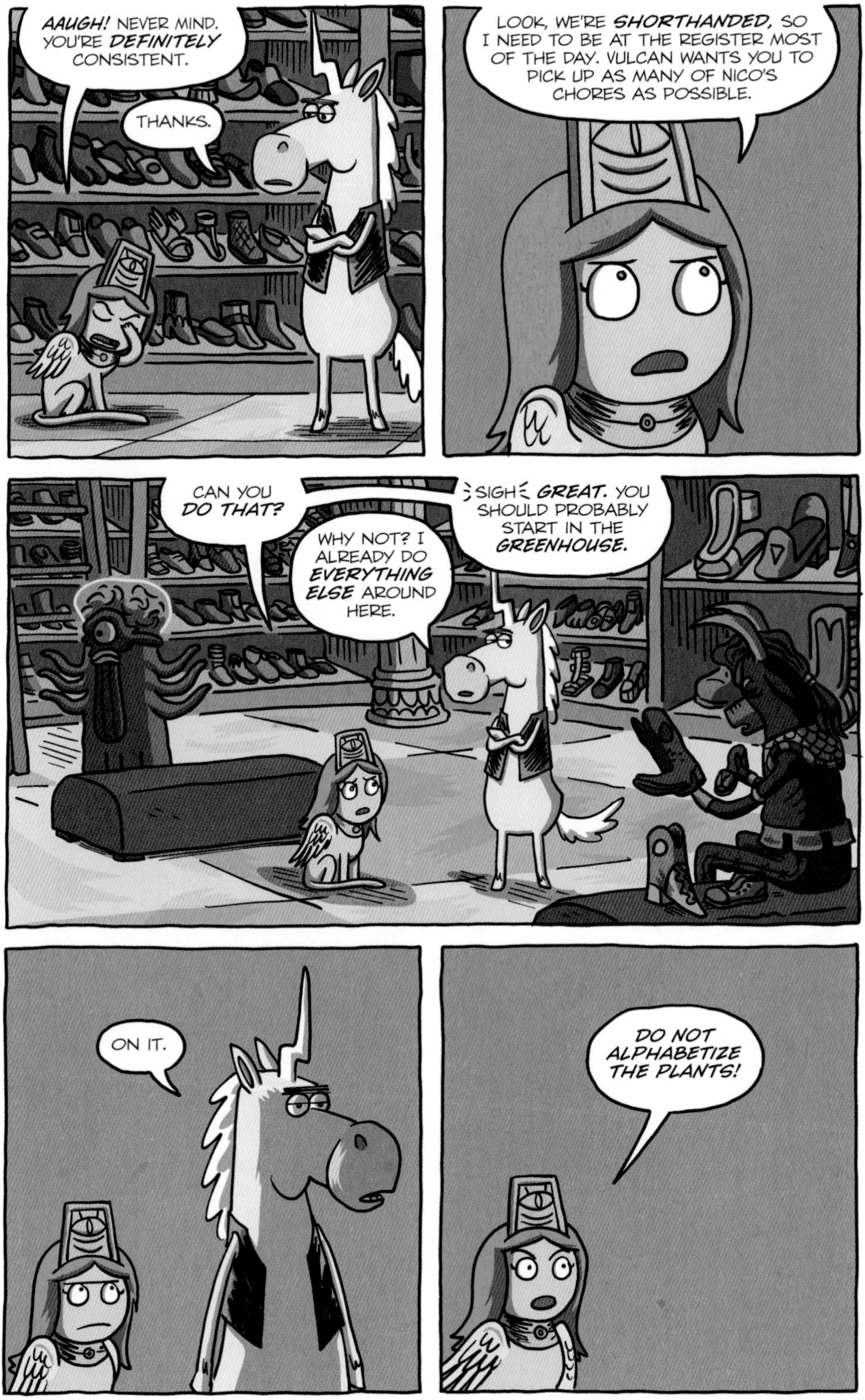
AAUGH! NEVER MIND. YOU'RE DEFINITELY CONSISTENT.
THANKS.
LOOK, WE'RE SHORTHANDED, SO I NEED TO BE AT THE REGISTER MOST OF THE DAY. VULCAN WANTS YOU TO PICK UP AS MANY OF NICO'S CHORES AS POSSIBLE.
CAN YOU DO THAT?
WHY NOT? I ALREADY DO EVERYTHING ELSE AROUND HERE.
SIGH GREAT. YOU SHOULD PROBABLY START IN THE GREENHOUSE.
ON IT.
DO NOT ALPHABETIZE THE PLANTS!

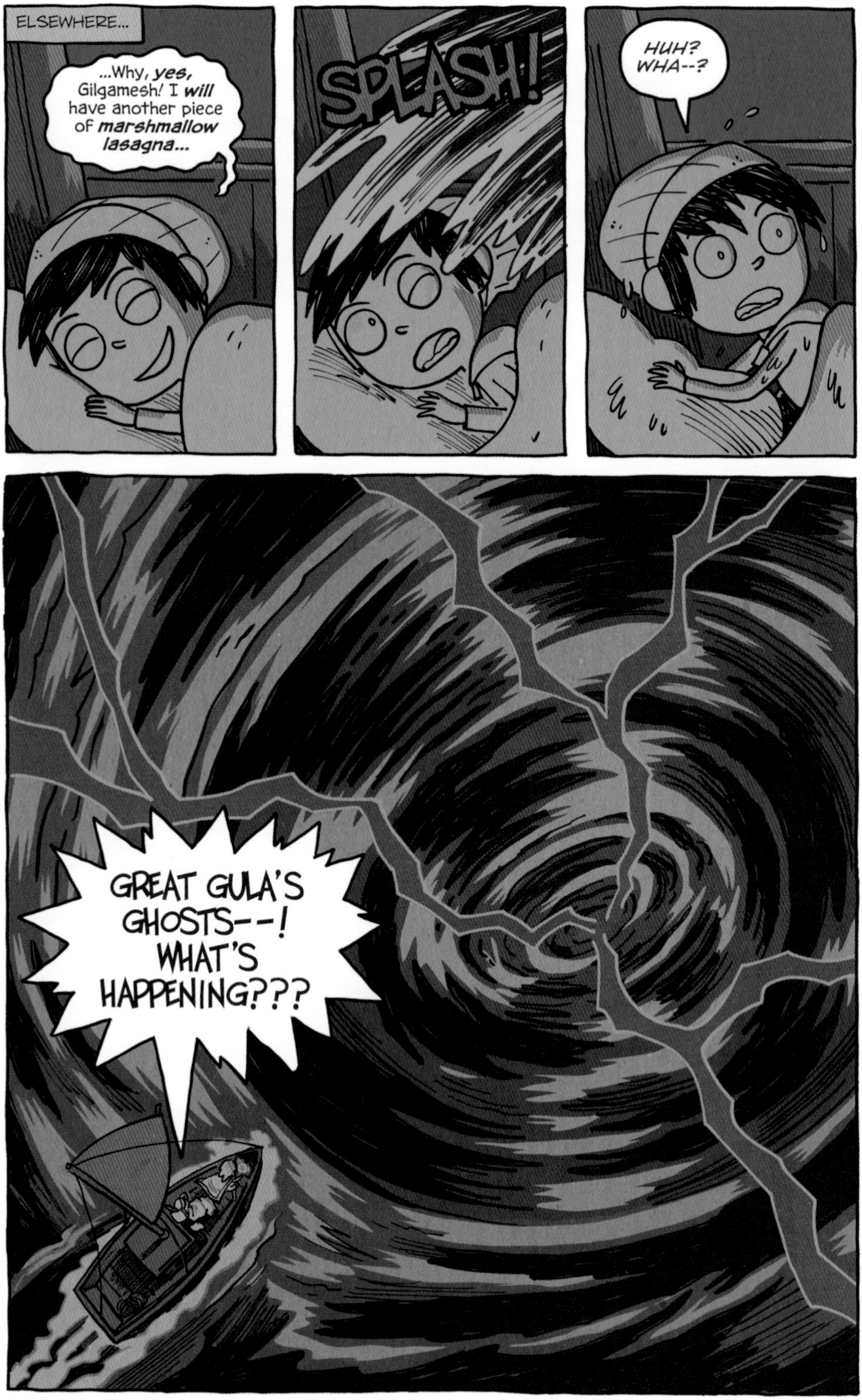
ELSEWHERE...
...Why, yes, Gilgamesh! I will have another piece of marshmallow lasagna...
SPLASH!
HUH? WHA--?
GREAT GULA'S GHOSTS--! WHAT'S HAPPENING???

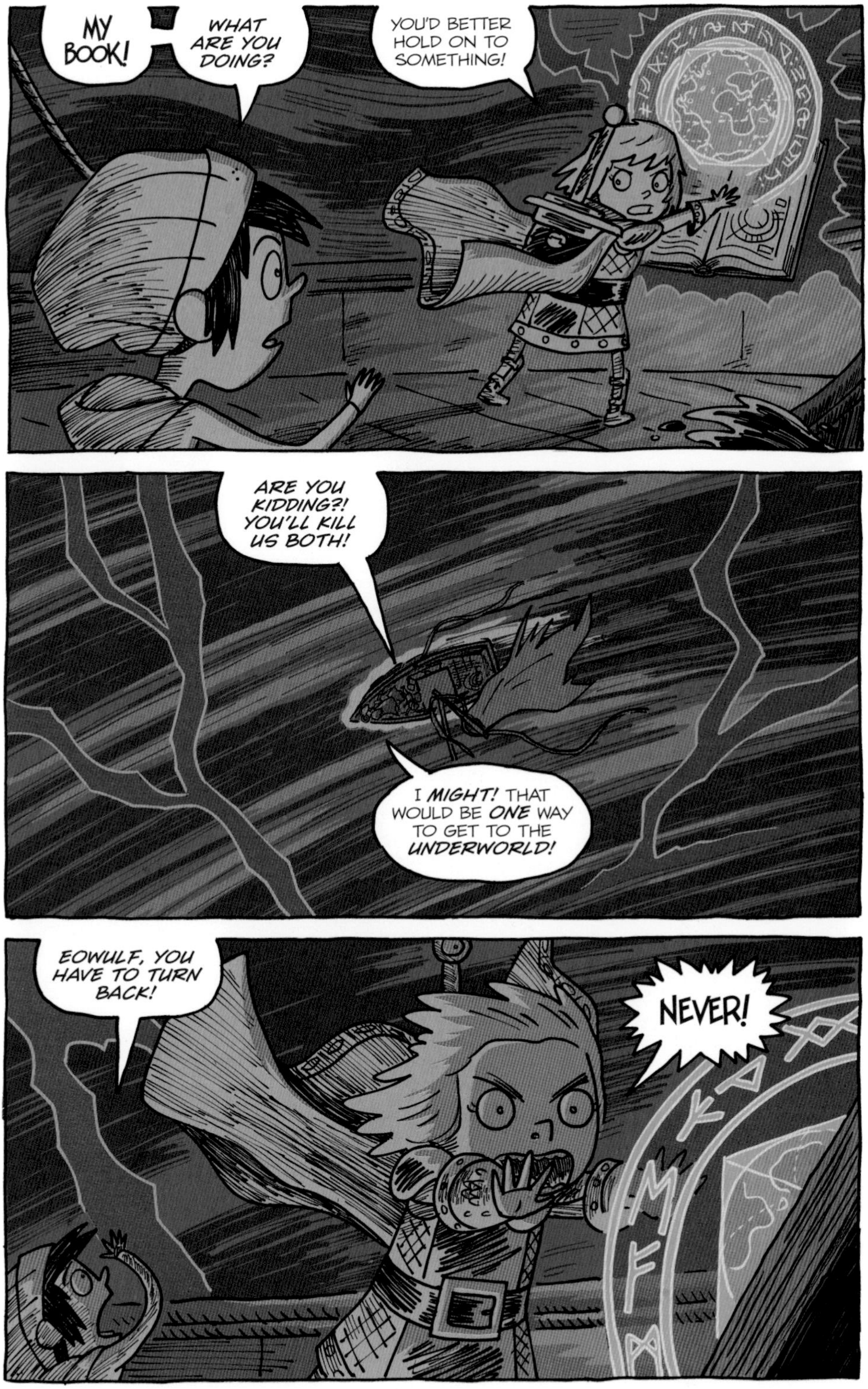
MY BOOK!
WHAT ARE YOU DOING?
YOU'D BETTER HOLD ON TO SOMETHING!
ARE YOU KIDDING?! YOU'LL KILL US BOTH!
I MIGHT! THAT WOULD BE ONE WAY TO GET TO THE UNDERWORLD!
EOWULF, YOU HAVE TO TURN BACK!
NEVER!

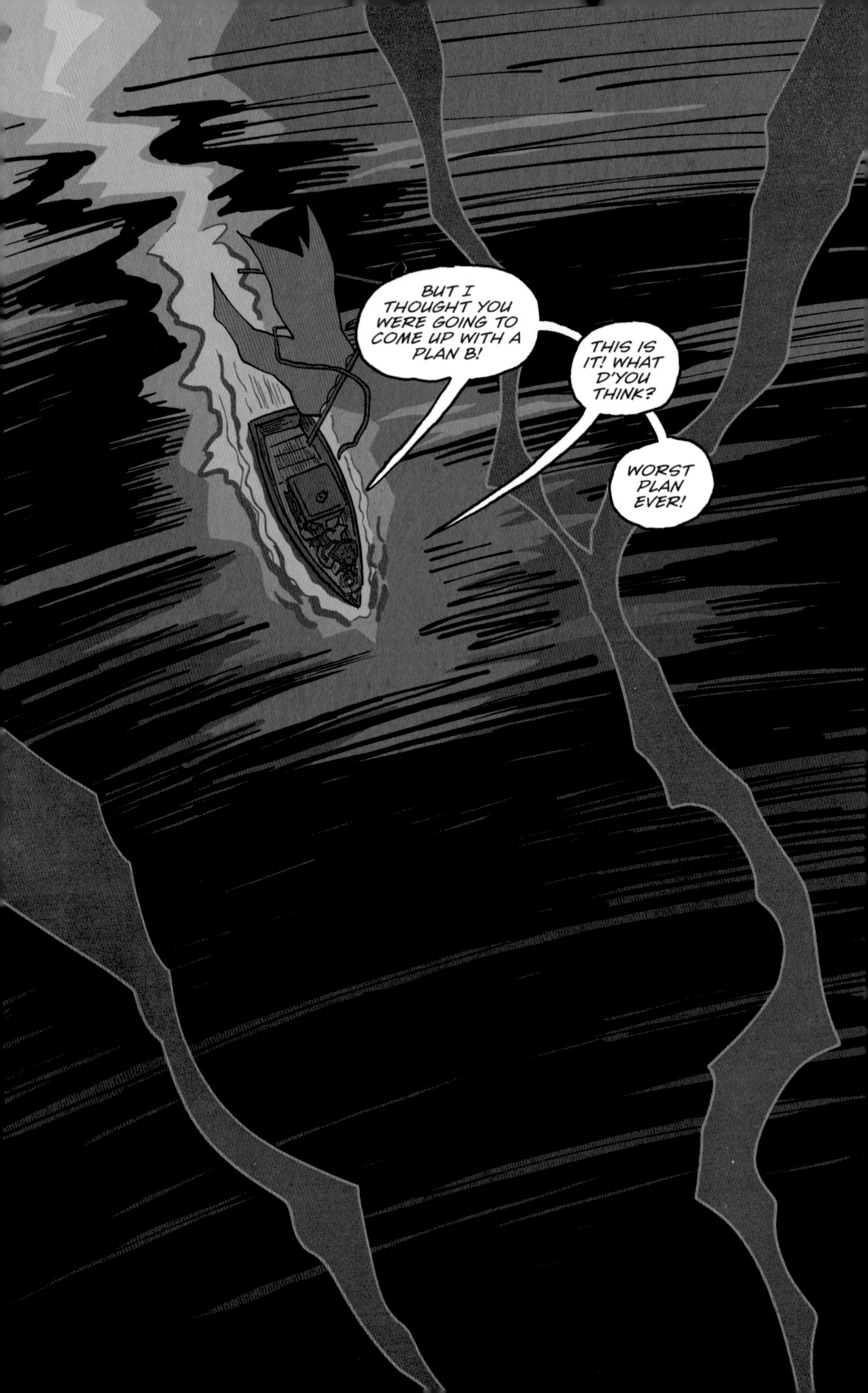
BUT I THOUGHT YOU WERE GOING TO COME UP WITH A PLAN B!
THIS IS IT! WHAT D'YOU THINK?
WORST PLAN EVER!

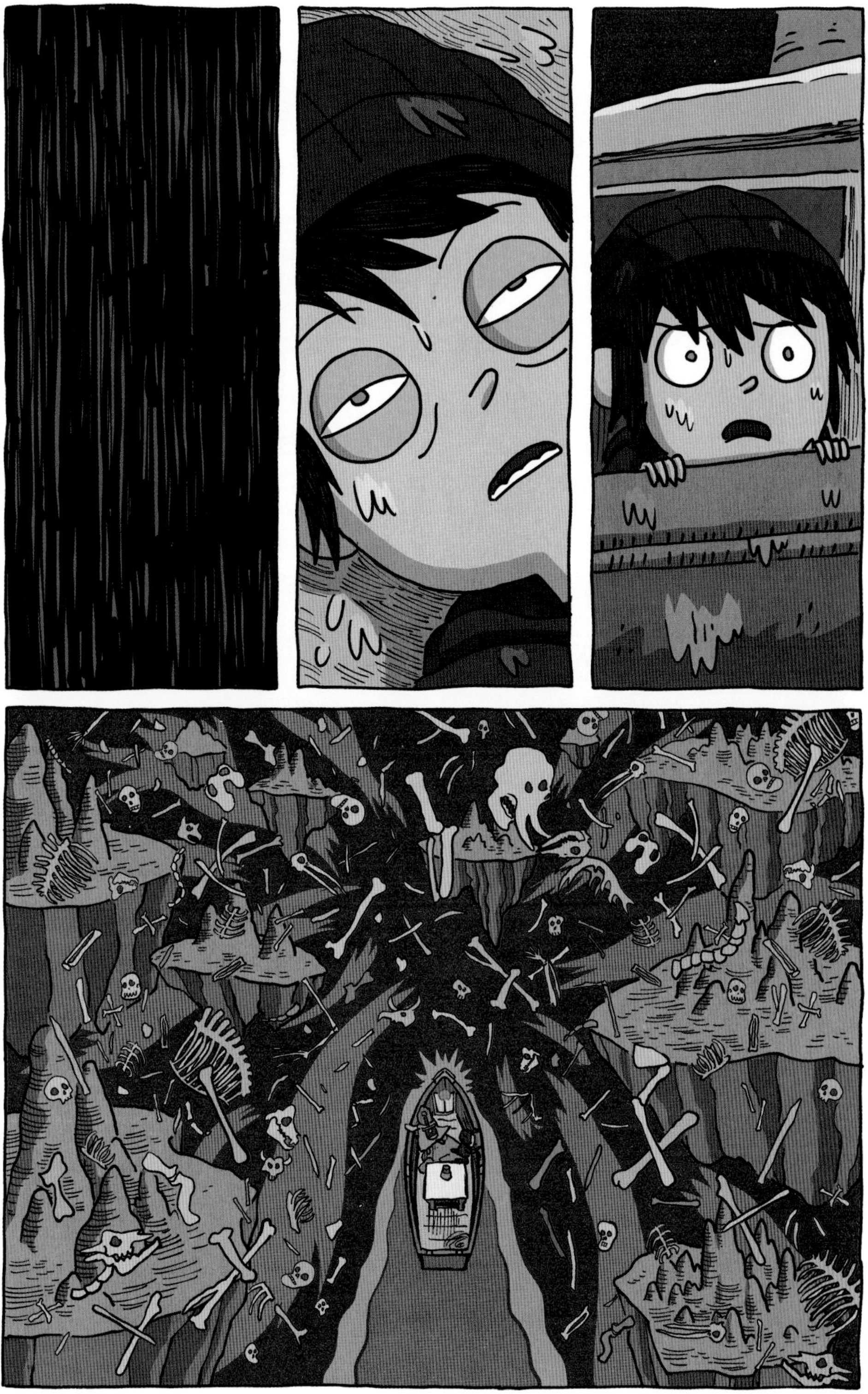

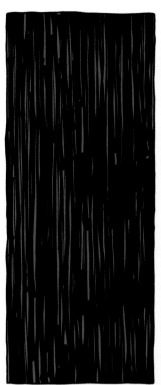

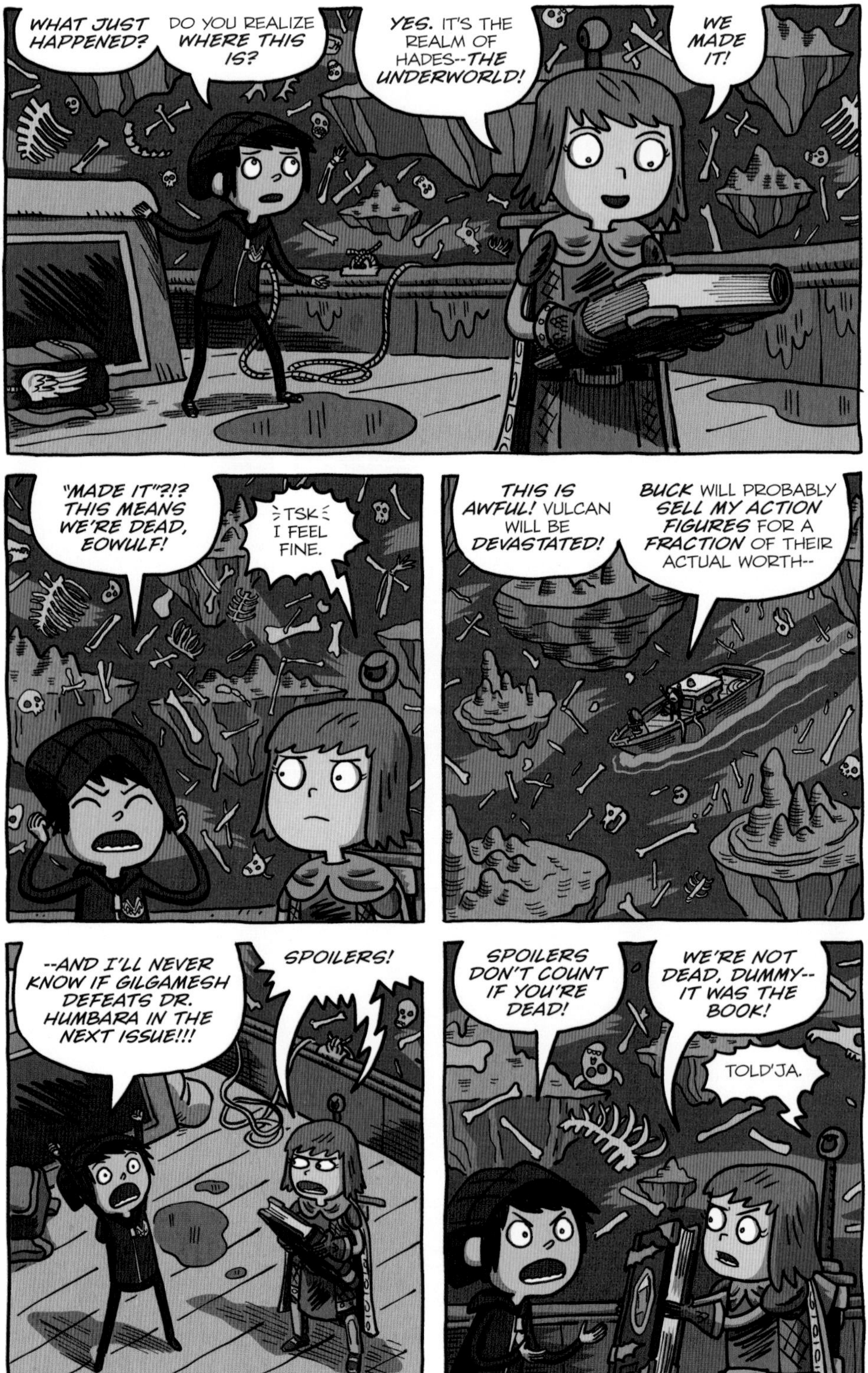
WHAT JUST HAPPENED?
DO YOU REALIZE WHERE THIS IS?
YES. IT'S THE REALM OF HADES--THE UNDERWORLD!
WE MADE IT!
"MADE IT"?!? THIS MEANS WE'RE DEAD, EOWULF!
TSK I FEEL FINE.
THIS IS AWFUL! VULCAN WILL BE DEVASTATED!
BUCK WILL PROBABLY SELL MY ACTION FIGURES FOR A FRACTION OF THEIR ACTUAL WORTH--
--AND I'LL NEVER KNOW IF GILGAMESH DEFEATS DR. HUMBARA IN THE NEXT ISSUE!!!
SPOILERS!
SPOILERS DON'T COUNT IF YOU'RE DEAD!
WE'RE NOT DEAD, DUMMY--IT WAS THE BOOK!
TOLD'JA.

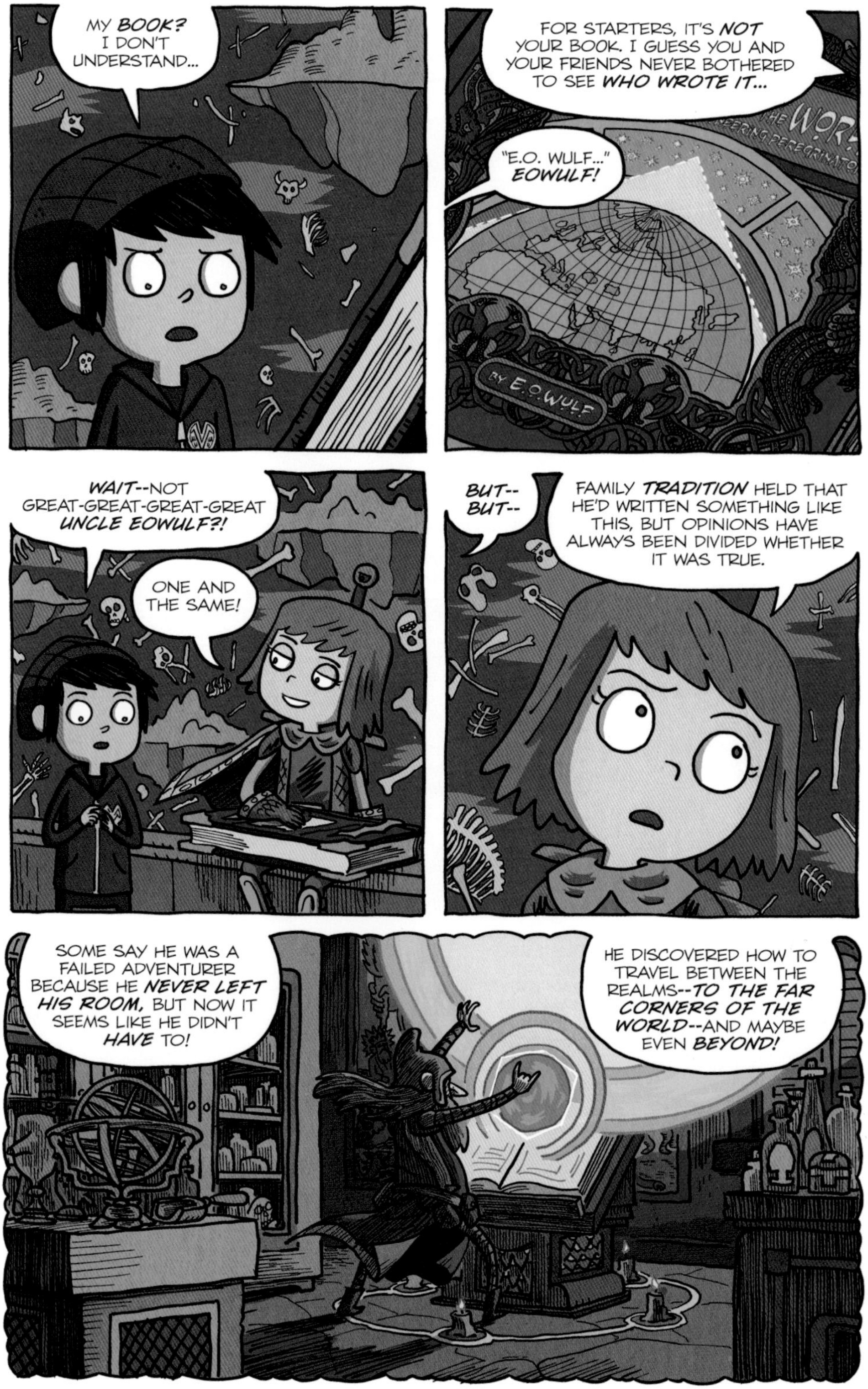
MY *BOOK?* I DON'T UNDERSTAND...
FOR STARTERS, IT'S *NOT* YOUR BOOK. I GUESS YOU AND YOUR FRIENDS NEVER BOTHERED TO SEE *WHO WROTE IT...*
"E.O. WULF..." *EOWULF!*
BY E.O. WULF
*WAIT*--NOT GREAT-GREAT-GREAT-GREAT *UNCLE EOWULF?!*
ONE AND THE SAME!
*BUT--* *BUT--*
FAMILY *TRADITION* HELD THAT HE'D WRITTEN SOMETHING LIKE THIS, BUT OPINIONS HAVE ALWAYS BEEN DIVIDED WHETHER IT WAS TRUE.
SOME SAY HE WAS A FAILED ADVENTURER BECAUSE HE *NEVER LEFT HIS ROOM,* BUT NOW IT SEEMS LIKE HE DIDN'T *HAVE* TO!
HE DISCOVERED HOW TO TRAVEL BETWEEN THE REALMS--*TO THE FAR CORNERS OF THE WORLD*--AND MAYBE EVEN *BEYOND!*

HE WROTE IT ALL DOWN IN THAT BOOK...

IT'S NOT JUST A *BOOK*--IT'S A *DOORWAY* TO *ALL* THE CELESTIAL REALMS!

BUT IT ONLY WORKS FOR US *WULFS!* FOR ANYONE ELSE, IT'S JUST A *WEIRD OLD BOOK!*

GAH! AND I BROUGHT IT RIGHT *TO YOU!*

*FACT IS*--IF YOU HAD MINDED YOUR *OWN BUSINESS,* MY QUEST WOULD ALREADY HAVE *FAILED!*

I GUESS I OWE YOU SOME *THANKS!* NOW I'M ONE STEP *CLOSER...*

*YEAH*-- ONE STEP CLOSER TO *SLAYING!*

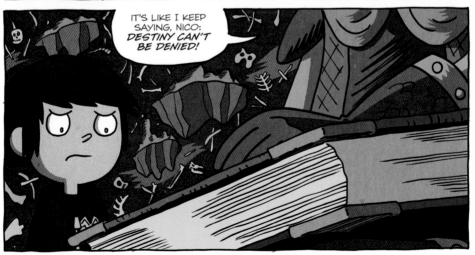

IT'S LIKE I KEEP SAYING, NICO: *DESTINY CAN'T BE DENIED!*

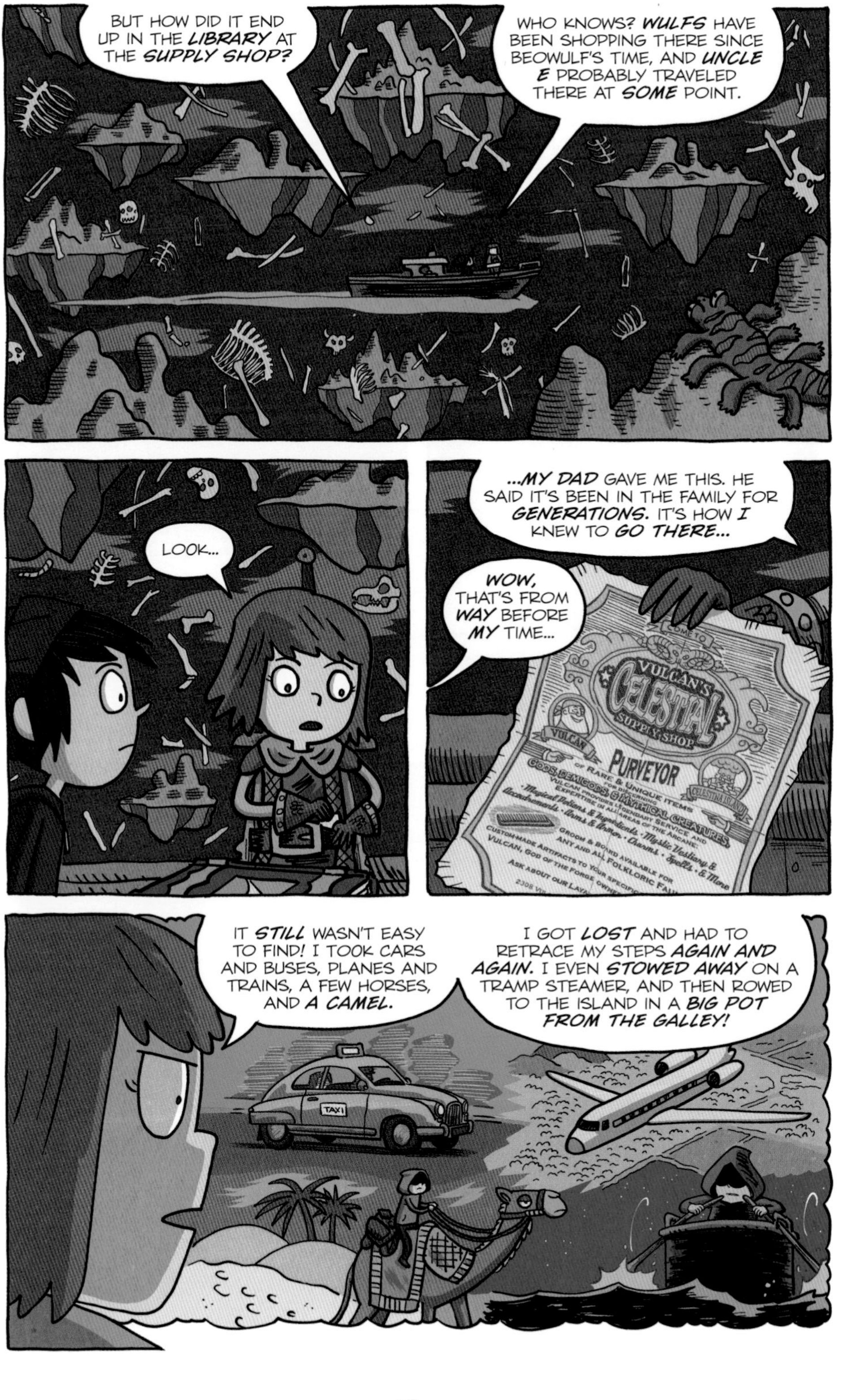
BUT HOW DID IT END UP IN THE *LIBRARY* AT THE *SUPPLY SHOP?*
WHO KNOWS? *WULFS* HAVE BEEN SHOPPING THERE SINCE BEOWULF'S TIME, AND *UNCLE E* PROBABLY TRAVELED THERE AT *SOME* POINT.
LOOK...
*...MY DAD* GAVE ME THIS. HE SAID IT'S BEEN IN THE FAMILY FOR *GENERATIONS.* IT'S HOW *I* KNEW TO *GO THERE...*
*WOW,* THAT'S FROM *WAY* BEFORE *MY* TIME...
VULCAN'S CELESTIAL SUPPLY SHOP
PURVEYOR
OF RARE & UNIQUE ITEMS
IT *STILL* WASN'T EASY TO FIND! I TOOK CARS AND BUSES, PLANES AND TRAINS, A FEW HORSES, AND *A CAMEL.*
I GOT *LOST* AND HAD TO RETRACE MY STEPS *AGAIN AND AGAIN.* I EVEN *STOWED AWAY* ON A TRAMP STEAMER, AND THEN ROWED TO THE ISLAND IN A *BIG POT FROM THE GALLEY!*
TAXI

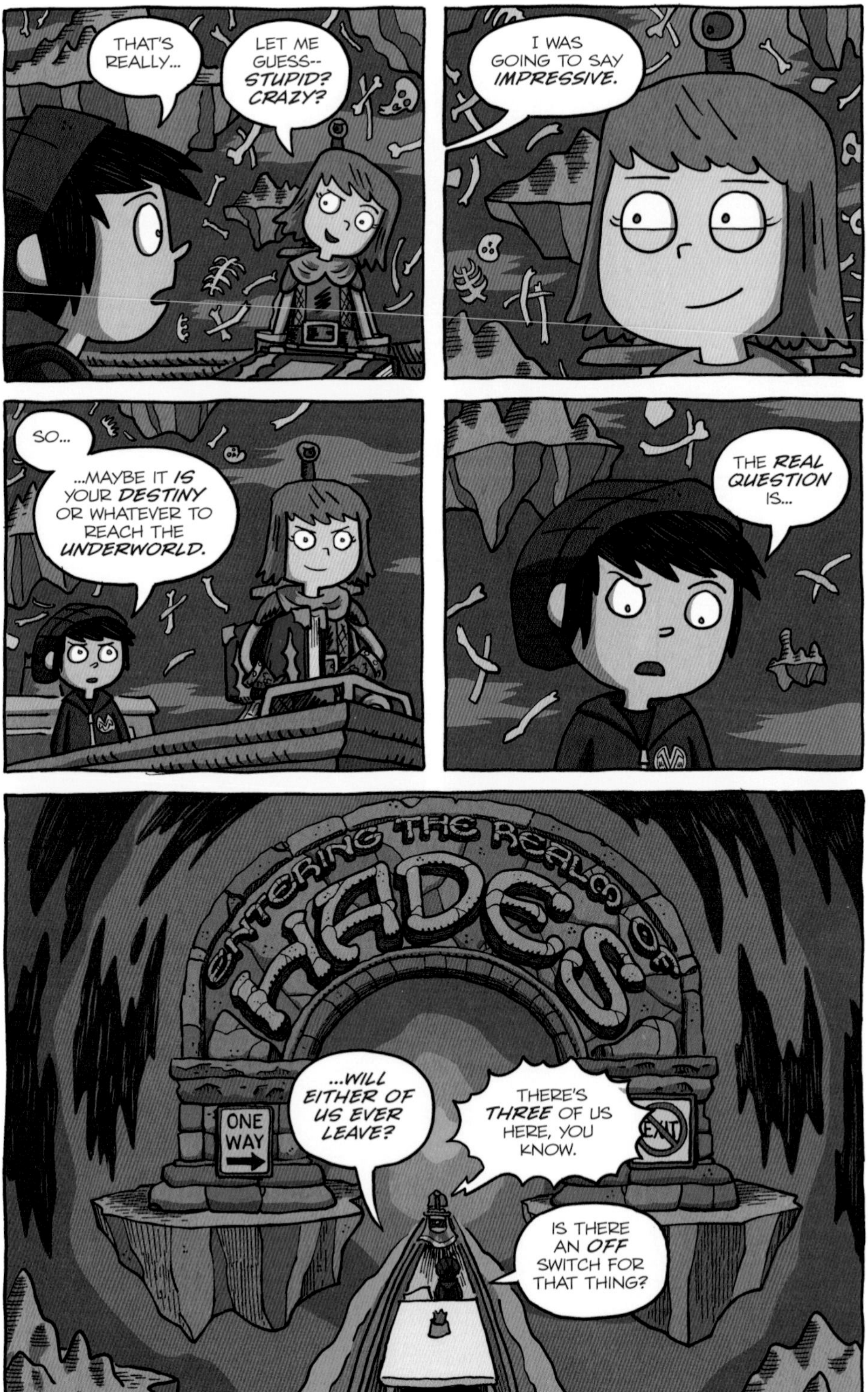
THAT'S REALLY...
LET ME GUESS-- STUPID? CRAZY?
I WAS GOING TO SAY IMPRESSIVE.
SO...
...MAYBE IT IS YOUR DESTINY OR WHATEVER TO REACH THE UNDERWORLD.
THE REAL QUESTION IS...
ENTERING THE REALM OF HADES
ONE WAY
EXIT
...WILL EITHER OF US EVER LEAVE?
THERE'S THREE OF US HERE, YOU KNOW.
IS THERE AN OFF SWITCH FOR THAT THING?

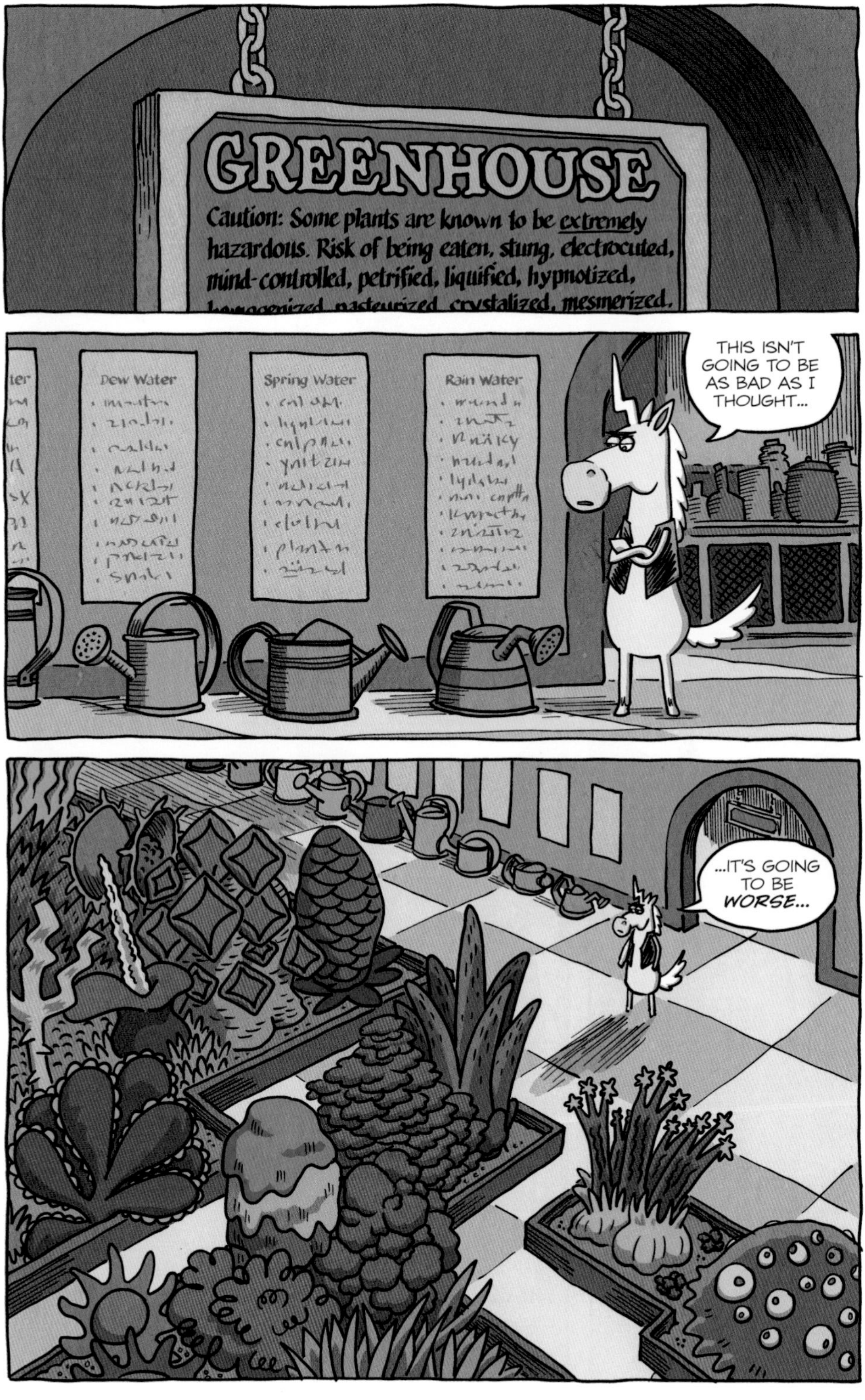
GREENHOUSE
Caution: Some plants are known to be extremely hazardous. Risk of being eaten, stung, electrocuted, mind-controlled, petrified, liquified, hypnotized,
pasteurized, crystalized, mesmerized,
Dew Water
Spring Water
Rain Water
THIS ISN'T GOING TO BE AS BAD AS I THOUGHT...
...IT'S GOING TO BE *WORSE...*

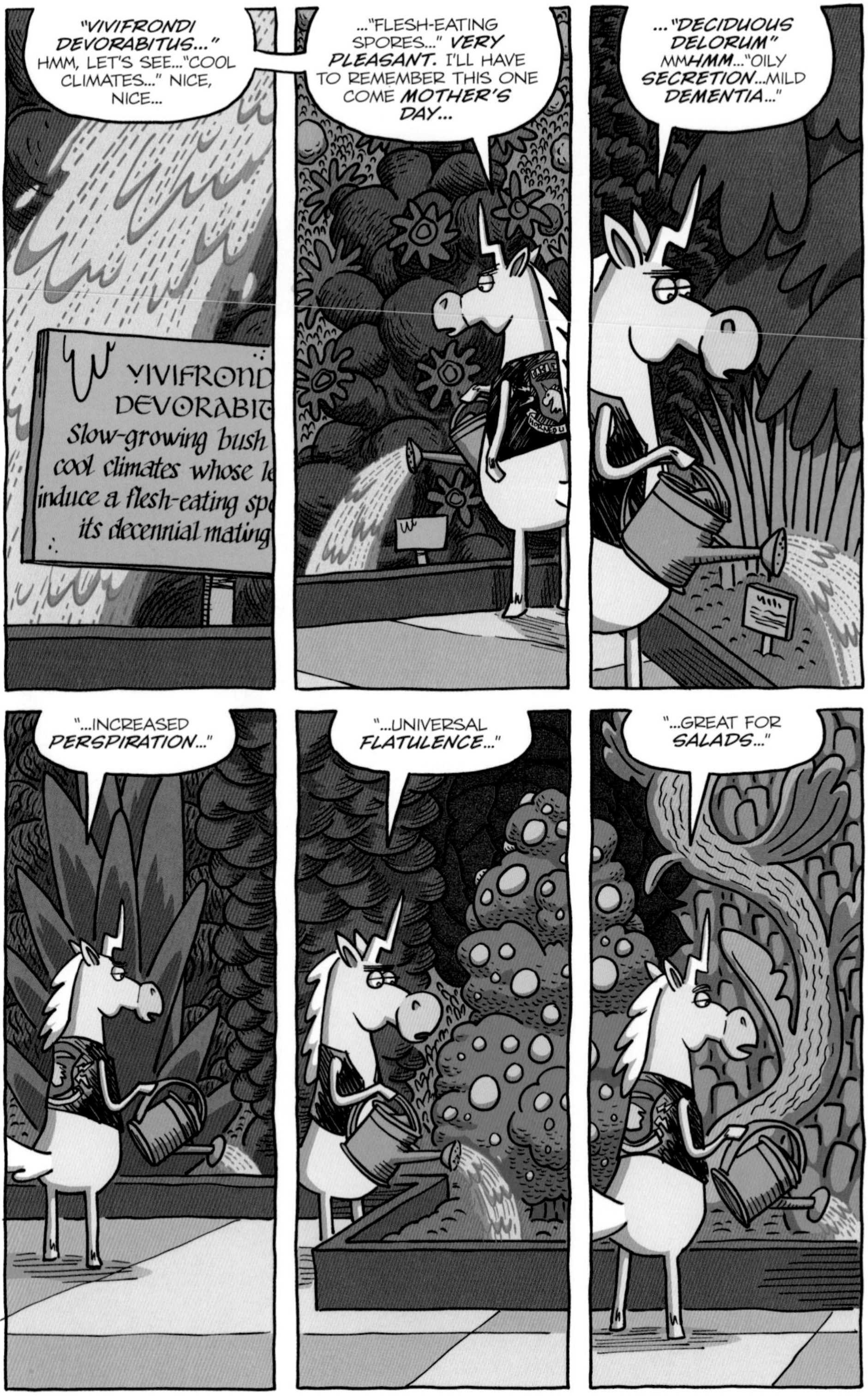
"VIVIFRONDI DEVORABITUS..." HMM, LET'S SEE..."COOL CLIMATES..." NICE, NICE...
VIVIFROND
DEVORABIT
Slow-growing bush
cool climates whose le
induce a flesh-eating sp
its decennial mating
..."FLESH-EATING SPORES..." VERY PLEASANT. I'LL HAVE TO REMEMBER THIS ONE COME MOTHER'S DAY...
..."DECIDUOUS DELORUM" MMHMM..."OILY SECRETION...MILD DEMENTIA..."
"...INCREASED PERSPIRATION..."
"...UNIVERSAL FLATULENCE..."
"...GREAT FOR SALADS..."

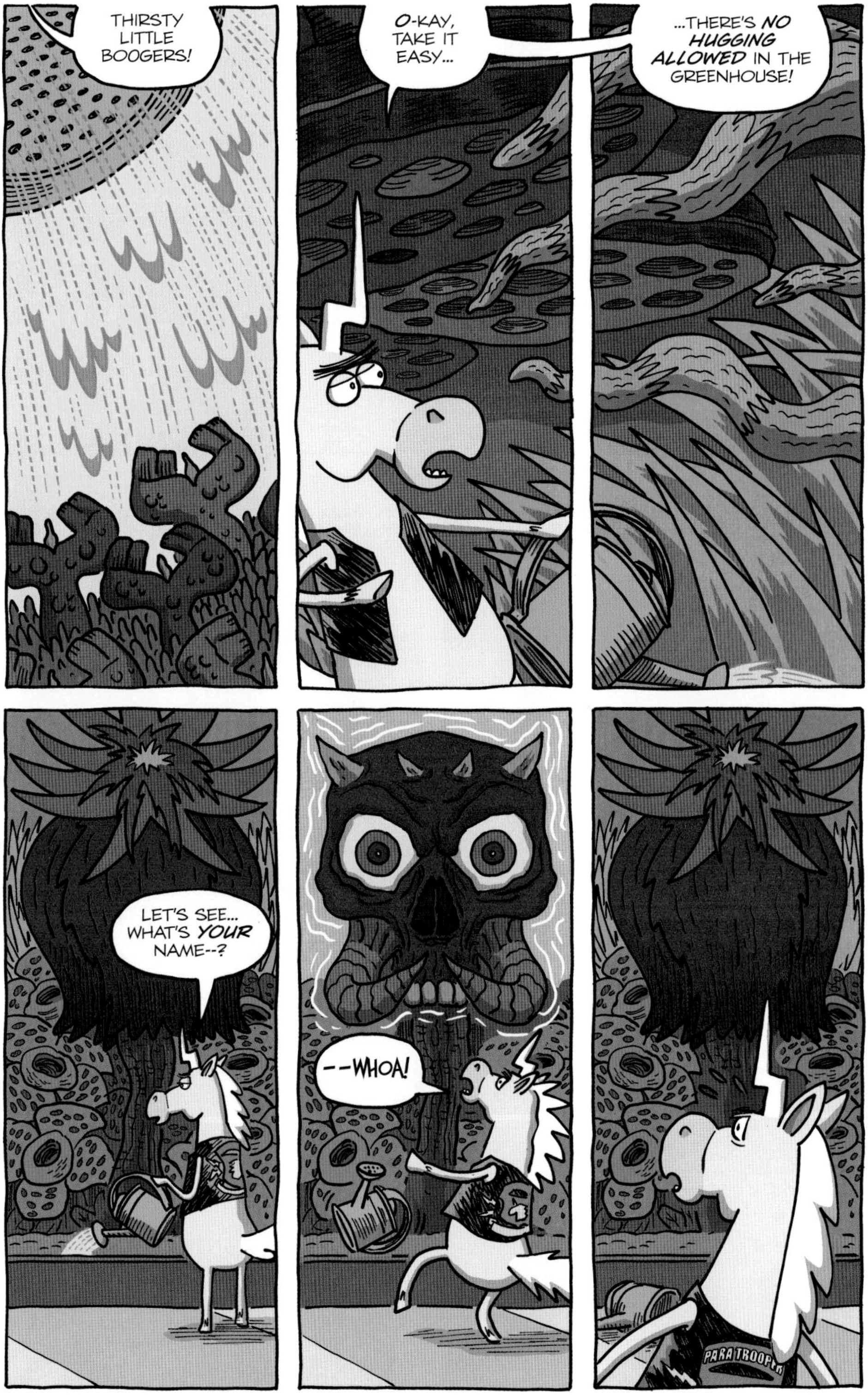
THIRSTY LITTLE BOOGERS!
O-KAY, TAKE IT EASY...
...THERE'S NO HUGGING ALLOWED IN THE GREENHOUSE!
LET'S SEE... WHAT'S YOUR NAME--?
--WHOA!
PARA TROOPER

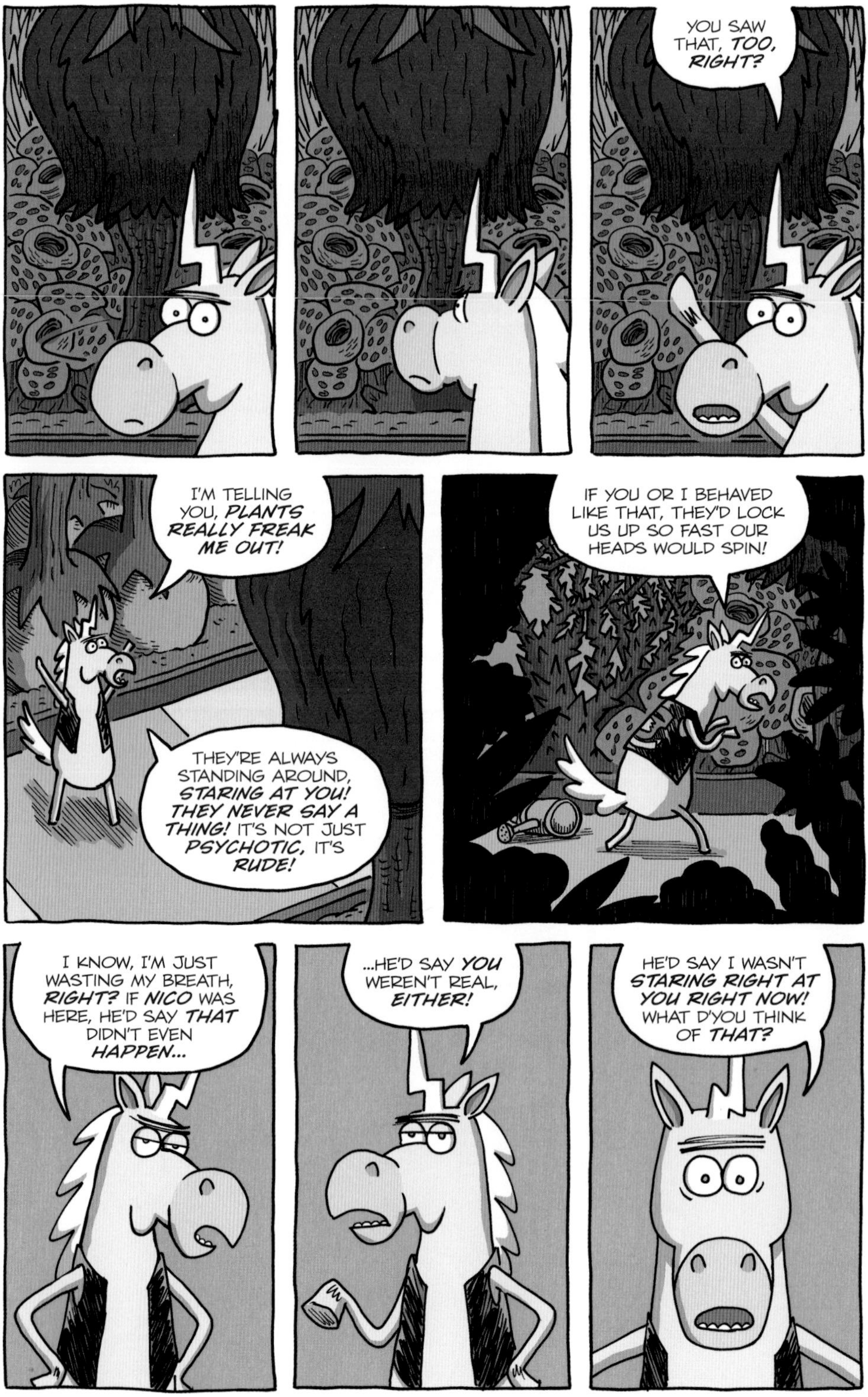
YOU SAW THAT, TOO, RIGHT?
I'M TELLING YOU, PLANTS REALLY FREAK ME OUT!
THEY'RE ALWAYS STANDING AROUND, STARING AT YOU! THEY NEVER SAY A THING! IT'S NOT JUST PSYCHOTIC, IT'S RUDE!
IF YOU OR I BEHAVED LIKE THAT, THEY'D LOCK US UP SO FAST OUR HEADS WOULD SPIN!
I KNOW, I'M JUST WASTING MY BREATH, RIGHT? IF NICO WAS HERE, HE'D SAY THAT DIDN'T EVEN HAPPEN...
...HE'D SAY YOU WEREN'T REAL, EITHER!
HE'D SAY I WASN'T STARING RIGHT AT YOU RIGHT NOW! WHAT D'YOU THINK OF THAT?

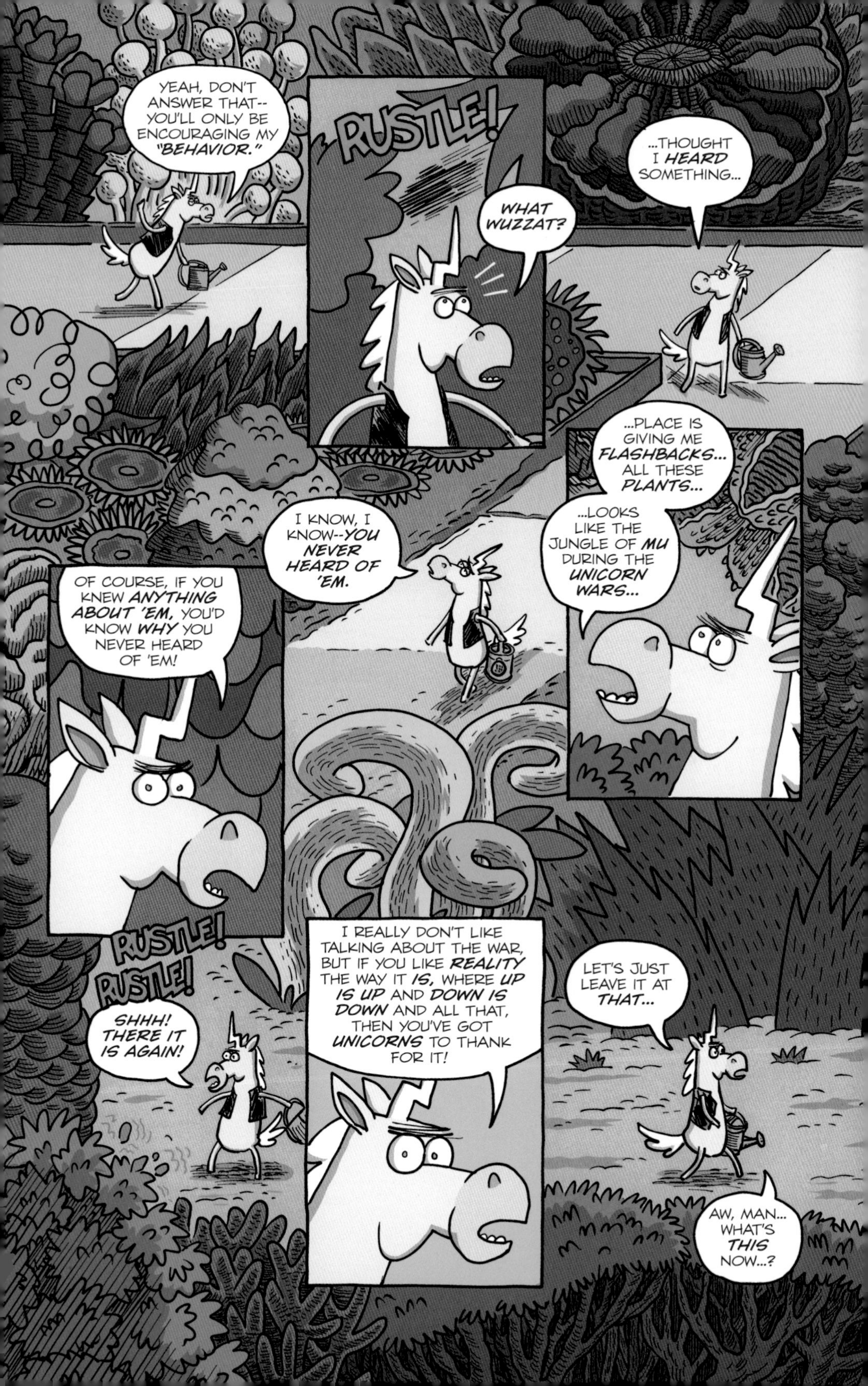

YEAH, DON'T ANSWER THAT-- YOU'LL ONLY BE ENCOURAGING MY *"BEHAVIOR."*
RUSTLE!
*WHAT WUZZAT?*
...THOUGHT I ***HEARD*** SOMETHING...
...PLACE IS GIVING ME ***FLASHBACKS...*** ALL THESE ***PLANTS...***
...LOOKS LIKE THE JUNGLE OF ***MU*** DURING THE ***UNICORN WARS...***
I KNOW, I KNOW--***YOU NEVER HEARD OF 'EM.***
OF COURSE, IF YOU KNEW ***ANYTHING ABOUT 'EM,*** YOU'D KNOW ***WHY*** YOU NEVER HEARD OF 'EM!
RUSTLE! RUSTLE!
***SHHH! THERE IT IS AGAIN!***
I REALLY DON'T LIKE TALKING ABOUT THE WAR, BUT IF YOU LIKE ***REALITY*** THE WAY IT ***IS,*** WHERE ***UP IS UP*** AND ***DOWN IS DOWN*** AND ALL THAT, THEN YOU'VE GOT ***UNICORNS*** TO THANK FOR IT!
LET'S JUST LEAVE IT AT ***THAT...***
AW, MAN... WHAT'S ***THIS*** NOW...?

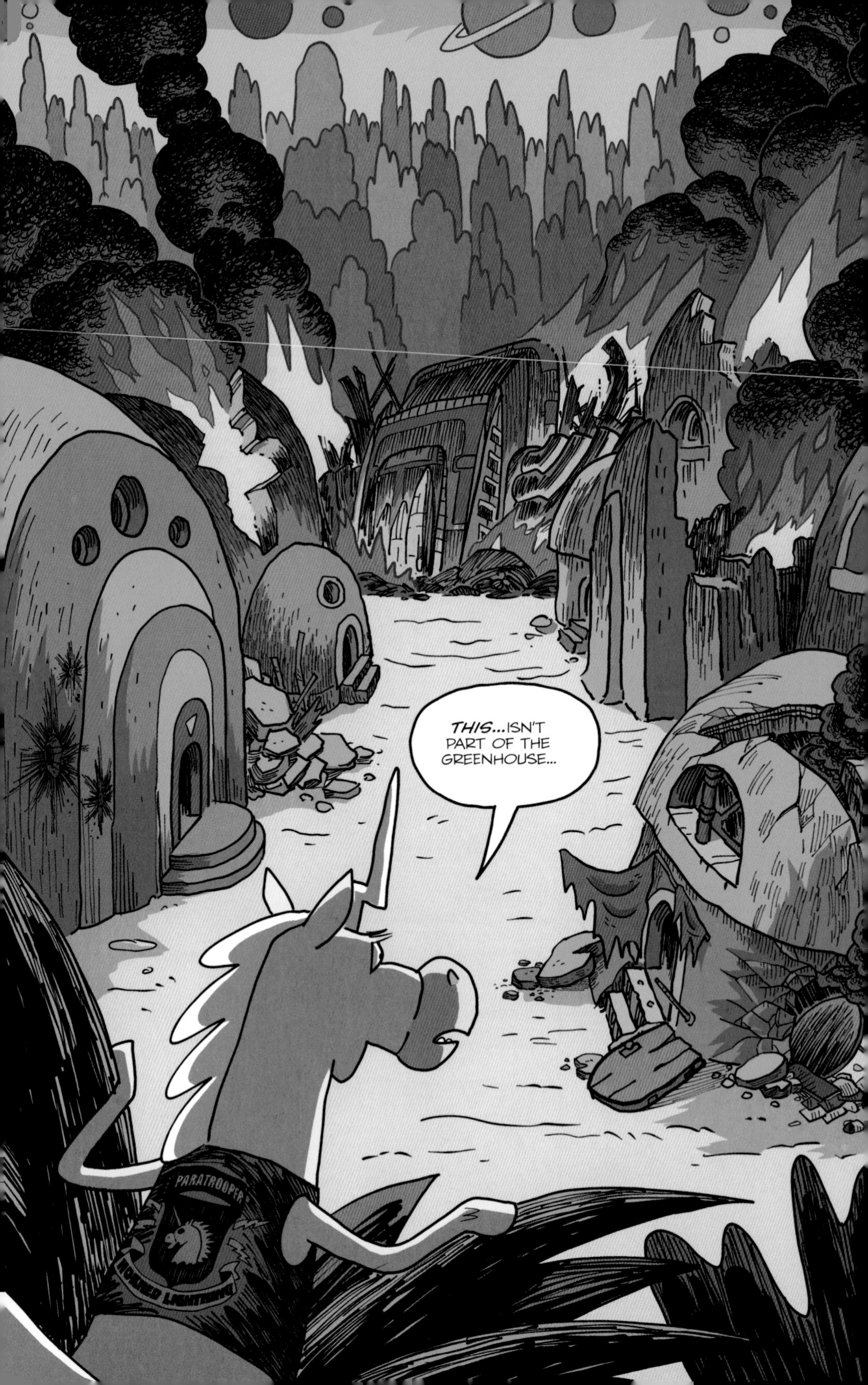
THIS...ISN'T PART OF THE GREENHOUSE...
PARATROOPER
HORNED LIGHTNING

# PART 2:
# KNIT TOGETHER.

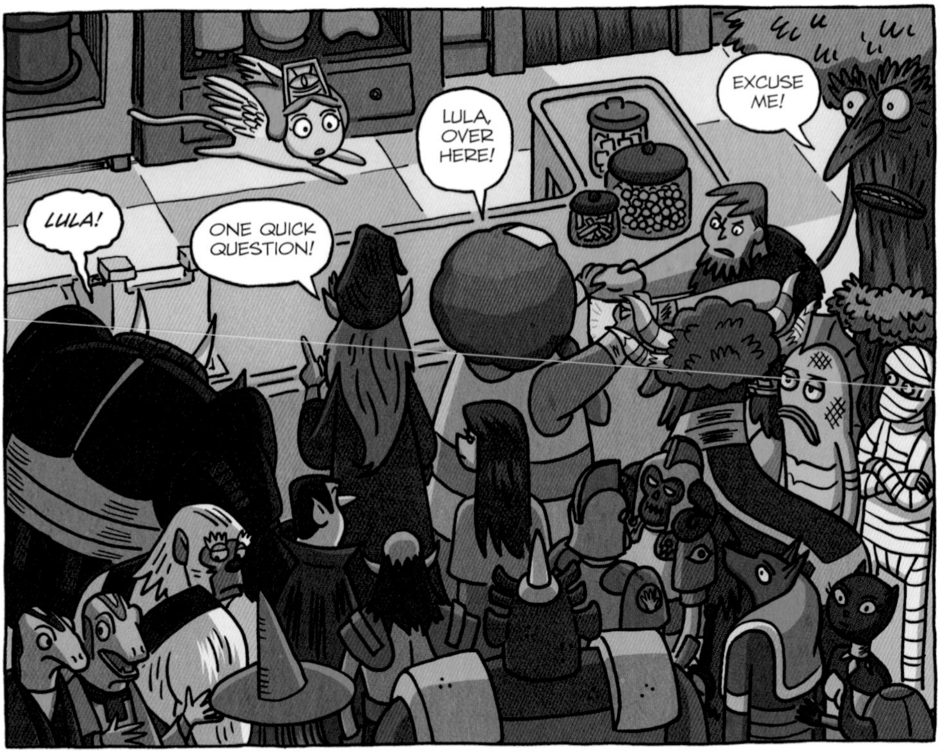
LULA!
ONE QUICK QUESTION!
LULA, OVER HERE!
EXCUSE ME!

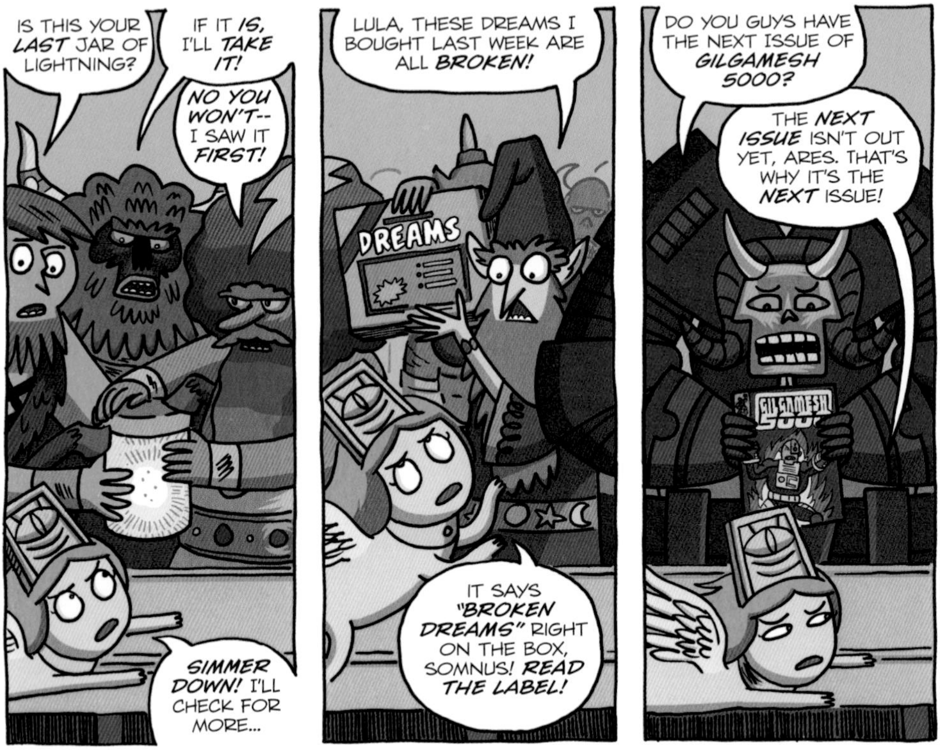
IS THIS YOUR LAST JAR OF LIGHTNING?
IF IT IS, I'LL TAKE IT!
NO YOU WON'T-- I SAW IT FIRST!
SIMMER DOWN! I'LL CHECK FOR MORE...
LULA, THESE DREAMS I BOUGHT LAST WEEK ARE ALL BROKEN!
DREAMS
IT SAYS "BROKEN DREAMS" RIGHT ON THE BOX, SOMNUS! READ THE LABEL!
DO YOU GUYS HAVE THE NEXT ISSUE OF GILGAMESH 5000?
THE NEXT ISSUE ISN'T OUT YET, ARES. THAT'S WHY IT'S THE NEXT ISSUE!

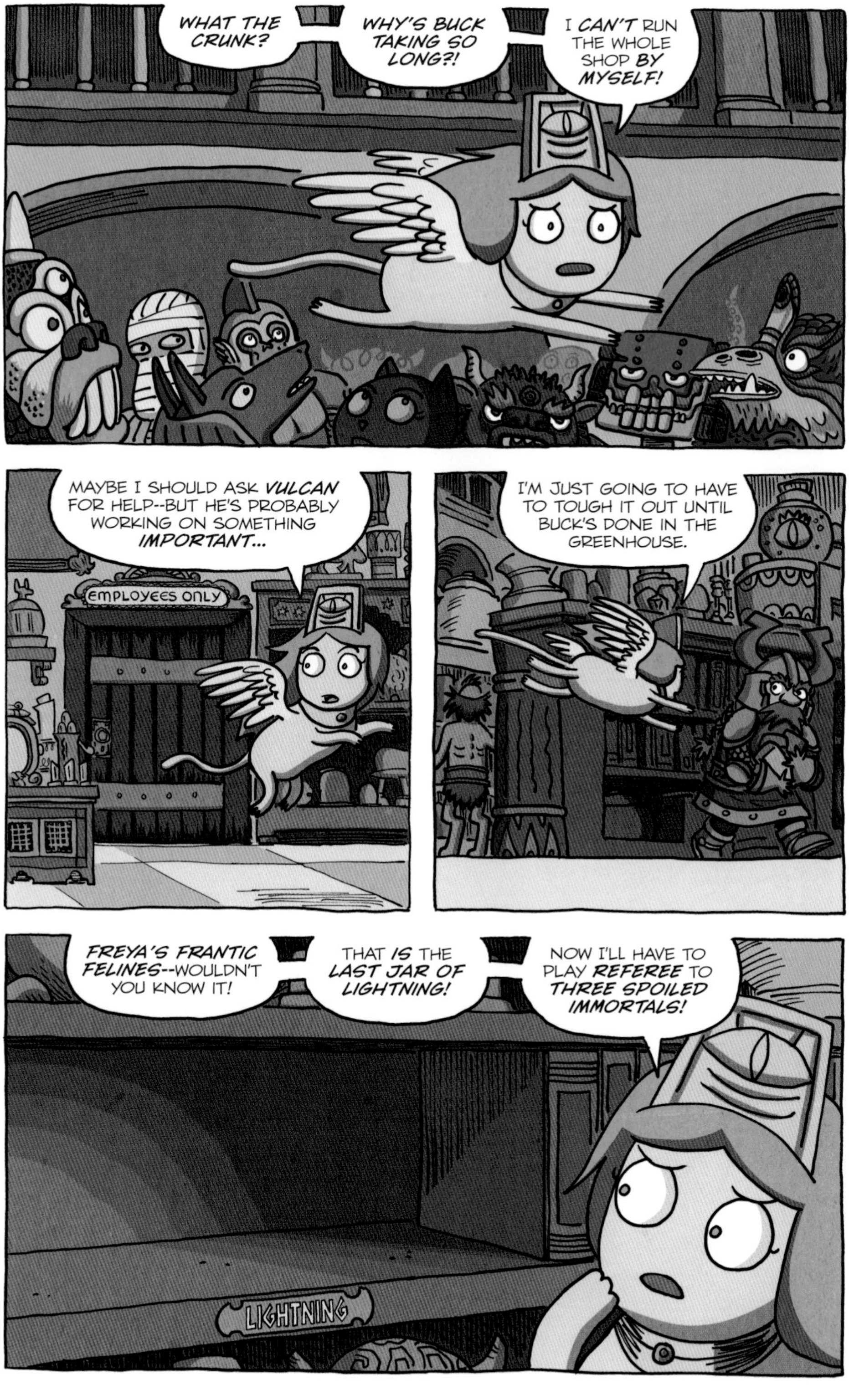
WHAT THE CRUNK?
WHY'S BUCK TAKING SO LONG?!
I CAN'T RUN THE WHOLE SHOP BY MYSELF!
MAYBE I SHOULD ASK VULCAN FOR HELP--BUT HE'S PROBABLY WORKING ON SOMETHING IMPORTANT...
EMPLOYEES ONLY
I'M JUST GOING TO HAVE TO TOUGH IT OUT UNTIL BUCK'S DONE IN THE GREENHOUSE.
FREYA'S FRANTIC FELINES--WOULDN'T YOU KNOW IT!
THAT IS THE LAST JAR OF LIGHTNING!
NOW I'LL HAVE TO PLAY REFEREE TO THREE SPOILED IMMORTALS!
LIGHTNING

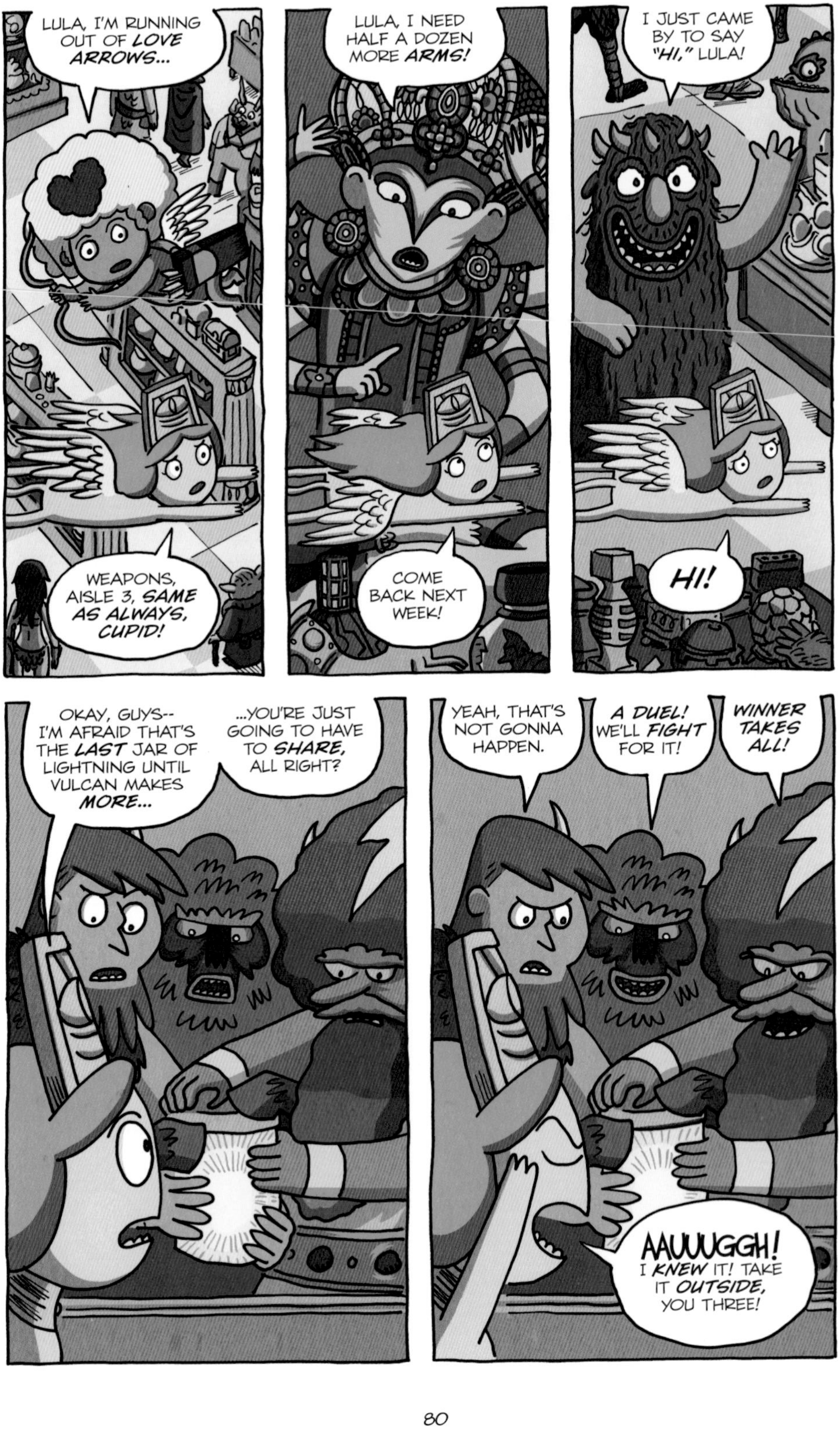
LULA, I'M RUNNING OUT OF LOVE ARROWS...
WEAPONS, AISLE 3, SAME AS ALWAYS, CUPID!
LULA, I NEED HALF A DOZEN MORE ARMS!
COME BACK NEXT WEEK!
I JUST CAME BY TO SAY "HI," LULA!
HI!
OKAY, GUYS-- I'M AFRAID THAT'S THE LAST JAR OF LIGHTNING UNTIL VULCAN MAKES MORE...
...YOU'RE JUST GOING TO HAVE TO SHARE, ALL RIGHT?
YEAH, THAT'S NOT GONNA HAPPEN.
A DUEL! WE'LL FIGHT FOR IT!
WINNER TAKES ALL!
AAUUUGGH! I KNEW IT! TAKE IT OUTSIDE, YOU THREE!

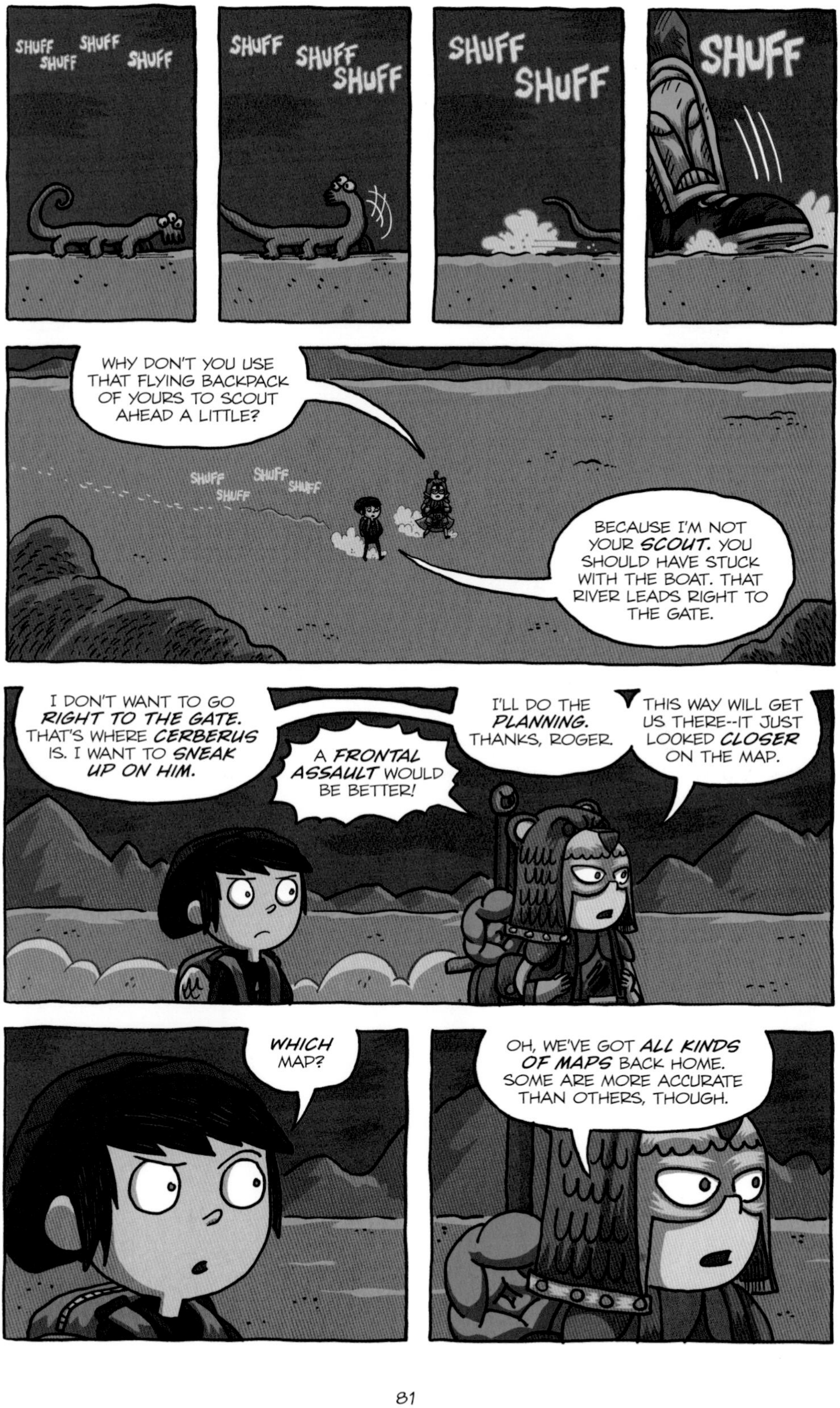
SHUFF SHUFF SHUFF SHUFF
SHUFF SHUFF SHUFF
SHUFF SHUFF
SHUFF
WHY DON'T YOU USE THAT FLYING BACKPACK OF YOURS TO SCOUT AHEAD A LITTLE?
SHUFF SHUFF SHUFF SHUFF
BECAUSE I'M NOT YOUR SCOUT. YOU SHOULD HAVE STUCK WITH THE BOAT. THAT RIVER LEADS RIGHT TO THE GATE.
I DON'T WANT TO GO RIGHT TO THE GATE. THAT'S WHERE CERBERUS IS. I WANT TO SNEAK UP ON HIM.
A FRONTAL ASSAULT WOULD BE BETTER!
I'LL DO THE PLANNING. THANKS, ROGER.
THIS WAY WILL GET US THERE--IT JUST LOOKED CLOSER ON THE MAP.
WHICH MAP?
OH, WE'VE GOT ALL KINDS OF MAPS BACK HOME. SOME ARE MORE ACCURATE THAN OTHERS, THOUGH.

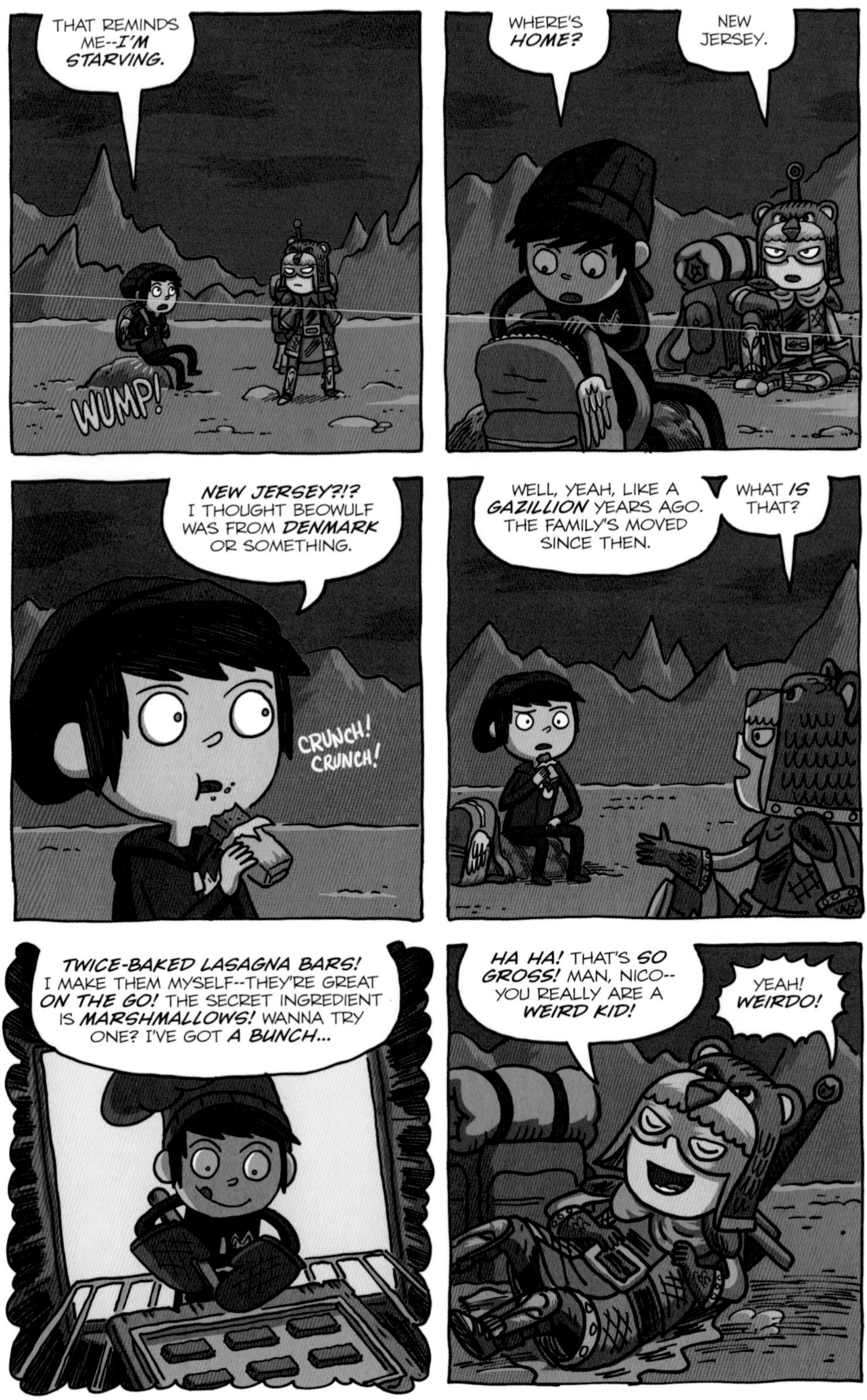
THAT REMINDS ME--I'M STARVING.
WUMP!
WHERE'S HOME?
NEW JERSEY.
NEW JERSEY?!? I THOUGHT BEOWULF WAS FROM DENMARK OR SOMETHING.
CRUNCH! CRUNCH!
WELL, YEAH, LIKE A GAZILLION YEARS AGO. THE FAMILY'S MOVED SINCE THEN.
WHAT IS THAT?
TWICE-BAKED LASAGNA BARS! I MAKE THEM MYSELF--THEY'RE GREAT ON THE GO! THE SECRET INGREDIENT IS MARSHMALLOWS! WANNA TRY ONE? I'VE GOT A BUNCH...
HA HA! THAT'S SO GROSS! MAN, NICO-- YOU REALLY ARE A WEIRD KID!
YEAH! WEIRDO!

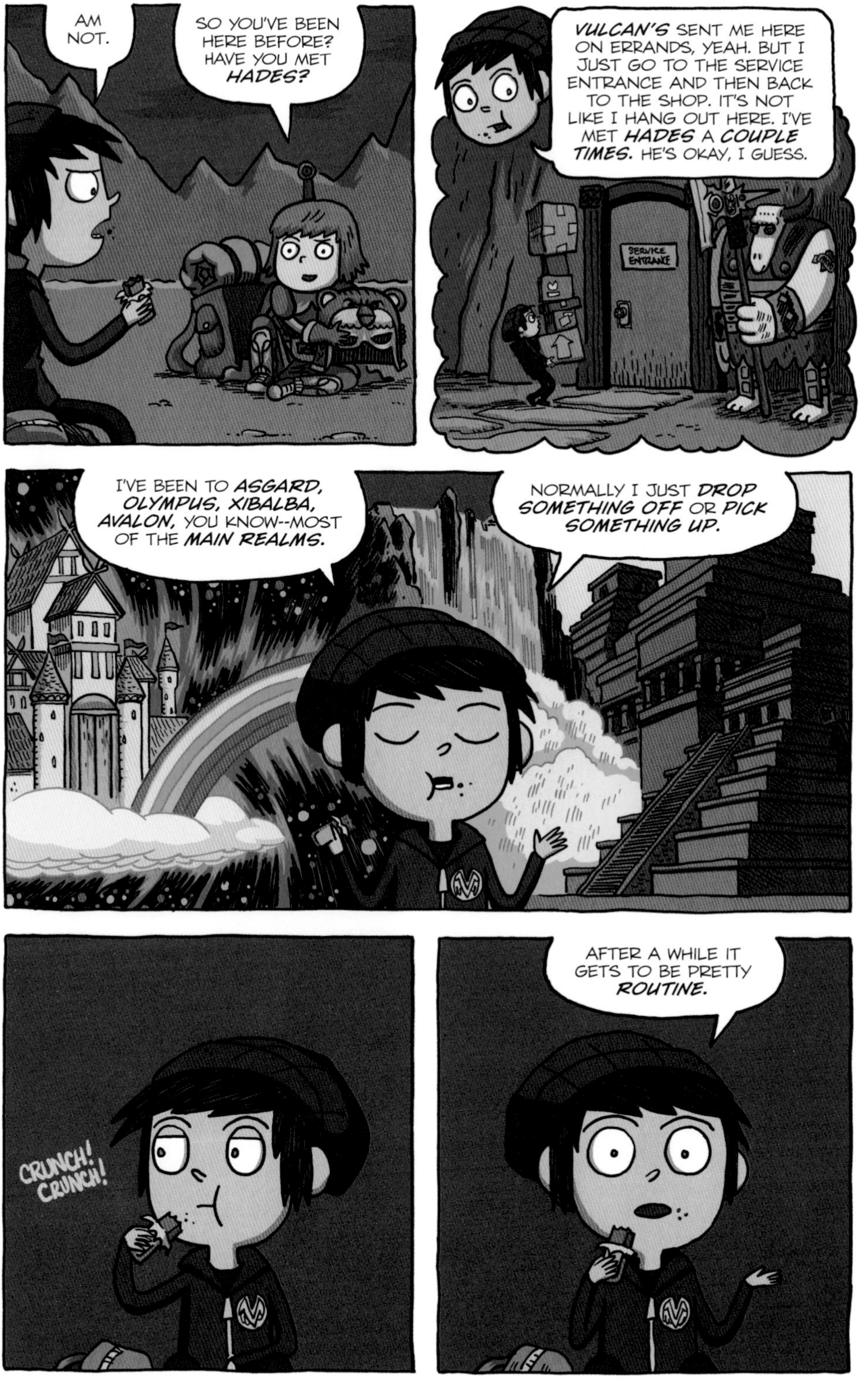
AM NOT.
SO YOU'VE BEEN HERE BEFORE? HAVE YOU MET HADES?
VULCAN'S SENT ME HERE ON ERRANDS, YEAH. BUT I JUST GO TO THE SERVICE ENTRANCE AND THEN BACK TO THE SHOP. IT'S NOT LIKE I HANG OUT HERE. I'VE MET HADES A COUPLE TIMES. HE'S OKAY, I GUESS.
SERVICE ENTRANCE
I'VE BEEN TO ASGARD, OLYMPUS, XIBALBA, AVALON, YOU KNOW--MOST OF THE MAIN REALMS.
NORMALLY I JUST DROP SOMETHING OFF OR PICK SOMETHING UP.
CRUNCH! CRUNCH!
AFTER A WHILE IT GETS TO BE PRETTY ROUTINE.

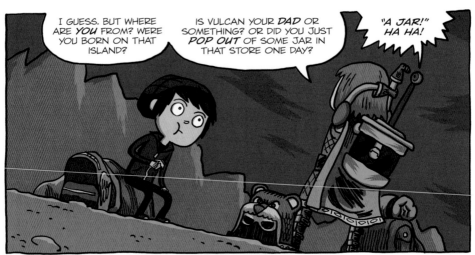

I GUESS. BUT WHERE ARE *YOU* FROM? WERE YOU BORN ON THAT ISLAND?

IS VULCAN YOUR *DAD* OR SOMETHING? OR DID YOU JUST *POP OUT* OF SOME JAR IN THAT STORE ONE DAY?

*"A JAR!"* HA HA!

IF *VULCAN* WAS MY DAD THAT WOULD MAKE ME A GOD, *TOO.* I'M JUST A KID WHO WORKS IN HIS SHOP.

WHOEVER MY *REAL PARENTS* WERE, THEY LEFT ME *IN A BOX* ON VULCAN'S DOORSTEP. HE'S RAISED ME EVER SINCE.

WAAAAAAA!

*BUCK* ALREADY WORKED THERE, AND VULCAN HIRED *LULA* A COUPLE YEARS AGO.

YEAH, *WHAT'S UP* WITH THAT UNICORN? HE'S *WEIRDER THAN YOU!*

WELL, A UNICORN'S *HORN* IS THE ROOT OF THEIR *MAGIC*, BUT BUCK'S WAS DAMAGED DURING THE *UNICORN WARS...*

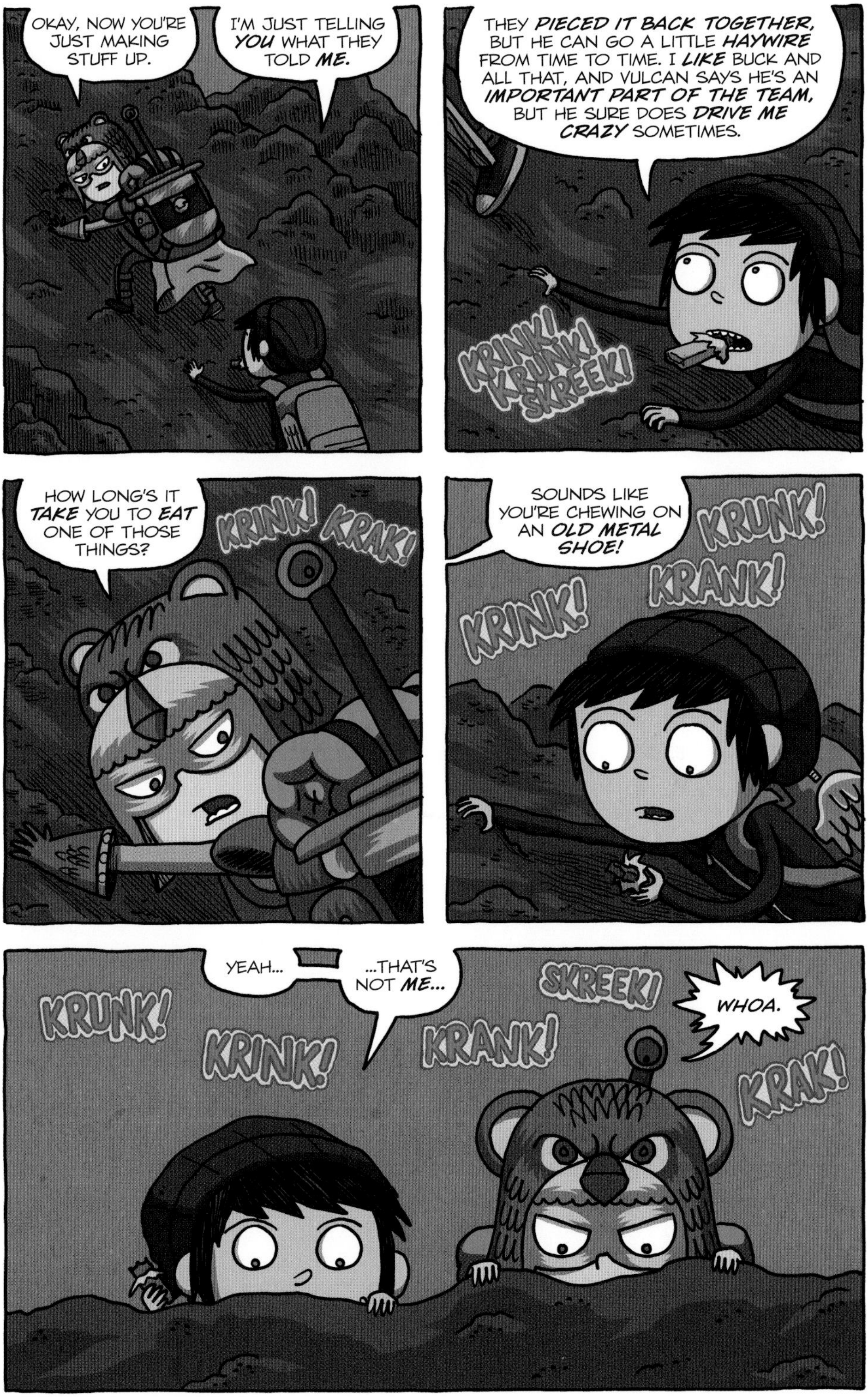
OKAY, NOW YOU'RE JUST MAKING STUFF UP.
I'M JUST TELLING *YOU* WHAT THEY TOLD *ME.*
THEY *PIECED IT BACK TOGETHER,* BUT HE CAN GO A LITTLE *HAYWIRE* FROM TIME TO TIME. I *LIKE* BUCK AND ALL THAT, AND VULCAN SAYS HE'S AN *IMPORTANT PART OF THE TEAM,* BUT HE SURE DOES *DRIVE ME CRAZY* SOMETIMES.
KRINK! KRUNK! SKREEK!
HOW LONG'S IT *TAKE* YOU TO *EAT* ONE OF THOSE THINGS?
KRINK! KRAK!
SOUNDS LIKE YOU'RE CHEWING ON AN *OLD METAL SHOE!*
KRUNK! KRANK! KRINK!
YEAH...
...THAT'S NOT *ME...*
KRUNK! KRINK! KRANK! SKREEK!
WHOA.
KRAK!

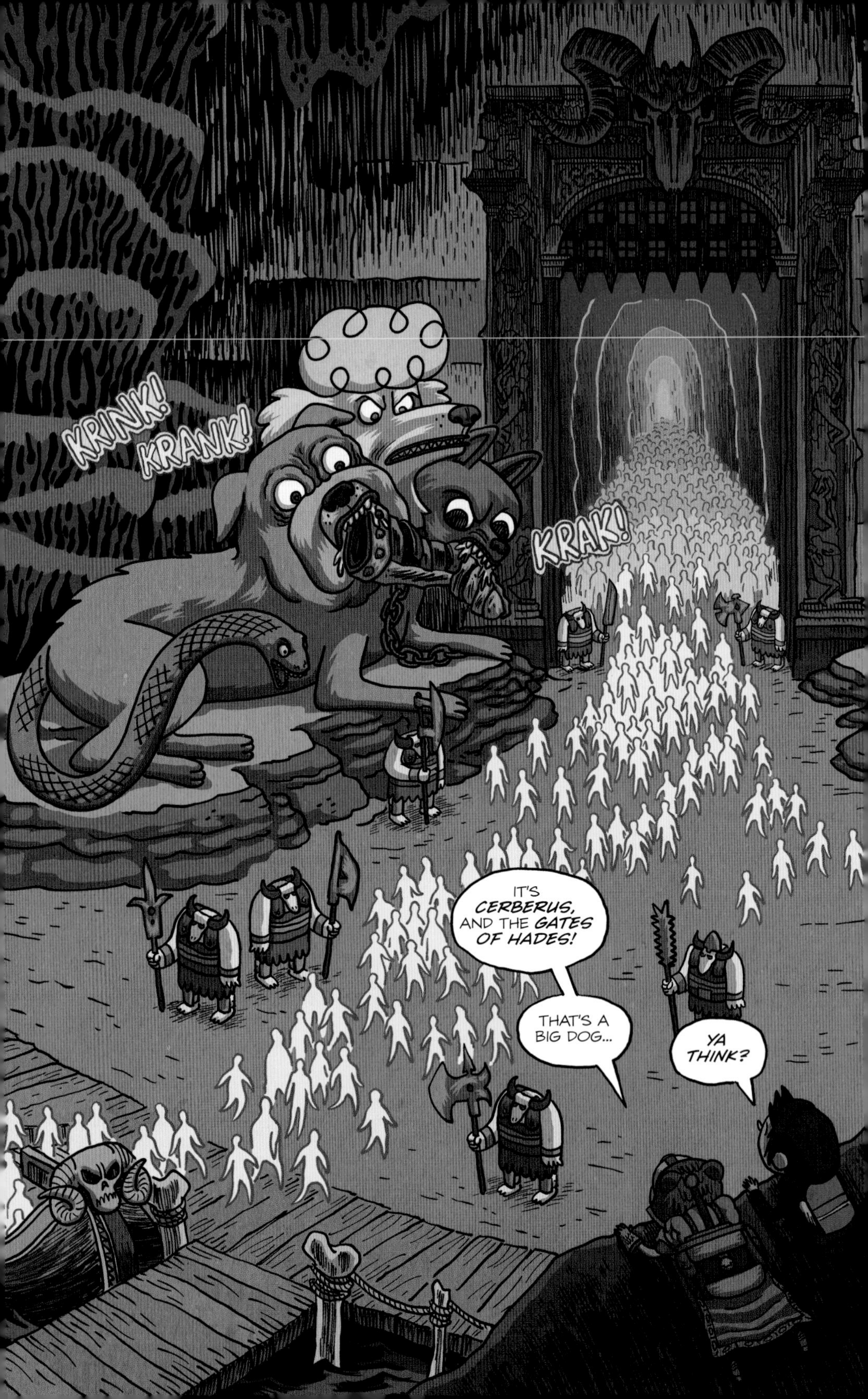
KRINK! KRANK!
KRAK!
IT'S CERBERUS, AND THE GATES OF HADES!
THAT'S A BIG DOG...
YA THINK?

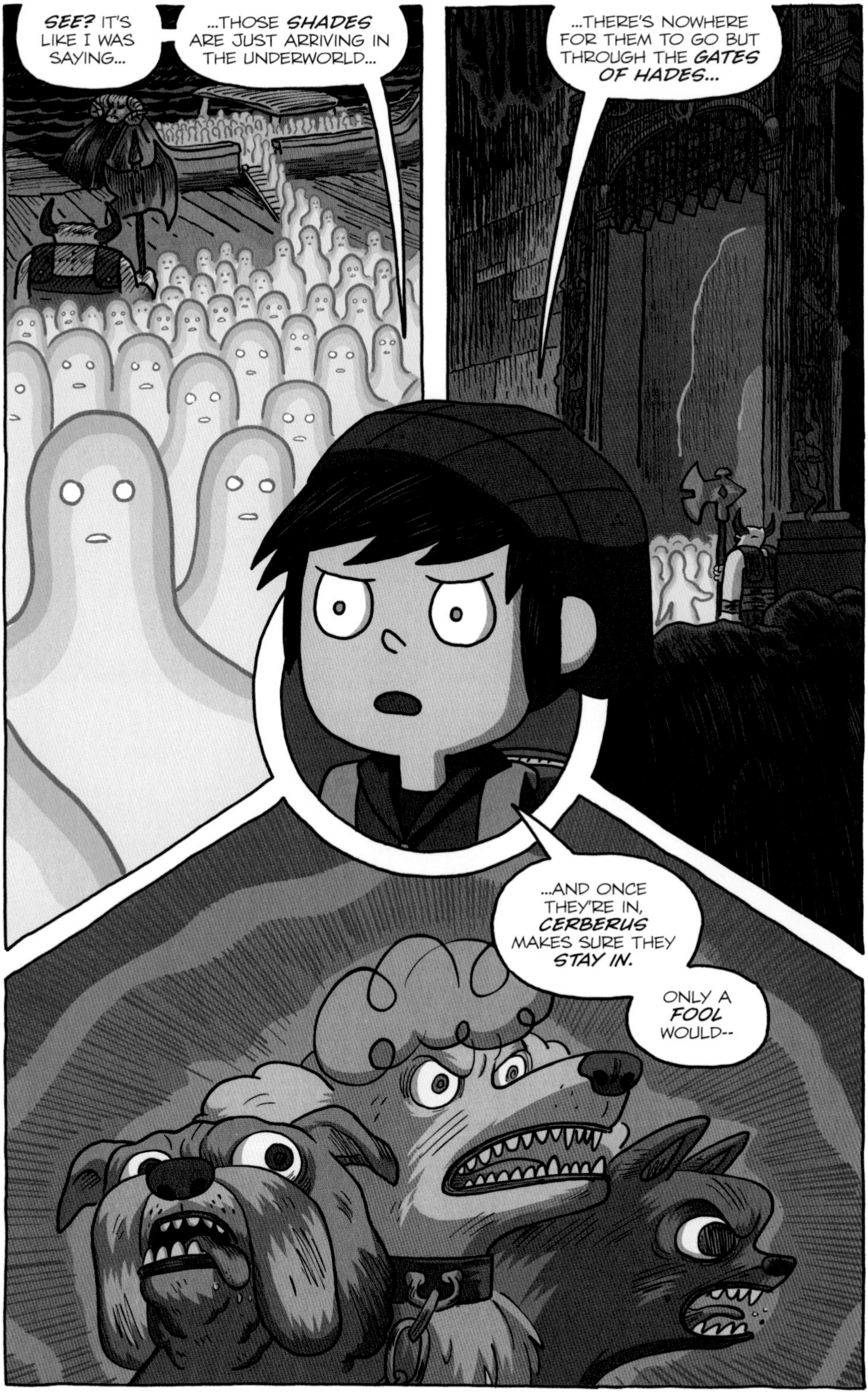
SEE? IT'S LIKE I WAS SAYING...
...THOSE SHADES ARE JUST ARRIVING IN THE UNDERWORLD...
...THERE'S NOWHERE FOR THEM TO GO BUT THROUGH THE GATES OF HADES...
...AND ONCE THEY'RE IN, CERBERUS MAKES SURE THEY STAY IN.
ONLY A FOOL WOULD--

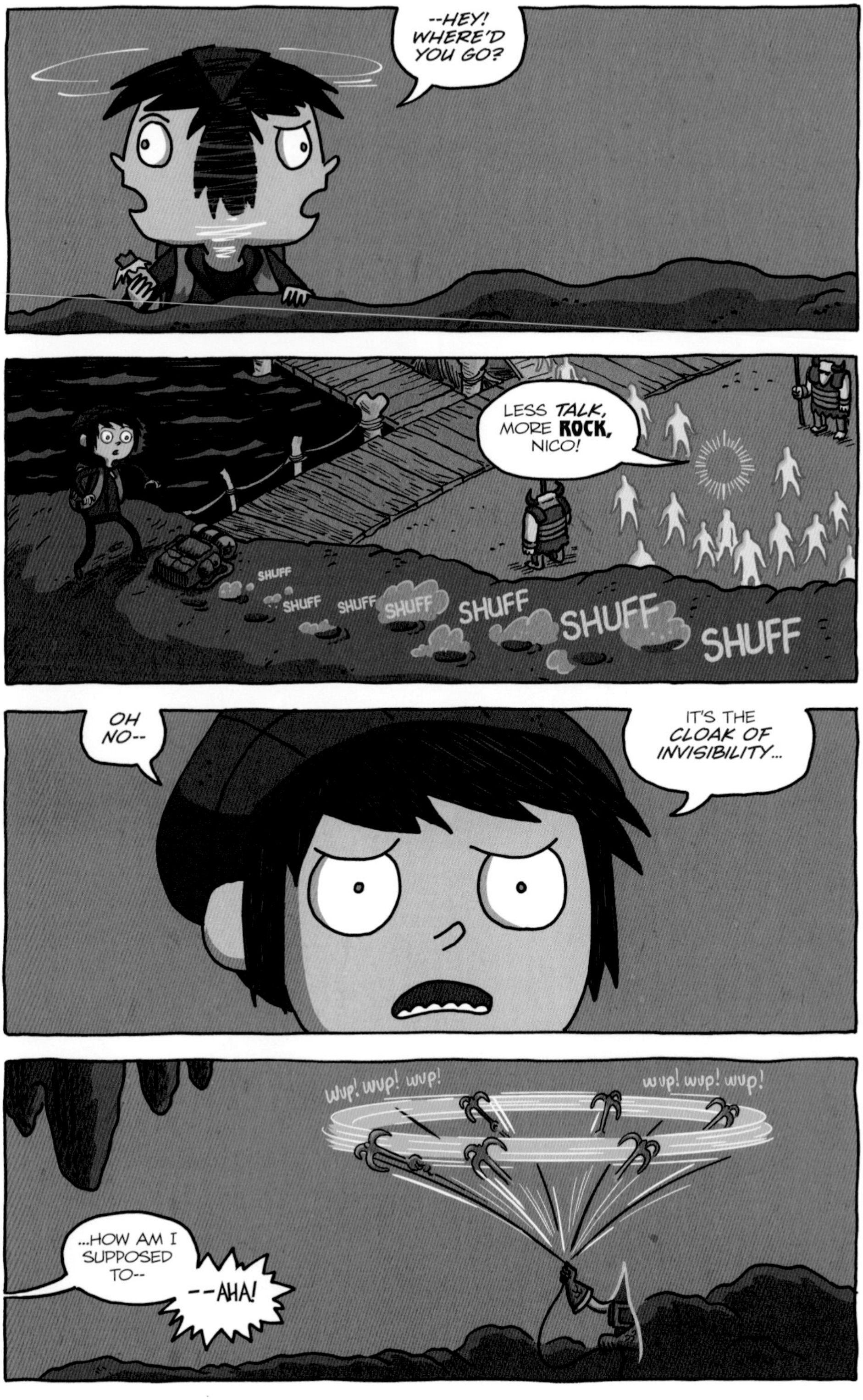
--HEY! WHERE'D YOU GO?
LESS TALK, MORE ROCK, NICO!
SHUFF SHUFF SHUFF SHUFF SHUFF SHUFF SHUFF
OH NO--
IT'S THE CLOAK OF INVISIBILITY...
wup! wup! wup!
wup! wup! wup!
...HOW AM I SUPPOSED TO--
--AHA!

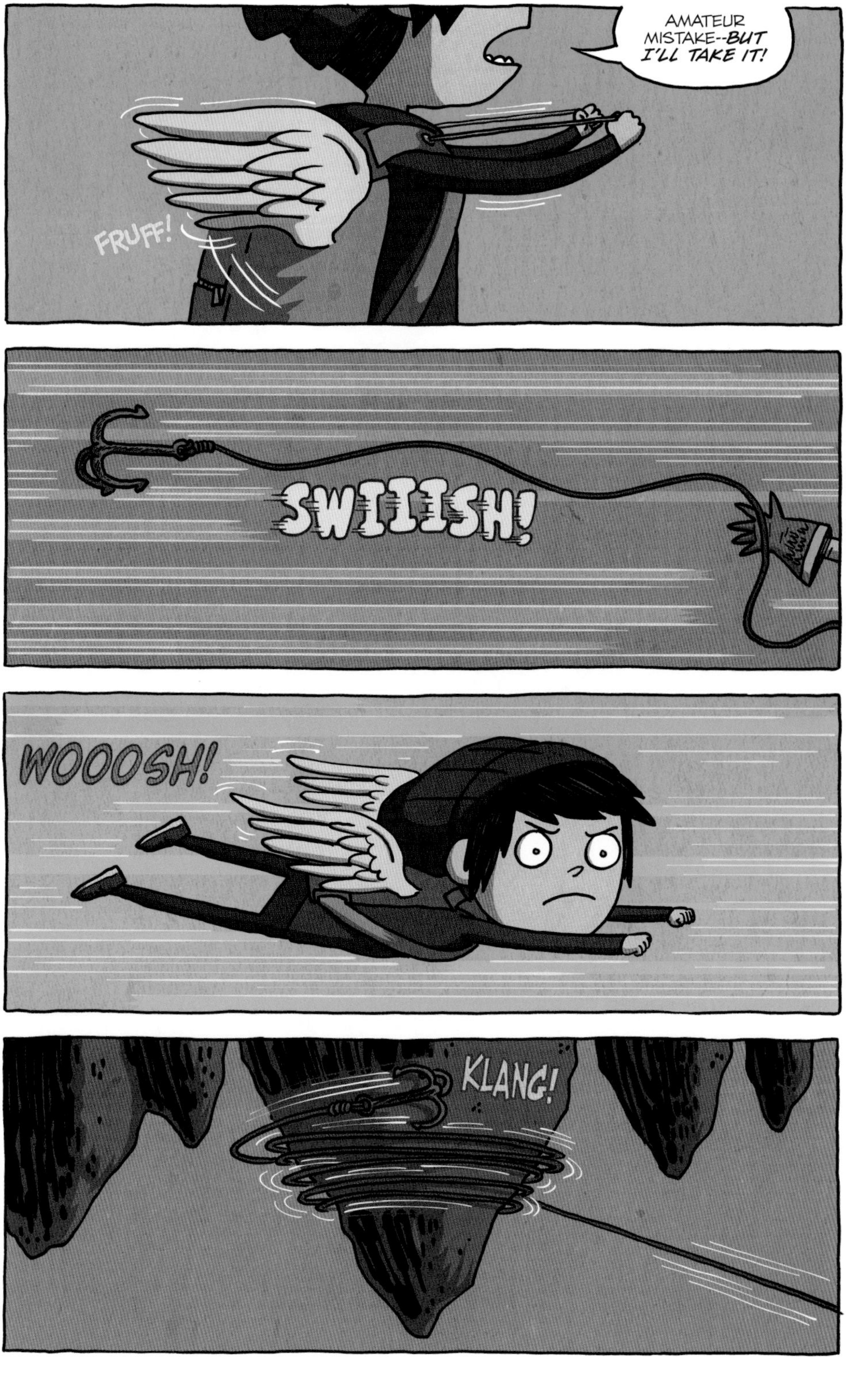
AMATEUR MISTAKE--BUT I'LL TAKE IT!
FRUFF!
SWIIISH!
WOOOSH!
KLANG!

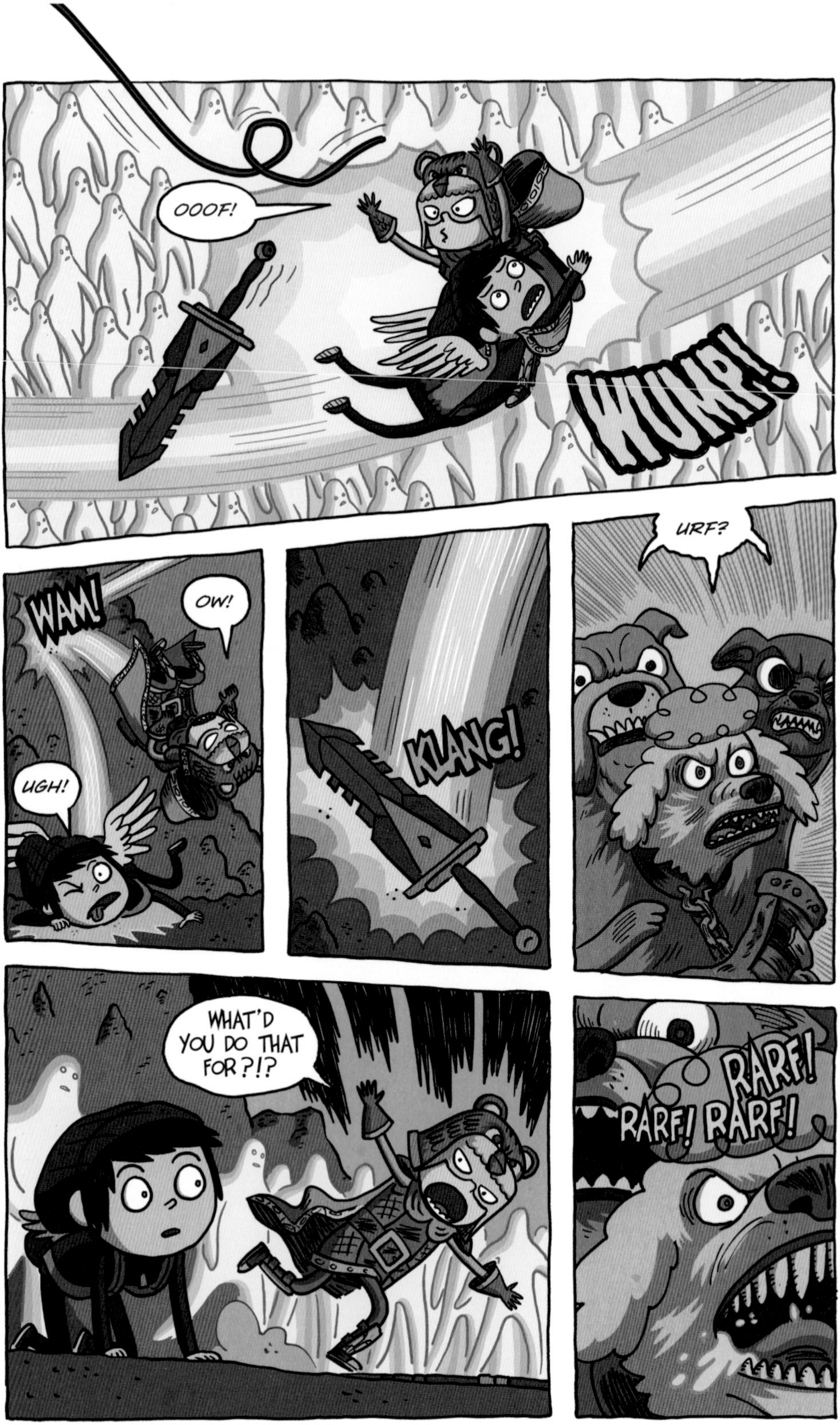
OOOF!
WUMP!
WAM!
OW!
UGH!
KLANG!
URF?
WHAT'D YOU DO THAT FOR?!?
RARF!
RARF! RARF!

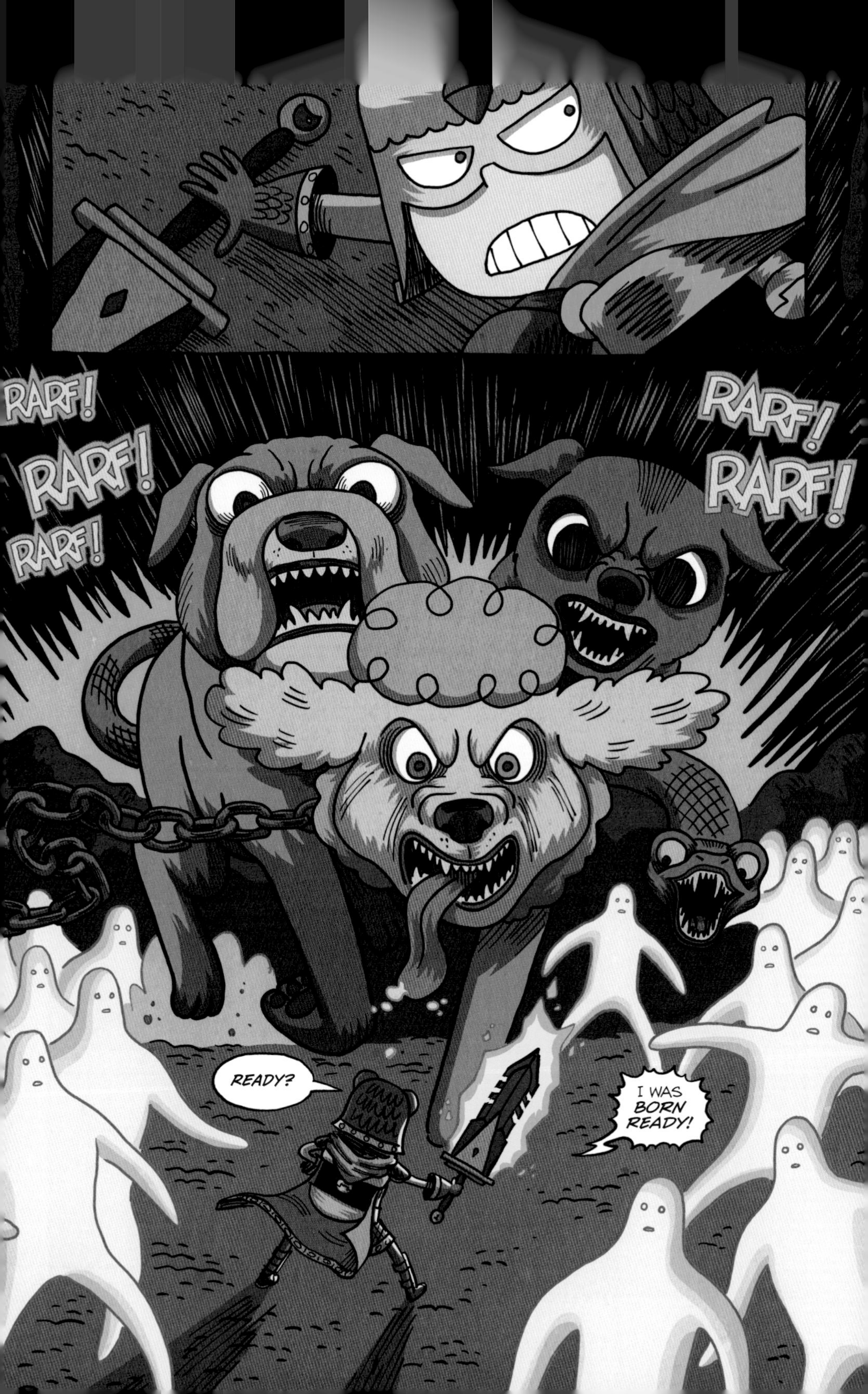
RARF!
RARF!
RARF!
RARF!
RARF!
READY?
I WAS BORN READY!

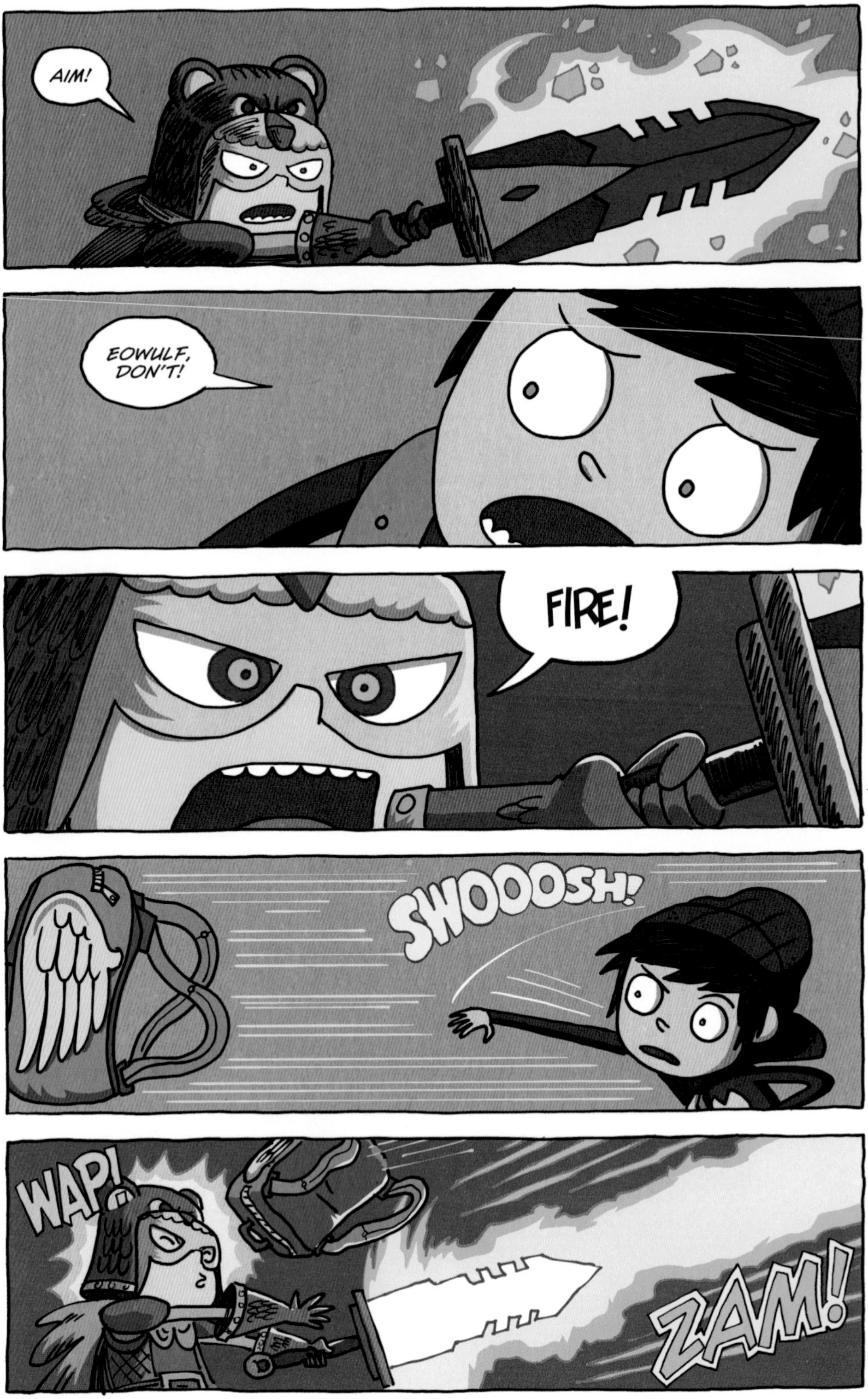
AIM!
EOWULF, DON'T!
FIRE!
SHOOOSH!
WAP!
ZAM!

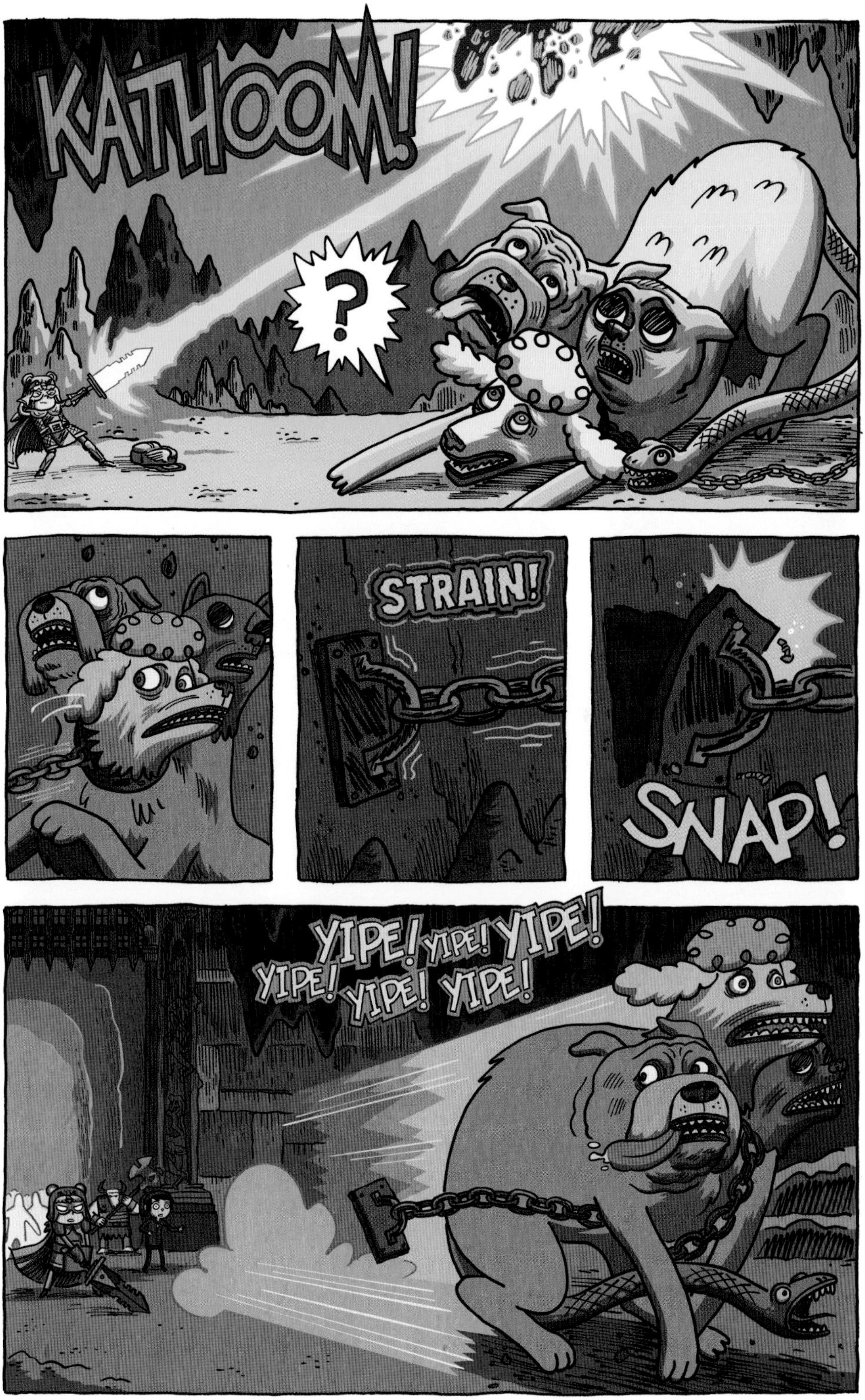
KATHOOM!
?
STRAIN!
SNAP!
YIPE! YIPE! YIPE!
YIPE! YIPE! YIPE!

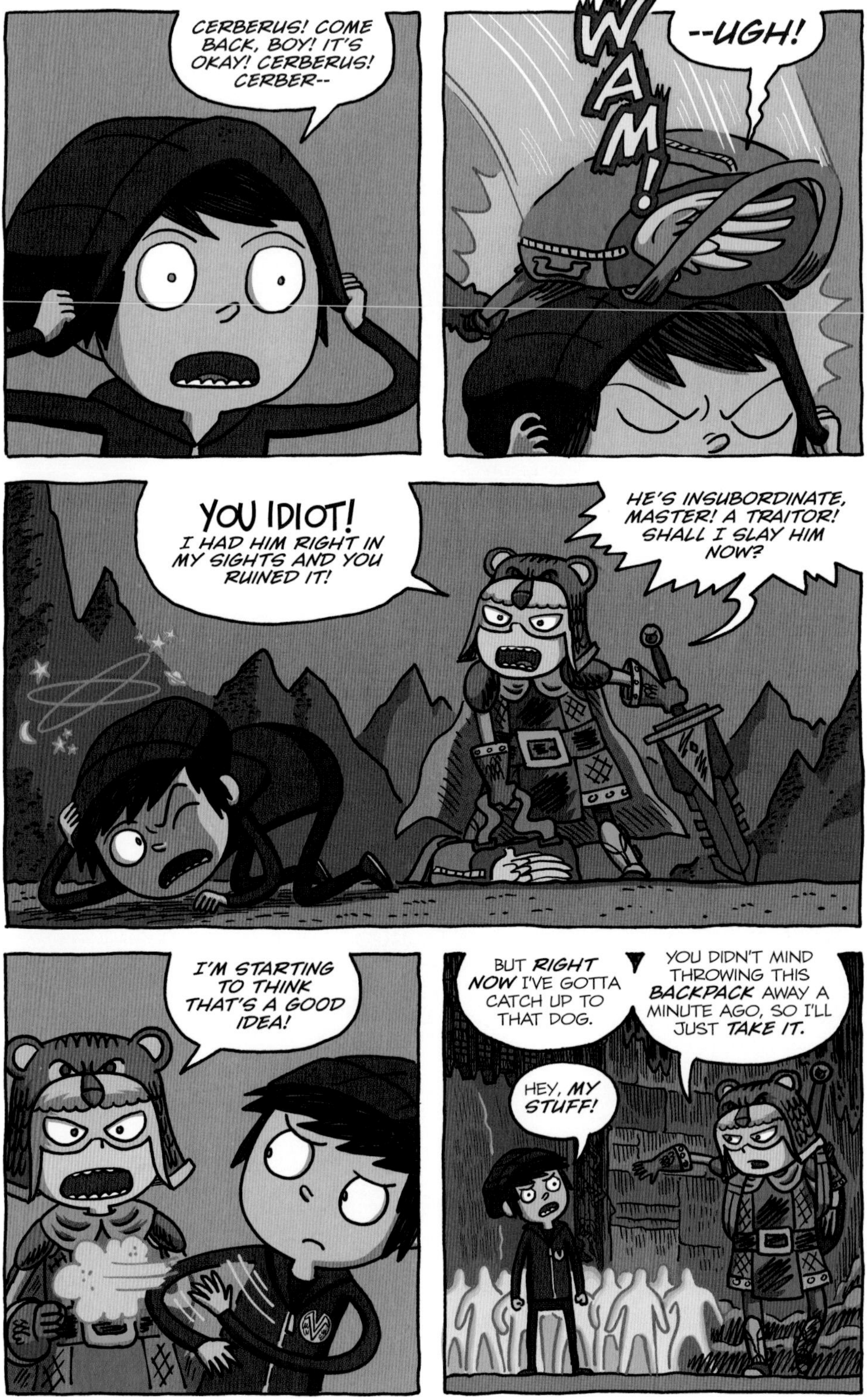
CERBERUS! COME BACK, BOY! IT'S OKAY! CERBERUS! CERBER--
WAM!
--UGH!
YOU IDIOT! I HAD HIM RIGHT IN MY SIGHTS AND YOU RUINED IT!
HE'S INSUBORDINATE, MASTER! A TRAITOR! SHALL I SLAY HIM NOW?
I'M STARTING TO THINK THAT'S A GOOD IDEA!
BUT RIGHT NOW I'VE GOTTA CATCH UP TO THAT DOG.
YOU DIDN'T MIND THROWING THIS BACKPACK AWAY A MINUTE AGO, SO I'LL JUST TAKE IT.
HEY, MY STUFF!

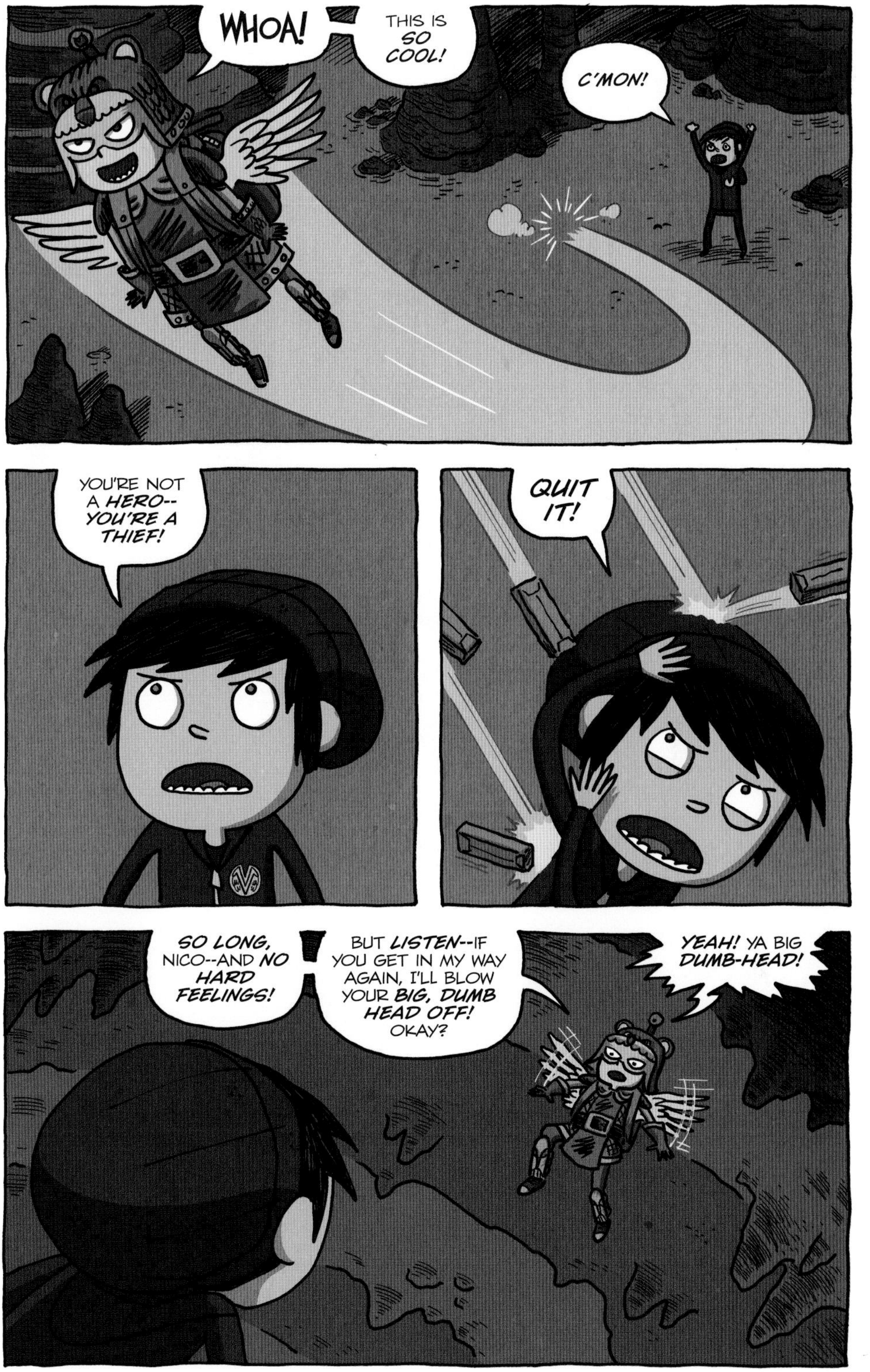
WHOA!
THIS IS SO COOL!
C'MON!
YOU'RE NOT A HERO--YOU'RE A THIEF!
QUIT IT!
SO LONG, NICO--AND NO HARD FEELINGS!
BUT LISTEN--IF YOU GET IN MY WAY AGAIN, I'LL BLOW YOUR BIG, DUMB HEAD OFF! OKAY?
YEAH! YA BIG DUMB-HEAD!

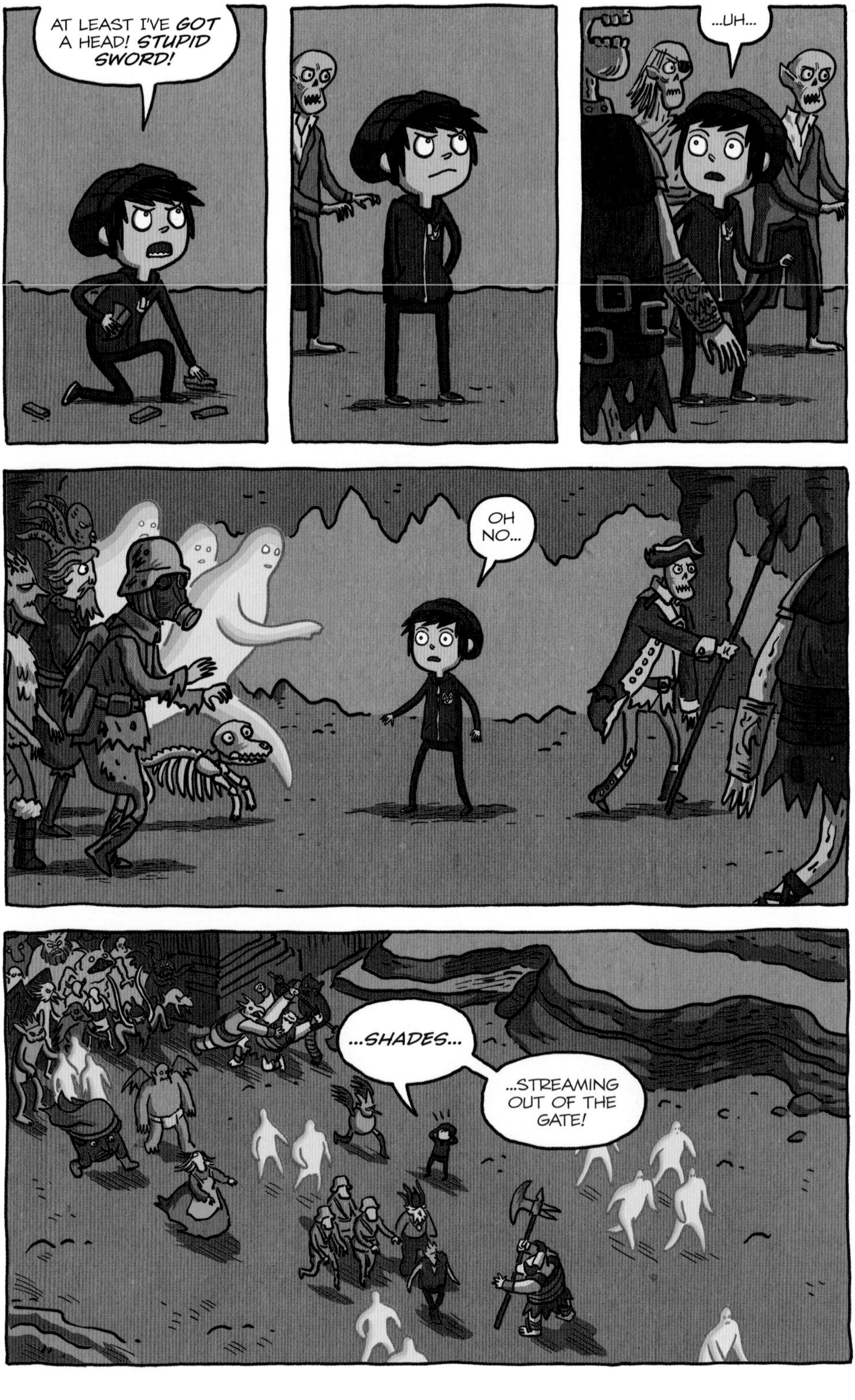
AT LEAST I'VE GOT A HEAD! STUPID SWORD!
...UH...
OH NO...
...SHADES...
...STREAMING OUT OF THE GATE!

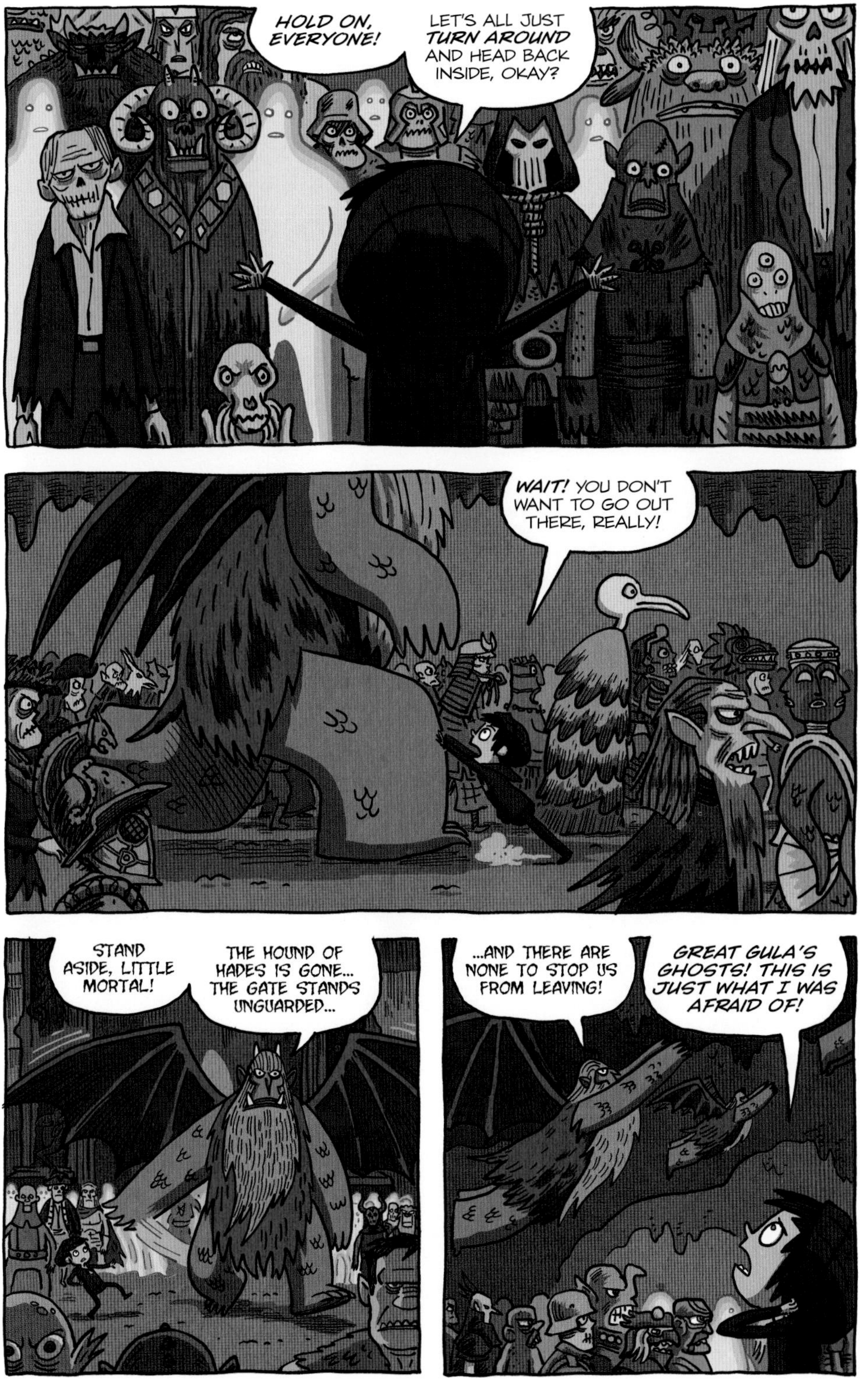
HOLD ON, EVERYONE!
LET'S ALL JUST TURN AROUND AND HEAD BACK INSIDE, OKAY?
WAIT! YOU DON'T WANT TO GO OUT THERE, REALLY!
STAND ASIDE, LITTLE MORTAL!
THE HOUND OF HADES IS GONE... THE GATE STANDS UNGUARDED...
...AND THERE ARE NONE TO STOP US FROM LEAVING!
GREAT GULA'S GHOSTS! THIS IS JUST WHAT I WAS AFRAID OF!

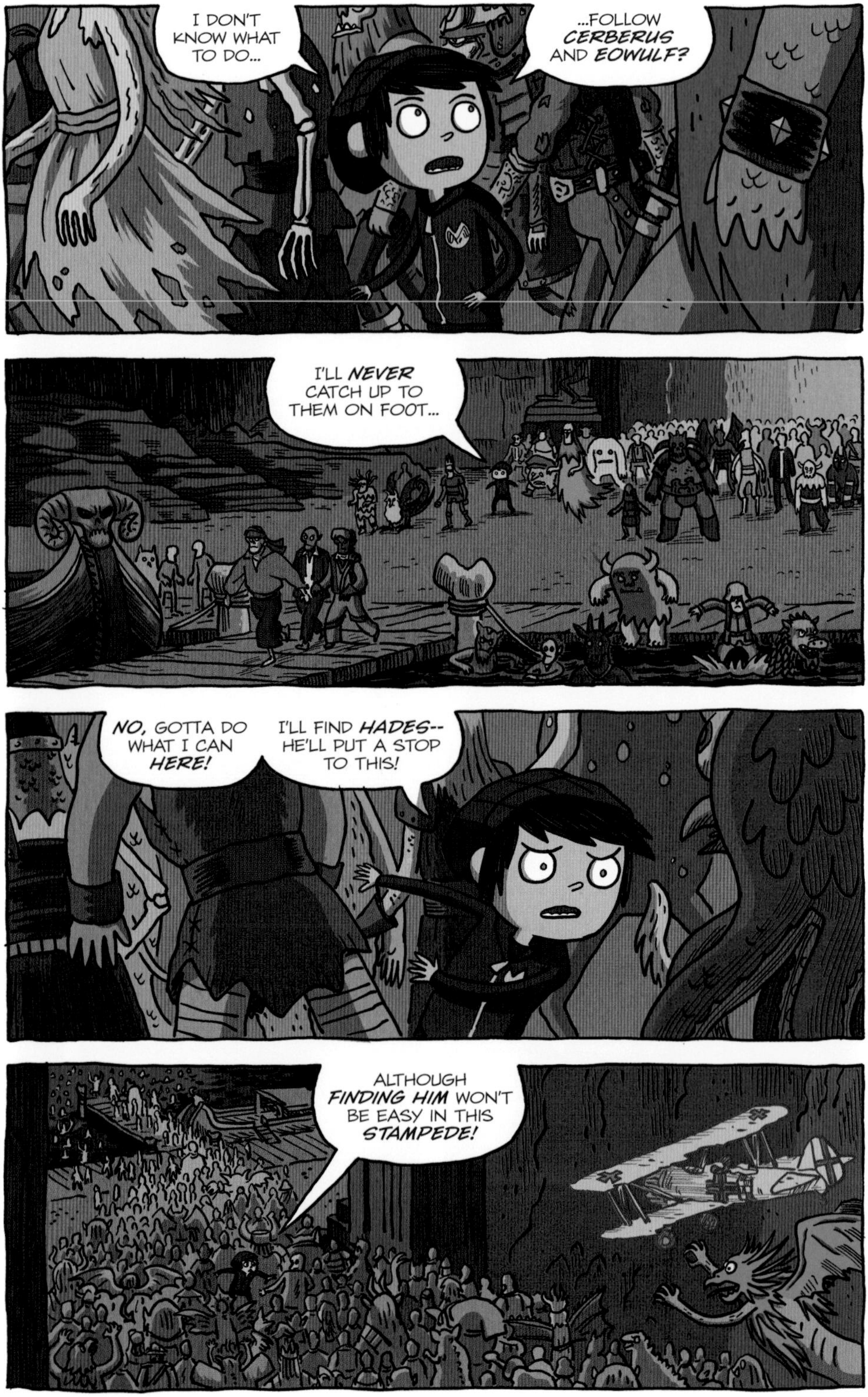
I DON'T KNOW WHAT TO DO...
...FOLLOW CERBERUS AND EOWULF?
I'LL NEVER CATCH UP TO THEM ON FOOT...
NO, GOTTA DO WHAT I CAN HERE!
I'LL FIND HADES-- HE'LL PUT A STOP TO THIS!
ALTHOUGH FINDING HIM WON'T BE EASY IN THIS STAMPEDE!

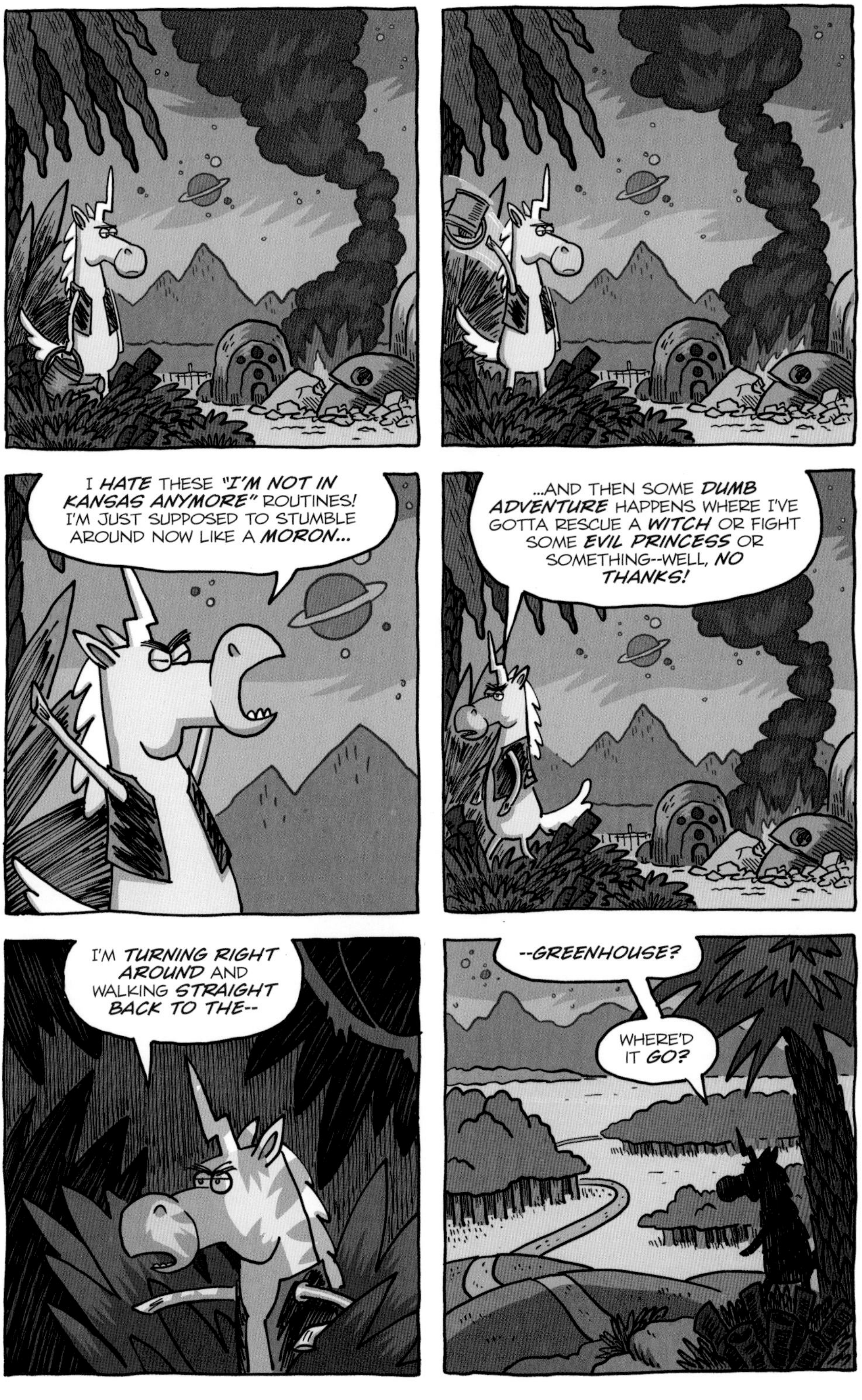
I HATE THESE "I'M NOT IN KANSAS ANYMORE" ROUTINES! I'M JUST SUPPOSED TO STUMBLE AROUND NOW LIKE A MORON...
...AND THEN SOME DUMB ADVENTURE HAPPENS WHERE I'VE GOTTA RESCUE A WITCH OR FIGHT SOME EVIL PRINCESS OR SOMETHING--WELL, NO THANKS!
I'M TURNING RIGHT AROUND AND WALKING STRAIGHT BACK TO THE--
--GREENHOUSE?
WHERE'D IT GO?

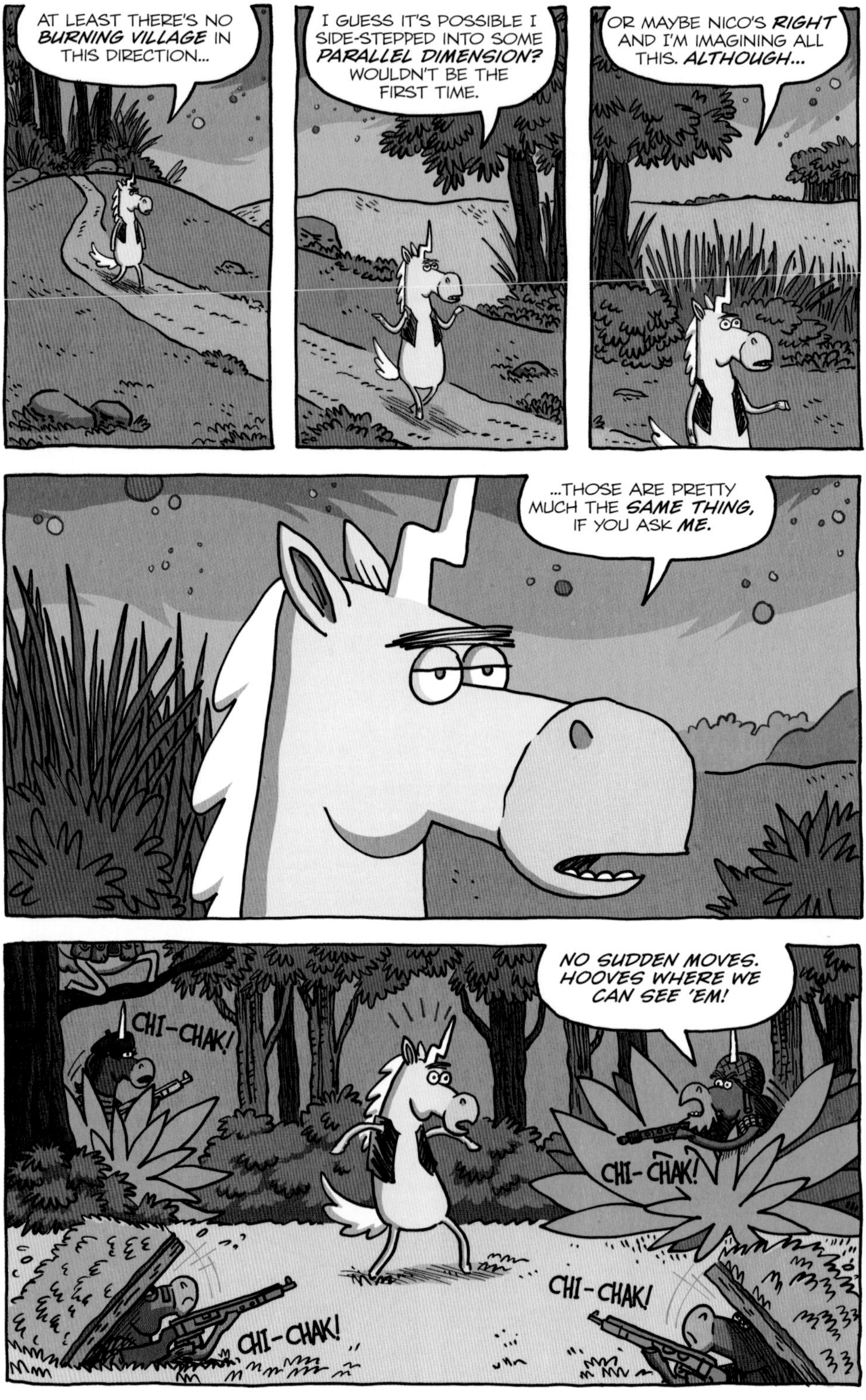
AT LEAST THERE'S NO BURNING VILLAGE IN THIS DIRECTION...
I GUESS IT'S POSSIBLE I SIDE-STEPPED INTO SOME PARALLEL DIMENSION? WOULDN'T BE THE FIRST TIME.
OR MAYBE NICO'S RIGHT AND I'M IMAGINING ALL THIS. ALTHOUGH...
...THOSE ARE PRETTY MUCH THE SAME THING, IF YOU ASK ME.
CHI-CHAK!
NO SUDDEN MOVES. HOOVES WHERE WE CAN SEE 'EM!
CHI-CHAK!
CHI-CHAK!
CHI-CHAK!

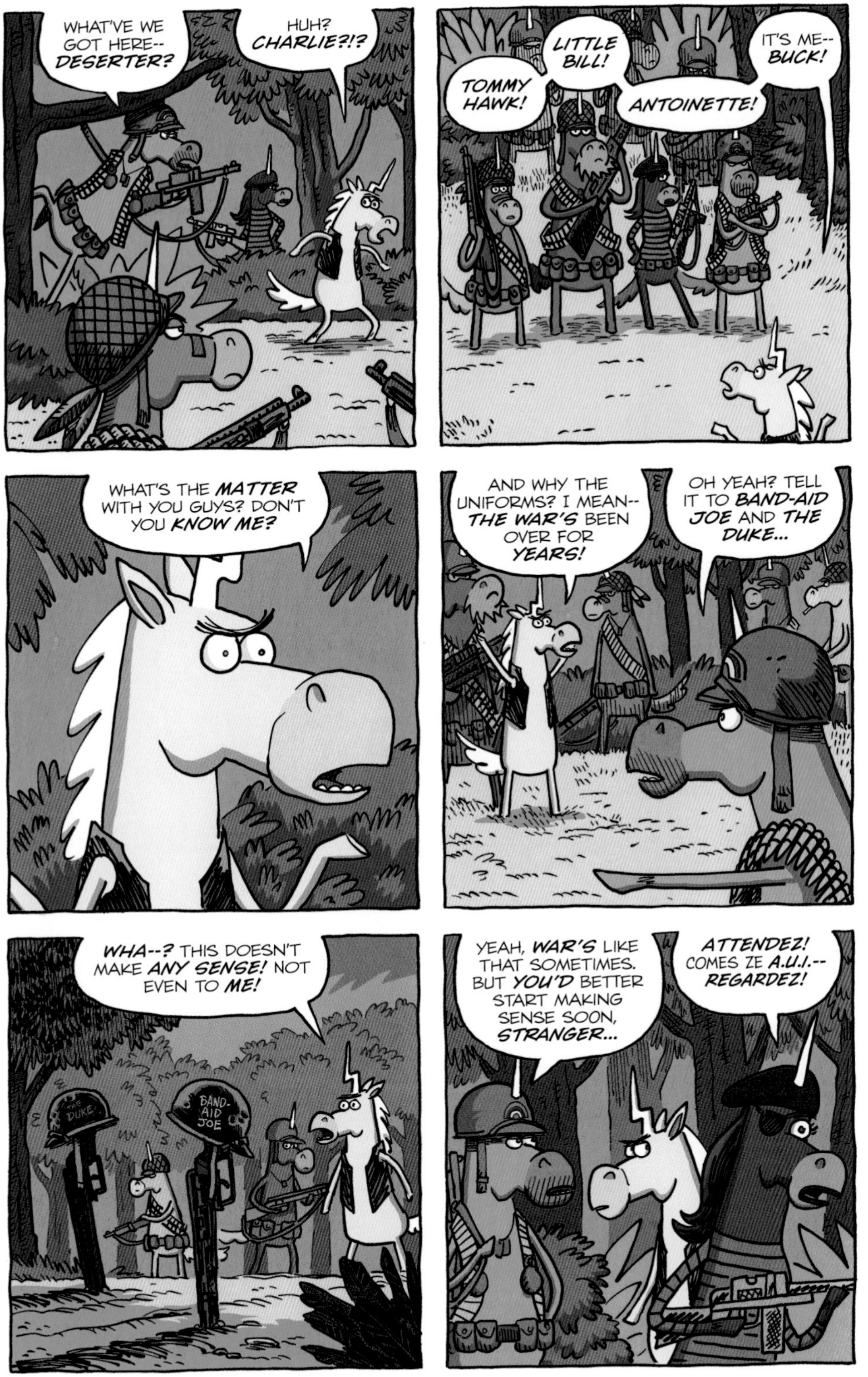
WHAT'VE WE GOT HERE-- DESERTER?
HUH? CHARLIE?!?
TOMMY HAWK!
LITTLE BILL!
ANTOINETTE!
IT'S ME-- BUCK!
WHAT'S THE MATTER WITH YOU GUYS? DON'T YOU KNOW ME?
AND WHY THE UNIFORMS? I MEAN-- THE WAR'S BEEN OVER FOR YEARS!
OH YEAH? TELL IT TO BAND-AID JOE AND THE DUKE...
WHA--? THIS DOESN'T MAKE ANY SENSE! NOT EVEN TO ME!
THE DUKE
BAND-AID JOE
YEAH, WAR'S LIKE THAT SOMETIMES. BUT YOU'D BETTER START MAKING SENSE SOON, STRANGER...
ATTENDEZ! COMES ZE A.U.I.-- REGARDEZ!

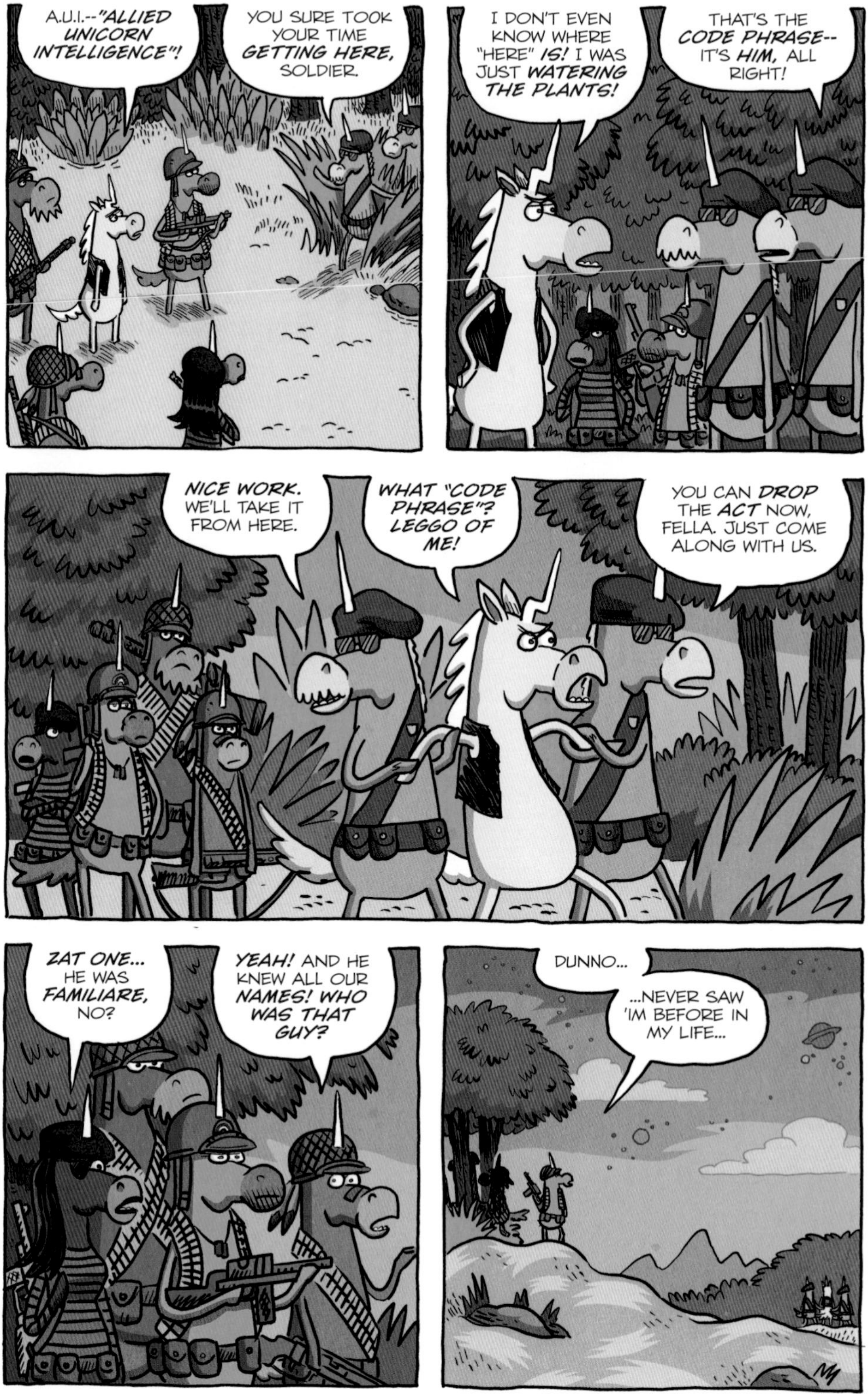
A.U.I.--"ALLIED UNICORN INTELLIGENCE"!
YOU SURE TOOK YOUR TIME GETTING HERE, SOLDIER.
I DON'T EVEN KNOW WHERE "HERE" IS! I WAS JUST WATERING THE PLANTS!
THAT'S THE CODE PHRASE-- IT'S HIM, ALL RIGHT!
NICE WORK. WE'LL TAKE IT FROM HERE.
WHAT "CODE PHRASE"? LEGGO OF ME!
YOU CAN DROP THE ACT NOW, FELLA. JUST COME ALONG WITH US.
ZAT ONE... HE WAS FAMILIARE, NO?
YEAH! AND HE KNEW ALL OUR NAMES! WHO WAS THAT GUY?
DUNNO...
...NEVER SAW 'IM BEFORE IN MY LIFE...

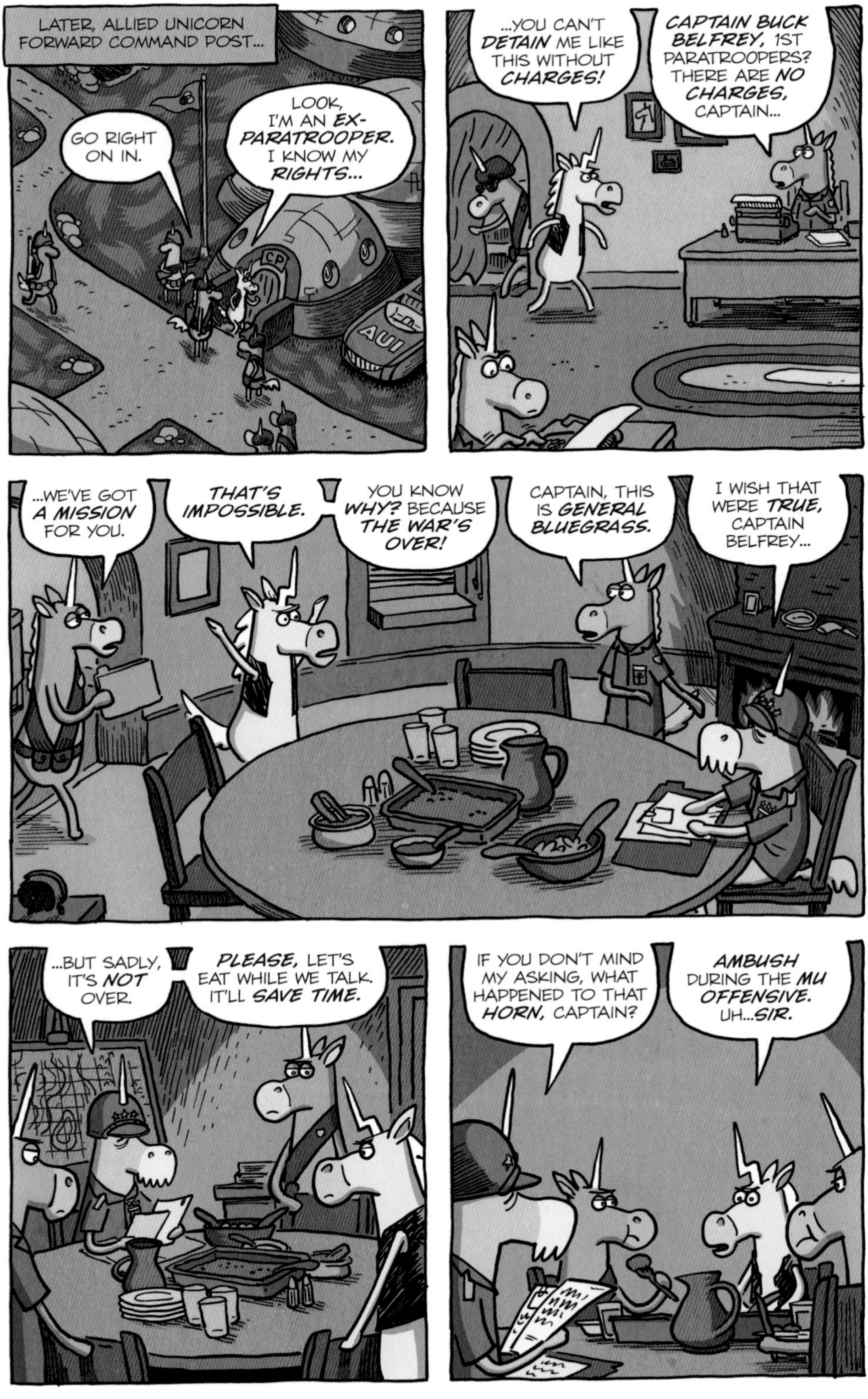
LATER, ALLIED UNICORN FORWARD COMMAND POST...
GO RIGHT ON IN.
LOOK, I'M AN EX-PARATROOPER. I KNOW MY RIGHTS...
CP
AUI
...YOU CAN'T DETAIN ME LIKE THIS WITHOUT CHARGES!
CAPTAIN BUCK BELFREY, 1ST PARATROOPERS? THERE ARE NO CHARGES, CAPTAIN...
...WE'VE GOT A MISSION FOR YOU.
THAT'S IMPOSSIBLE.
YOU KNOW WHY? BECAUSE THE WAR'S OVER!
CAPTAIN, THIS IS GENERAL BLUEGRASS.
I WISH THAT WERE TRUE, CAPTAIN BELFREY...
...BUT SADLY, IT'S NOT OVER.
PLEASE, LET'S EAT WHILE WE TALK. IT'LL SAVE TIME.
IF YOU DON'T MIND MY ASKING, WHAT HAPPENED TO THAT HORN, CAPTAIN?
AMBUSH DURING THE MU OFFENSIVE. UH...SIR.

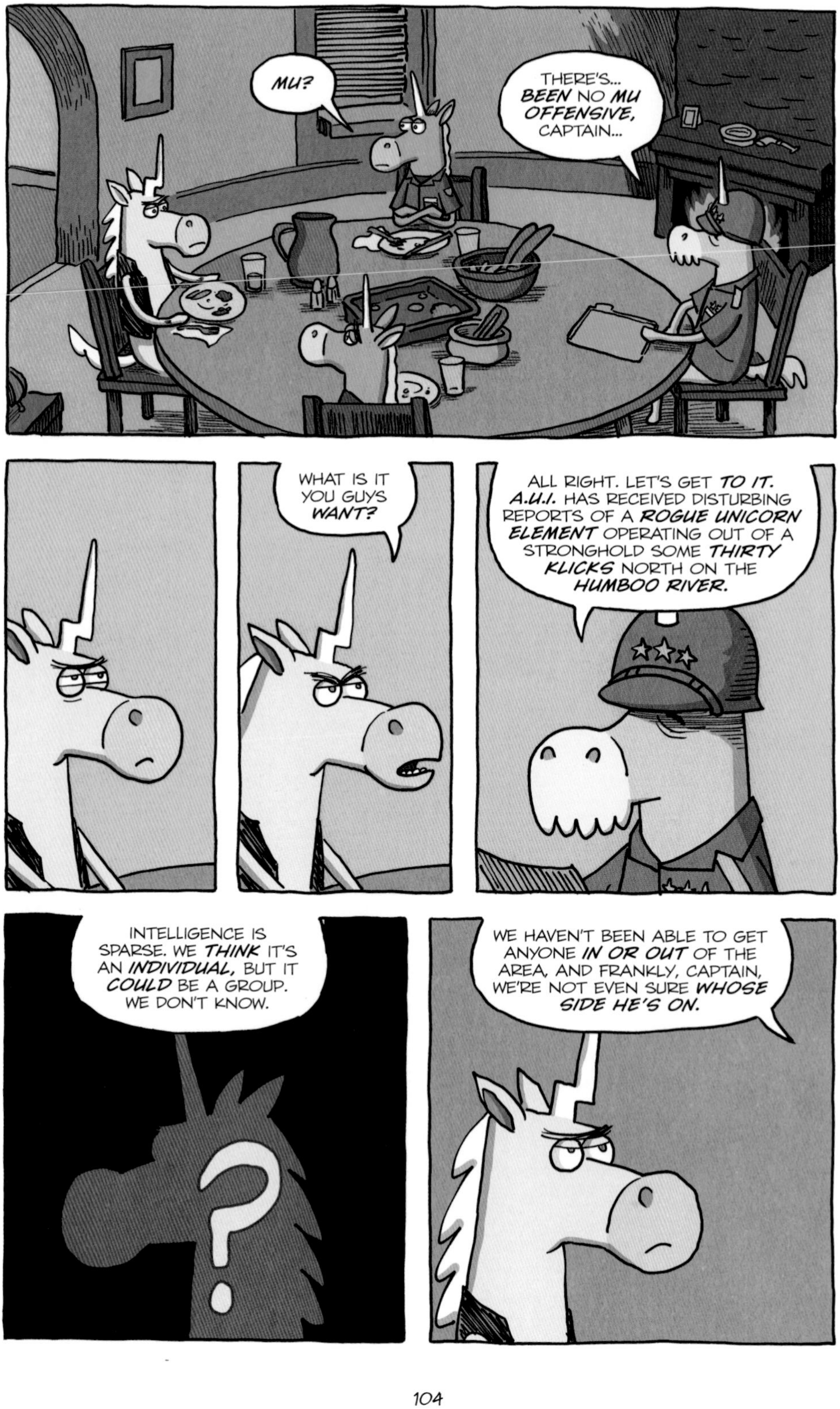
MU?
THERE'S... BEEN NO MU OFFENSIVE, CAPTAIN...
WHAT IS IT YOU GUYS WANT?
ALL RIGHT. LET'S GET TO IT. A.U.I. HAS RECEIVED DISTURBING REPORTS OF A ROGUE UNICORN ELEMENT OPERATING OUT OF A STRONGHOLD SOME THIRTY KLICKS NORTH ON THE HUMBOO RIVER.
INTELLIGENCE IS SPARSE. WE THINK IT'S AN INDIVIDUAL, BUT IT COULD BE A GROUP. WE DON'T KNOW.
WE HAVEN'T BEEN ABLE TO GET ANYONE IN OR OUT OF THE AREA, AND FRANKLY, CAPTAIN, WE'RE NOT EVEN SURE WHOSE SIDE HE'S ON.

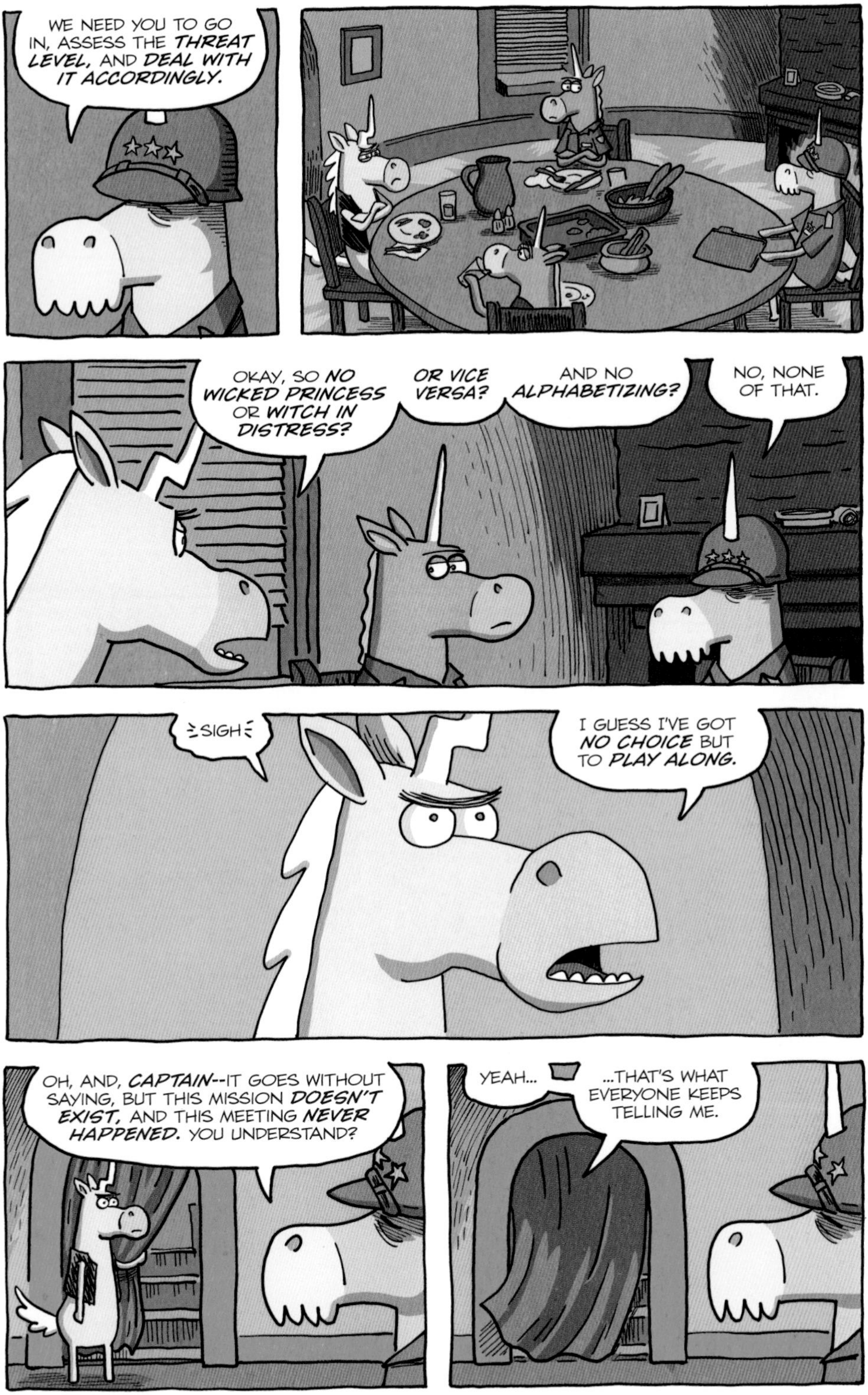
WE NEED YOU TO GO IN, ASSESS THE THREAT LEVEL, AND DEAL WITH IT ACCORDINGLY.
OKAY, SO NO WICKED PRINCESS OR WITCH IN DISTRESS?
OR VICE VERSA?
AND NO ALPHABETIZING?
NO, NONE OF THAT.
SIGH
I GUESS I'VE GOT NO CHOICE BUT TO PLAY ALONG.
OH, AND, CAPTAIN--IT GOES WITHOUT SAYING, BUT THIS MISSION DOESN'T EXIST, AND THIS MEETING NEVER HAPPENED. YOU UNDERSTAND?
YEAH...
...THAT'S WHAT EVERYONE KEEPS TELLING ME.

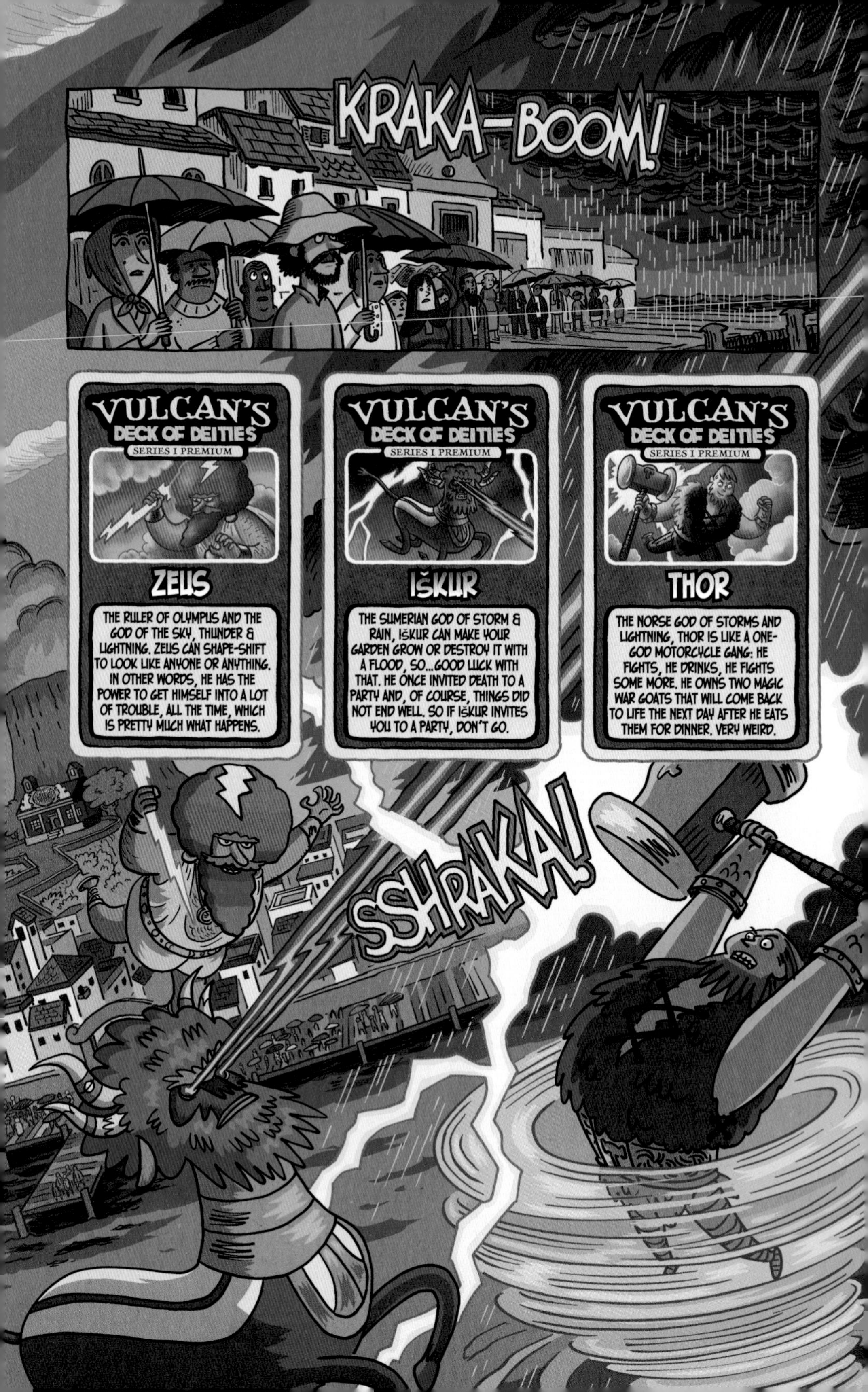
KRAKA-BOOM!
VULCAN'S
DECK OF DEITIES
SERIES I PREMIUM
ZEUS
THE RULER OF OLYMPUS AND THE GOD OF THE SKY, THUNDER & LIGHTNING. ZEUS CAN SHAPE-SHIFT TO LOOK LIKE ANYONE OR ANYTHING. IN OTHER WORDS, HE HAS THE POWER TO GET HIMSELF INTO A LOT OF TROUBLE, ALL THE TIME, WHICH IS PRETTY MUCH WHAT HAPPENS.
VULCAN'S
DECK OF DEITIES
SERIES I PREMIUM
IŠKUR
THE SUMERIAN GOD OF STORM & RAIN, IŠKUR CAN MAKE YOUR GARDEN GROW OR DESTROY IT WITH A FLOOD, SO...GOOD LUCK WITH THAT. HE ONCE INVITED DEATH TO A PARTY AND, OF COURSE, THINGS DID NOT END WELL. SO IF IŠKUR INVITES YOU TO A PARTY, DON'T GO.
VULCAN'S
DECK OF DEITIES
SERIES I PREMIUM
THOR
THE NORSE GOD OF STORMS AND LIGHTNING, THOR IS LIKE A ONE-GOD MOTORCYCLE GANG: HE FIGHTS, HE DRINKS, HE FIGHTS SOME MORE. HE OWNS TWO MAGIC WAR GOATS THAT WILL COME BACK TO LIFE THE NEXT DAY AFTER HE EATS THEM FOR DINNER. VERY WEIRD.
SSHRAKA!

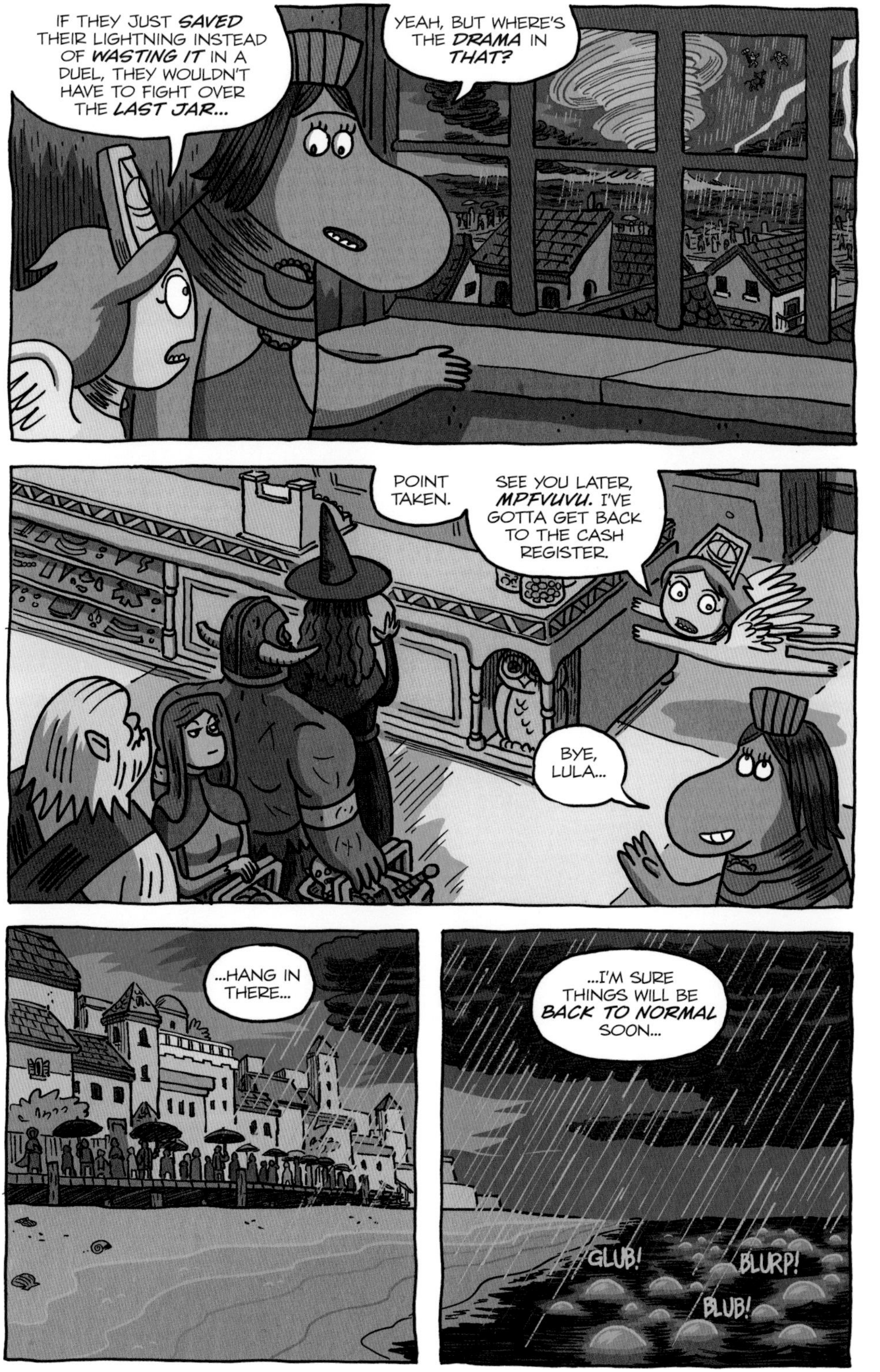
IF THEY JUST SAVED THEIR LIGHTNING INSTEAD OF WASTING IT IN A DUEL, THEY WOULDN'T HAVE TO FIGHT OVER THE LAST JAR...
YEAH, BUT WHERE'S THE DRAMA IN THAT?
POINT TAKEN.
SEE YOU LATER, MPFVUVU. I'VE GOTTA GET BACK TO THE CASH REGISTER.
BYE, LULA...
...HANG IN THERE...
...I'M SURE THINGS WILL BE BACK TO NORMAL SOON...
GLUB!
BLURP!
BLUB!

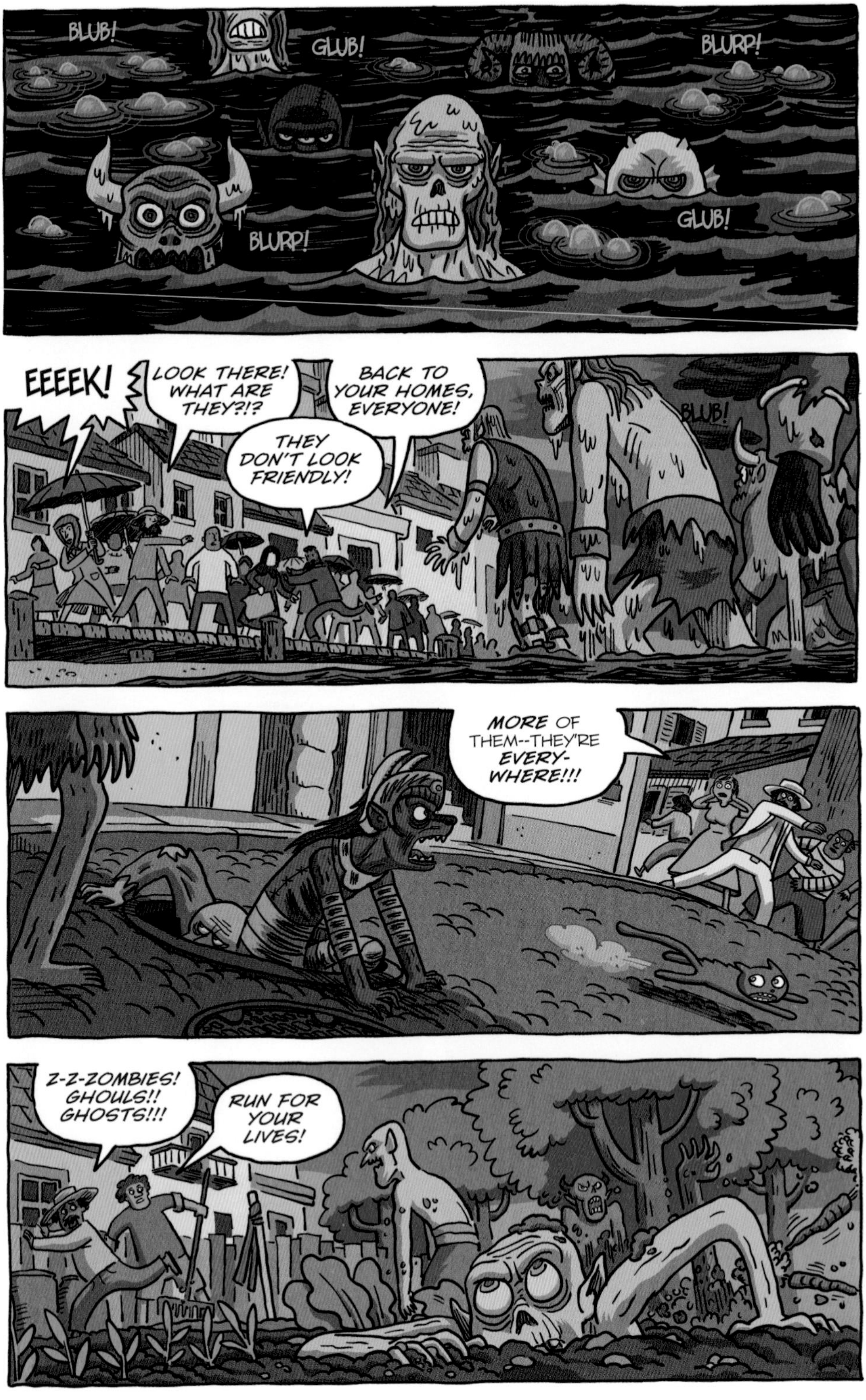
BLUB!
GLUB!
BLURP!
BLURP!
GLUB!
EEEEK!
LOOK THERE! WHAT ARE THEY?!?
THEY DON'T LOOK FRIENDLY!
BACK TO YOUR HOMES, EVERYONE!
BLUB!
MORE OF THEM--THEY'RE EVERY-WHERE!!!
Z-Z-ZOMBIES! GHOULS!! GHOSTS!!!
RUN FOR YOUR LIVES!

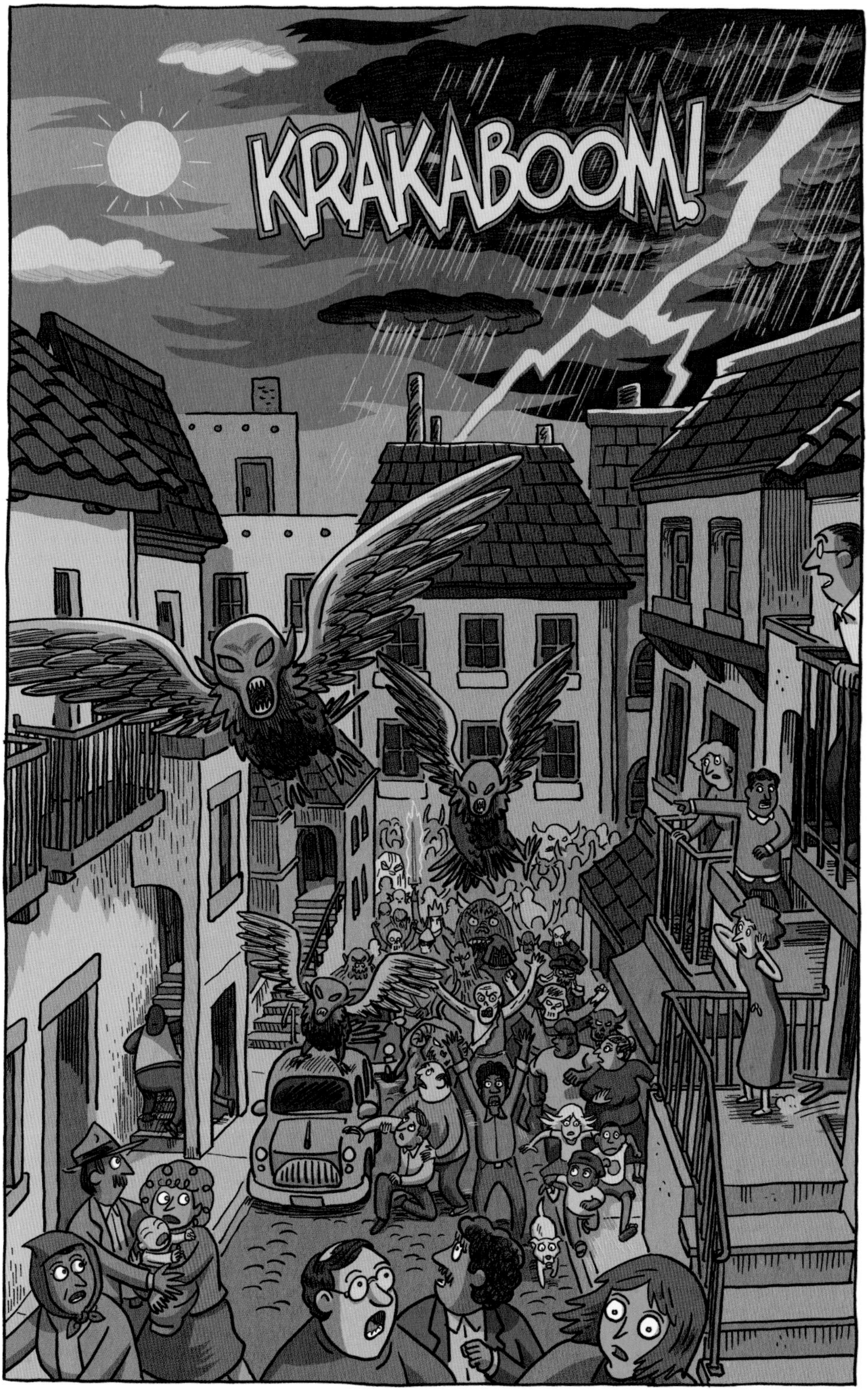
KRAKABOOM!

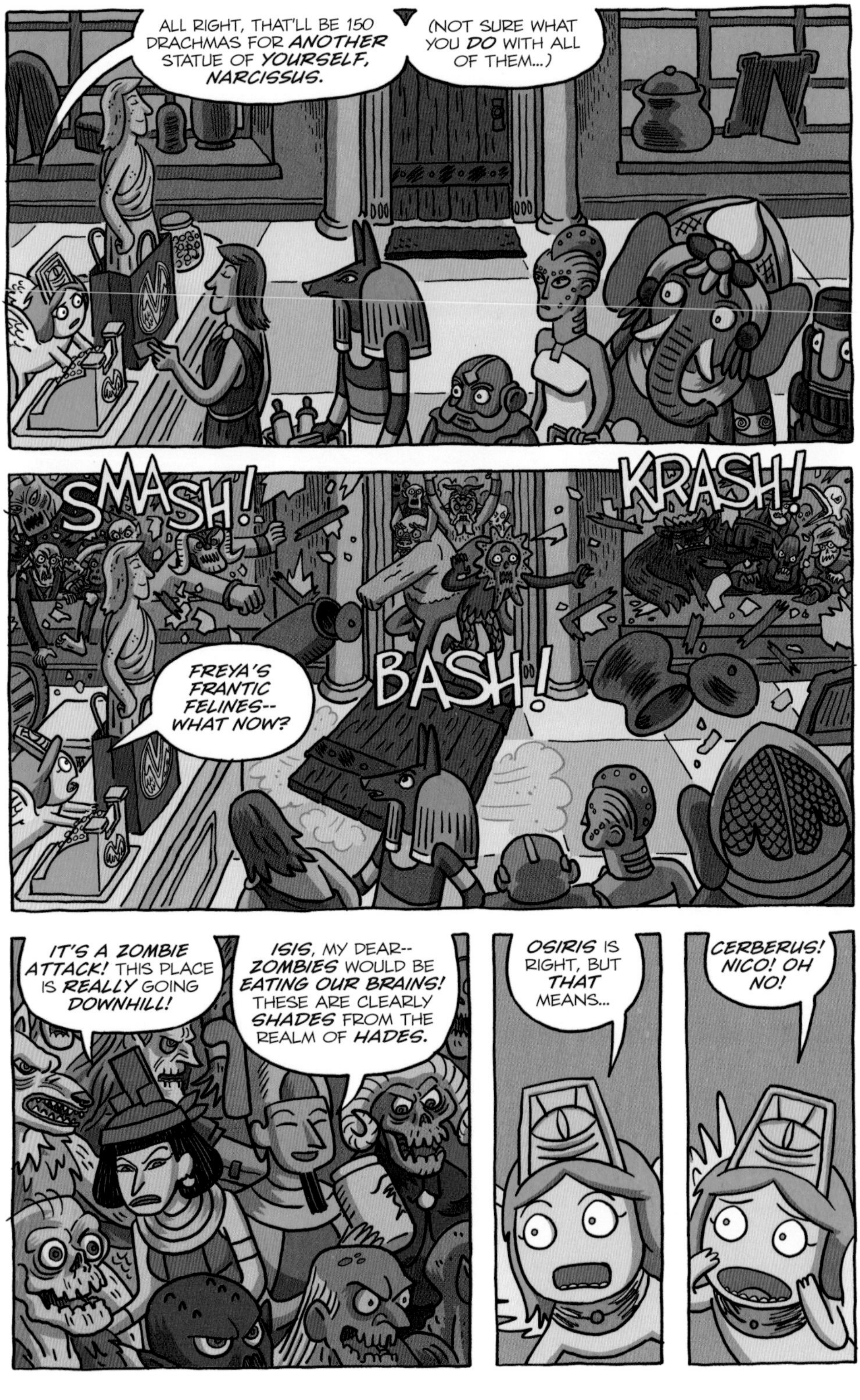
ALL RIGHT, THAT'LL BE 150 DRACHMAS FOR ANOTHER STATUE OF YOURSELF, NARCISSUS.
(NOT SURE WHAT YOU DO WITH ALL OF THEM...)
SMASH!
KRASH!
BASH!
FREYA'S FRANTIC FELINES--WHAT NOW?
IT'S A ZOMBIE ATTACK! THIS PLACE IS REALLY GOING DOWNHILL!
ISIS, MY DEAR--ZOMBIES WOULD BE EATING OUR BRAINS! THESE ARE CLEARLY SHADES FROM THE REALM OF HADES.
OSIRIS IS RIGHT, BUT THAT MEANS...
CERBERUS! NICO! OH NO!

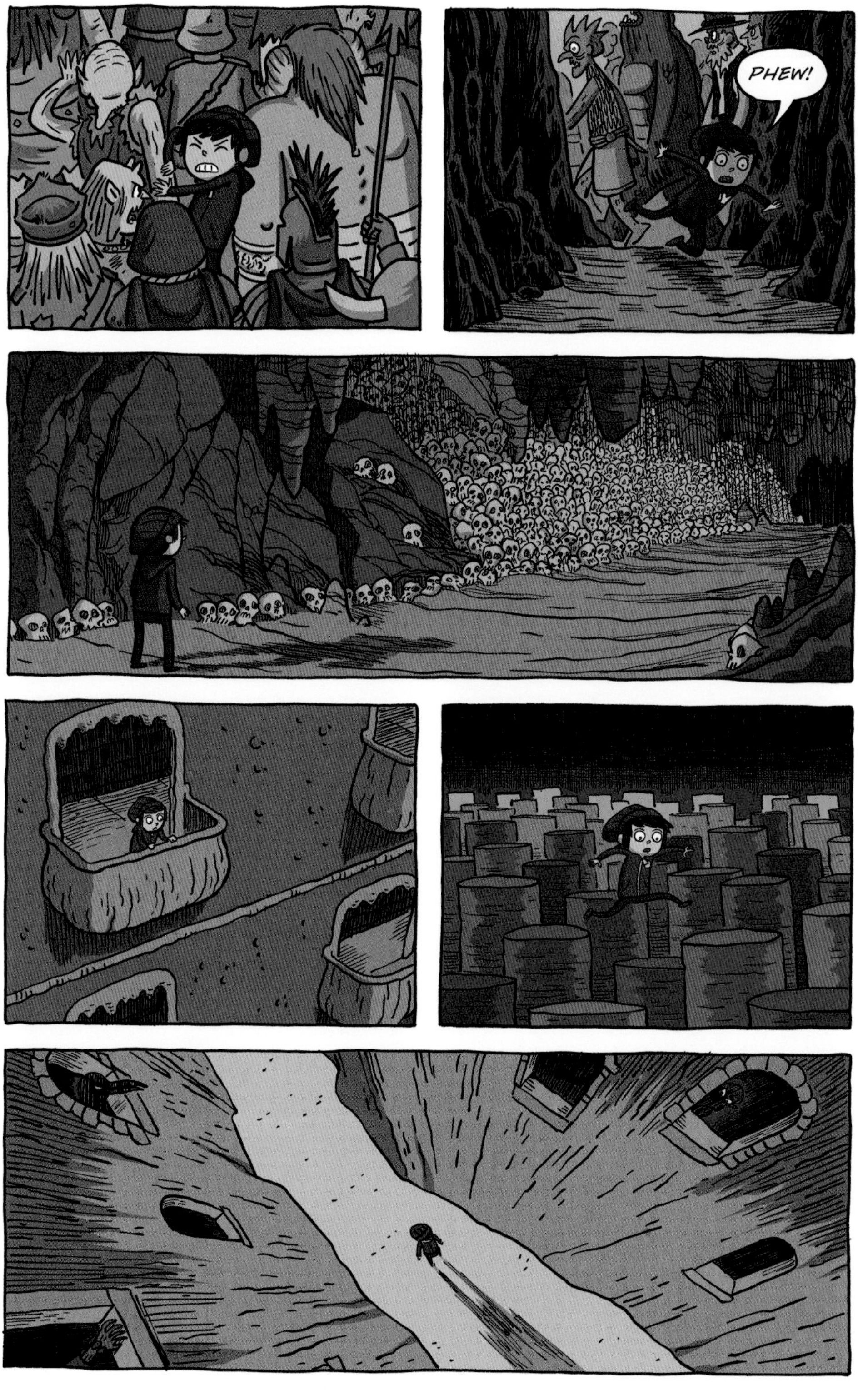
PHEW!

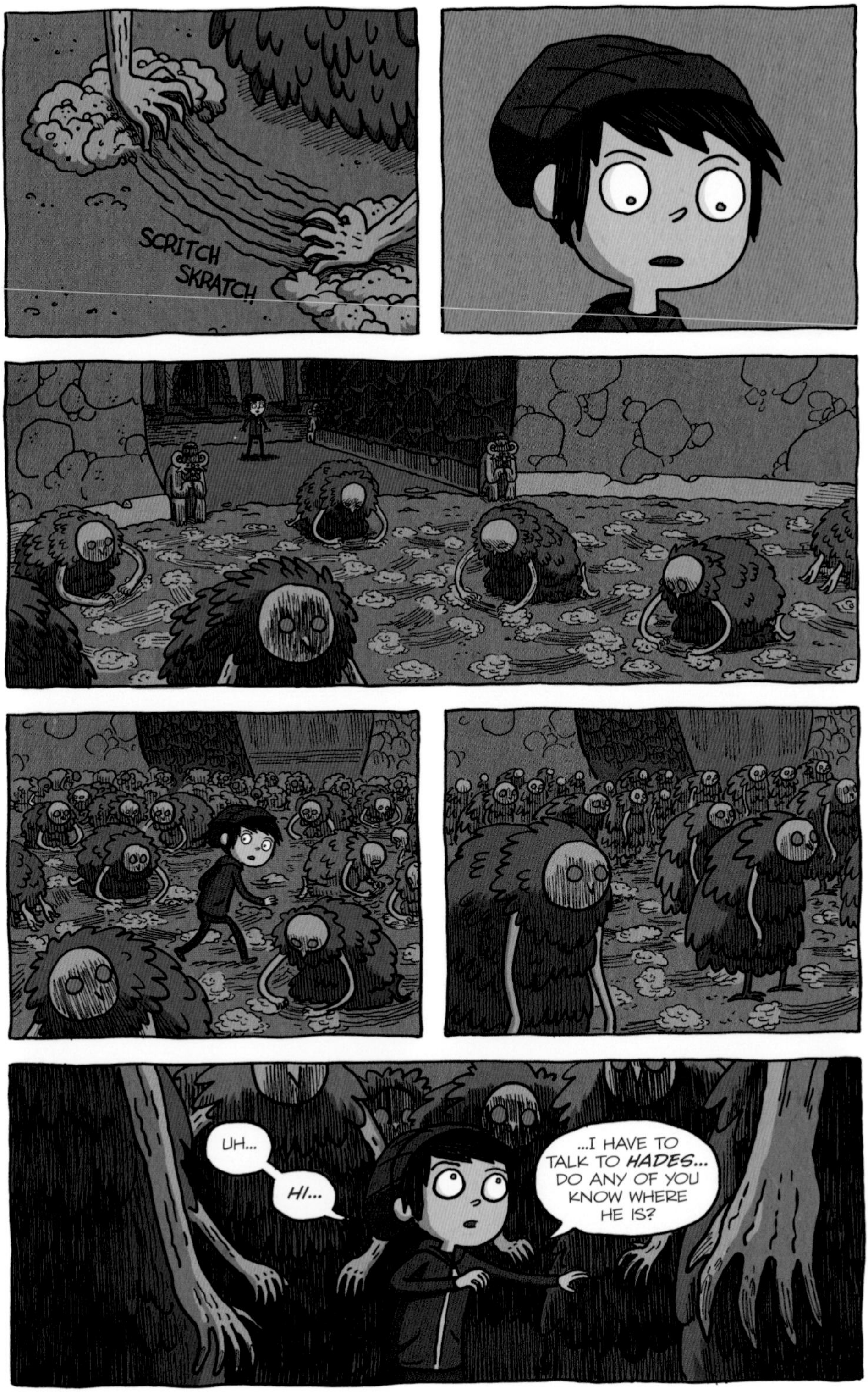
SCRITCH
SKRATCH!
UH...
HI...
...I HAVE TO TALK TO HADES... DO ANY OF YOU KNOW WHERE HE IS?

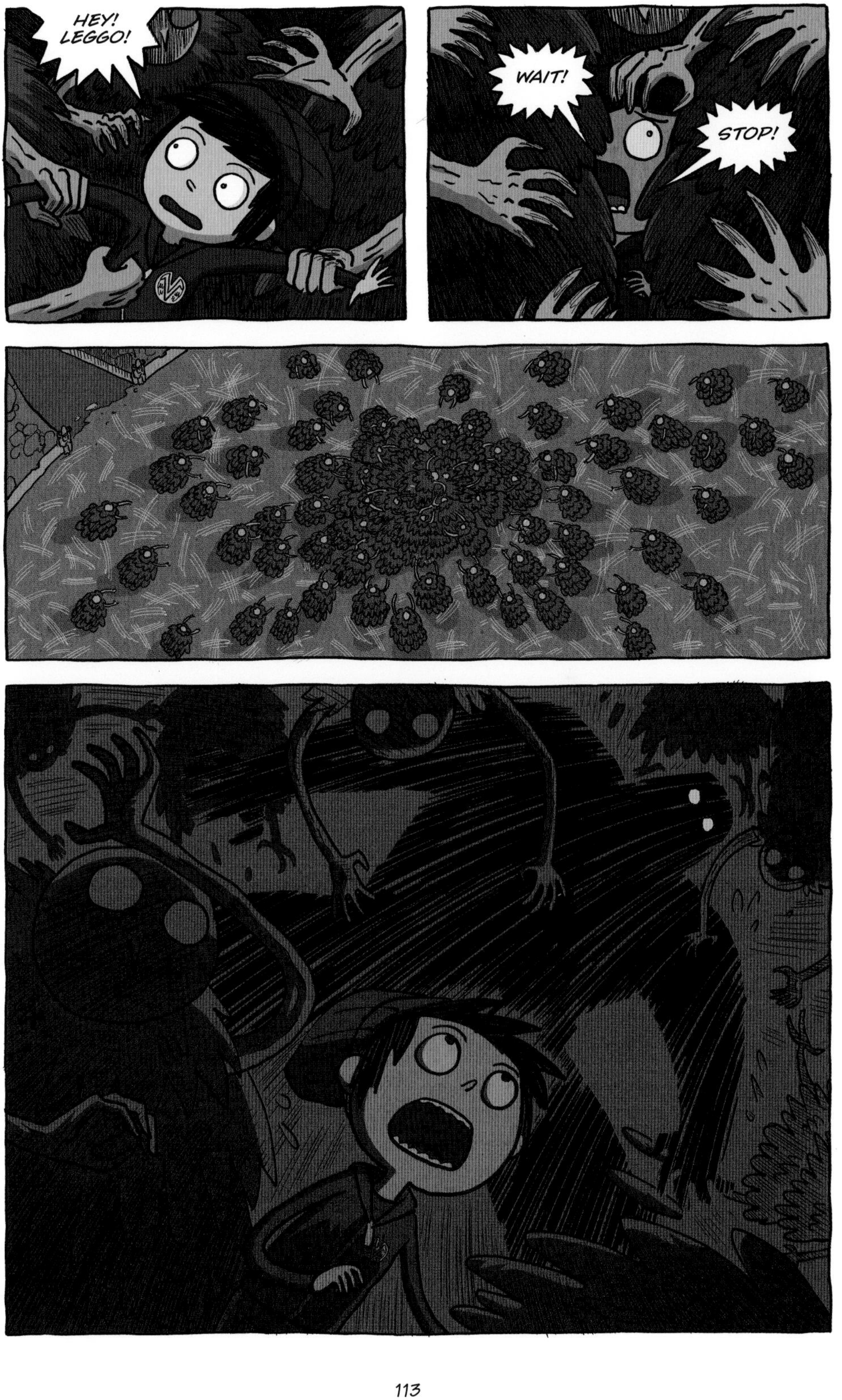
HEY! LEGGO!
WAIT!
STOP!

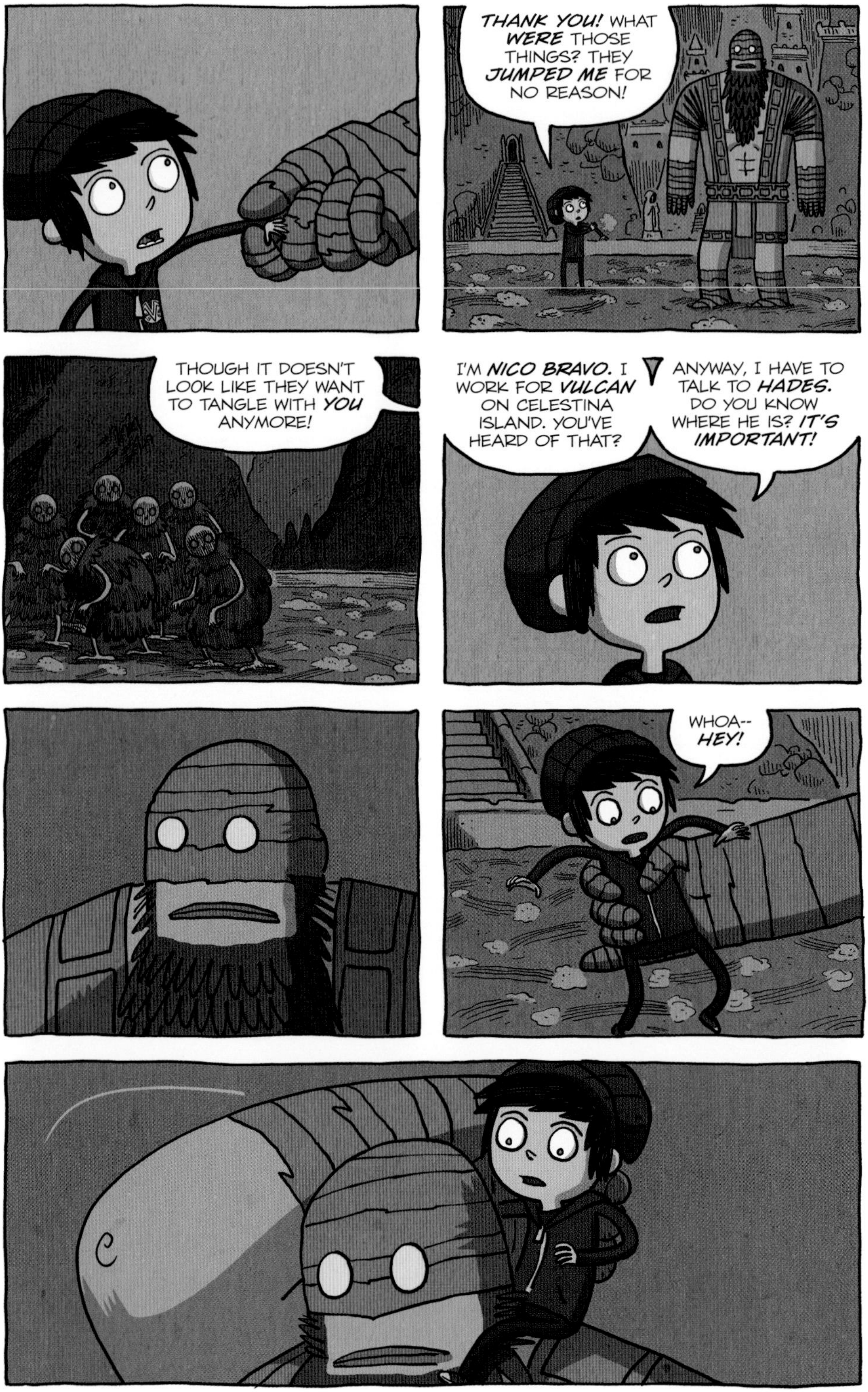
THANK YOU! WHAT WERE THOSE THINGS? THEY JUMPED ME FOR NO REASON!
THOUGH IT DOESN'T LOOK LIKE THEY WANT TO TANGLE WITH YOU ANYMORE!
I'M NICO BRAVO. I WORK FOR VULCAN ON CELESTINA ISLAND. YOU'VE HEARD OF THAT?
ANYWAY, I HAVE TO TALK TO HADES. DO YOU KNOW WHERE HE IS? IT'S IMPORTANT!
WHOA-- HEY!

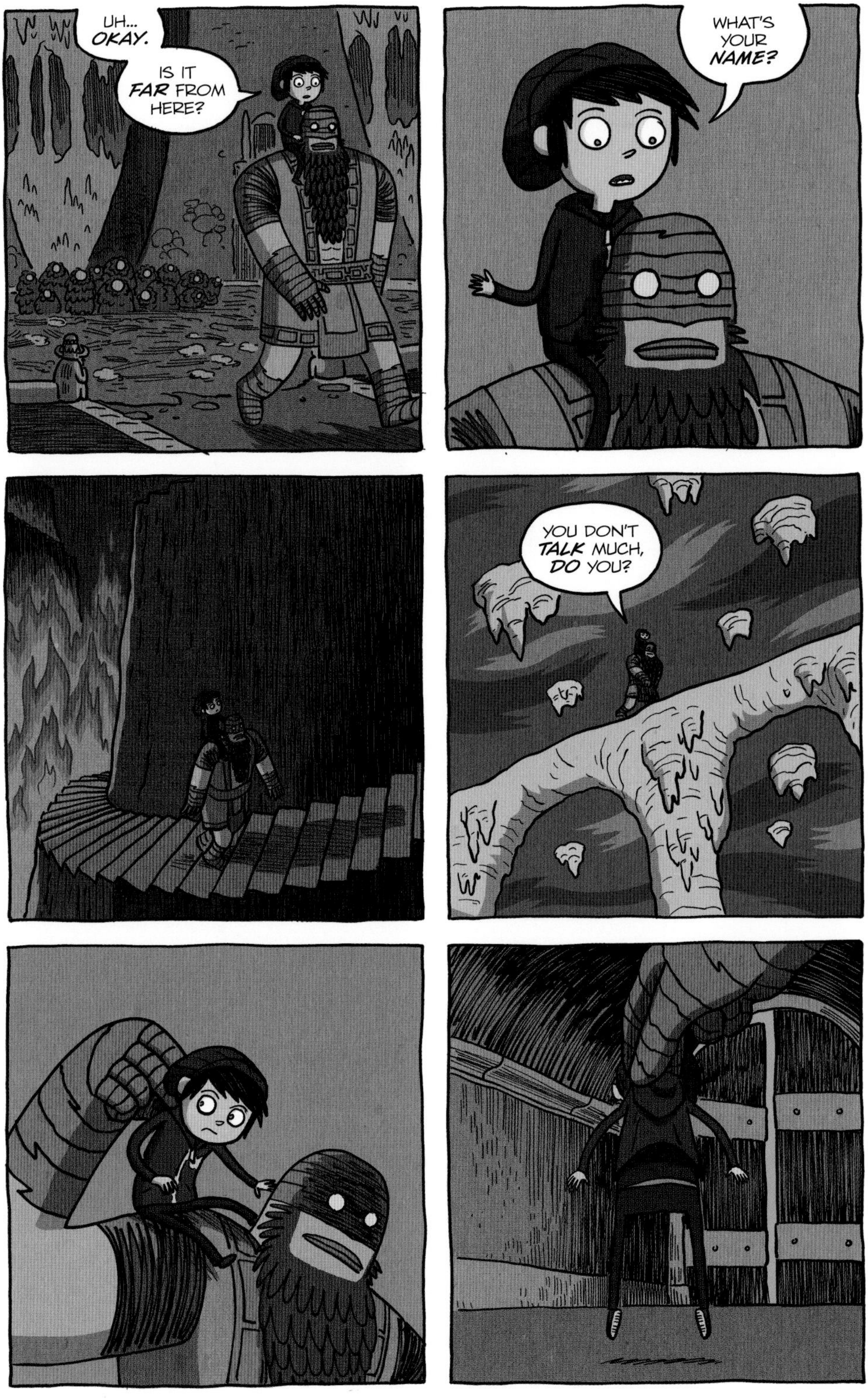
UH... OKAY.
IS IT FAR FROM HERE?
WHAT'S YOUR NAME?
YOU DON'T TALK MUCH, DO YOU?

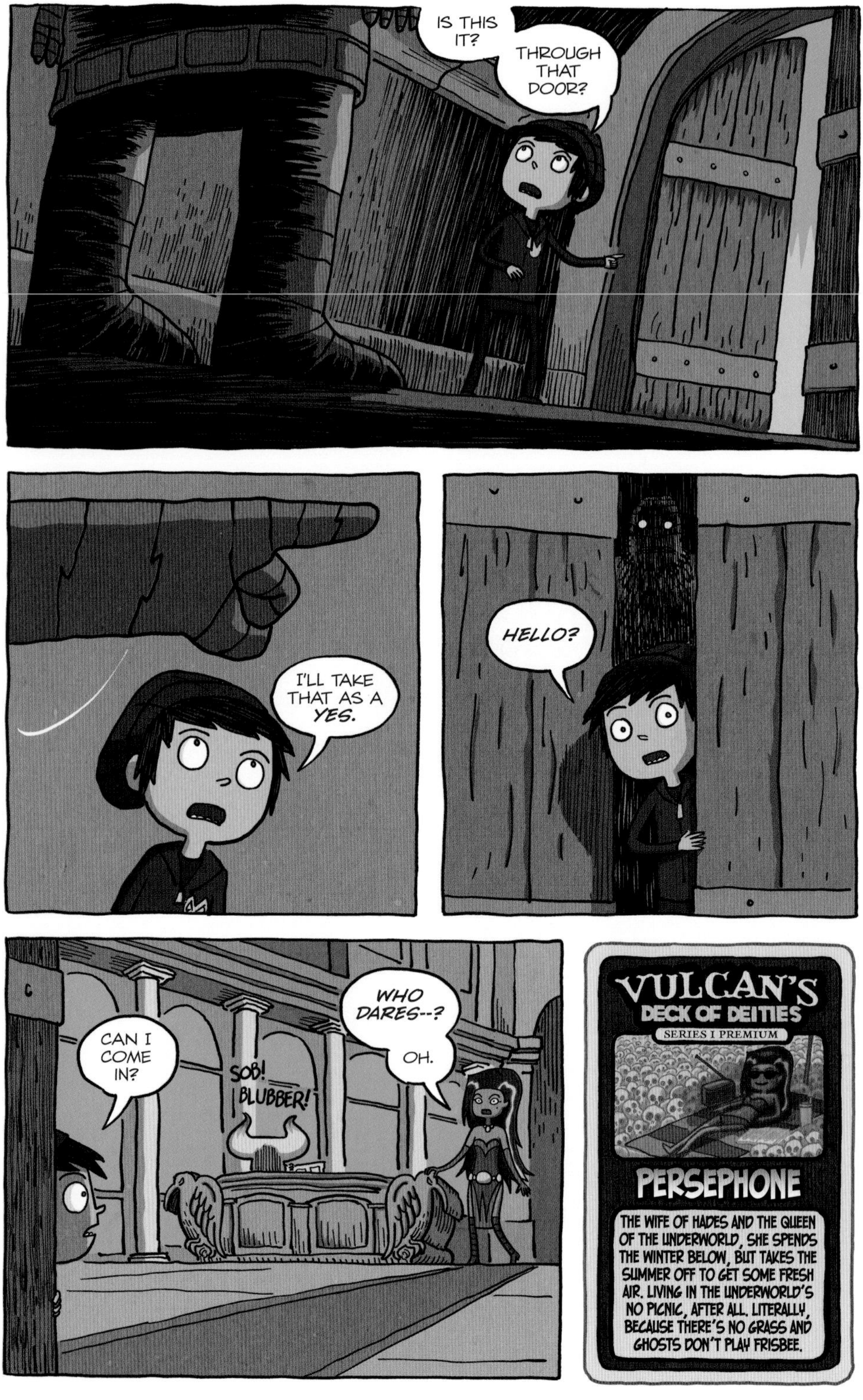
IS THIS IT?
THROUGH THAT DOOR?
I'LL TAKE THAT AS A YES.
HELLO?
CAN I COME IN?
SOB! BLUBBER!
WHO DARES--?
OH.
VULCAN'S DECK OF DEITIES
SERIES I PREMIUM
PERSEPHONE
THE WIFE OF HADES AND THE QUEEN OF THE UNDERWORLD, SHE SPENDS THE WINTER BELOW, BUT TAKES THE SUMMER OFF TO GET SOME FRESH AIR. LIVING IN THE UNDERWORLD'S NO PICNIC, AFTER ALL. LITERALLY, BECAUSE THERE'S NO GRASS AND GHOSTS DON'T PLAY FRISBEE.

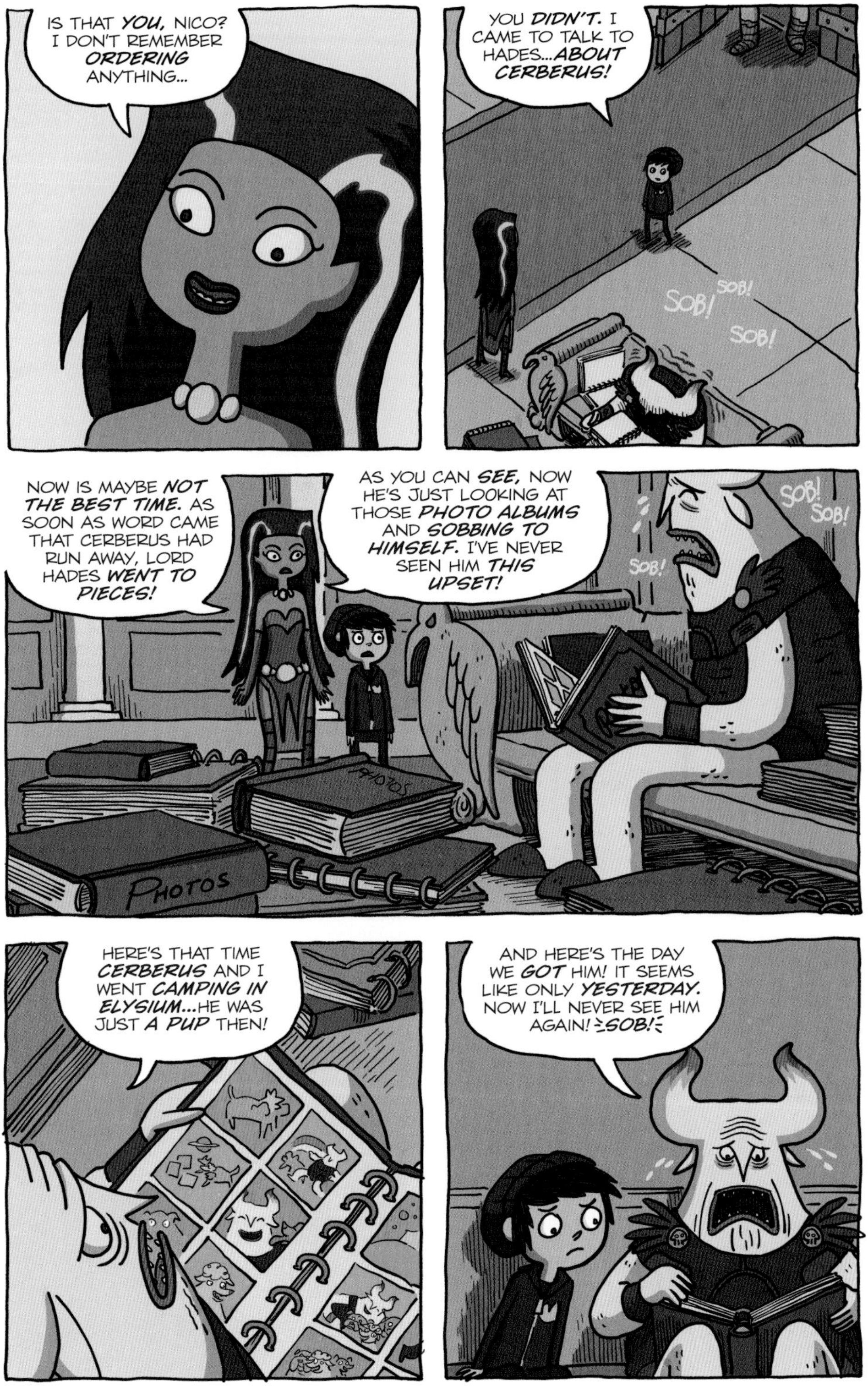
IS THAT YOU, NICO? I DON'T REMEMBER ORDERING ANYTHING...
YOU DIDN'T. I CAME TO TALK TO HADES...ABOUT CERBERUS!
SOB! SOB! SOB!
NOW IS MAYBE NOT THE BEST TIME. AS SOON AS WORD CAME THAT CERBERUS HAD RUN AWAY, LORD HADES WENT TO PIECES!
AS YOU CAN SEE, NOW HE'S JUST LOOKING AT THOSE PHOTO ALBUMS AND SOBBING TO HIMSELF. I'VE NEVER SEEN HIM THIS UPSET!
SOB! SOB! SOB!
PHOTOS
PHOTOS
HERE'S THAT TIME CERBERUS AND I WENT CAMPING IN ELYSIUM...HE WAS JUST A PUP THEN!
AND HERE'S THE DAY WE GOT HIM! IT SEEMS LIKE ONLY YESTERDAY. NOW I'LL NEVER SEE HIM AGAIN! SOB!

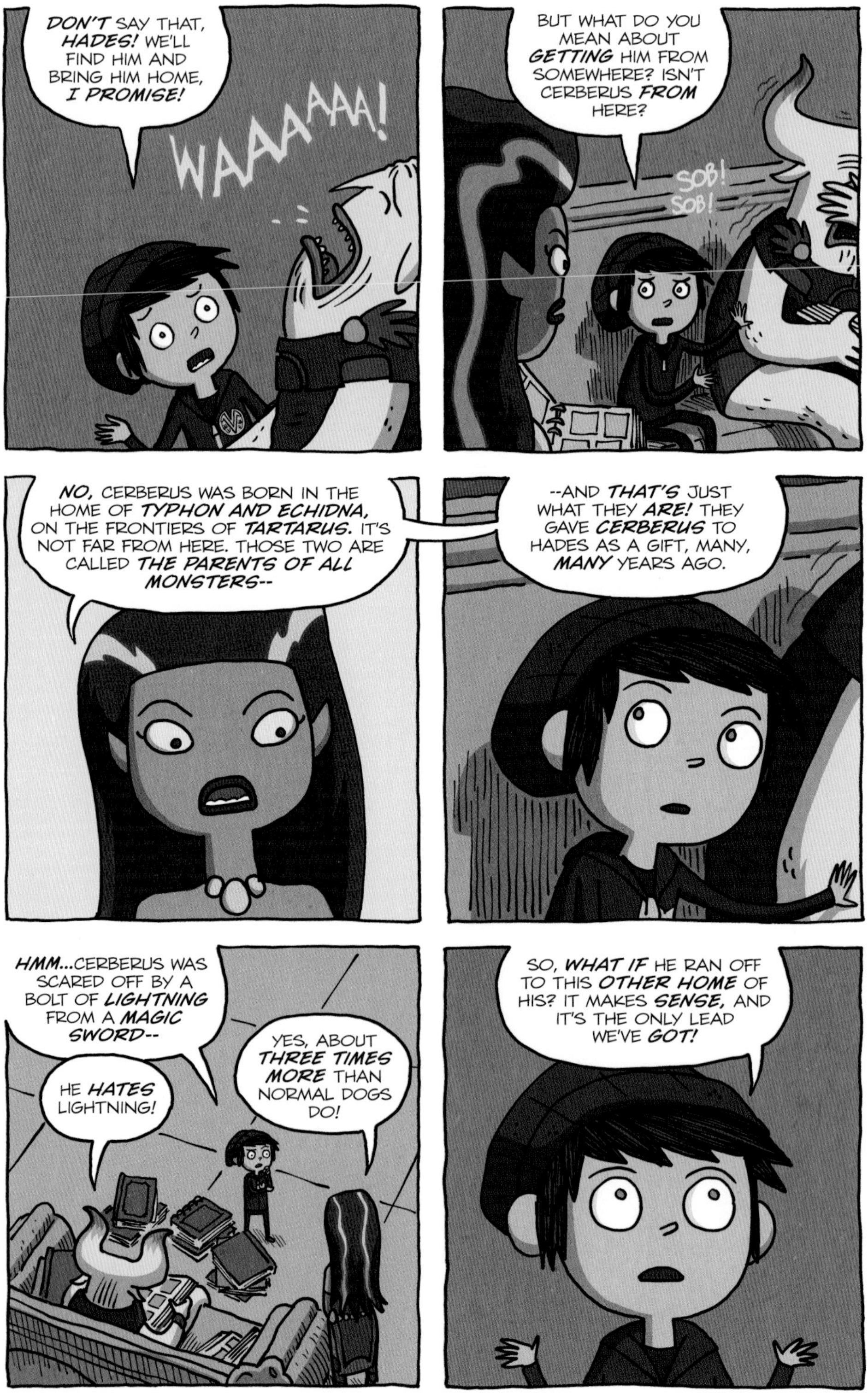
DON'T SAY THAT, HADES! WE'LL FIND HIM AND BRING HIM HOME, I PROMISE!
WAAAAAA!
BUT WHAT DO YOU MEAN ABOUT GETTING HIM FROM SOMEWHERE? ISN'T CERBERUS FROM HERE?
SOB! SOB!
NO, CERBERUS WAS BORN IN THE HOME OF TYPHON AND ECHIDNA, ON THE FRONTIERS OF TARTARUS. IT'S NOT FAR FROM HERE. THOSE TWO ARE CALLED THE PARENTS OF ALL MONSTERS--
--AND THAT'S JUST WHAT THEY ARE! THEY GAVE CERBERUS TO HADES AS A GIFT, MANY, MANY YEARS AGO.
HMM...CERBERUS WAS SCARED OFF BY A BOLT OF LIGHTNING FROM A MAGIC SWORD--
HE HATES LIGHTNING!
YES, ABOUT THREE TIMES MORE THAN NORMAL DOGS DO!
SO, WHAT IF HE RAN OFF TO THIS OTHER HOME OF HIS? IT MAKES SENSE, AND IT'S THE ONLY LEAD WE'VE GOT!

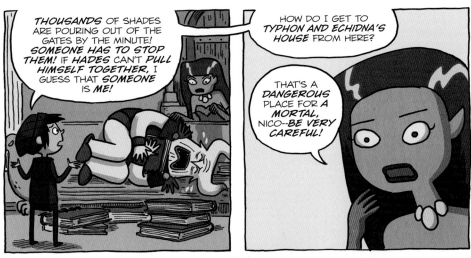

THOUSANDS OF SHADES ARE POURING OUT OF THE GATES BY THE MINUTE! SOMEONE HAS TO STOP THEM! IF HADES CAN'T PULL HIMSELF TOGETHER, I GUESS THAT SOMEONE IS ME!

HOW DO I GET TO TYPHON AND ECHIDNA'S HOUSE FROM HERE?

THAT'S A DANGEROUS PLACE FOR A MORTAL, NICO--BE VERY CAREFUL!

HERE, SINCE YOU'VE ALREADY MET GILGAMESH, HE WILL GUIDE YOU TO TARTARUS--!

GREAT GULA'S GHOSTS-- GILGAMESH?!?

## VULCAN'S
### DECK OF DEITIES
SERIES II PREMIUM

## GILGAMESH

POSSESSING SUPERHUMAN STRENGTH AND ABILITIES, HE'S 2/3 GOD AND 1/3 HUMAN, THE KING OF URUK, AND THE FIRST AND GREATEST OF THE LEGENDARY HEROES. THOUGH HE DIED CENTURIES AGO, HIS COMIC BOOK STILL COMES OUT ONCE A MONTH--AND IT ROCKS!

YOU MEAN--THE GILGAMESH?!?

YOU LOOK TOTALLY DIFFERENT IN THE COMICS!

GOOD LUCK, NICO! FIND CERBERUS AND BRING HIM HOME!

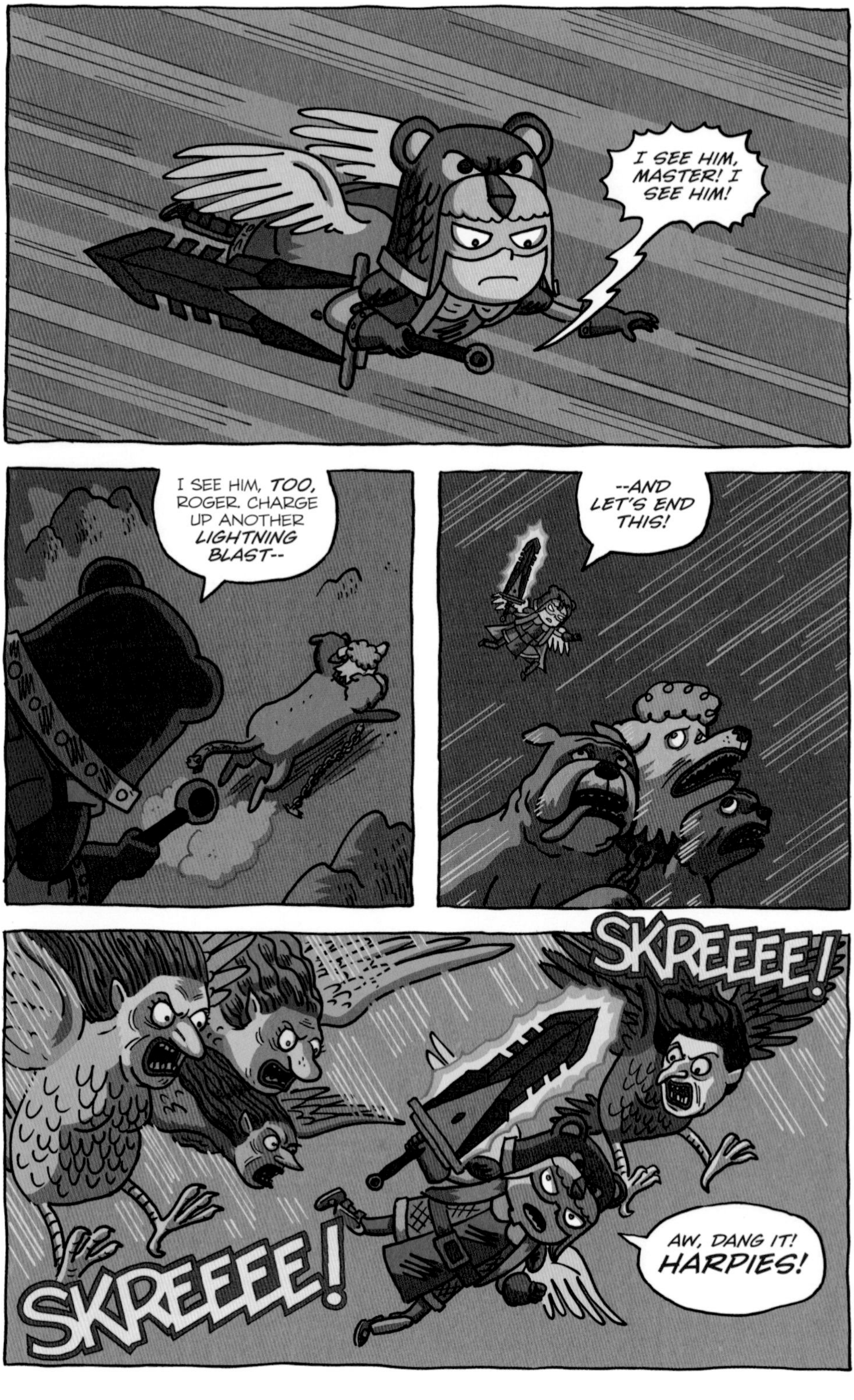
I SEE HIM, MASTER! I SEE HIM!
I SEE HIM, TOO, ROGER. CHARGE UP ANOTHER LIGHTNING BLAST--
--AND LET'S END THIS!
SKREEEEE!
SKREEEEE!
AW, DANG IT! HARPIES!

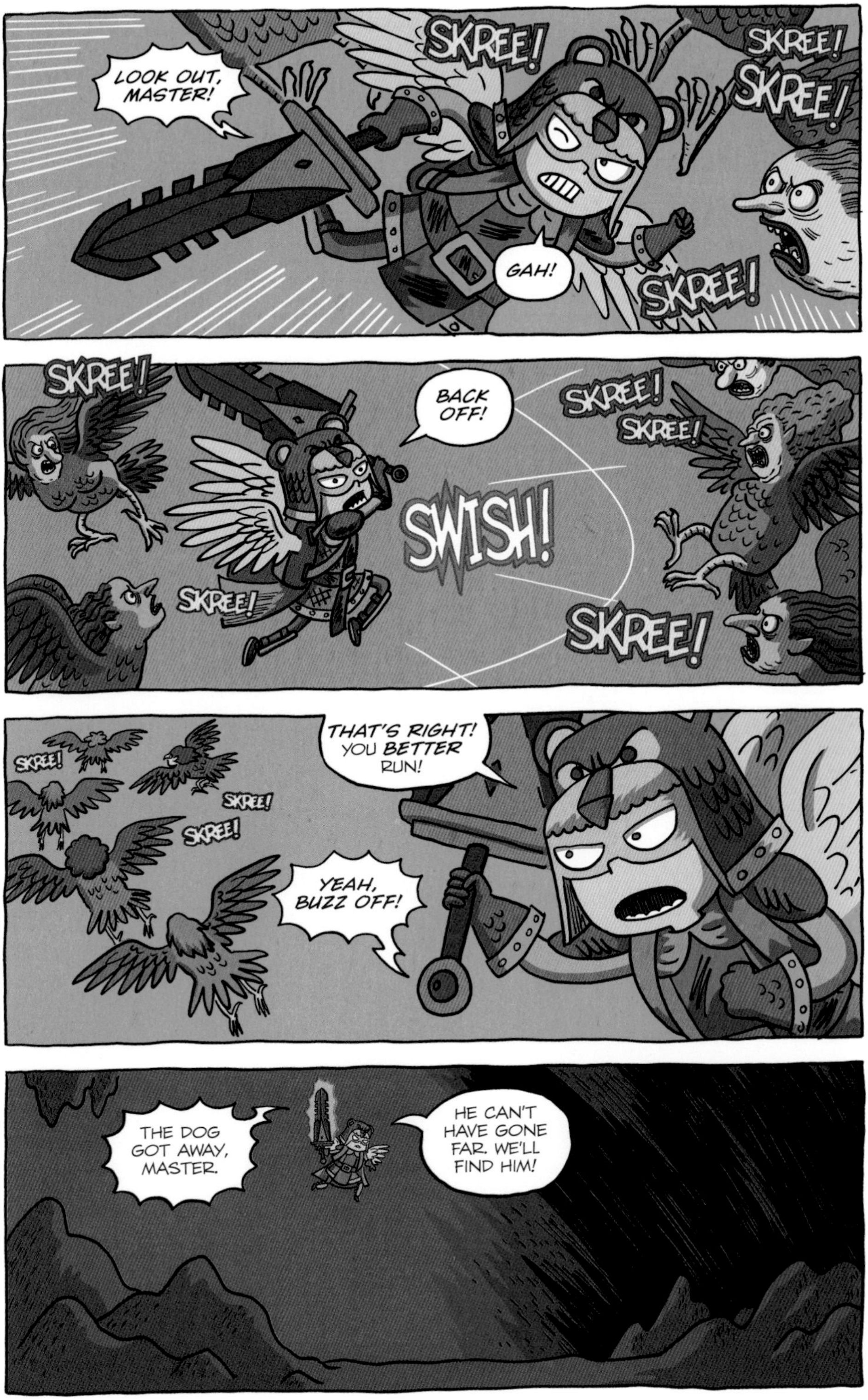
LOOK OUT, MASTER!
SKREE!
SKREE!
SKREE!
GAH!
SKREE!
SKREE!
BACK OFF!
SKREE!
SKREE!
SWISH!
SKREE!
SKREE!
SKREE!
THAT'S RIGHT! YOU BETTER RUN!
SKREE!
SKREE!
YEAH, BUZZ OFF!
THE DOG GOT AWAY, MASTER.
HE CAN'T HAVE GONE FAR. WE'LL FIND HIM!

RRRRRRRRRRRRRRRRRRRRRRRRR

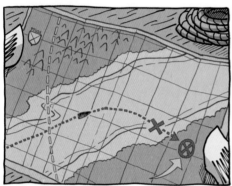

RRRRRRRRR

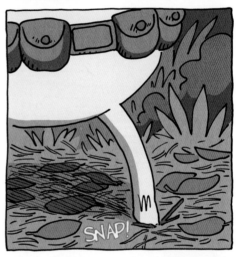

SNAP!

OH CRUD!

WAAAAAA!

123

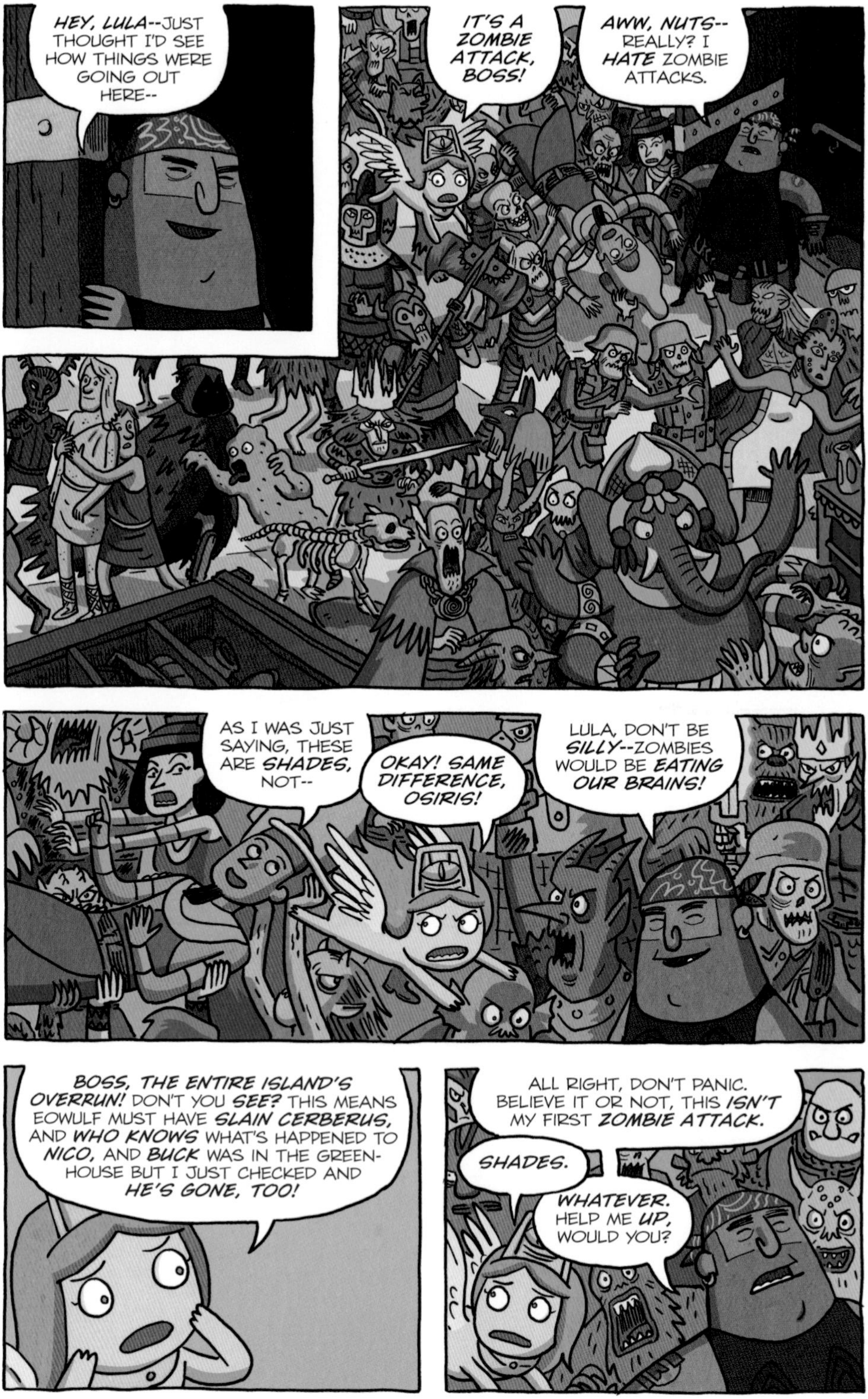
HEY, LULA--JUST THOUGHT I'D SEE HOW THINGS WERE GOING OUT HERE--
IT'S A ZOMBIE ATTACK, BOSS!
AWW, NUTS--REALLY? I HATE ZOMBIE ATTACKS.
AS I WAS JUST SAYING, THESE ARE SHADES, NOT--
OKAY! SAME DIFFERENCE, OSIRIS!
LULA, DON'T BE SILLY--ZOMBIES WOULD BE EATING OUR BRAINS!
BOSS, THE ENTIRE ISLAND'S OVERRUN! DON'T YOU SEE? THIS MEANS EOWULF MUST HAVE SLAIN CERBERUS, AND WHO KNOWS WHAT'S HAPPENED TO NICO, AND BUCK WAS IN THE GREEN-HOUSE BUT I JUST CHECKED AND HE'S GONE, TOO!
ALL RIGHT, DON'T PANIC. BELIEVE IT OR NOT, THIS ISN'T MY FIRST ZOMBIE ATTACK.
SHADES.
WHATEVER. HELP ME UP, WOULD YOU?

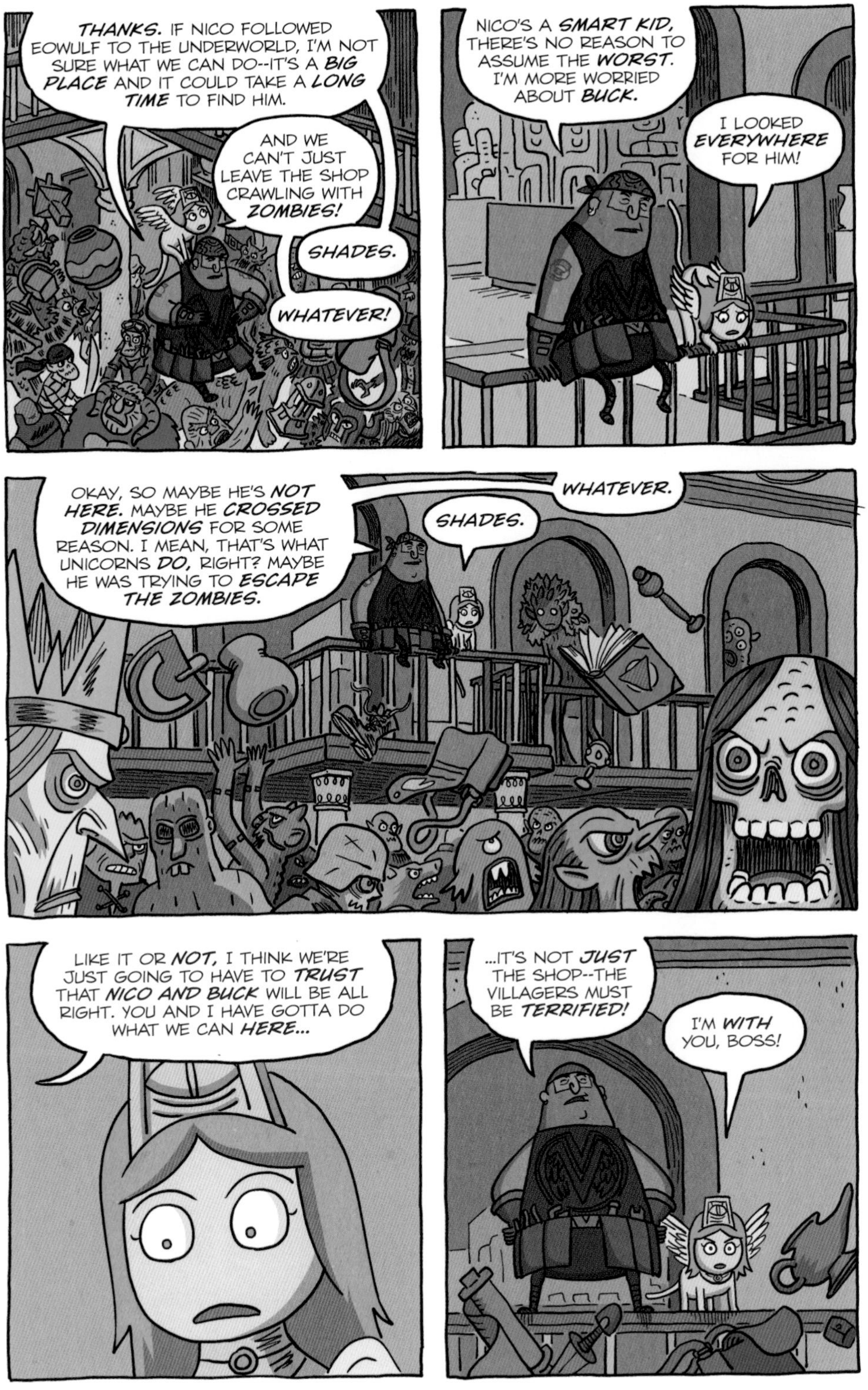
THANKS. IF NICO FOLLOWED EOWULF TO THE UNDERWORLD, I'M NOT SURE WHAT WE CAN DO--IT'S A BIG PLACE AND IT COULD TAKE A LONG TIME TO FIND HIM.
AND WE CAN'T JUST LEAVE THE SHOP CRAWLING WITH ZOMBIES!
SHADES.
WHATEVER!
NICO'S A SMART KID, THERE'S NO REASON TO ASSUME THE WORST. I'M MORE WORRIED ABOUT BUCK.
I LOOKED EVERYWHERE FOR HIM!
OKAY, SO MAYBE HE'S NOT HERE. MAYBE HE CROSSED DIMENSIONS FOR SOME REASON. I MEAN, THAT'S WHAT UNICORNS DO, RIGHT? MAYBE HE WAS TRYING TO ESCAPE THE ZOMBIES.
SHADES.
WHATEVER.
LIKE IT OR NOT, I THINK WE'RE JUST GOING TO HAVE TO TRUST THAT NICO AND BUCK WILL BE ALL RIGHT. YOU AND I HAVE GOTTA DO WHAT WE CAN HERE...
...IT'S NOT JUST THE SHOP--THE VILLAGERS MUST BE TERRIFIED!
I'M WITH YOU, BOSS!

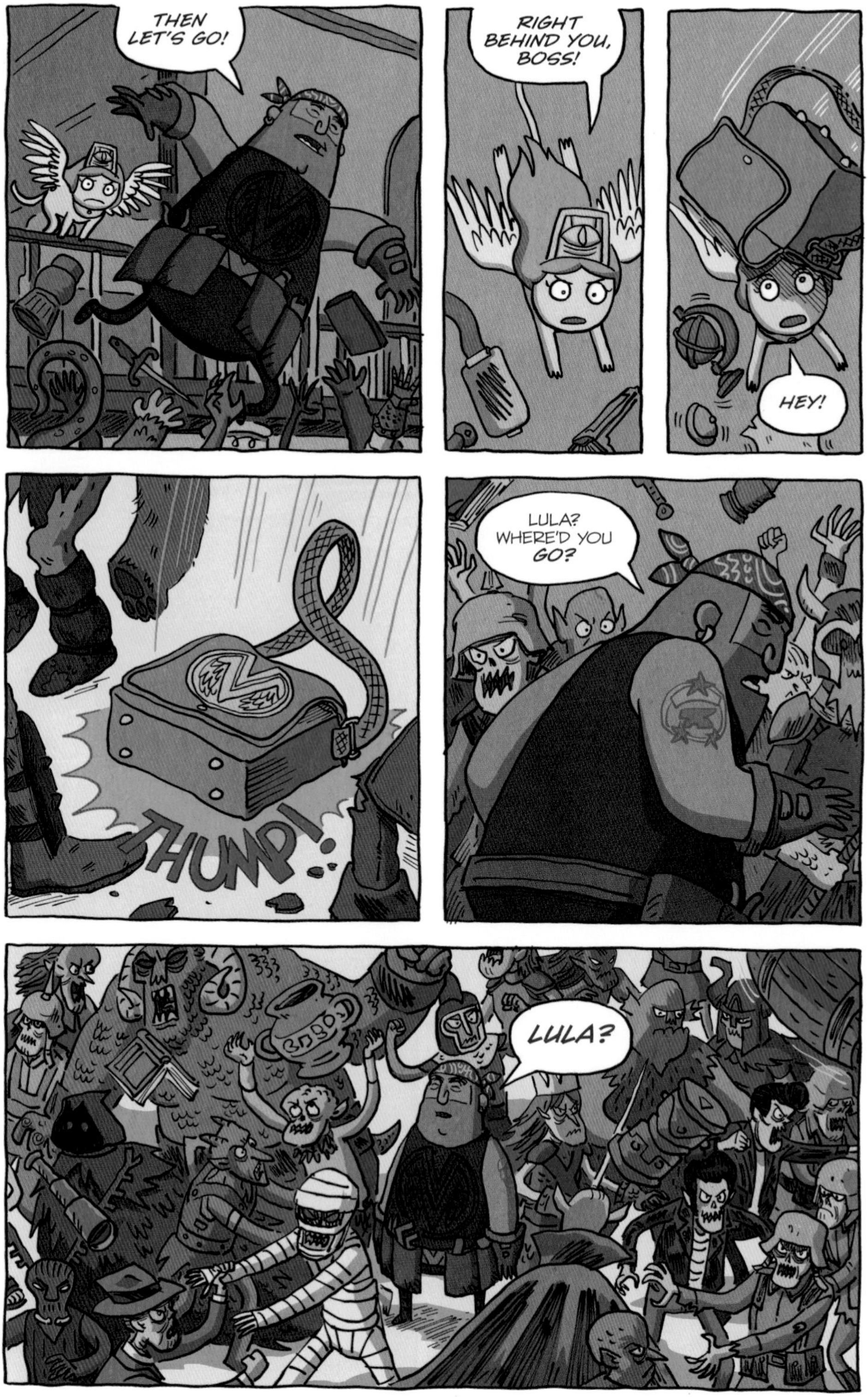
THEN LET'S GO!
RIGHT BEHIND YOU, BOSS!
HEY!
THUMP!
LULA? WHERE'D YOU GO?
LULA?

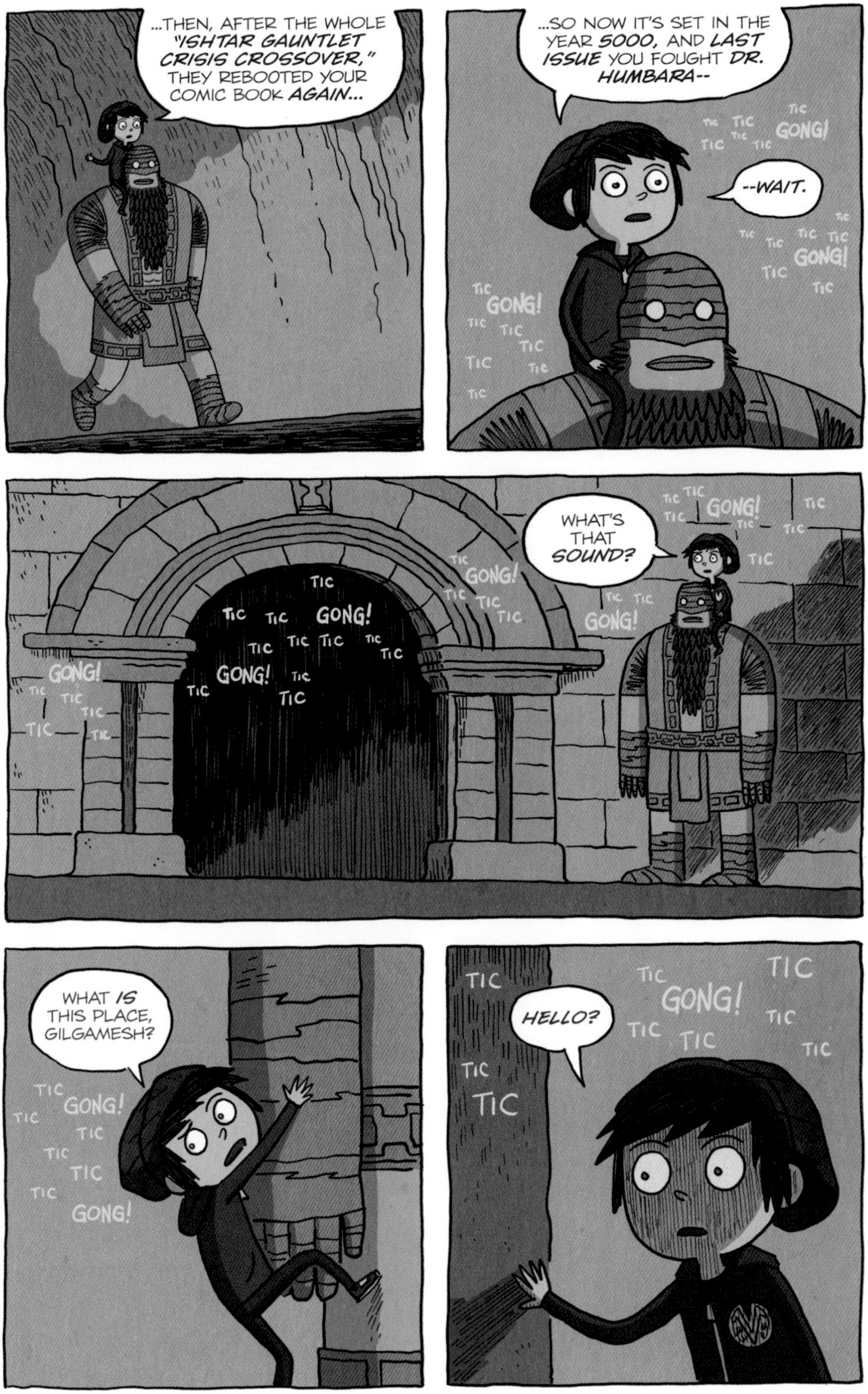
...THEN, AFTER THE WHOLE "ISHTAR GAUNTLET CRISIS CROSSOVER," THEY REBOOTED YOUR COMIC BOOK AGAIN...
...SO NOW IT'S SET IN THE YEAR 5000, AND LAST ISSUE YOU FOUGHT DR. HUMBARA--
TIC TIC TIC TIC TIC TIC GONG!
--WAIT.
TIC TIC TIC TIC GONG! TIC TIC
TIC GONG! TIC TIC TIC TIC TIC TIC
WHAT'S THAT SOUND?
TIC TIC TIC GONG!
TIC GONG! TIC TIC TIC
TIC TIC GONG! TIC TIC TIC TIC TIC TIC GONG! TIC TIC TIC
GONG! TIC TIC TIC TIC TIC
WHAT IS THIS PLACE, GILGAMESH?
TIC GONG! TIC TIC TIC TIC TIC GONG!
HELLO?
TIC TIC GONG! TIC TIC TIC TIC TIC TIC TIC

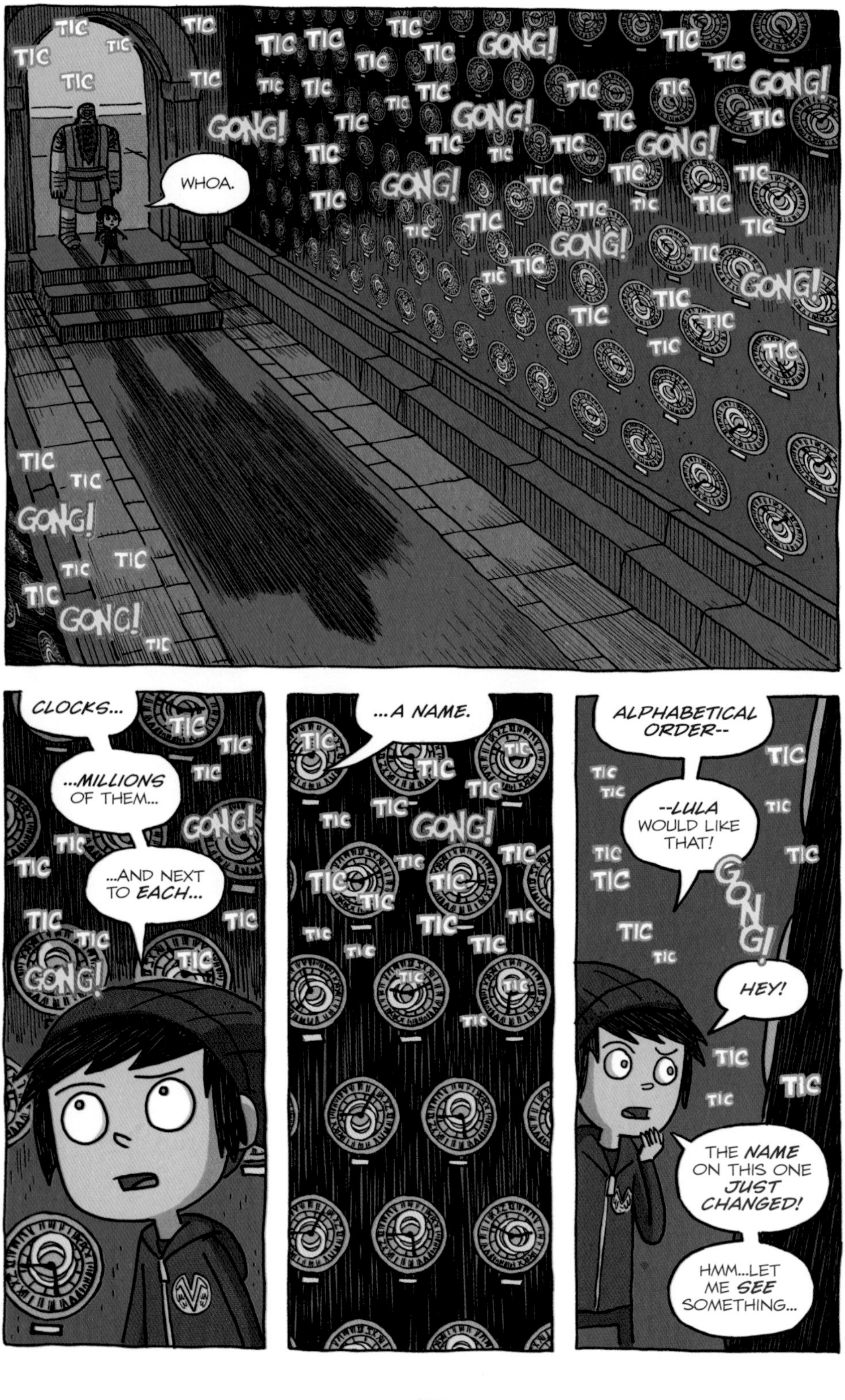
TIC
TIC
TIC
GONG!
WHOA.
CLOCKS...
...MILLIONS OF THEM...
...AND NEXT TO EACH...
...A NAME.
ALPHABETICAL ORDER--
--LULA WOULD LIKE THAT!
GONG!
HEY!
THE NAME ON THIS ONE JUST CHANGED!
HMM...LET ME SEE SOMETHING...

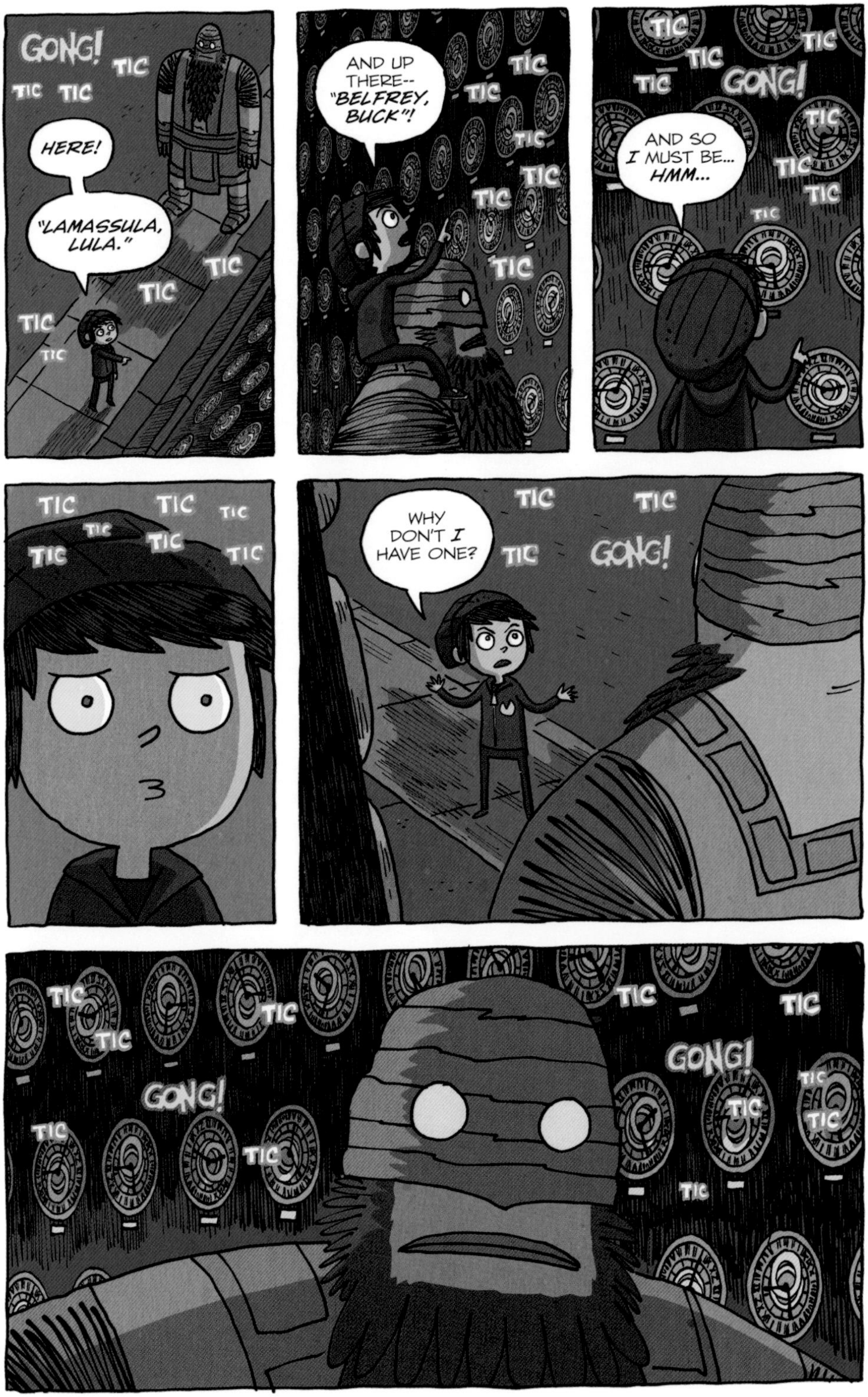
GONG!
TIC
TIC TIC
HERE!
"LAMASSULA, LULA."
TIC
TIC
TIC
TIC
AND UP THERE-- "BELFREY, BUCK"!
TIC
TIC
TIC
TIC
TIC
TIC
TIC TIC TIC
TIC GONG!
AND SO I MUST BE... HMM...
TIC
TIC
TIC
TIC
TIC TIC TIC
TIC TIC TIC
WHY DON'T I HAVE ONE?
TIC TIC
TIC GONG!
TIC TIC TIC TIC TIC
GONG!
GONG!
TIC TIC TIC TIC TIC TIC

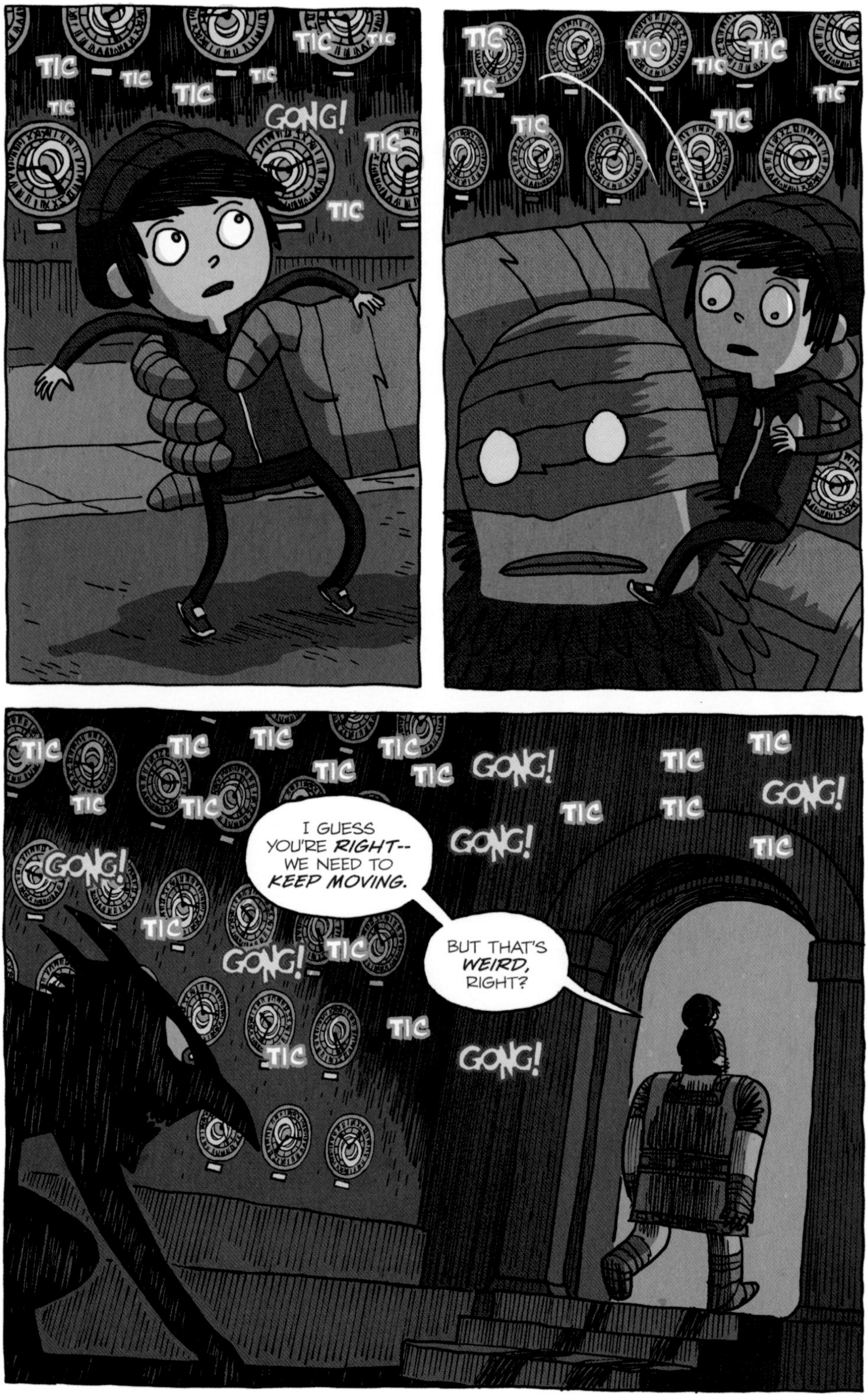
TIC
TIC
TIC
TIC
TIC
TIC
GONG!
TIC
TIC
TIC
TIC
TIC
TIC
TIC
TIC
TIC
TIC
TIC
TIC
TIC
TIC
TIC
TIC
TIC
GONG!
TIC
TIC
GONG!
I GUESS YOU'RE *RIGHT*-- WE NEED TO *KEEP MOVING.*
GONG!
BUT THAT'S *WEIRD,* RIGHT?
GONG!
TIC
GONG!
TIC
TIC
TIC
GONG!

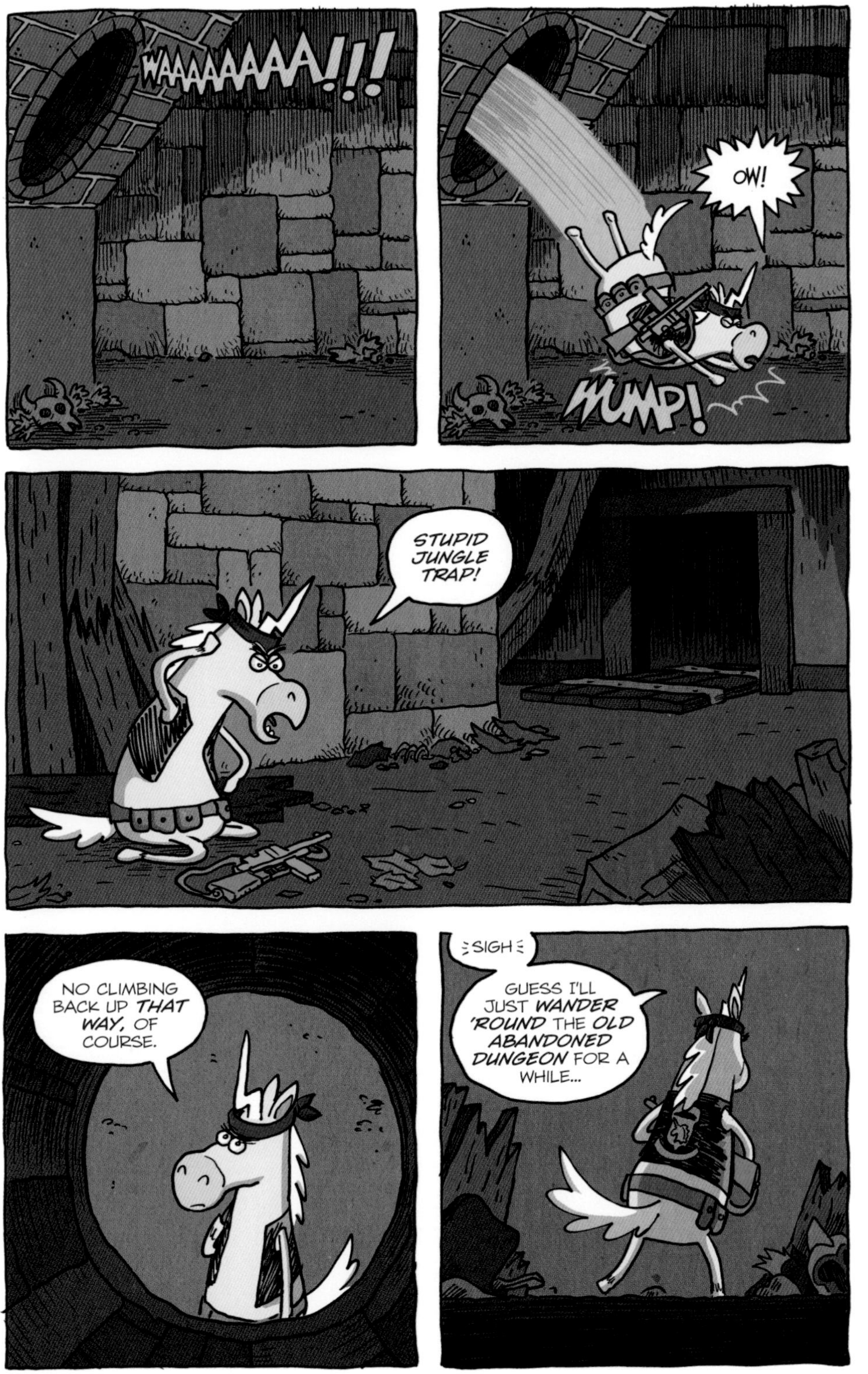
WAAAAAAAA!!!
OW!
WUMP!
STUPID JUNGLE TRAP!
NO CLIMBING BACK UP THAT WAY, OF COURSE.
SIGH
GUESS I'LL JUST WANDER 'ROUND THE OLD ABANDONED DUNGEON FOR A WHILE...

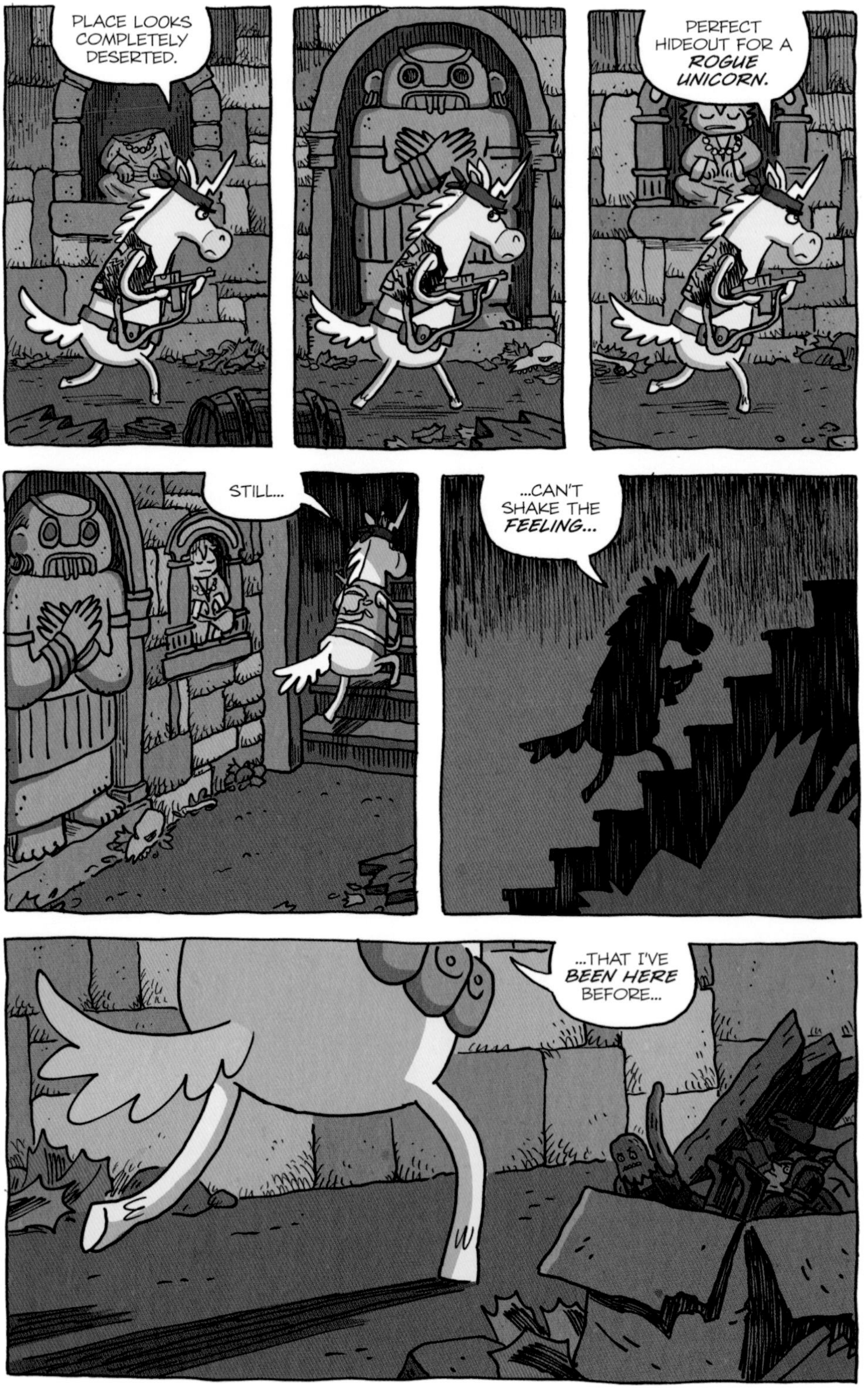
PLACE LOOKS COMPLETELY DESERTED.
PERFECT HIDEOUT FOR A *ROGUE UNICORN.*
STILL...
...CAN'T SHAKE THE *FEELING...*
...THAT I'VE *BEEN HERE* BEFORE...

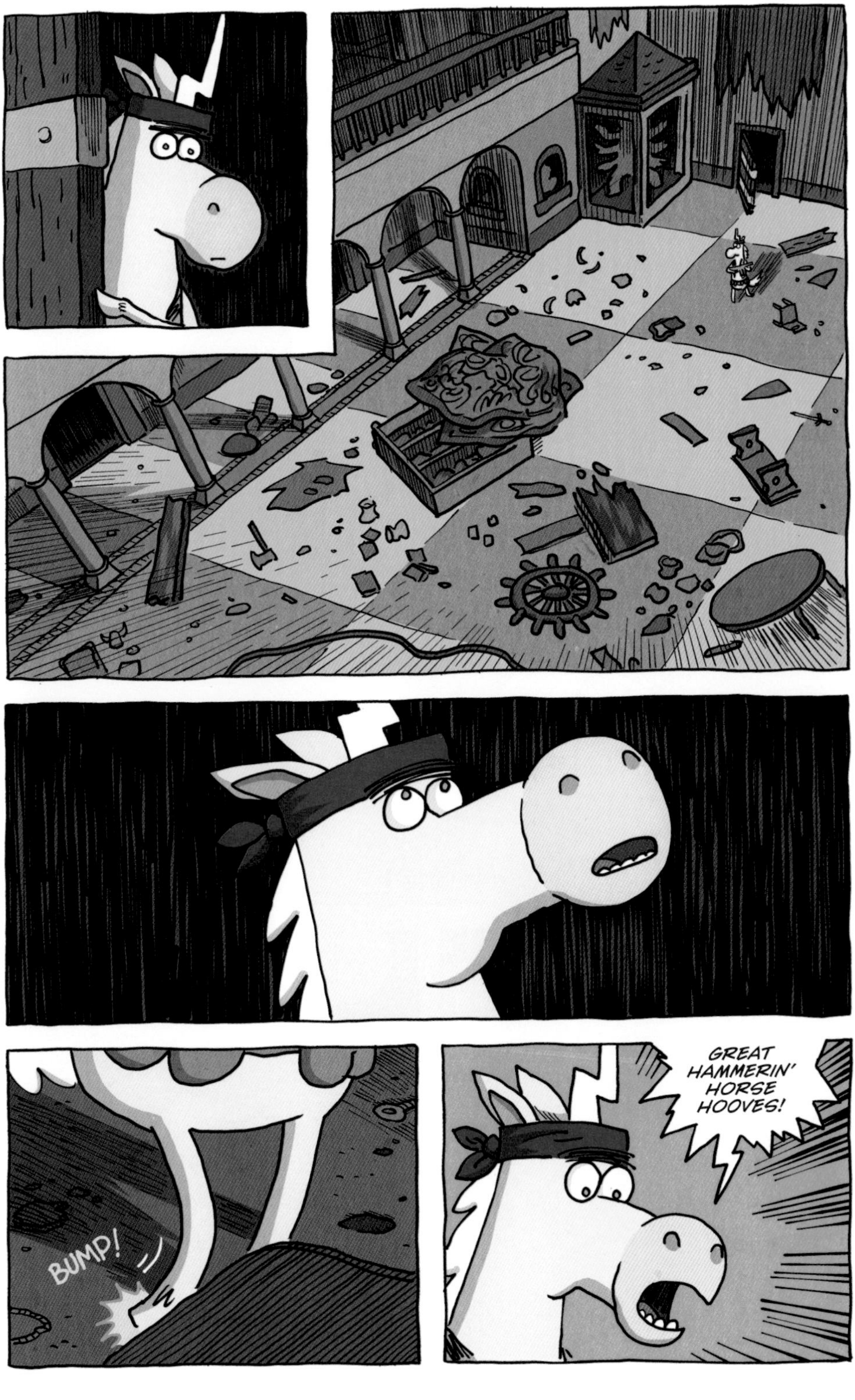
BUMP!
GREAT HAMMERIN' HORSE HOOVES!

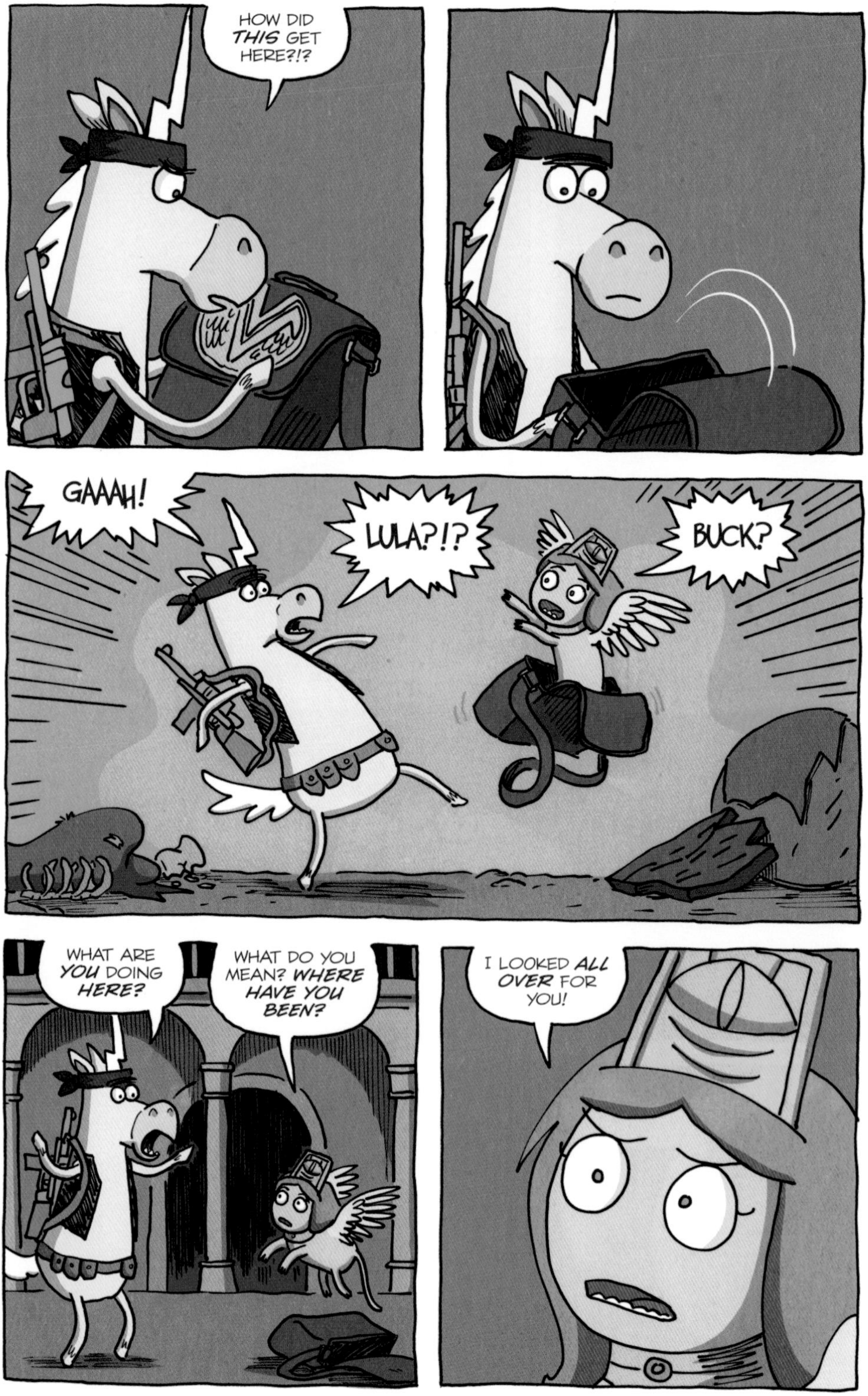
HOW DID THIS GET HERE?!?
GAAAH!
LULA?!?
BUCK?
WHAT ARE YOU DOING HERE?
WHAT DO YOU MEAN? WHERE HAVE YOU BEEN?
I LOOKED ALL OVER FOR YOU!

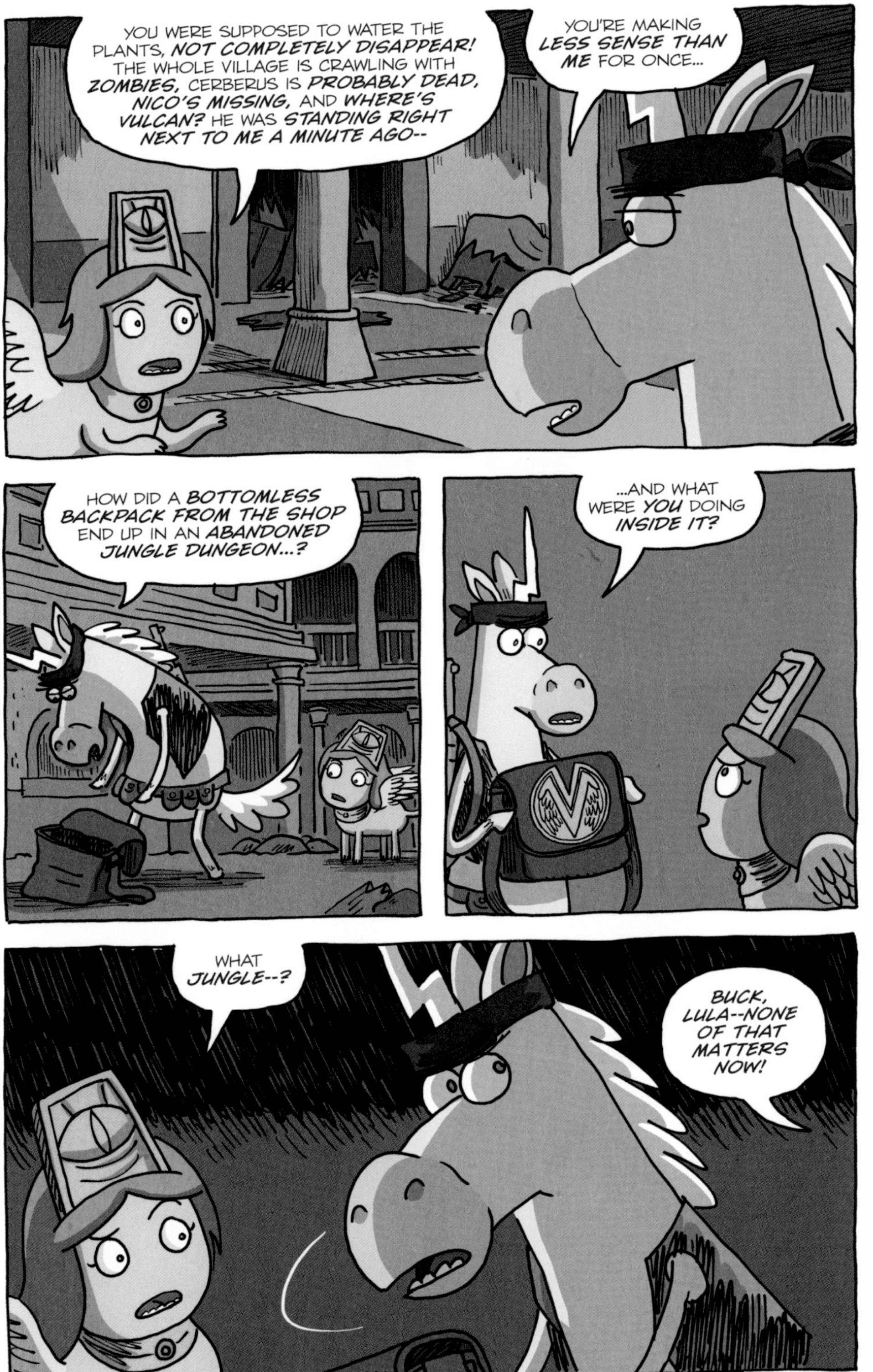
YOU WERE SUPPOSED TO WATER THE PLANTS, NOT COMPLETELY DISAPPEAR! THE WHOLE VILLAGE IS CRAWLING WITH ZOMBIES, CERBERUS IS PROBABLY DEAD, NICO'S MISSING, AND WHERE'S VULCAN? HE WAS STANDING RIGHT NEXT TO ME A MINUTE AGO--
YOU'RE MAKING LESS SENSE THAN ME FOR ONCE...
HOW DID A BOTTOMLESS BACKPACK FROM THE SHOP END UP IN AN ABANDONED JUNGLE DUNGEON...?
...AND WHAT WERE YOU DOING INSIDE IT?
WHAT JUNGLE--?
BUCK, LULA--NONE OF THAT MATTERS NOW!

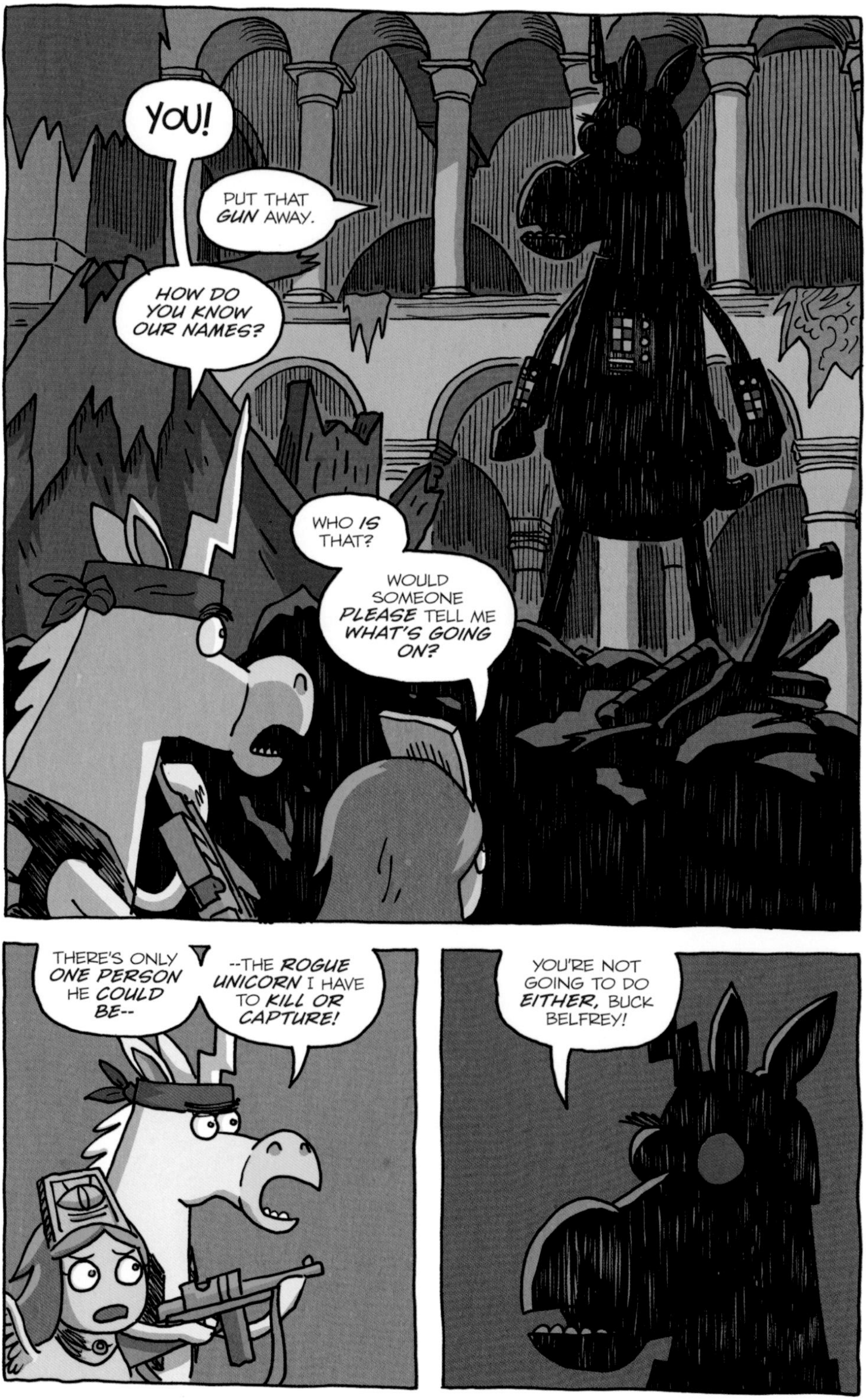
YOU!
PUT THAT GUN AWAY.
HOW DO YOU KNOW OUR NAMES?
WHO IS THAT?
WOULD SOMEONE PLEASE TELL ME WHAT'S GOING ON?
THERE'S ONLY ONE PERSON HE COULD BE--
--THE ROGUE UNICORN I HAVE TO KILL OR CAPTURE!
YOU'RE NOT GOING TO DO EITHER, BUCK BELFREY!

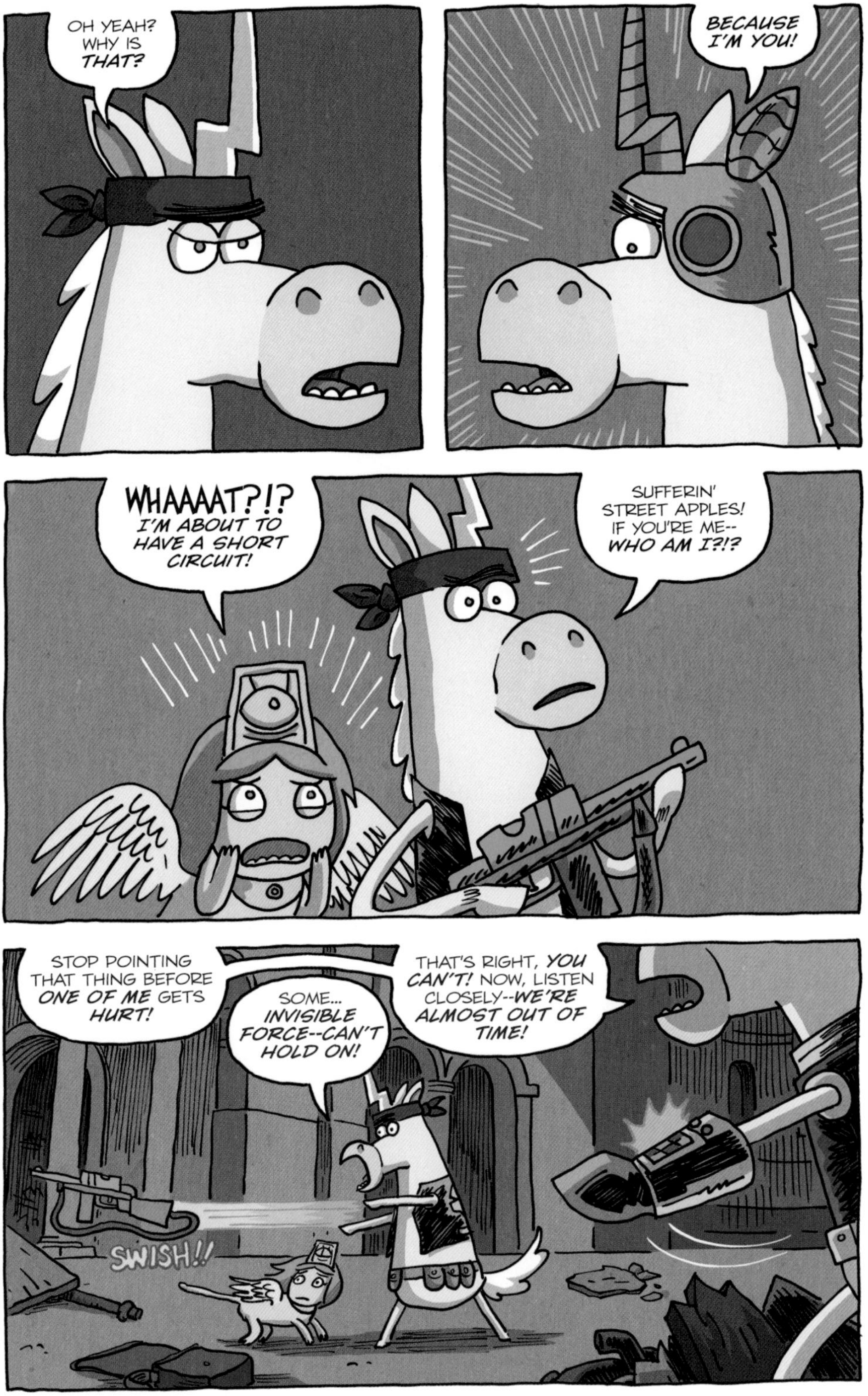
OH YEAH? WHY IS *THAT?*
*BECAUSE I'M YOU!*
WHAAAAT?!? *I'M ABOUT TO HAVE A SHORT CIRCUIT!*
SUFFERIN' STREET APPLES! IF YOU'RE ME-- *WHO AM I?!?*
STOP POINTING THAT THING BEFORE *ONE OF ME* GETS *HURT!*
SOME... *INVISIBLE FORCE--CAN'T HOLD ON!*
THAT'S RIGHT, *YOU CAN'T!* NOW, LISTEN CLOSELY--*WE'RE ALMOST OUT OF TIME!*
SWISH!!

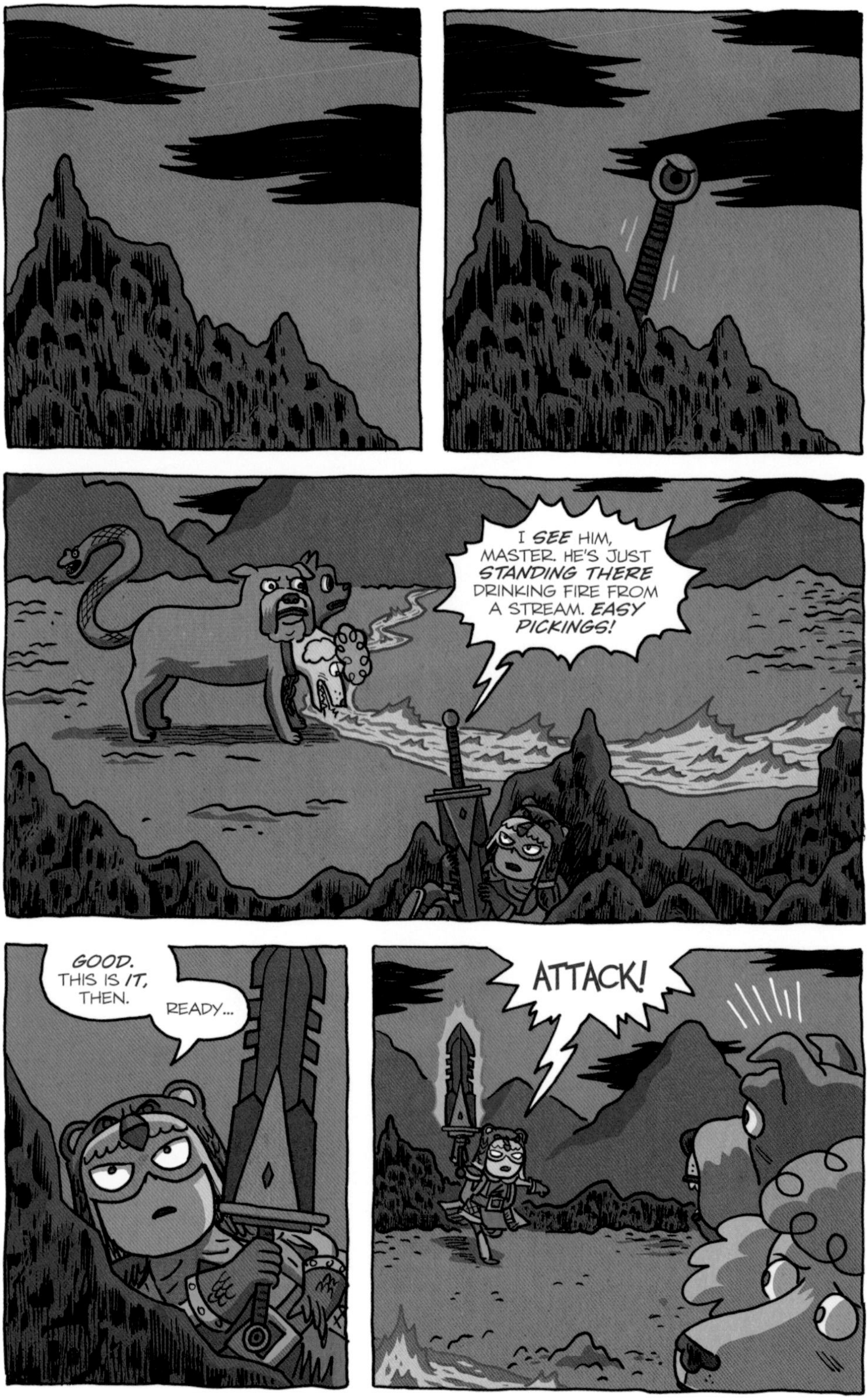
I SEE HIM, MASTER. HE'S JUST STANDING THERE DRINKING FIRE FROM A STREAM. EASY PICKINGS!
GOOD. THIS IS IT, THEN.
READY...
ATTACK!

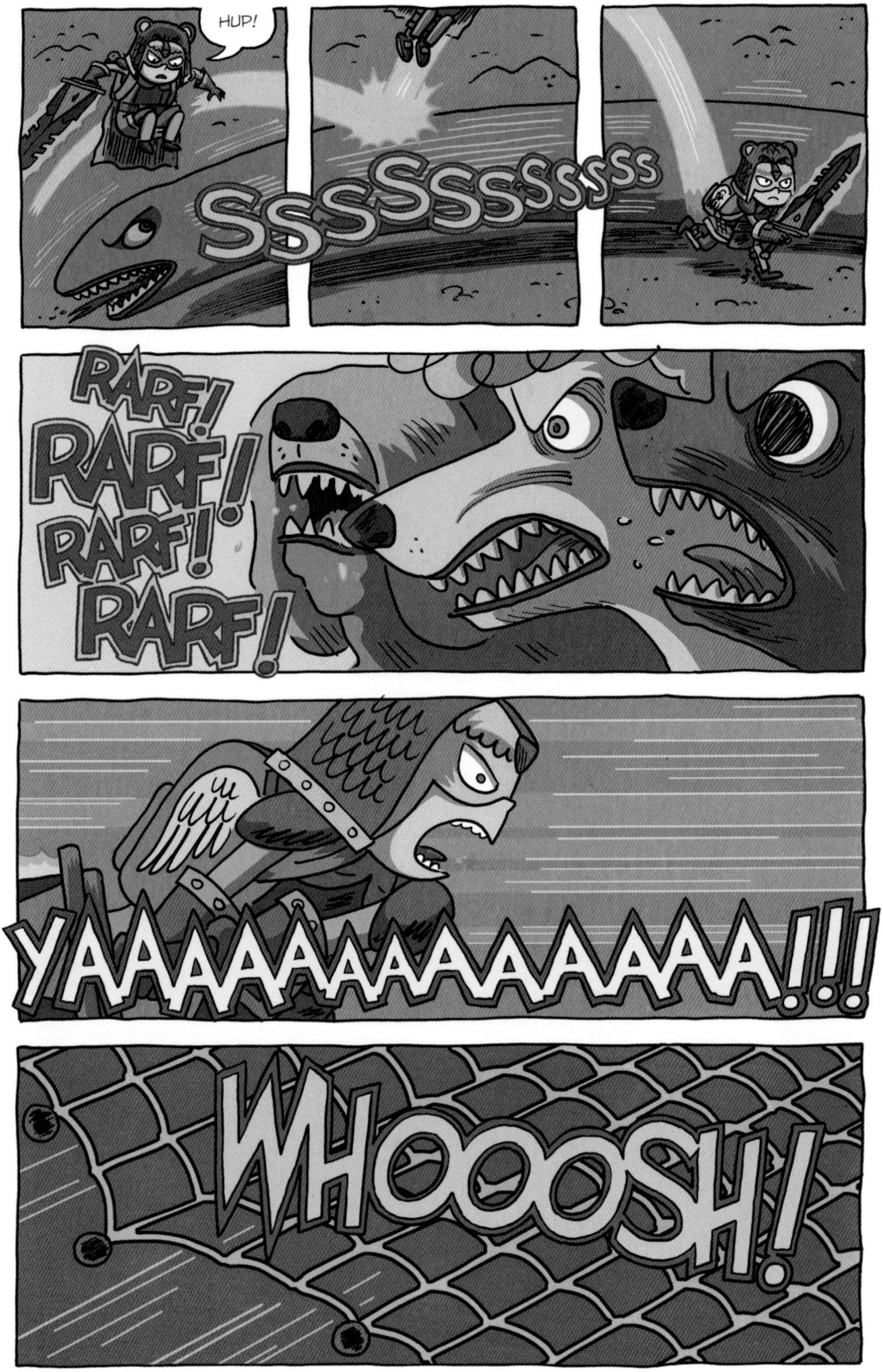
HUP!
SSSSSSSSSSSS
RARF!
RARF!
RARF!
RARF!
YAAAAAAAAAAAAA!!!
WHOOOSH!

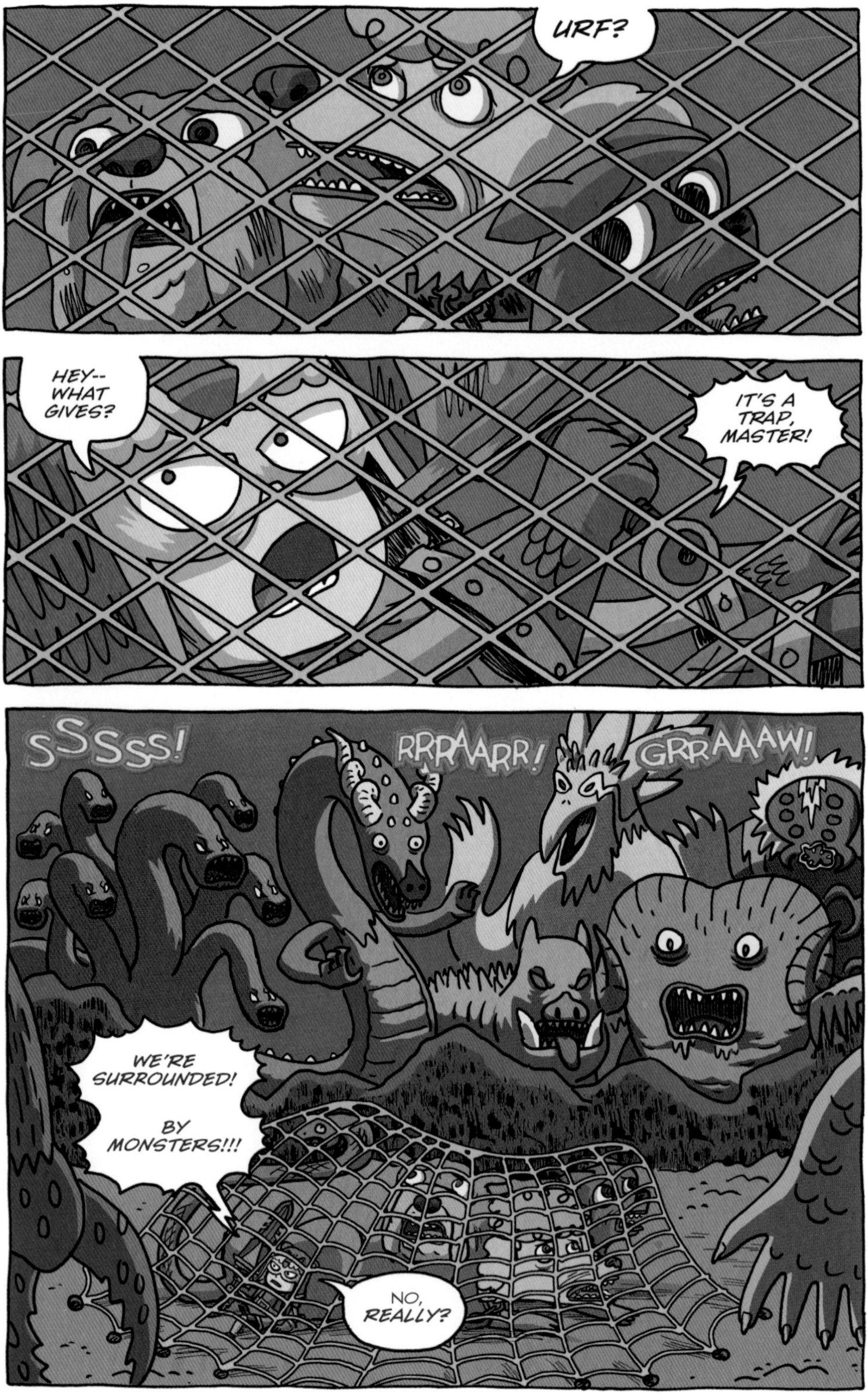
URF?
HEY-- WHAT GIVES?
IT'S A TRAP, MASTER!
SSSSS!
RRRAARR!
GRRAAAW!
WE'RE SURROUNDED!
BY MONSTERS!!!
NO, REALLY?

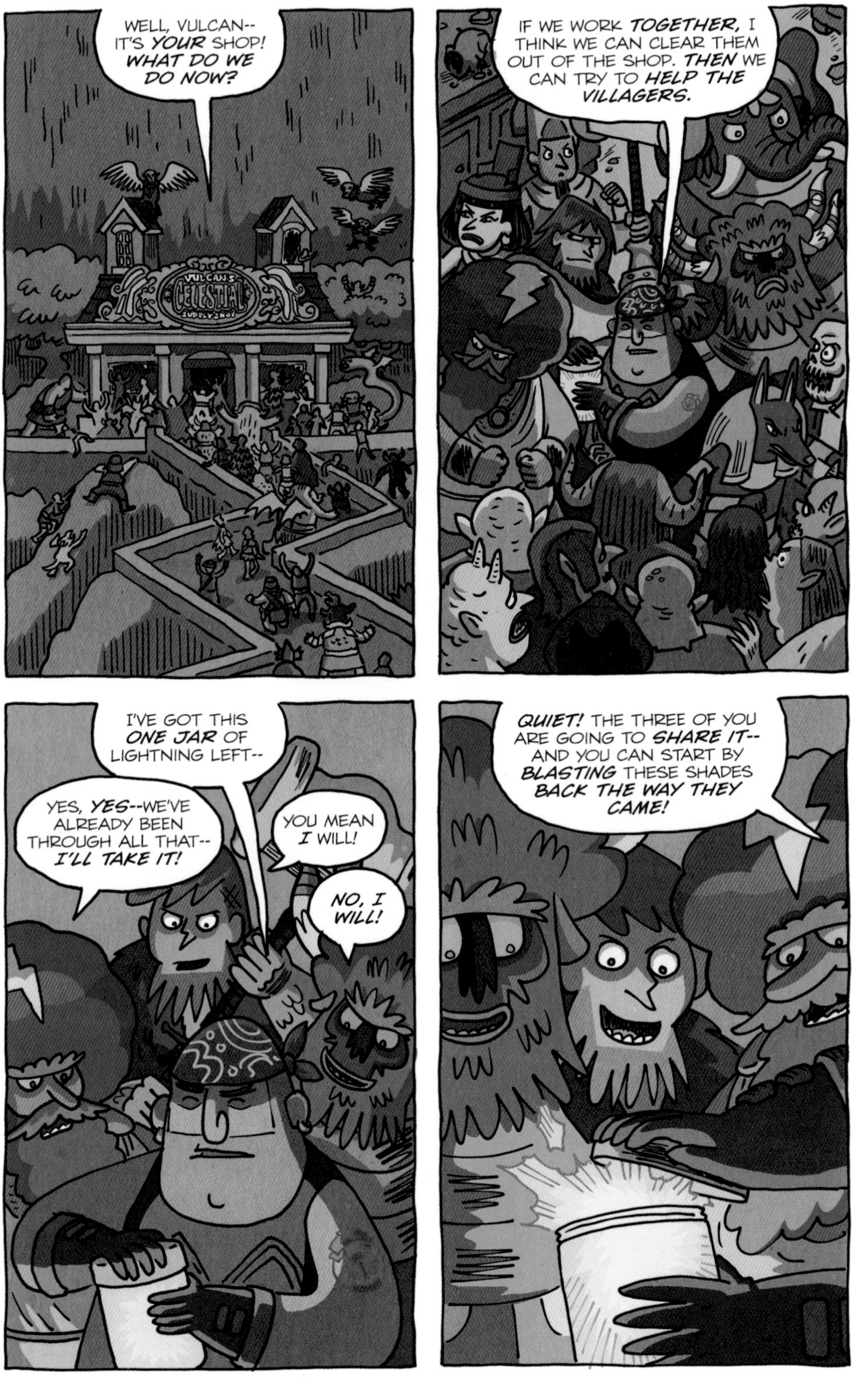
WELL, VULCAN-- IT'S YOUR SHOP! WHAT DO WE DO NOW?
VULCAN'S CELESTIAL SUPPLY SHOP
IF WE WORK TOGETHER, I THINK WE CAN CLEAR THEM OUT OF THE SHOP. THEN WE CAN TRY TO HELP THE VILLAGERS.
I'VE GOT THIS ONE JAR OF LIGHTNING LEFT--
YES, YES--WE'VE ALREADY BEEN THROUGH ALL THAT-- I'LL TAKE IT!
YOU MEAN I WILL!
NO, I WILL!
QUIET! THE THREE OF YOU ARE GOING TO SHARE IT-- AND YOU CAN START BY BLASTING THESE SHADES BACK THE WAY THEY CAME!

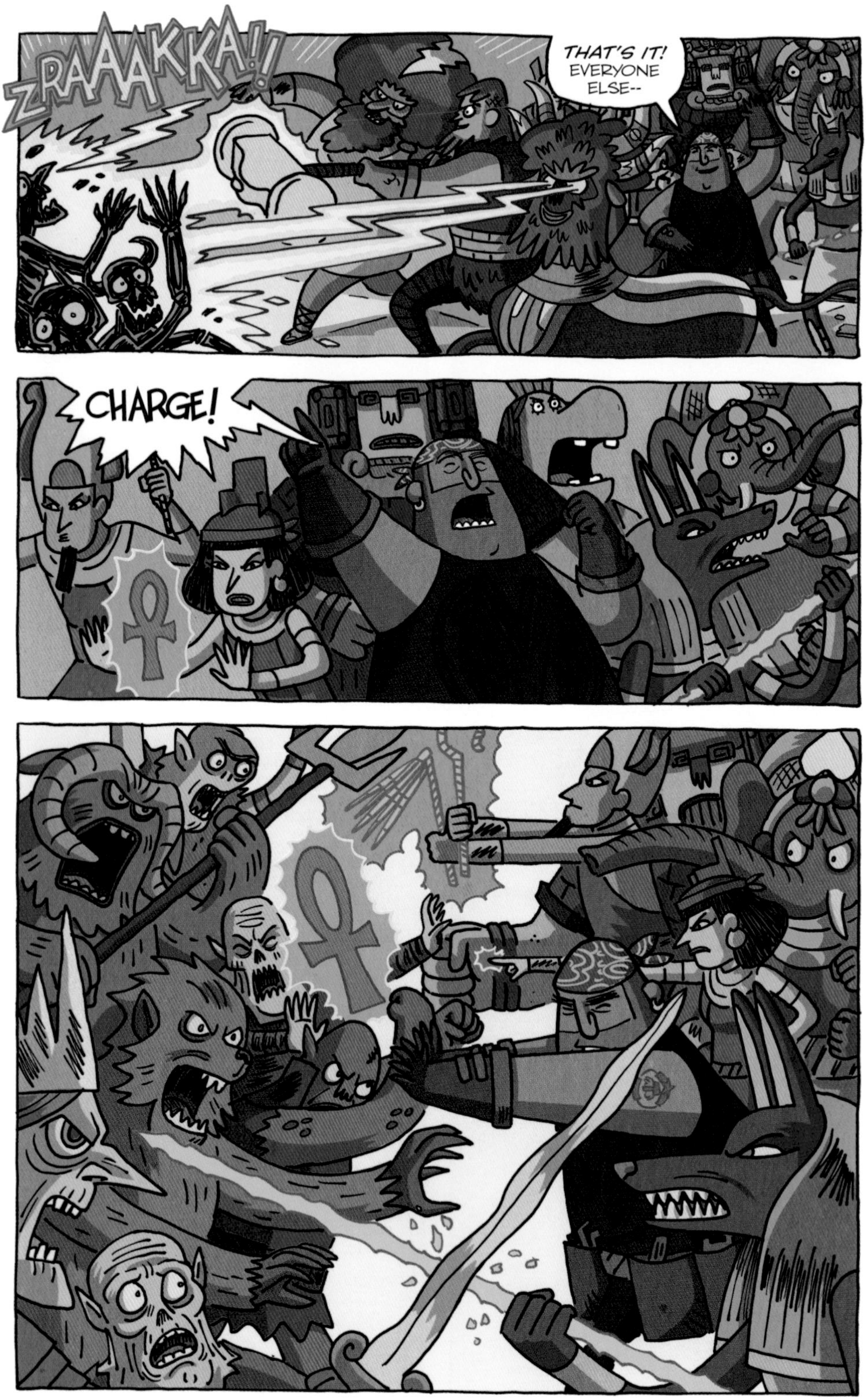
ZRAAAKKA!!
THAT'S IT! EVERYONE ELSE--
CHARGE!

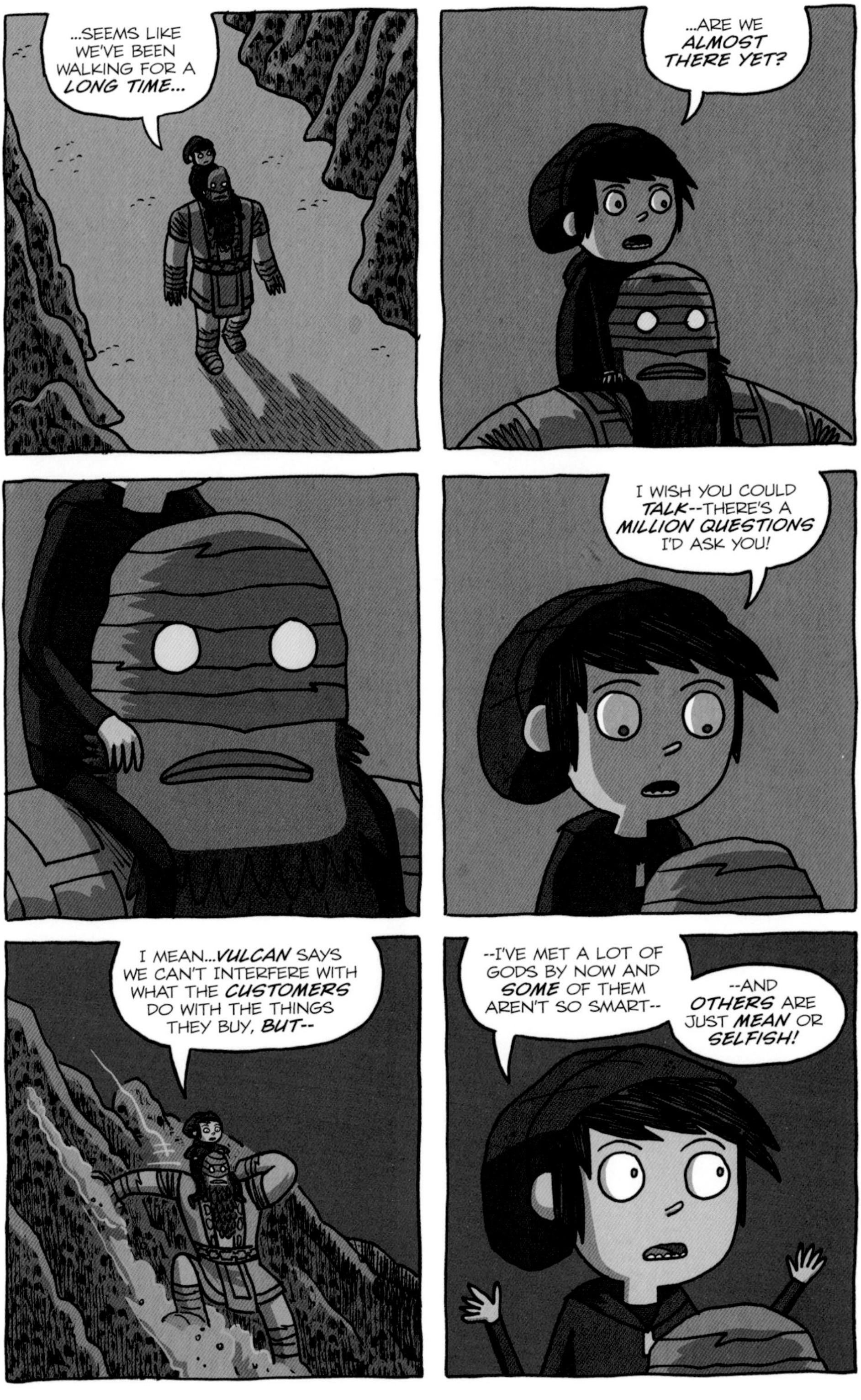
...SEEMS LIKE WE'VE BEEN WALKING FOR A LONG TIME...
...ARE WE ALMOST THERE YET?
I WISH YOU COULD TALK--THERE'S A MILLION QUESTIONS I'D ASK YOU!
I MEAN...VULCAN SAYS WE CAN'T INTERFERE WITH WHAT THE CUSTOMERS DO WITH THE THINGS THEY BUY, BUT--
--I'VE MET A LOT OF GODS BY NOW AND SOME OF THEM AREN'T SO SMART--
--AND OTHERS ARE JUST MEAN OR SELFISH!

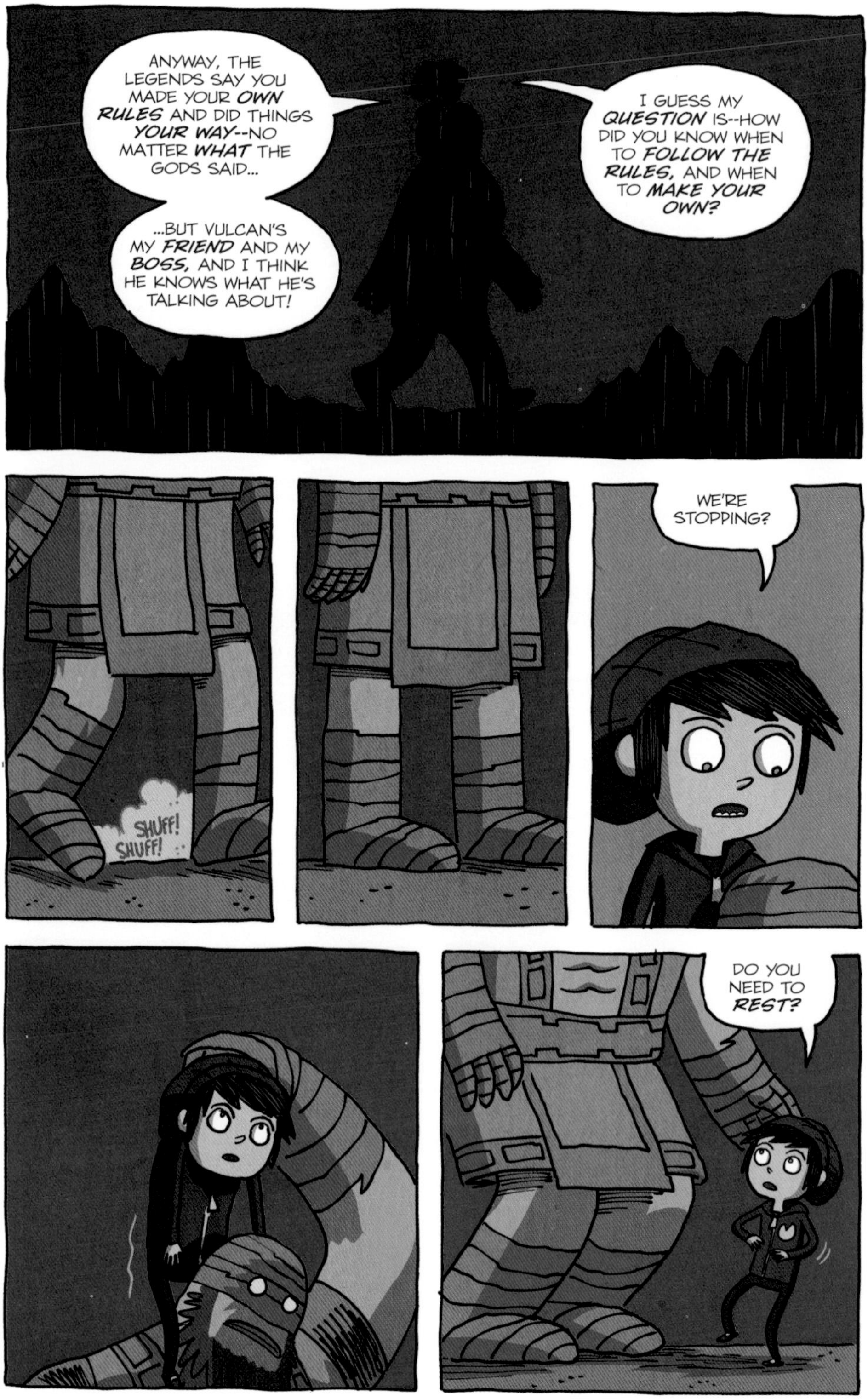
ANYWAY, THE LEGENDS SAY YOU MADE YOUR OWN RULES AND DID THINGS YOUR WAY--NO MATTER WHAT THE GODS SAID...
...BUT VULCAN'S MY FRIEND AND MY BOSS, AND I THINK HE KNOWS WHAT HE'S TALKING ABOUT!
I GUESS MY QUESTION IS--HOW DID YOU KNOW WHEN TO FOLLOW THE RULES, AND WHEN TO MAKE YOUR OWN?
SHUFF! SHUFF!
WE'RE STOPPING?
DO YOU NEED TO REST?

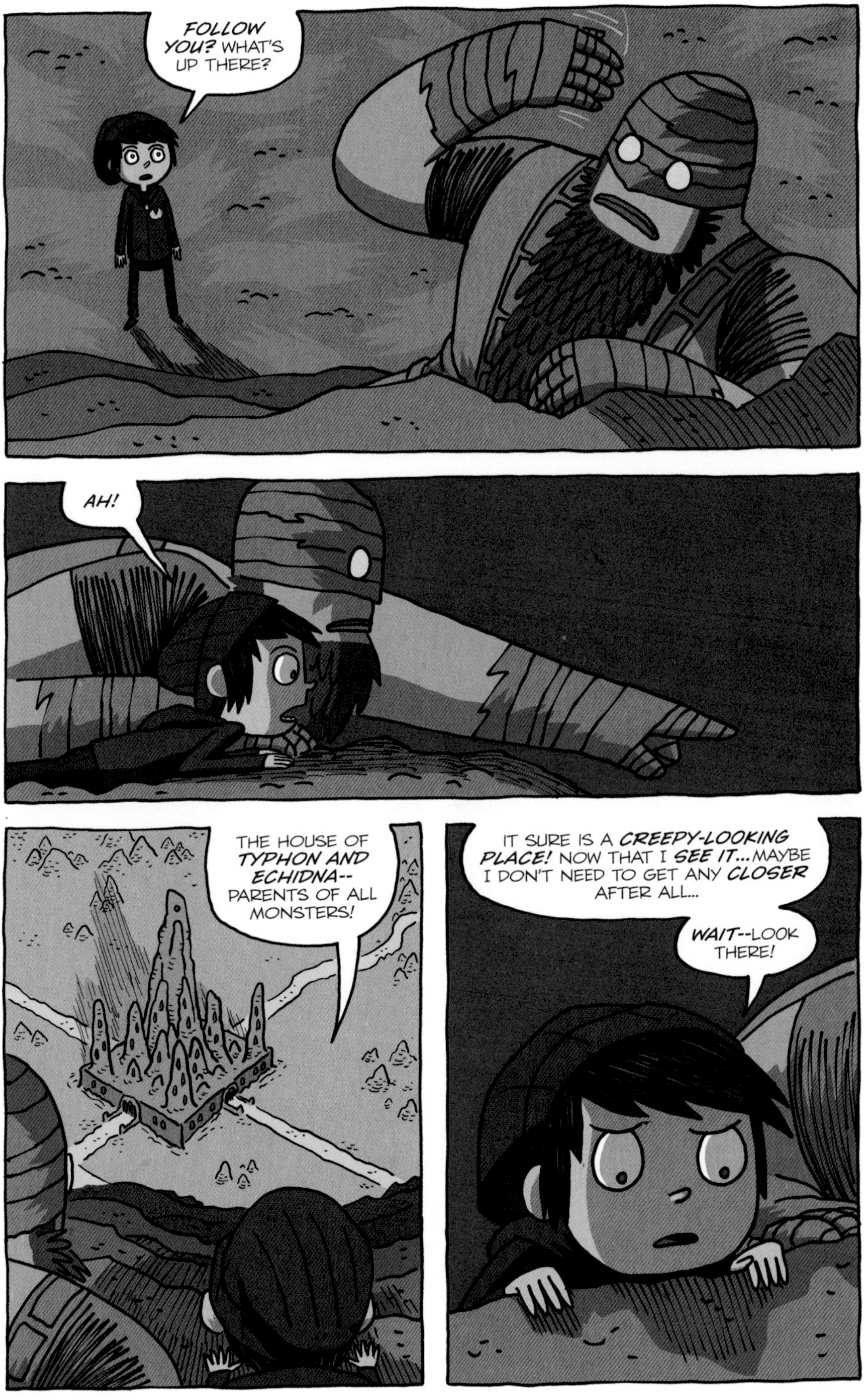
FOLLOW YOU? WHAT'S UP THERE?
AH!
THE HOUSE OF TYPHON AND ECHIDNA-- PARENTS OF ALL MONSTERS!
IT SURE IS A CREEPY-LOOKING PLACE! NOW THAT I SEE IT... MAYBE I DON'T NEED TO GET ANY CLOSER AFTER ALL...
WAIT--LOOK THERE!

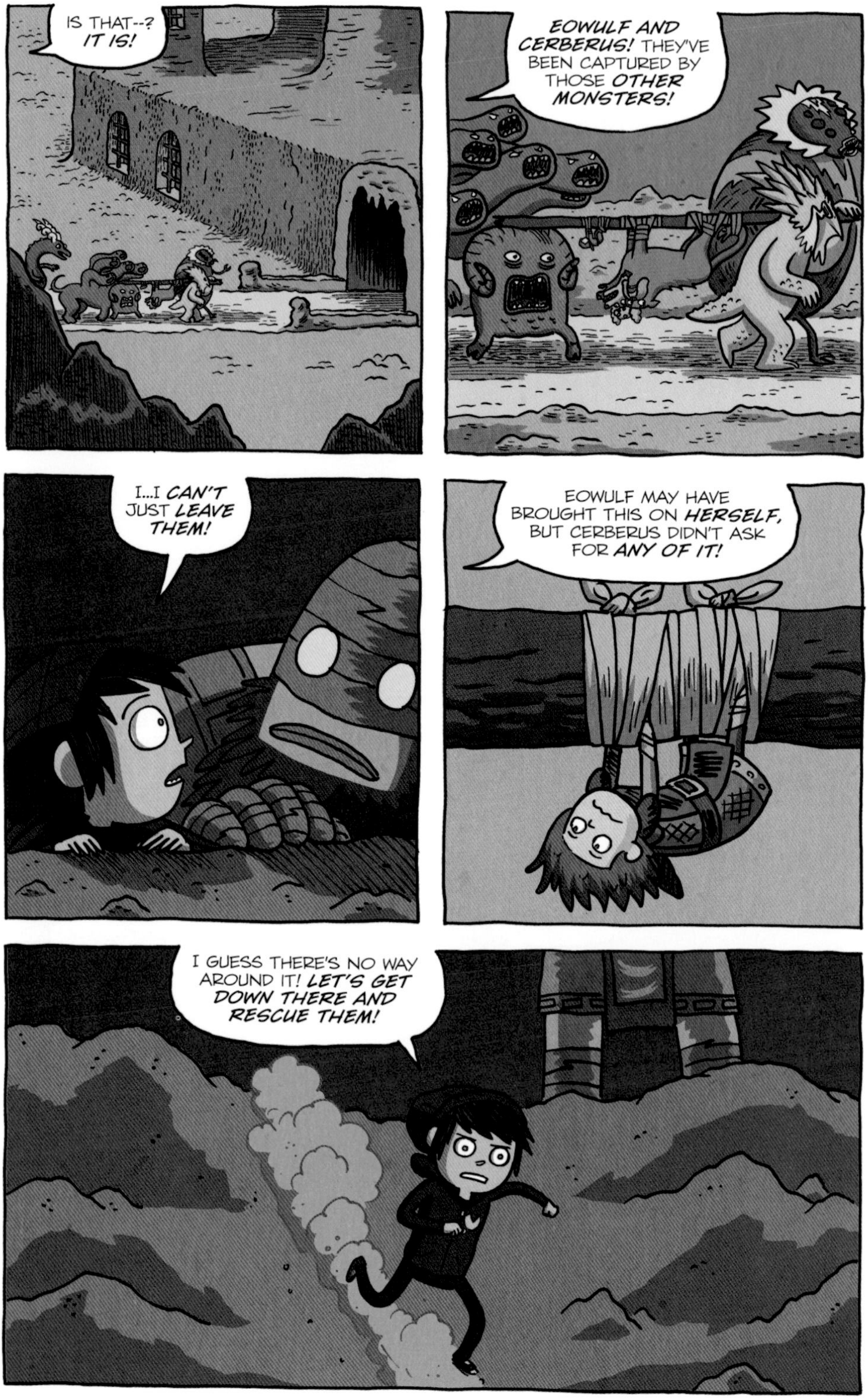
IS THAT--? IT IS!
EOWULF AND CERBERUS! THEY'VE BEEN CAPTURED BY THOSE OTHER MONSTERS!
I...I CAN'T JUST LEAVE THEM!
EOWULF MAY HAVE BROUGHT THIS ON HERSELF, BUT CERBERUS DIDN'T ASK FOR ANY OF IT!
I GUESS THERE'S NO WAY AROUND IT! LET'S GET DOWN THERE AND RESCUE THEM!

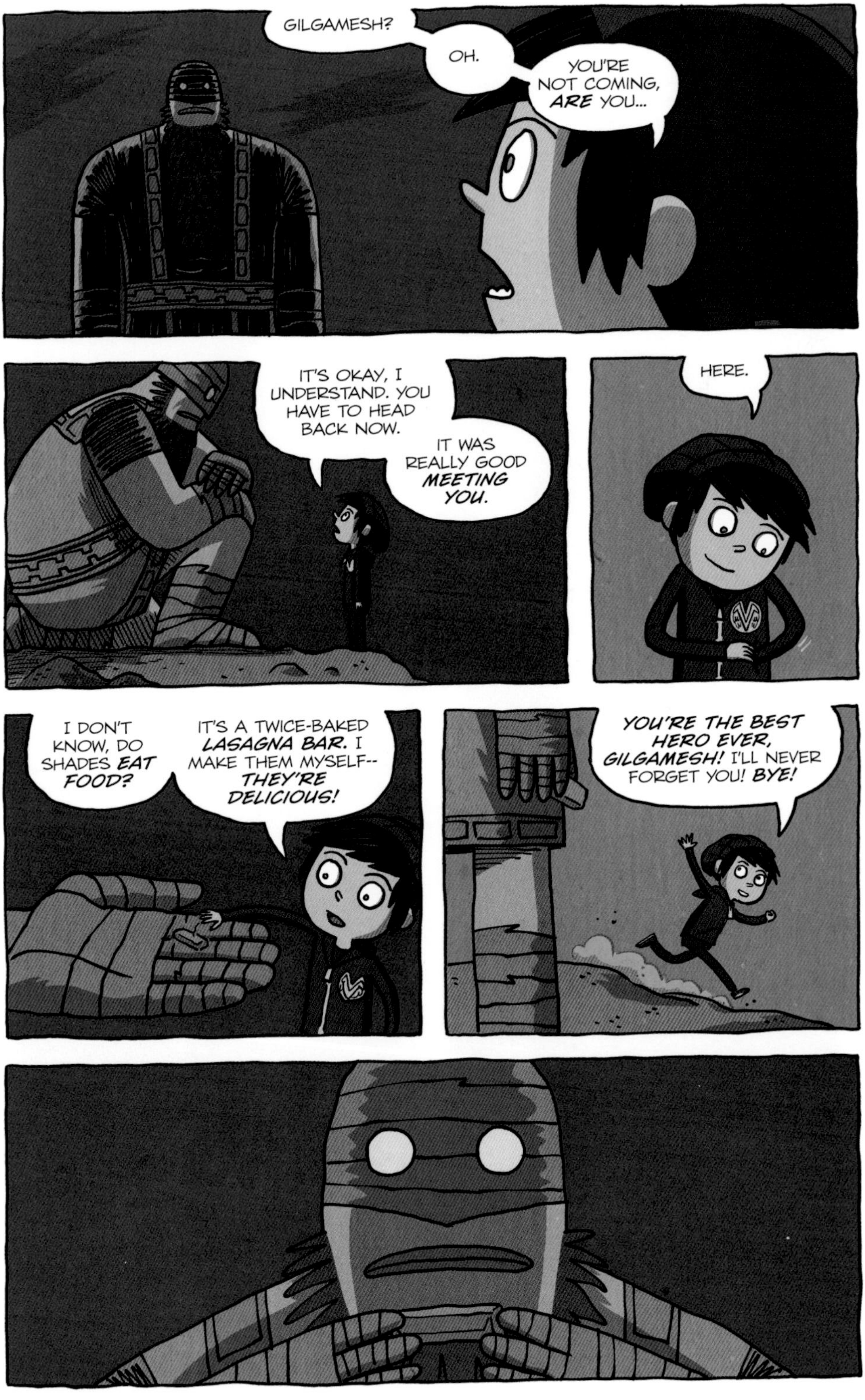
GILGAMESH?
OH.
YOU'RE NOT COMING, **ARE** YOU...
IT'S OKAY, I UNDERSTAND. YOU HAVE TO HEAD BACK NOW.
IT WAS REALLY GOOD **MEETING YOU.**
HERE.
I DON'T KNOW, DO SHADES **EAT FOOD?**
IT'S A TWICE-BAKED **LASAGNA BAR.** I MAKE THEM MYSELF-- **THEY'RE DELICIOUS!**
**YOU'RE THE BEST HERO EVER, GILGAMESH!** I'LL NEVER FORGET YOU! **BYE!**

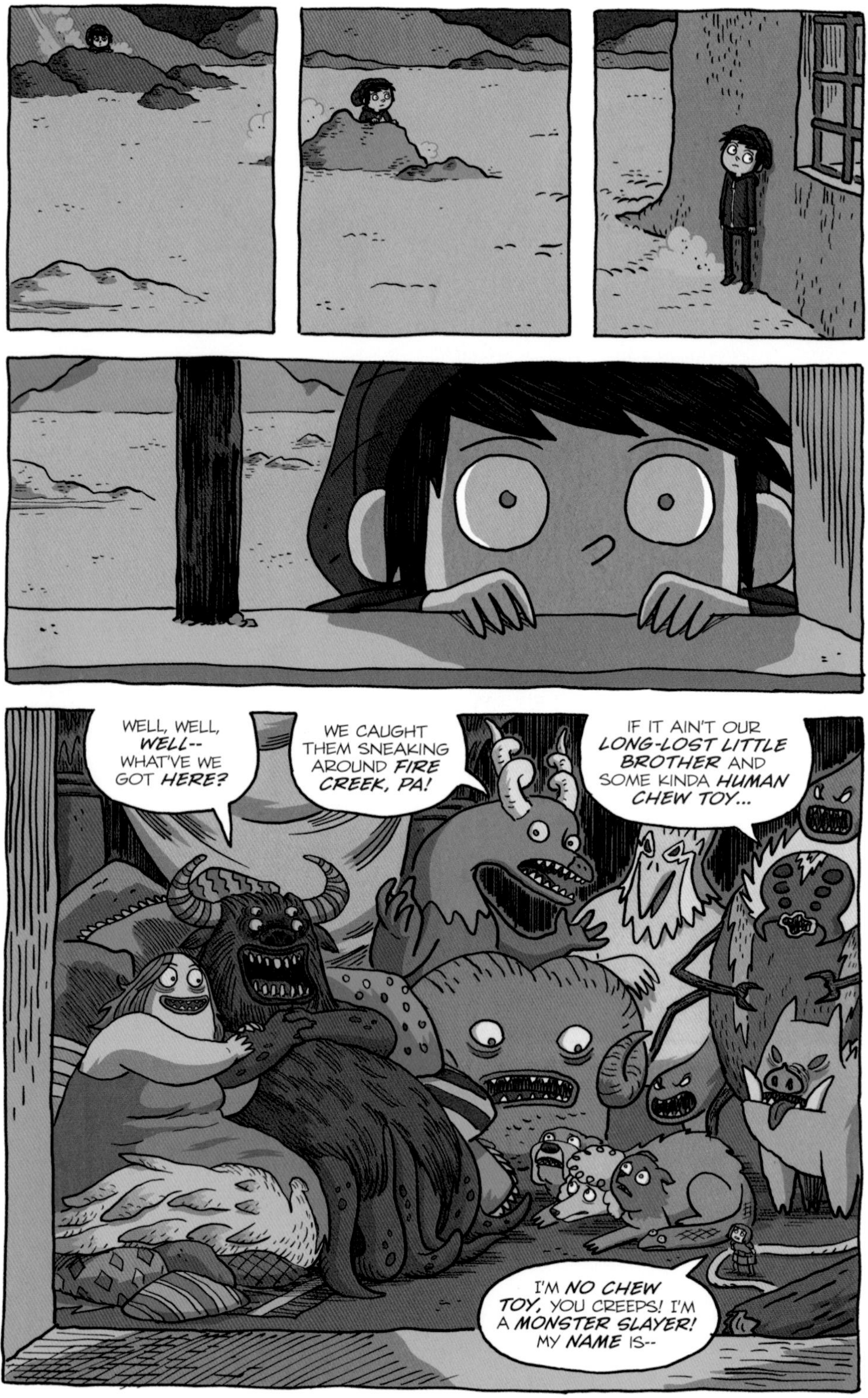
WELL, WELL, WELL-- WHAT'VE WE GOT HERE?
WE CAUGHT THEM SNEAKING AROUND FIRE CREEK, PA!
IF IT AIN'T OUR LONG-LOST LITTLE BROTHER AND SOME KINDA HUMAN CHEW TOY...
I'M NO CHEW TOY, YOU CREEPS! I'M A MONSTER SLAYER! MY NAME IS--

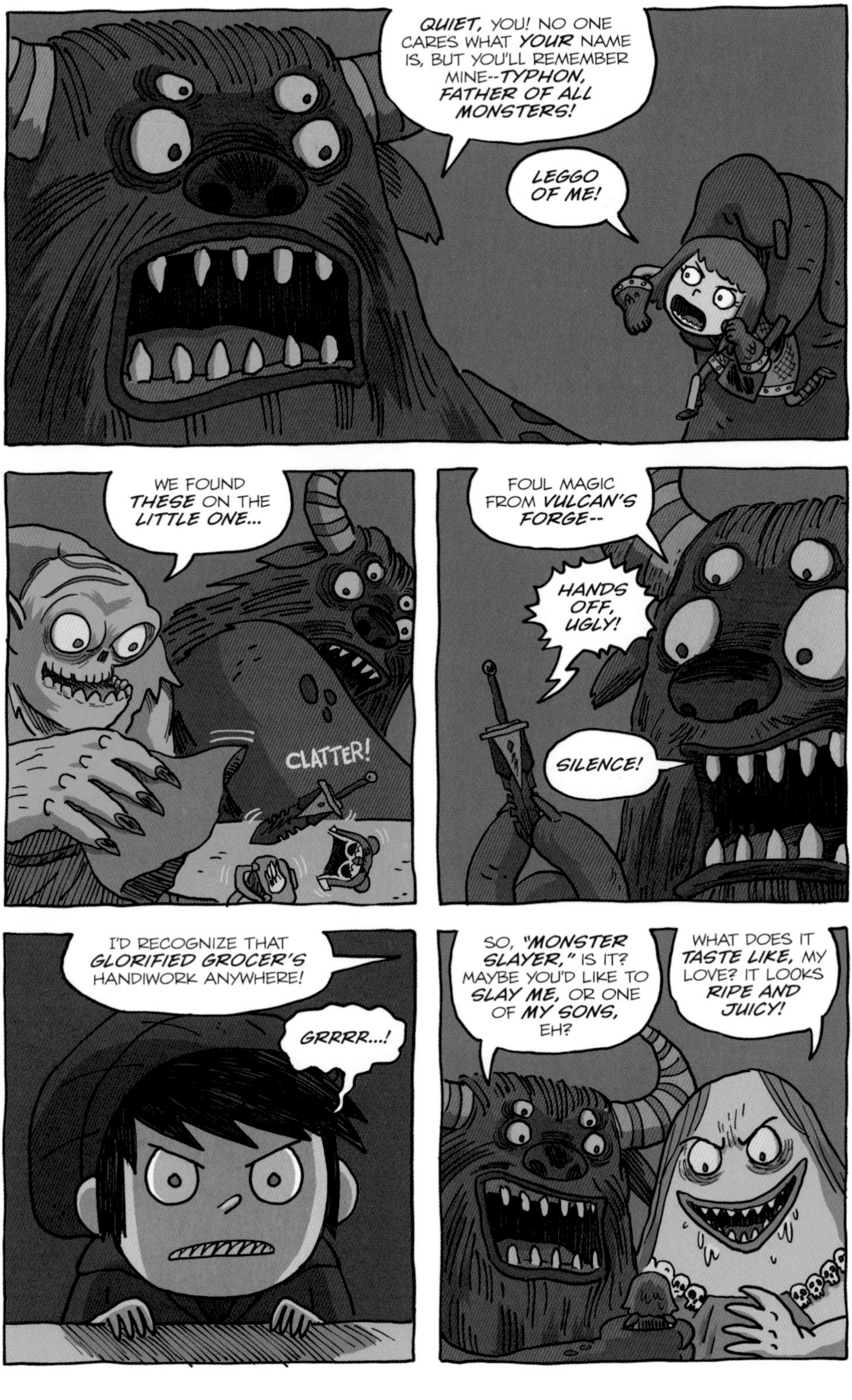
QUIET, YOU! NO ONE CARES WHAT YOUR NAME IS, BUT YOU'LL REMEMBER MINE--TYPHON, FATHER OF ALL MONSTERS!
LEGGO OF ME!
WE FOUND THESE ON THE LITTLE ONE...
CLATTER!
FOUL MAGIC FROM VULCAN'S FORGE--
HANDS OFF, UGLY!
SILENCE!
I'D RECOGNIZE THAT GLORIFIED GROCER'S HANDIWORK ANYWHERE!
GRRRR...!
SO, "MONSTER SLAYER," IS IT? MAYBE YOU'D LIKE TO SLAY ME, OR ONE OF MY SONS, EH?
WHAT DOES IT TASTE LIKE, MY LOVE? IT LOOKS RIPE AND JUICY!

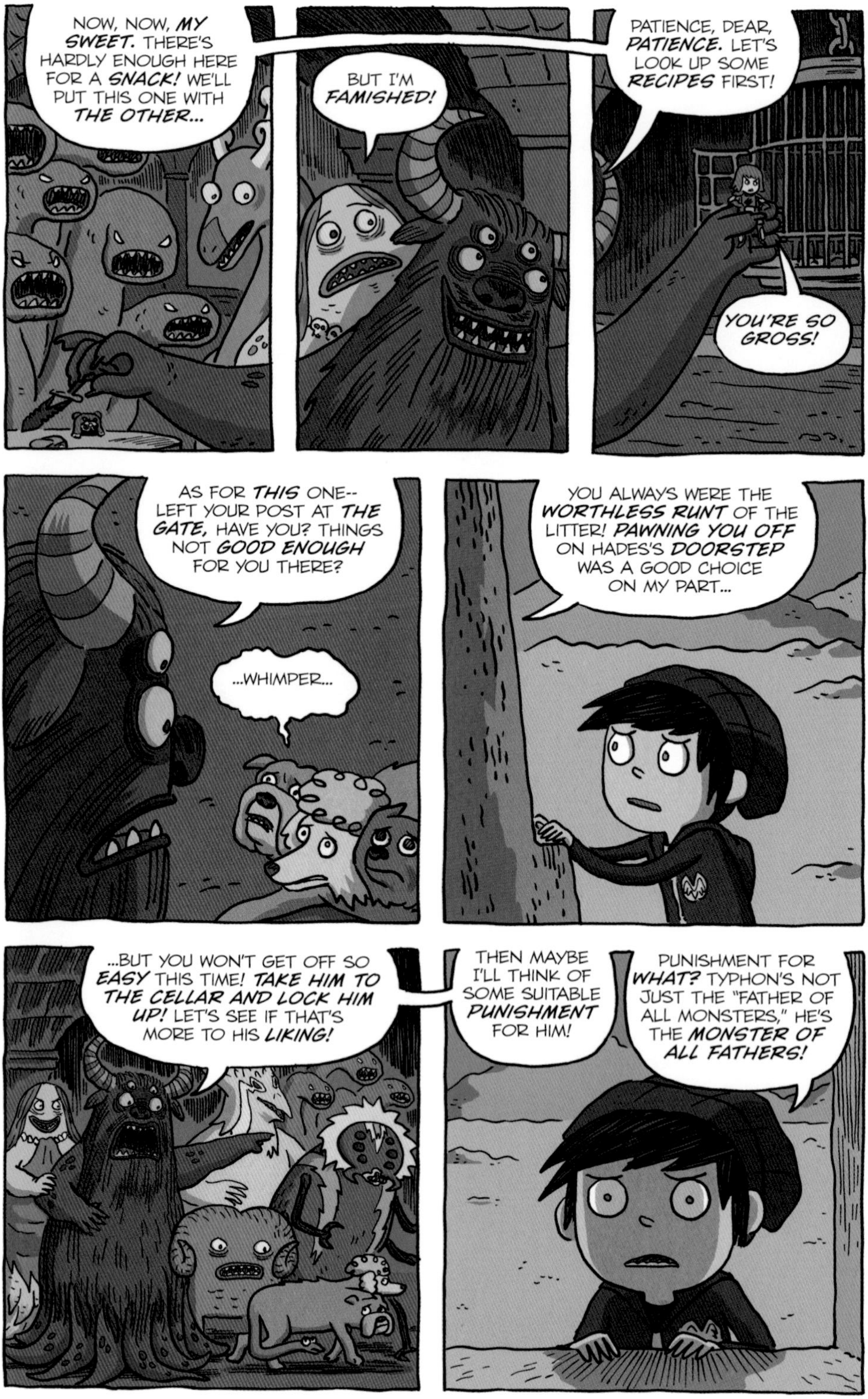
NOW, NOW, MY SWEET. THERE'S HARDLY ENOUGH HERE FOR A SNACK! WE'LL PUT THIS ONE WITH THE OTHER...
BUT I'M FAMISHED!
PATIENCE, DEAR, PATIENCE. LET'S LOOK UP SOME RECIPES FIRST!
YOU'RE SO GROSS!
AS FOR THIS ONE-- LEFT YOUR POST AT THE GATE, HAVE YOU? THINGS NOT GOOD ENOUGH FOR YOU THERE?
...WHIMPER...
YOU ALWAYS WERE THE WORTHLESS RUNT OF THE LITTER! PAWNING YOU OFF ON HADES'S DOORSTEP WAS A GOOD CHOICE ON MY PART...
...BUT YOU WON'T GET OFF SO EASY THIS TIME! TAKE HIM TO THE CELLAR AND LOCK HIM UP! LET'S SEE IF THAT'S MORE TO HIS LIKING!
THEN MAYBE I'LL THINK OF SOME SUITABLE PUNISHMENT FOR HIM!
PUNISHMENT FOR WHAT? TYPHON'S NOT JUST THE "FATHER OF ALL MONSTERS," HE'S THE MONSTER OF ALL FATHERS!

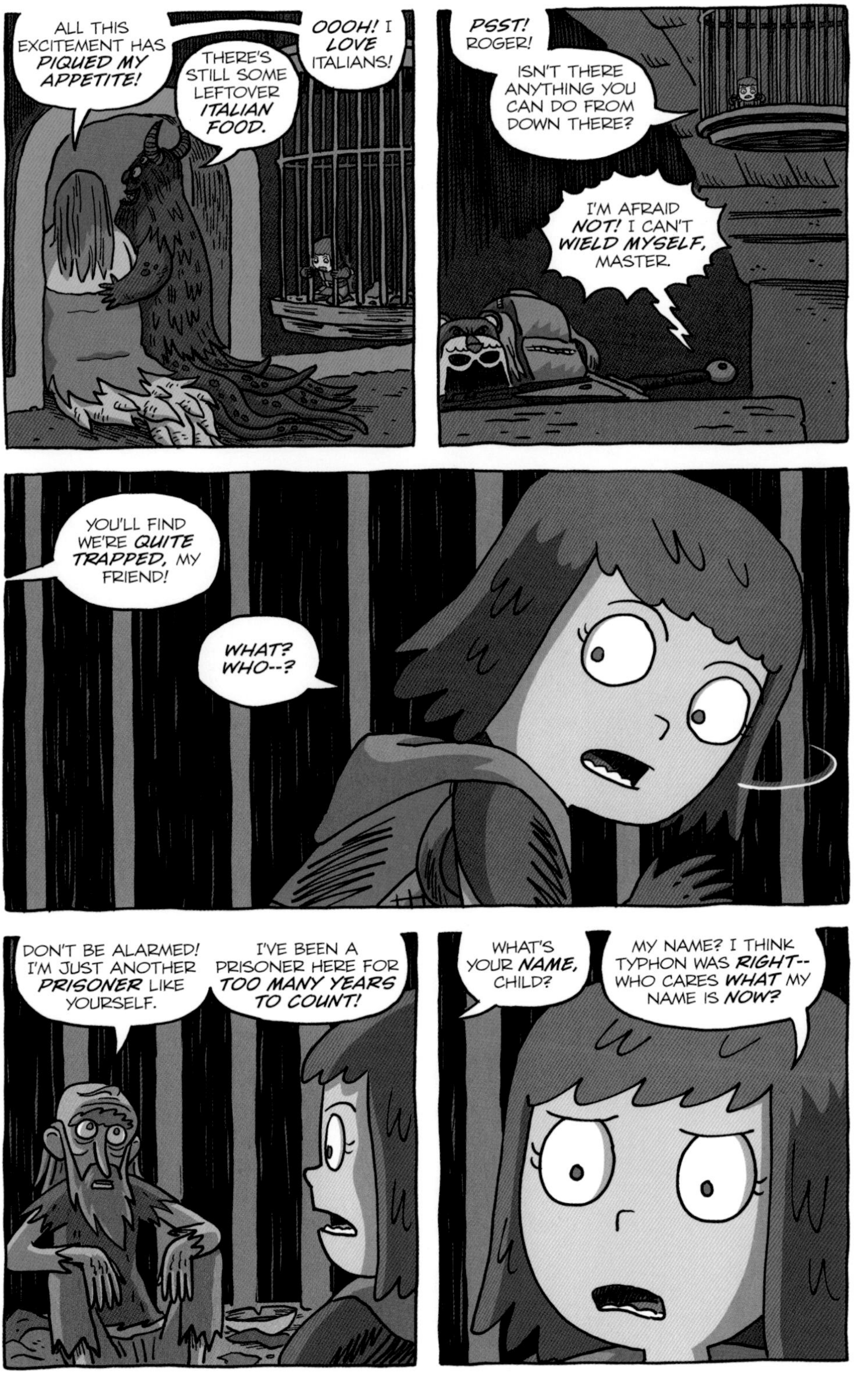

ALL THIS EXCITEMENT HAS PIQUED MY APPETITE!
THERE'S STILL SOME LEFTOVER ITALIAN FOOD.
OOOH! I LOVE ITALIANS!
PSST! ROGER!
ISN'T THERE ANYTHING YOU CAN DO FROM DOWN THERE?
I'M AFRAID NOT! I CAN'T WIELD MYSELF, MASTER.
YOU'LL FIND WE'RE QUITE TRAPPED, MY FRIEND!
WHAT? WHO--?
DON'T BE ALARMED! I'M JUST ANOTHER PRISONER LIKE YOURSELF.
I'VE BEEN A PRISONER HERE FOR TOO MANY YEARS TO COUNT!
WHAT'S YOUR NAME, CHILD?
MY NAME? I THINK TYPHON WAS RIGHT-- WHO CARES WHAT MY NAME IS NOW?

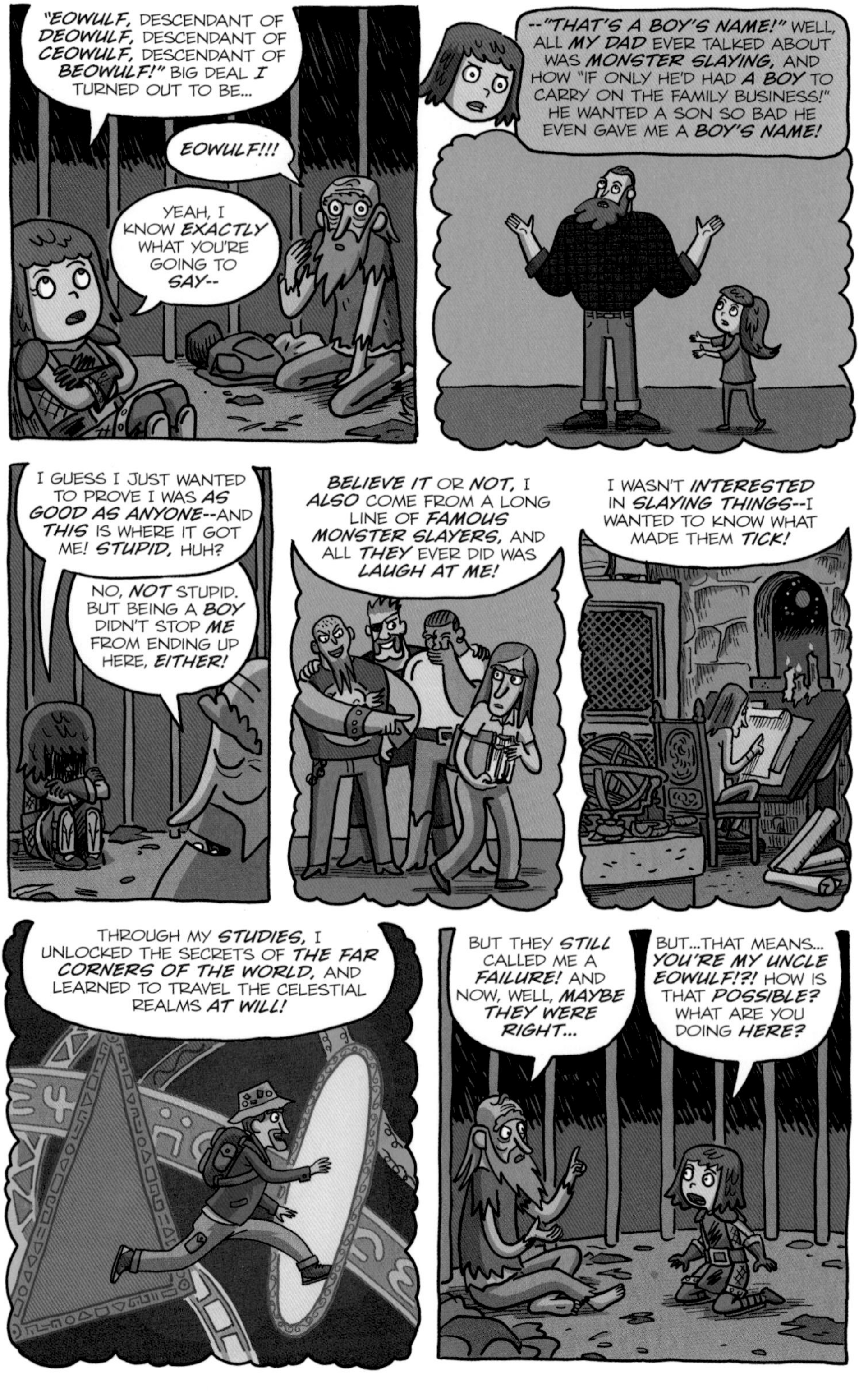
"EOWULF, DESCENDANT OF DEOWULF, DESCENDANT OF CEOWULF, DESCENDANT OF BEOWULF!" BIG DEAL I TURNED OUT TO BE...
EOWULF!!!
YEAH, I KNOW EXACTLY WHAT YOU'RE GOING TO SAY--
--"THAT'S A BOY'S NAME!" WELL, ALL MY DAD EVER TALKED ABOUT WAS MONSTER SLAYING, AND HOW "IF ONLY HE'D HAD A BOY TO CARRY ON THE FAMILY BUSINESS!" HE WANTED A SON SO BAD HE EVEN GAVE ME A BOY'S NAME!
I GUESS I JUST WANTED TO PROVE I WAS AS GOOD AS ANYONE--AND THIS IS WHERE IT GOT ME! STUPID, HUH?
NO, NOT STUPID. BUT BEING A BOY DIDN'T STOP ME FROM ENDING UP HERE, EITHER!
BELIEVE IT OR NOT, I ALSO COME FROM A LONG LINE OF FAMOUS MONSTER SLAYERS, AND ALL THEY EVER DID WAS LAUGH AT ME!
I WASN'T INTERESTED IN SLAYING THINGS--I WANTED TO KNOW WHAT MADE THEM TICK!
THROUGH MY STUDIES, I UNLOCKED THE SECRETS OF THE FAR CORNERS OF THE WORLD, AND LEARNED TO TRAVEL THE CELESTIAL REALMS AT WILL!
BUT THEY STILL CALLED ME A FAILURE! AND NOW, WELL, MAYBE THEY WERE RIGHT...
BUT...THAT MEANS... YOU'RE MY UNCLE EOWULF!?! HOW IS THAT POSSIBLE? WHAT ARE YOU DOING HERE?

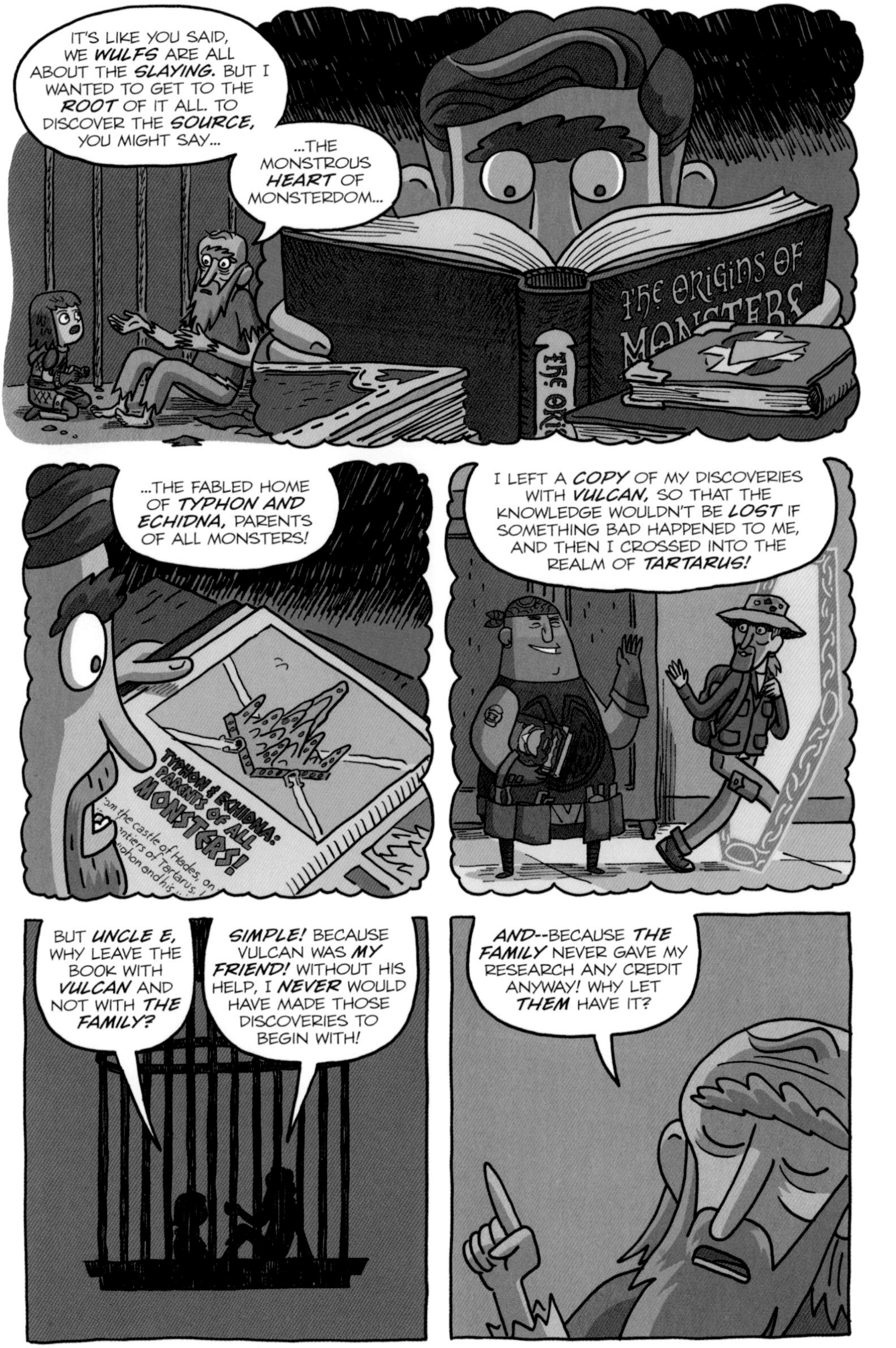
IT'S LIKE YOU SAID, WE WULFS ARE ALL ABOUT THE SLAYING. BUT I WANTED TO GET TO THE ROOT OF IT ALL. TO DISCOVER THE SOURCE, YOU MIGHT SAY...
...THE MONSTROUS HEART OF MONSTERDOM...
THE ORIGINS OF
...THE FABLED HOME OF TYPHON AND ECHIDNA, PARENTS OF ALL MONSTERS!
TYPHON & ECHIDNA: PARENTS OF ALL MONSTERS!
I LEFT A COPY OF MY DISCOVERIES WITH VULCAN, SO THAT THE KNOWLEDGE WOULDN'T BE LOST IF SOMETHING BAD HAPPENED TO ME, AND THEN I CROSSED INTO THE REALM OF TARTARUS!
BUT UNCLE E, WHY LEAVE THE BOOK WITH VULCAN AND NOT WITH THE FAMILY?
SIMPLE! BECAUSE VULCAN WAS MY FRIEND! WITHOUT HIS HELP, I NEVER WOULD HAVE MADE THOSE DISCOVERIES TO BEGIN WITH!
AND--BECAUSE THE FAMILY NEVER GAVE MY RESEARCH ANY CREDIT ANYWAY! WHY LET THEM HAVE IT?

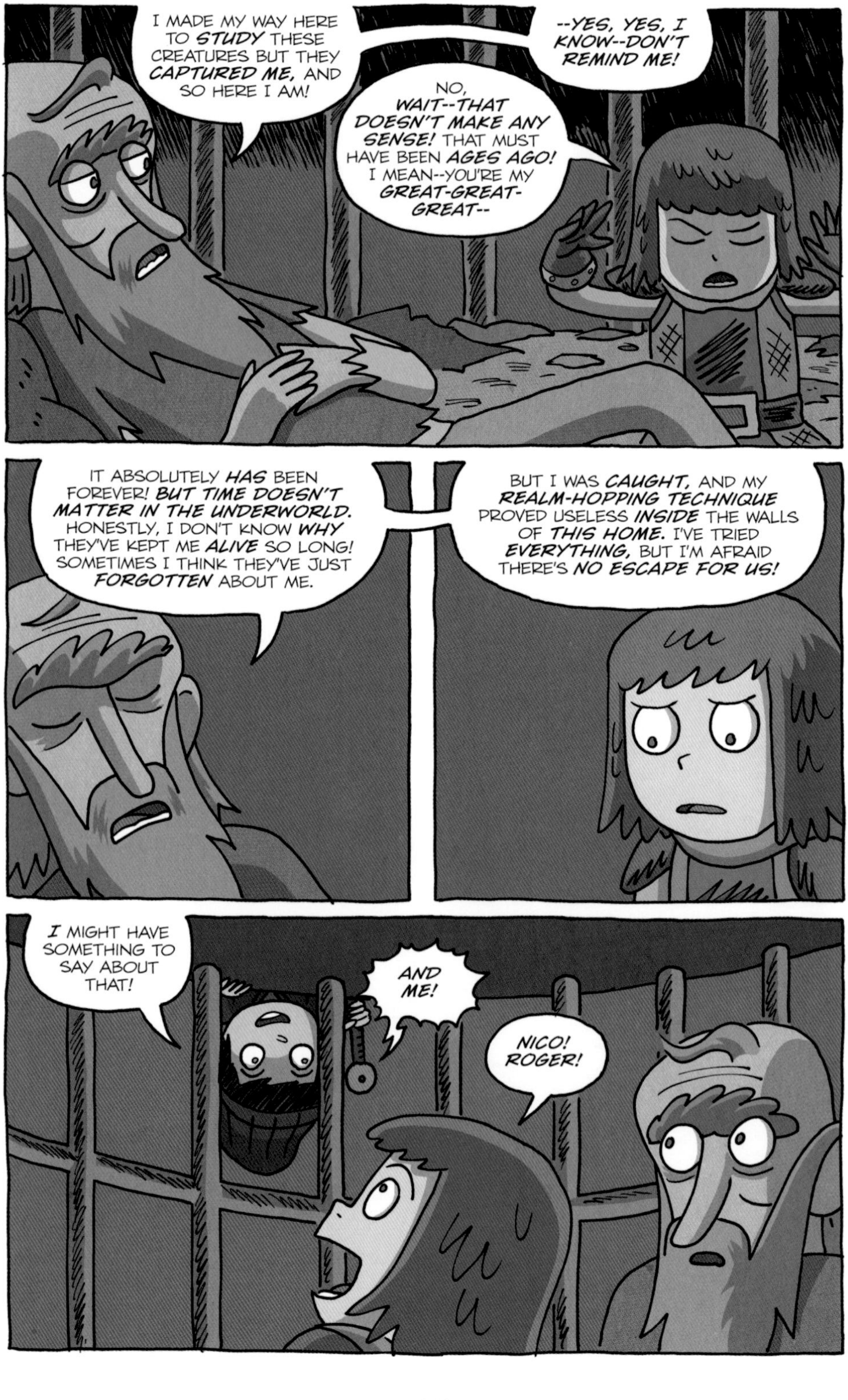
I MADE MY WAY HERE TO STUDY THESE CREATURES BUT THEY CAPTURED ME, AND SO HERE I AM!
NO, WAIT--THAT DOESN'T MAKE ANY SENSE! THAT MUST HAVE BEEN AGES AGO! I MEAN--YOU'RE MY GREAT-GREAT-GREAT--
--YES, YES, I KNOW--DON'T REMIND ME!
IT ABSOLUTELY HAS BEEN FOREVER! BUT TIME DOESN'T MATTER IN THE UNDERWORLD. HONESTLY, I DON'T KNOW WHY THEY'VE KEPT ME ALIVE SO LONG! SOMETIMES I THINK THEY'VE JUST FORGOTTEN ABOUT ME.
BUT I WAS CAUGHT, AND MY REALM-HOPPING TECHNIQUE PROVED USELESS INSIDE THE WALLS OF THIS HOME. I'VE TRIED EVERYTHING, BUT I'M AFRAID THERE'S NO ESCAPE FOR US!
I MIGHT HAVE SOMETHING TO SAY ABOUT THAT!
AND ME!
NICO! ROGER!

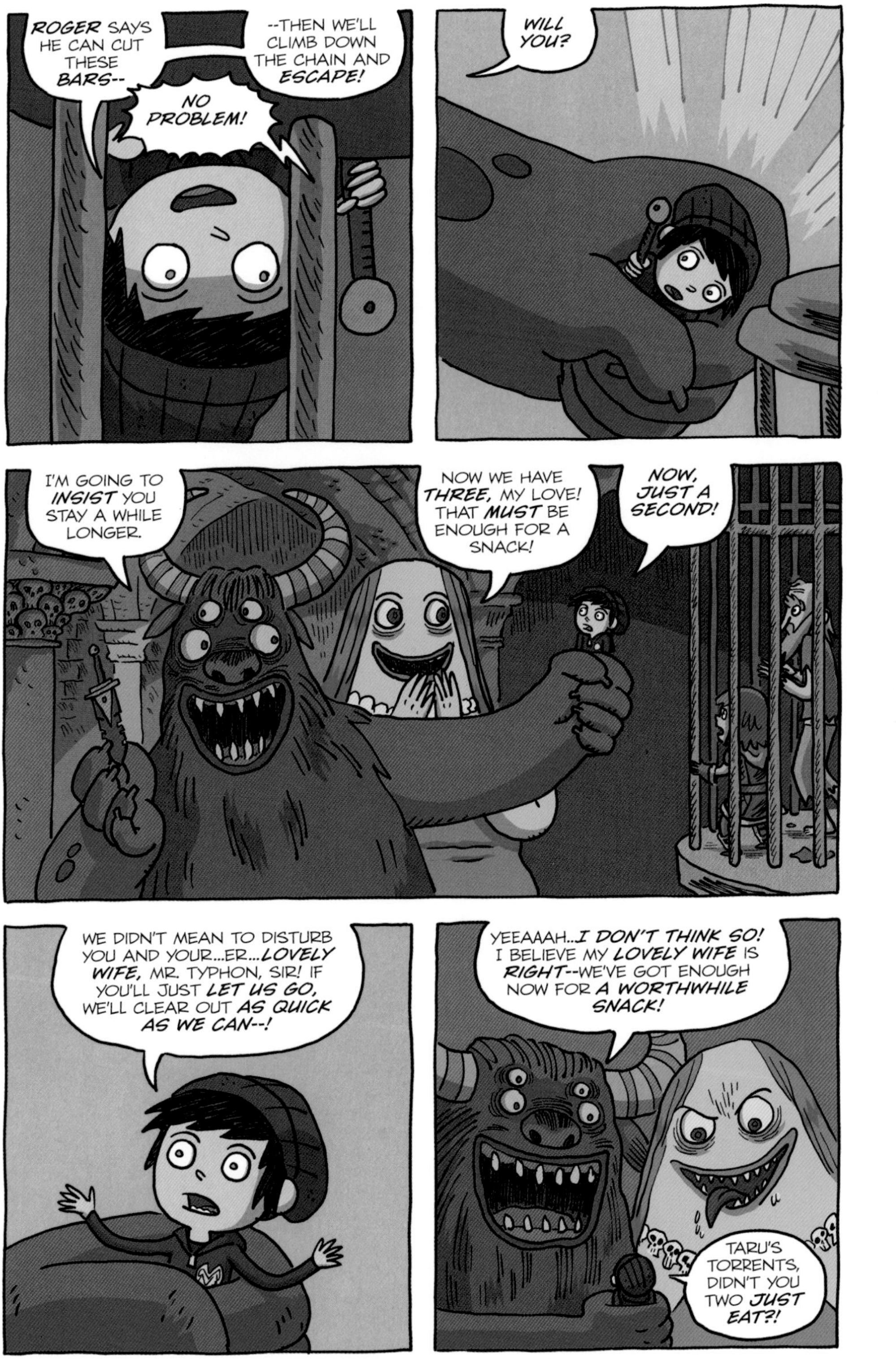
ROGER SAYS HE CAN CUT THESE BARS--
NO PROBLEM!
--THEN WE'LL CLIMB DOWN THE CHAIN AND ESCAPE!
WILL YOU?
I'M GOING TO INSIST YOU STAY A WHILE LONGER.
NOW WE HAVE THREE, MY LOVE! THAT MUST BE ENOUGH FOR A SNACK!
NOW, JUST A SECOND!
WE DIDN'T MEAN TO DISTURB YOU AND YOUR...ER...LOVELY WIFE, MR. TYPHON, SIR! IF YOU'LL JUST LET US GO, WE'LL CLEAR OUT AS QUICK AS WE CAN--!
YEEAAAH...I DON'T THINK SO! I BELIEVE MY LOVELY WIFE IS RIGHT--WE'VE GOT ENOUGH NOW FOR A WORTHWHILE SNACK!
TARU'S TORRENTS, DIDN'T YOU TWO JUST EAT?!

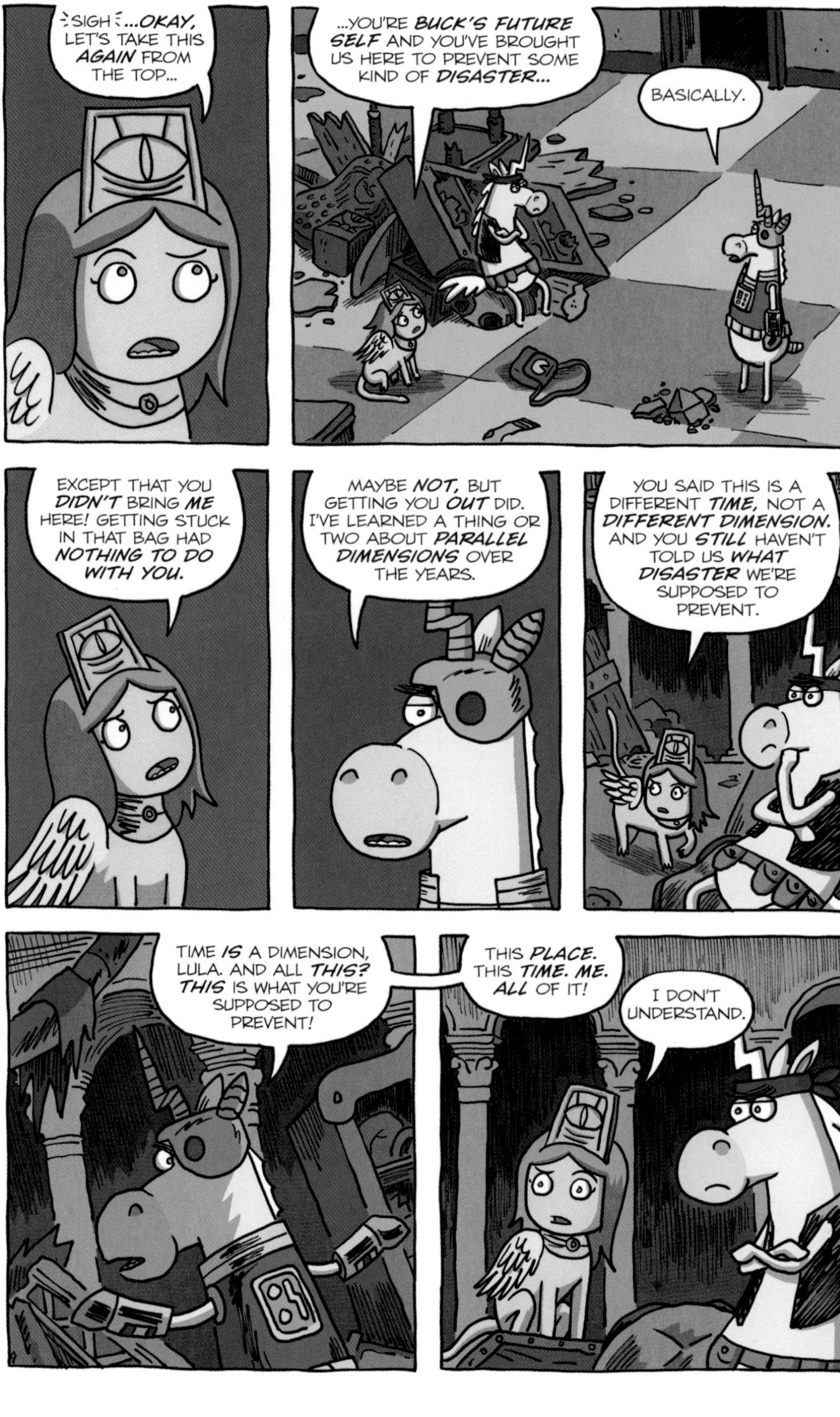
SIGH ...OKAY, LET'S TAKE THIS AGAIN FROM THE TOP...
...YOU'RE BUCK'S FUTURE SELF AND YOU'VE BROUGHT US HERE TO PREVENT SOME KIND OF DISASTER...
BASICALLY.
EXCEPT THAT YOU DIDN'T BRING ME HERE! GETTING STUCK IN THAT BAG HAD NOTHING TO DO WITH YOU.
MAYBE NOT, BUT GETTING YOU OUT DID. I'VE LEARNED A THING OR TWO ABOUT PARALLEL DIMENSIONS OVER THE YEARS.
YOU SAID THIS IS A DIFFERENT TIME, NOT A DIFFERENT DIMENSION. AND YOU STILL HAVEN'T TOLD US WHAT DISASTER WE'RE SUPPOSED TO PREVENT.
TIME IS A DIMENSION, LULA. AND ALL THIS? THIS IS WHAT YOU'RE SUPPOSED TO PREVENT!
THIS PLACE. THIS TIME. ME. ALL OF IT!
I DON'T UNDERSTAND.

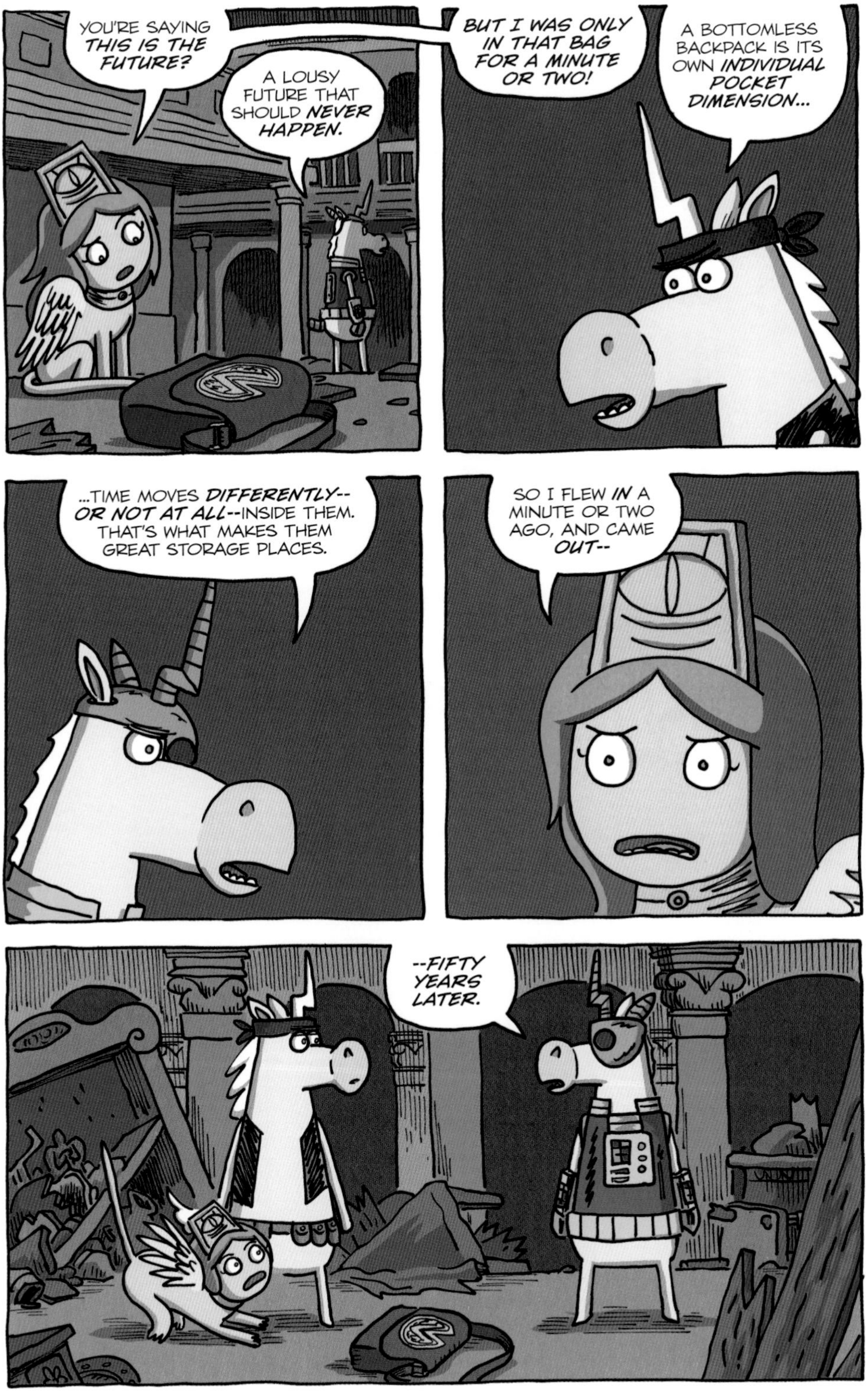
YOU'RE SAYING THIS IS THE FUTURE?
A LOUSY FUTURE THAT SHOULD NEVER HAPPEN.
BUT I WAS ONLY IN THAT BAG FOR A MINUTE OR TWO!
A BOTTOMLESS BACKPACK IS ITS OWN INDIVIDUAL POCKET DIMENSION...
...TIME MOVES DIFFERENTLY-- OR NOT AT ALL--INSIDE THEM. THAT'S WHAT MAKES THEM GREAT STORAGE PLACES.
SO I FLEW IN A MINUTE OR TWO AGO, AND CAME OUT--
--FIFTY YEARS LATER.

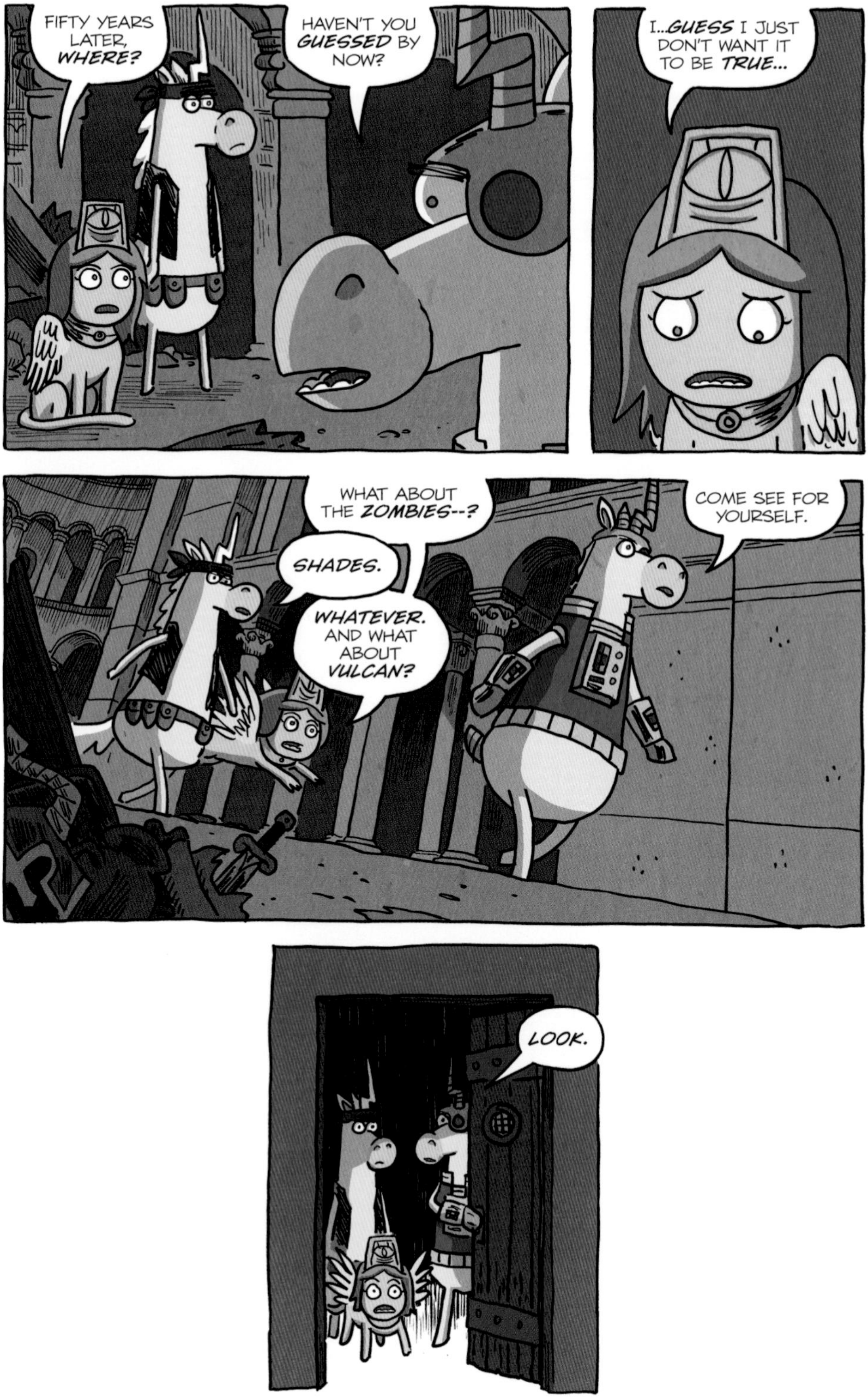
FIFTY YEARS LATER, WHERE?
HAVEN'T YOU GUESSED BY NOW?
I...GUESS I JUST DON'T WANT IT TO BE TRUE...
WHAT ABOUT THE ZOMBIES--?
SHADES.
WHATEVER. AND WHAT ABOUT VULCAN?
COME SEE FOR YOURSELF.
LOOK.

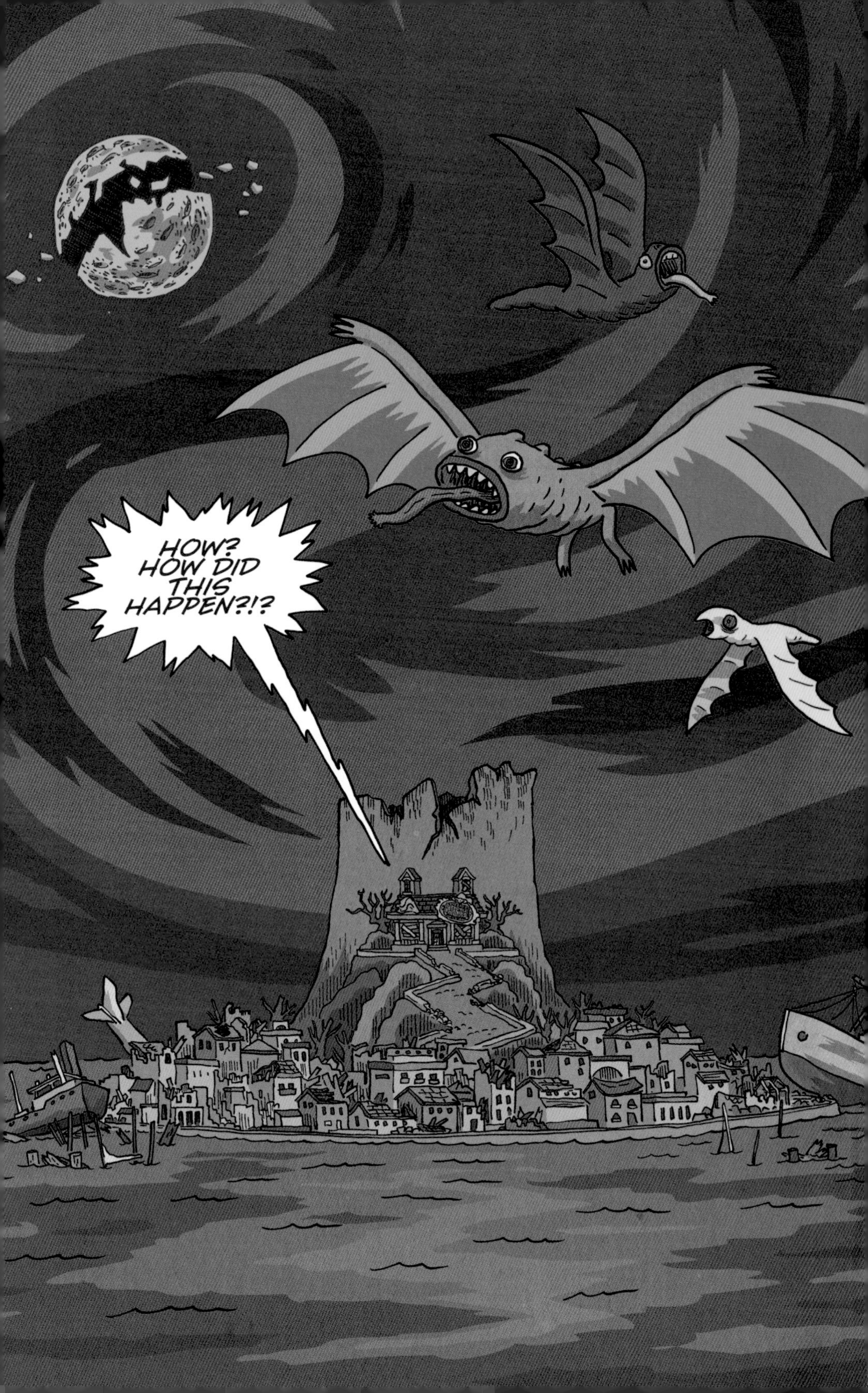
HOW? HOW DID THIS HAPPEN?!?

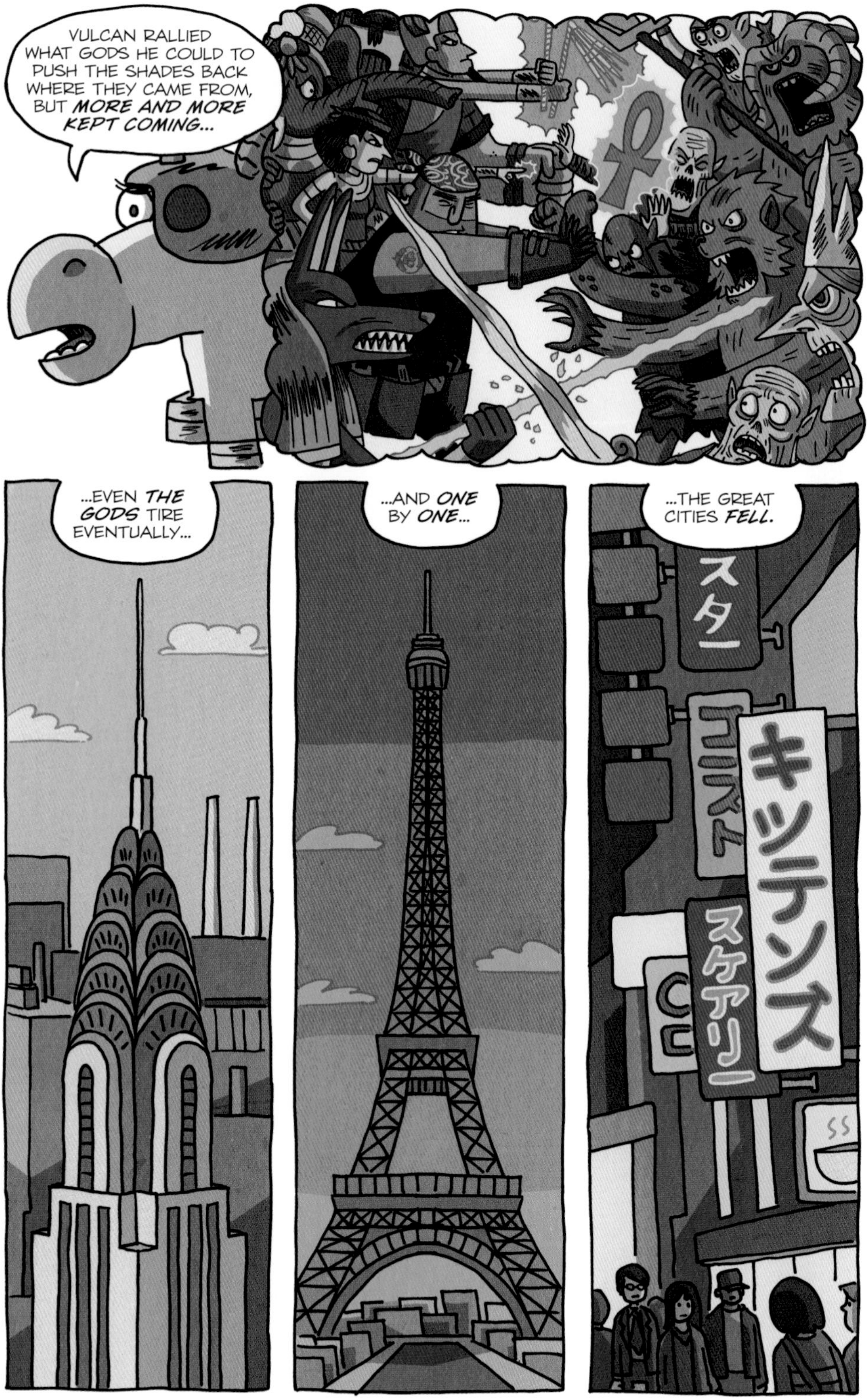
VULCAN RALLIED WHAT GODS HE COULD TO PUSH THE SHADES BACK WHERE THEY CAME FROM, BUT **MORE AND MORE KEPT COMING...**
...EVEN ***THE GODS*** TIRE EVENTUALLY...
...AND ***ONE*** BY ***ONE***...
...THE GREAT CITIES ***FELL.***
スター
スケアリー

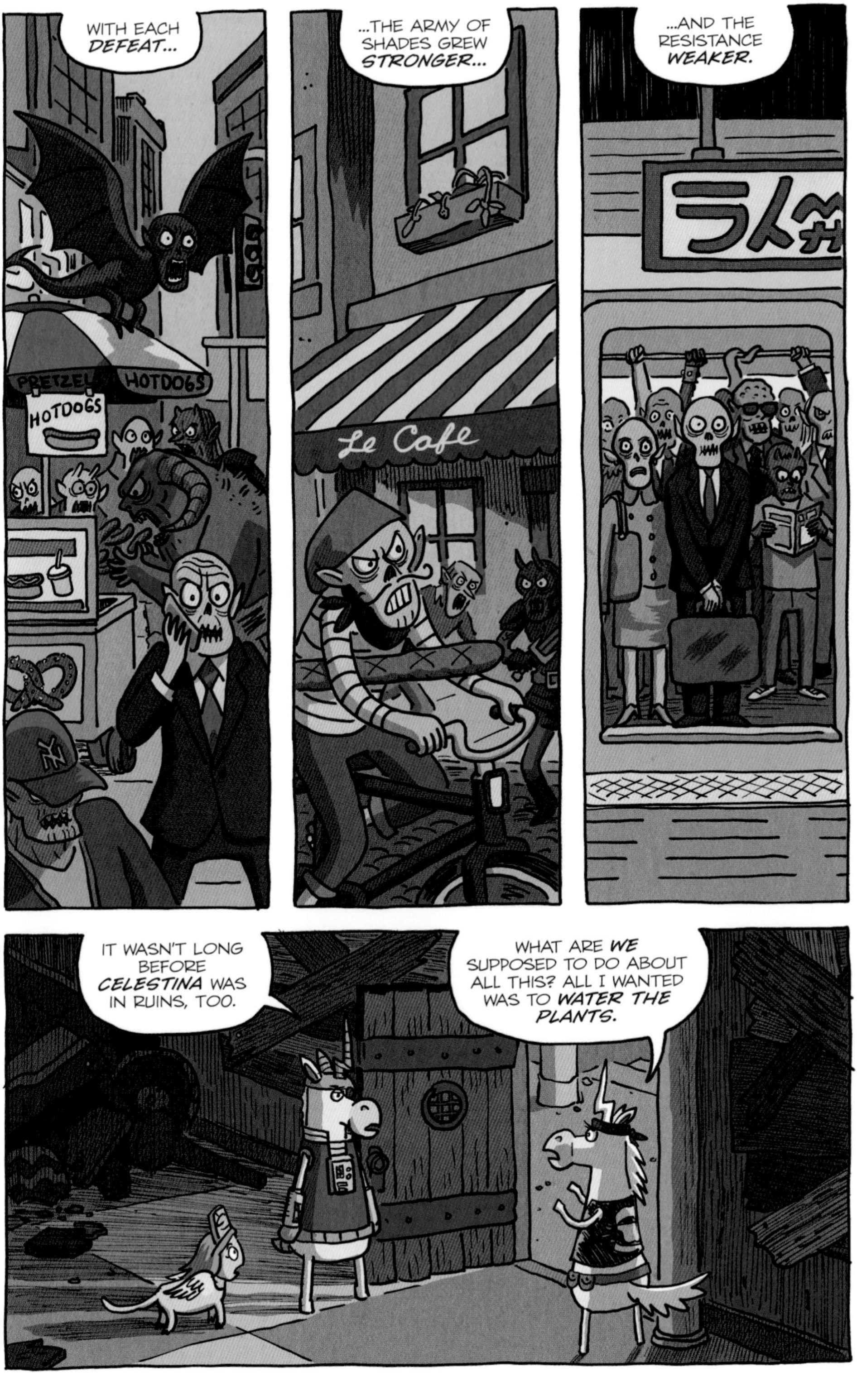
WITH EACH DEFEAT...
PRETZELS HOTDOGS
HOTDOGS
...THE ARMY OF SHADES GREW STRONGER...
Le Cafe
...AND THE RESISTANCE WEAKER.
IT WASN'T LONG BEFORE CELESTINA WAS IN RUINS, TOO.
WHAT ARE WE SUPPOSED TO DO ABOUT ALL THIS? ALL I WANTED WAS TO WATER THE PLANTS.

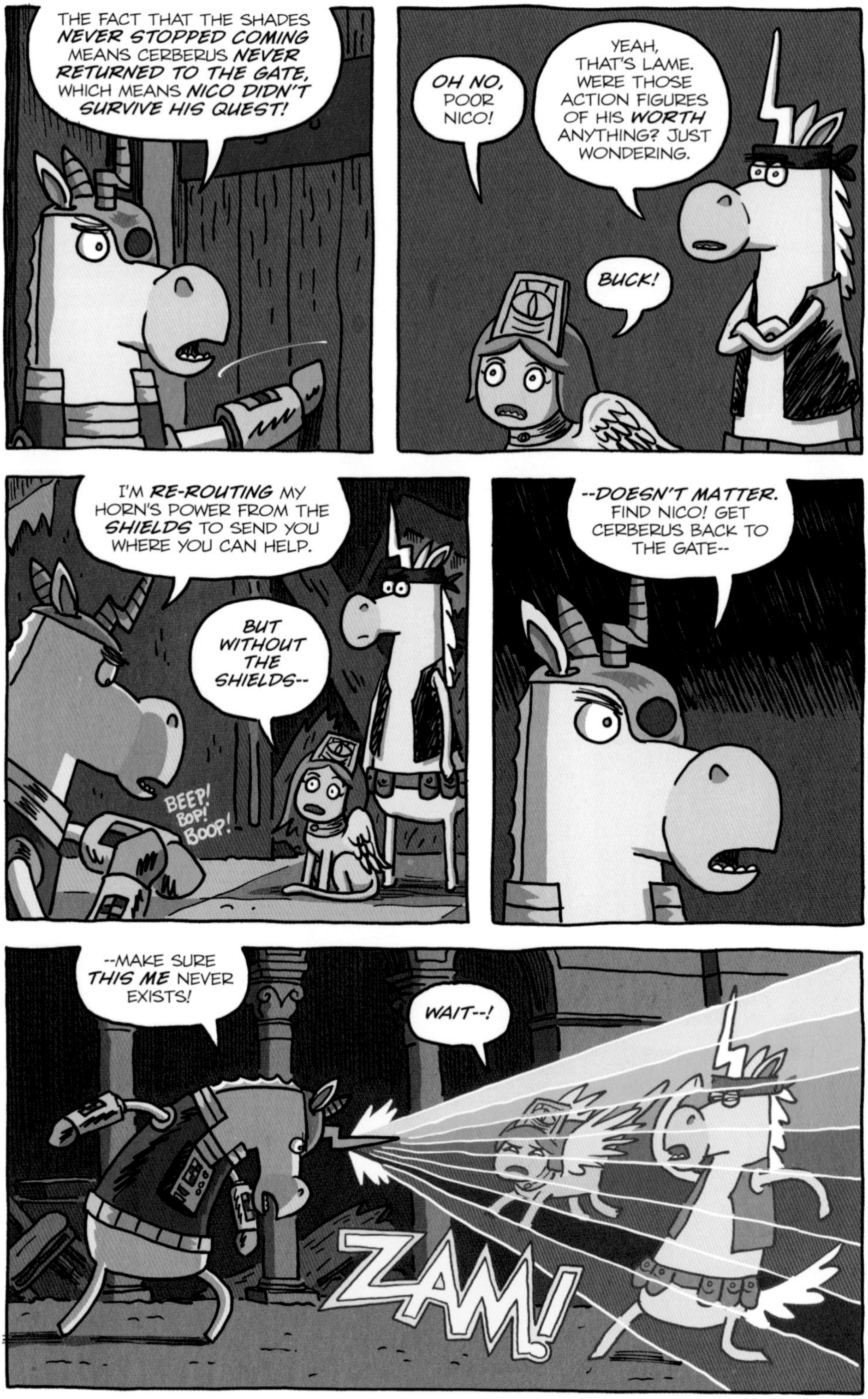
THE FACT THAT THE SHADES NEVER STOPPED COMING MEANS CERBERUS NEVER RETURNED TO THE GATE, WHICH MEANS NICO DIDN'T SURVIVE HIS QUEST!
OH NO, POOR NICO!
YEAH, THAT'S LAME. WERE THOSE ACTION FIGURES OF HIS WORTH ANYTHING? JUST WONDERING.
BUCK!
I'M RE-ROUTING MY HORN'S POWER FROM THE SHIELDS TO SEND YOU WHERE YOU CAN HELP.
BUT WITHOUT THE SHIELDS--
BEEP! BOP! BOOP!
--DOESN'T MATTER. FIND NICO! GET CERBERUS BACK TO THE GATE--
--MAKE SURE THIS ME NEVER EXISTS!
WAIT--!
ZAM!

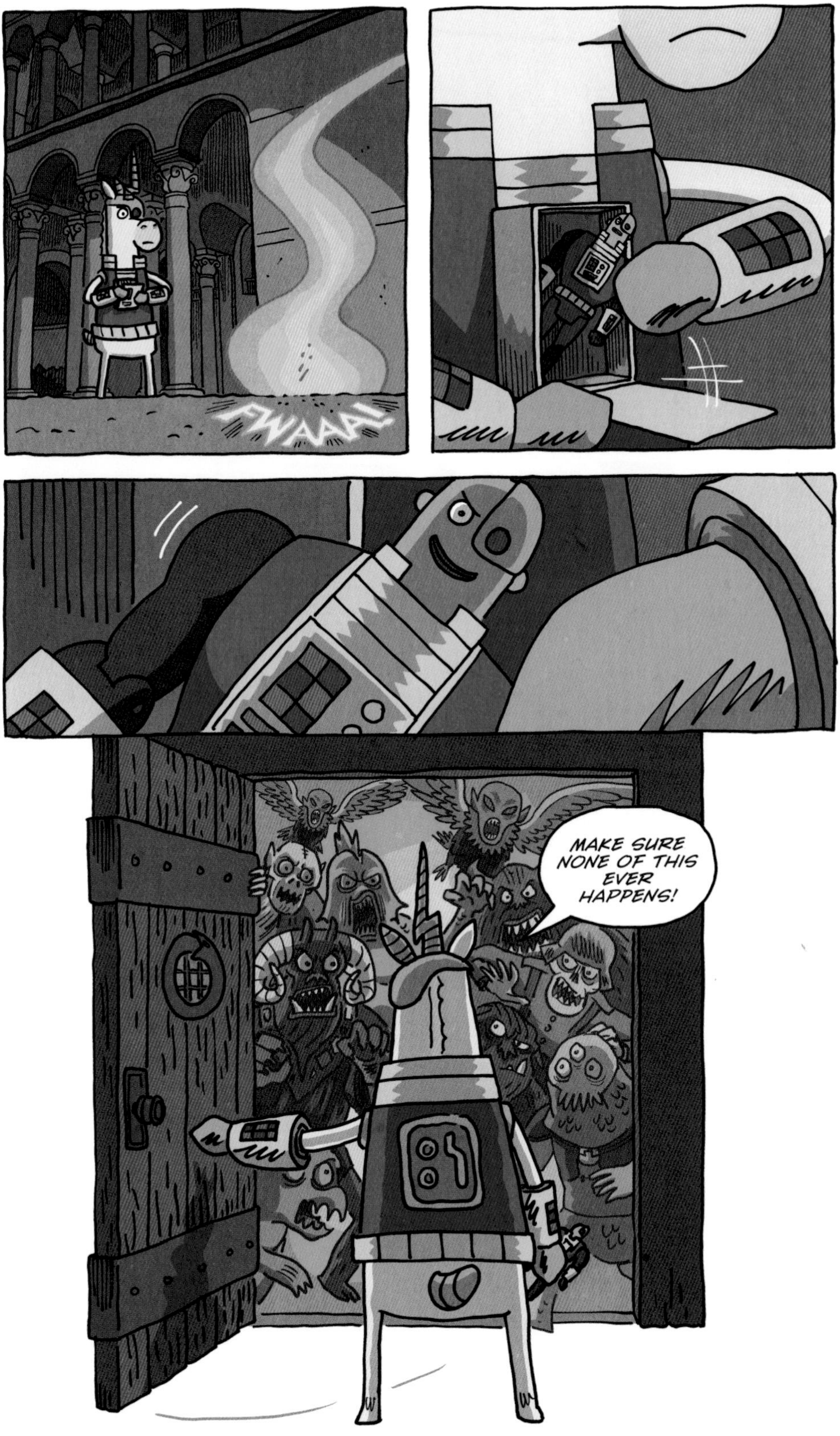
FWAAAL!
MAKE SURE NONE OF THIS EVER HAPPENS!

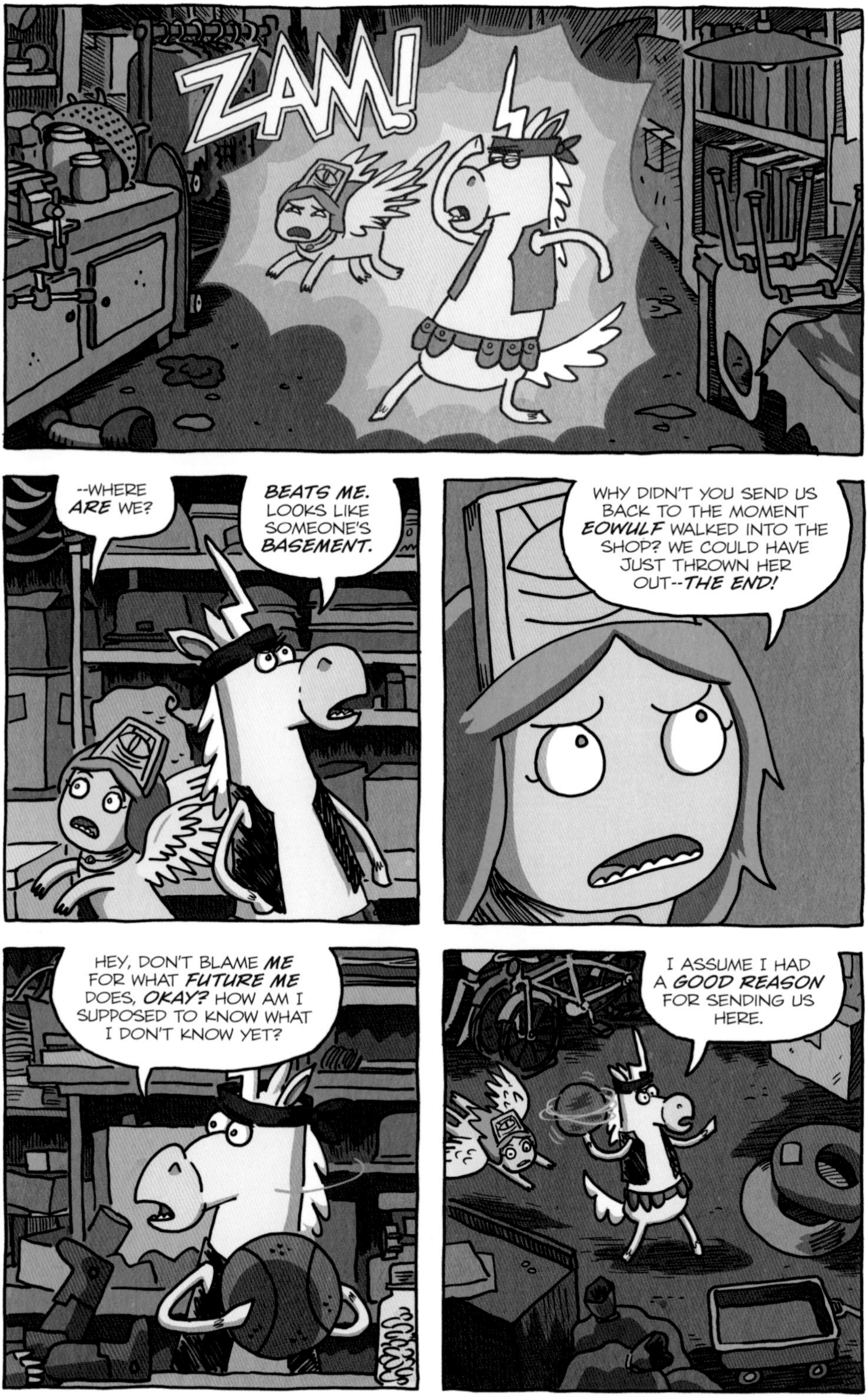
ZAM!
--WHERE ARE WE?
BEATS ME. LOOKS LIKE SOMEONE'S BASEMENT.
WHY DIDN'T YOU SEND US BACK TO THE MOMENT EOWULF WALKED INTO THE SHOP? WE COULD HAVE JUST THROWN HER OUT--THE END!
HEY, DON'T BLAME ME FOR WHAT FUTURE ME DOES, OKAY? HOW AM I SUPPOSED TO KNOW WHAT I DON'T KNOW YET?
I ASSUME I HAD A GOOD REASON FOR SENDING US HERE.

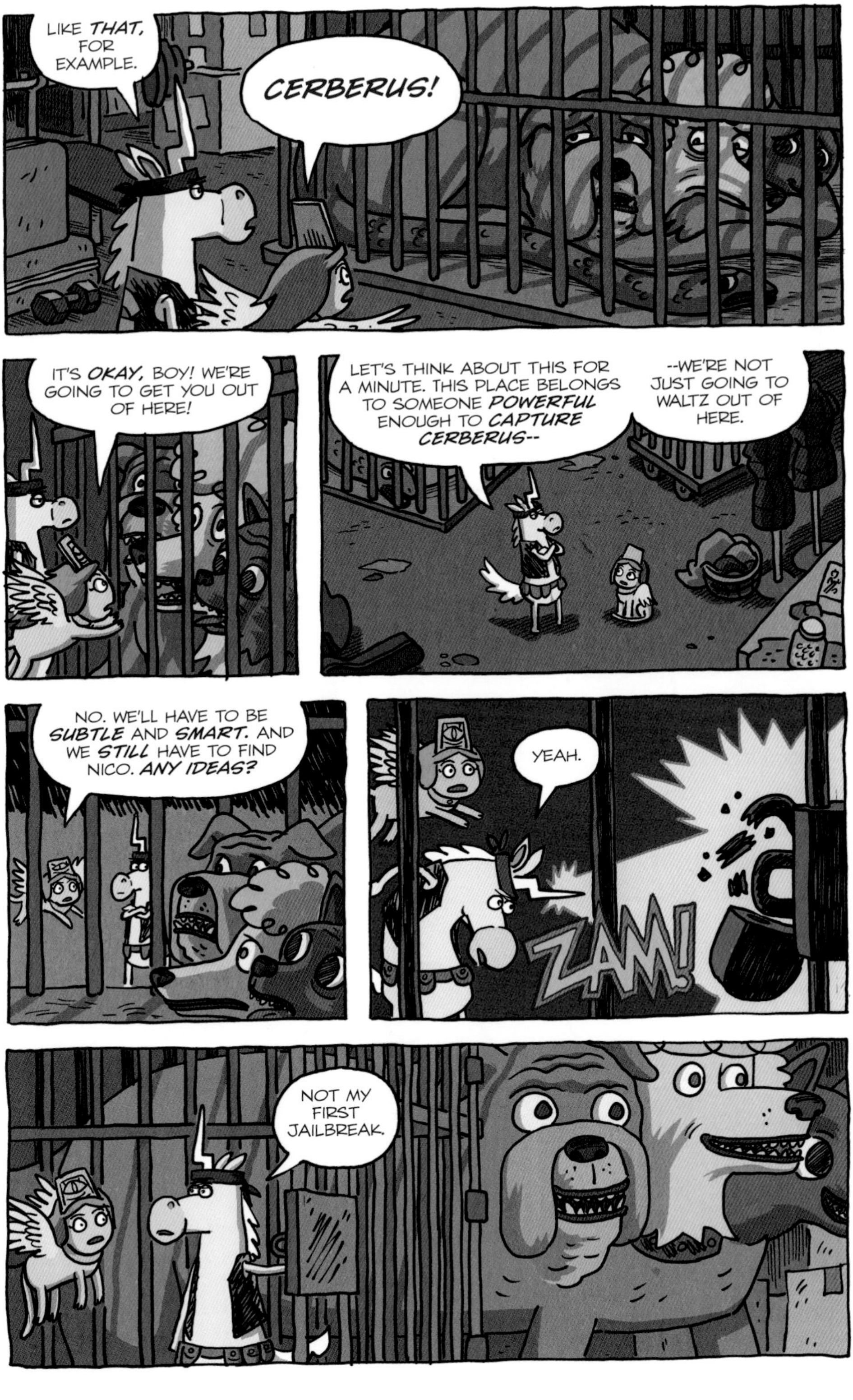
LIKE THAT, FOR EXAMPLE.
CERBERUS!
IT'S OKAY, BOY! WE'RE GOING TO GET YOU OUT OF HERE!
LET'S THINK ABOUT THIS FOR A MINUTE. THIS PLACE BELONGS TO SOMEONE POWERFUL ENOUGH TO CAPTURE CERBERUS--
--WE'RE NOT JUST GOING TO WALTZ OUT OF HERE.
NO. WE'LL HAVE TO BE SUBTLE AND SMART. AND WE STILL HAVE TO FIND NICO. ANY IDEAS?
YEAH.
ZAM!
NOT MY FIRST JAILBREAK.

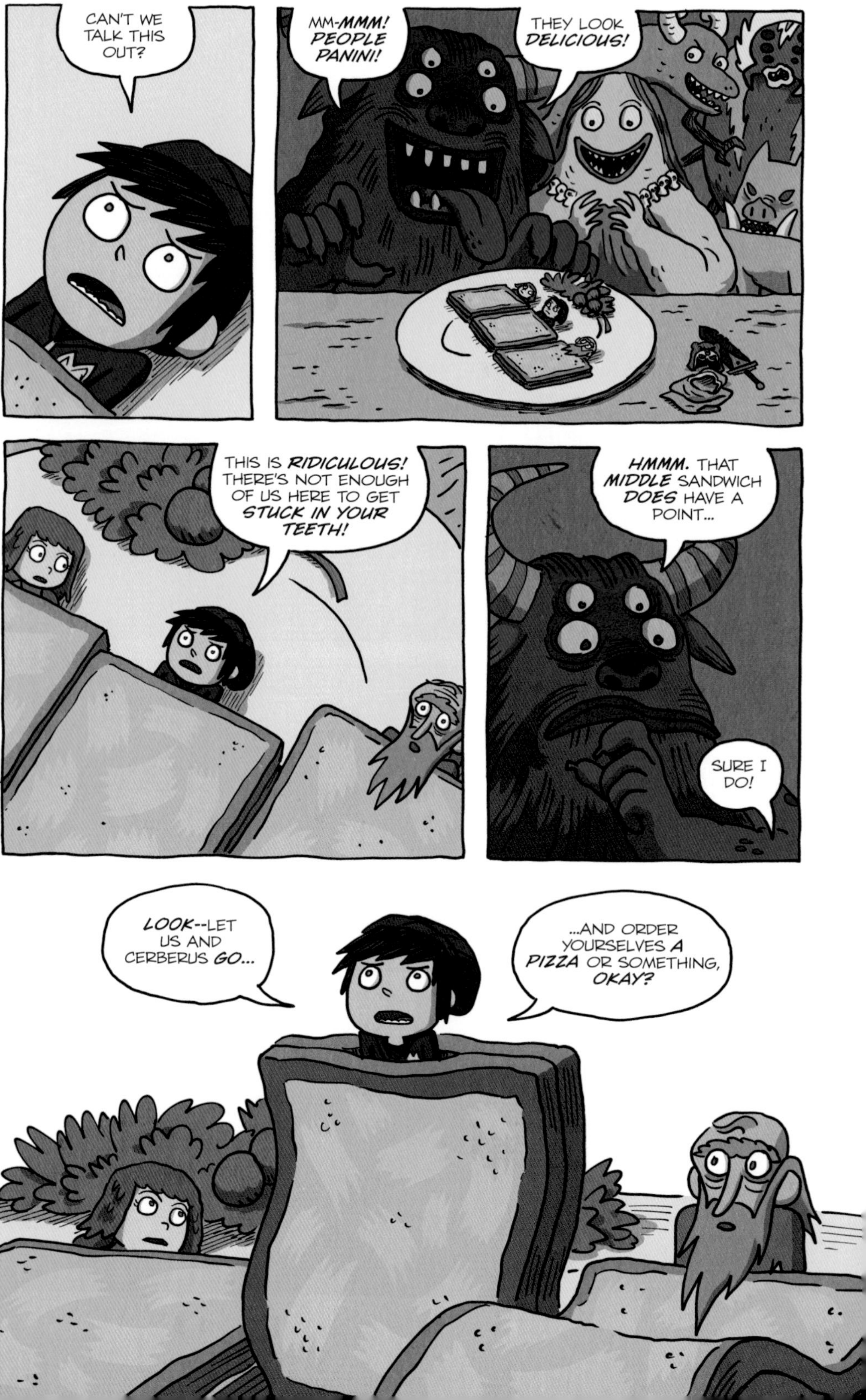
CAN'T WE TALK THIS OUT?
MM-MMM! PEOPLE PANINI!
THEY LOOK DELICIOUS!
THIS IS RIDICULOUS! THERE'S NOT ENOUGH OF US HERE TO GET STUCK IN YOUR TEETH!
HMMM. THAT MIDDLE SANDWICH DOES HAVE A POINT...
SURE I DO!
LOOK--LET US AND CERBERUS GO...
...AND ORDER YOURSELVES A PIZZA OR SOMETHING, OKAY?

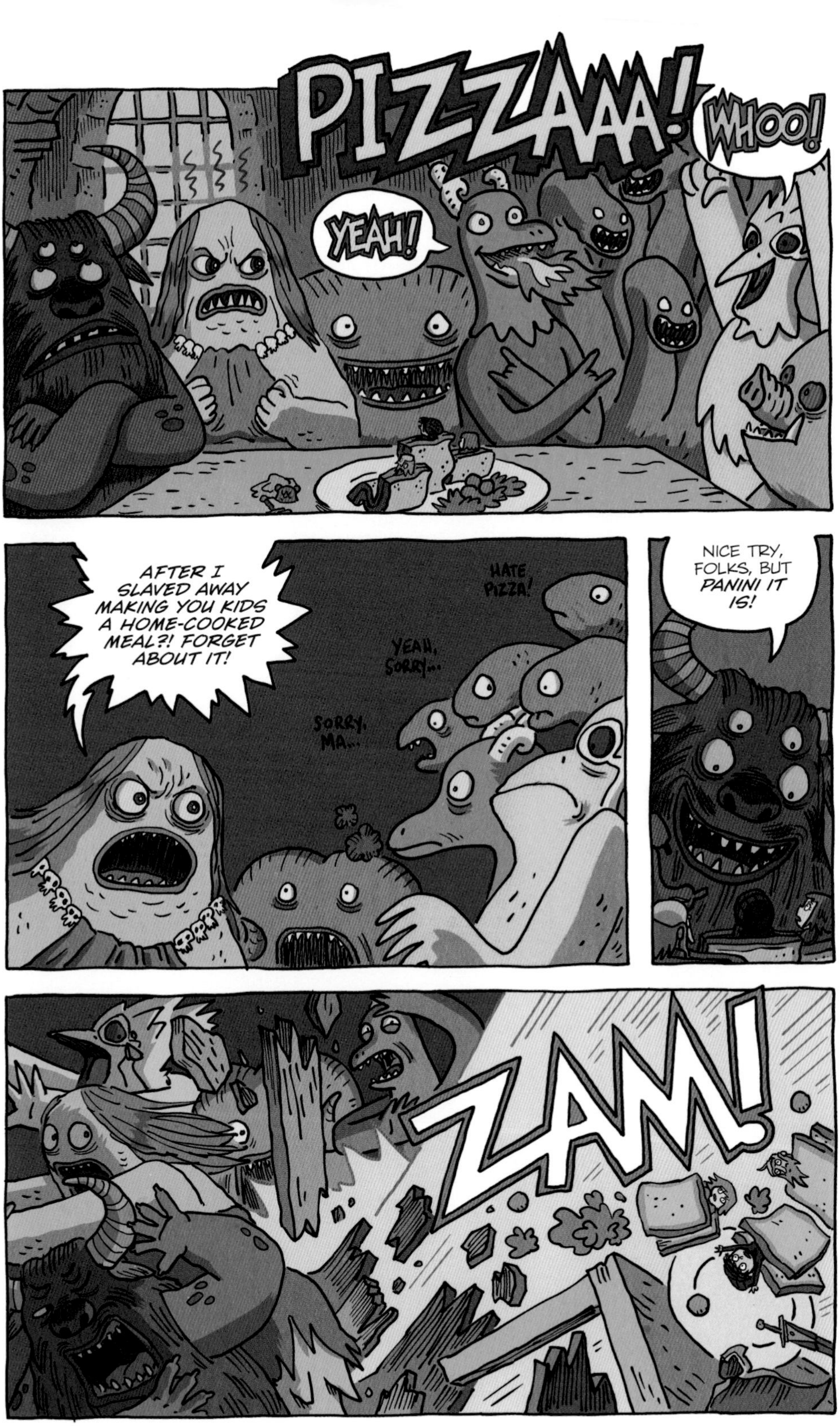
PIZZAAA!
WHOO!
YEAH!
AFTER I SLAVED AWAY MAKING YOU KIDS A HOME-COOKED MEAL?! FORGET ABOUT IT!
HATE PIZZA!
YEAH, SORRY...
SORRY, MA...
NICE TRY, FOLKS, BUT *PANINI* IT IS!
ZAM!

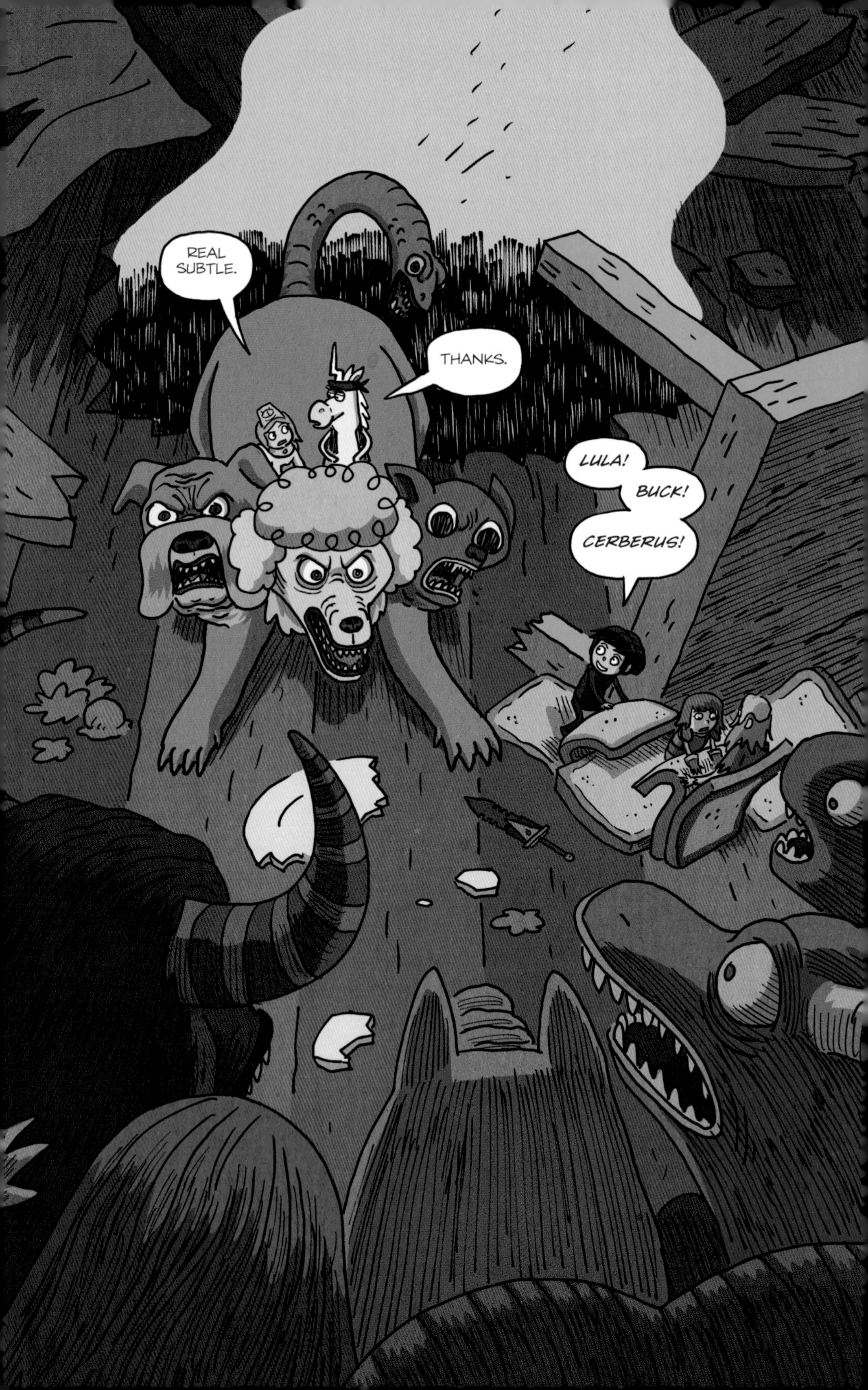
REAL SUBTLE.
THANKS.
LULA!
BUCK!
CERBERUS!

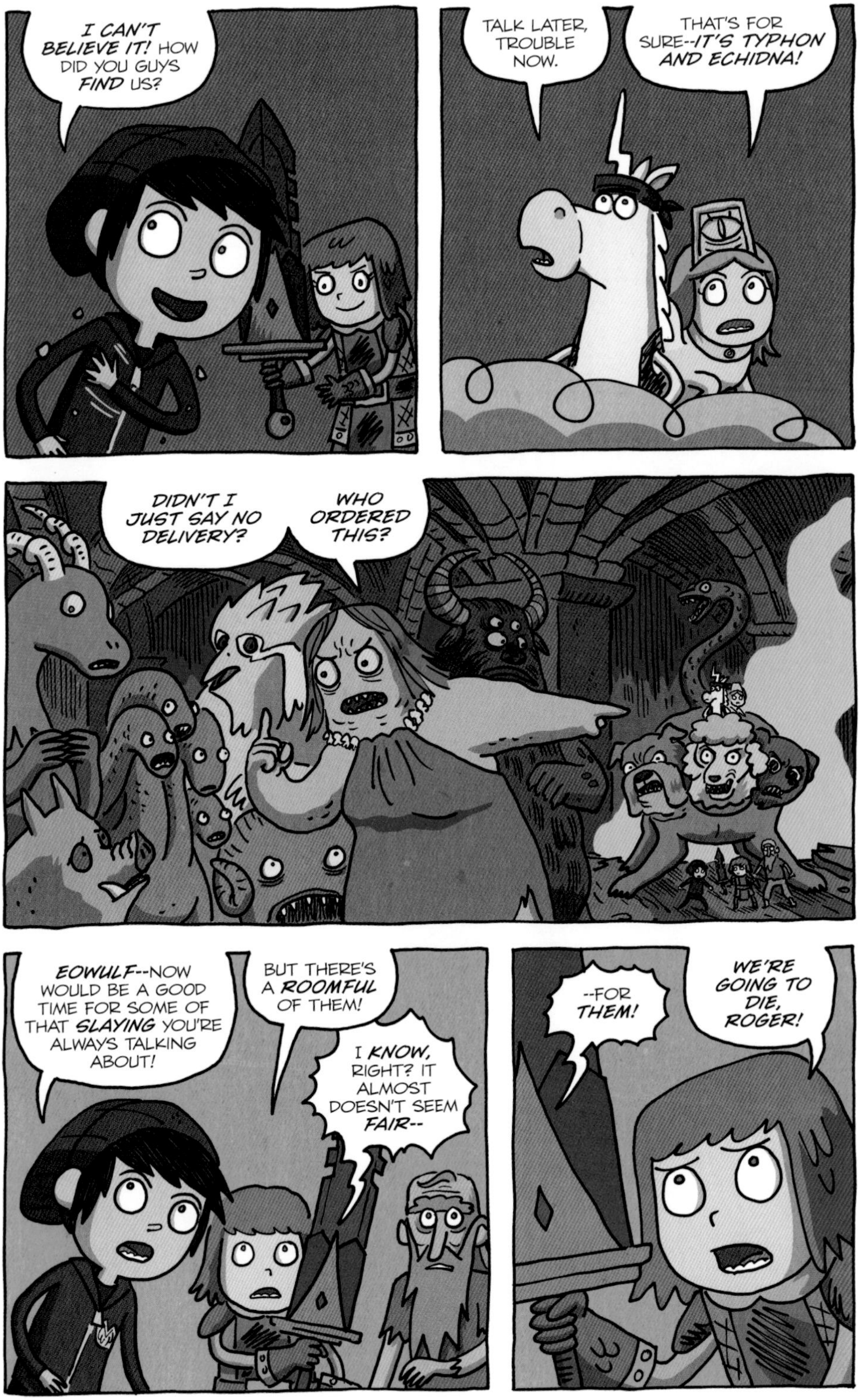
I CAN'T BELIEVE IT! HOW DID YOU GUYS FIND US?
TALK LATER, TROUBLE NOW.
THAT'S FOR SURE--IT'S TYPHON AND ECHIDNA!
DIDN'T I JUST SAY NO DELIVERY?
WHO ORDERED THIS?
EOWULF--NOW WOULD BE A GOOD TIME FOR SOME OF THAT SLAYING YOU'RE ALWAYS TALKING ABOUT!
BUT THERE'S A ROOMFUL OF THEM!
I KNOW, RIGHT? IT ALMOST DOESN'T SEEM FAIR--
--FOR THEM!
WE'RE GOING TO DIE, ROGER!

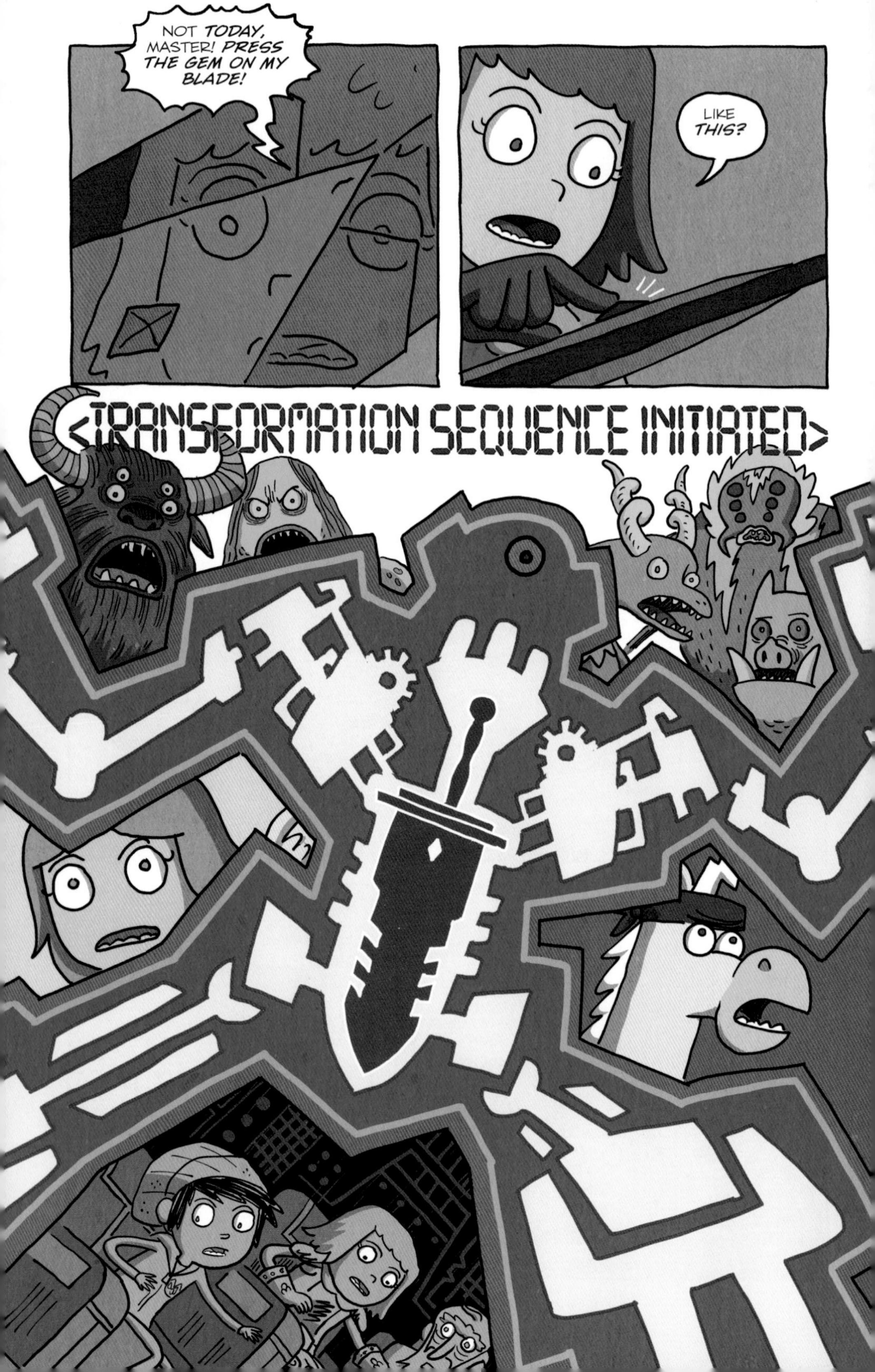
NOT TODAY, MASTER! PRESS THE GEM ON MY BLADE!
LIKE THIS?
<TRANSFORMATION SEQUENCE INITIATED>

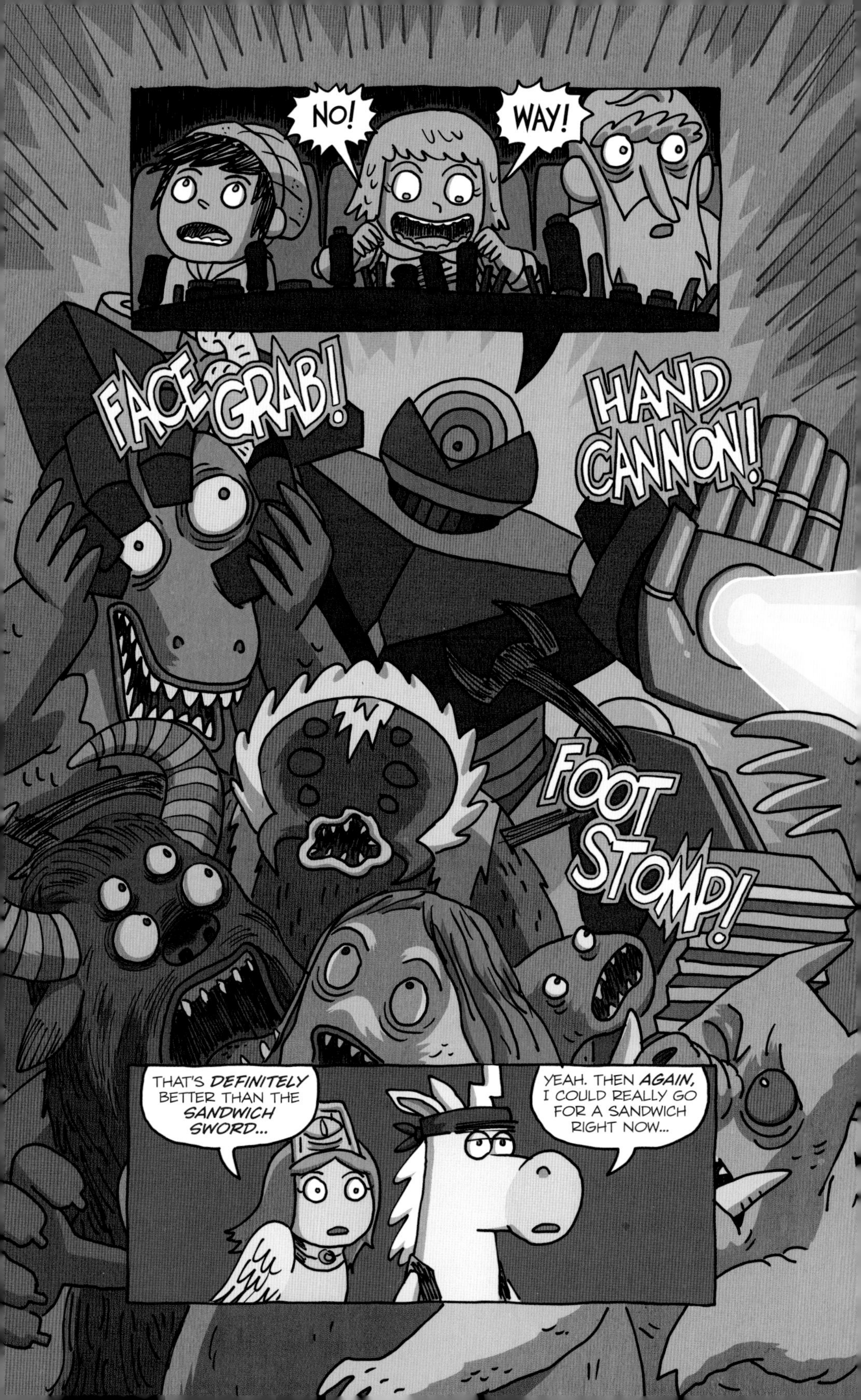
NO!
WAY!
FACE GRAB!
HAND CANNON!
FOOT STOMP!
THAT'S *DEFINITELY* BETTER THAN THE *SANDWICH SWORD*...
YEAH. THEN *AGAIN,* I COULD REALLY GO FOR A SANDWICH RIGHT NOW...

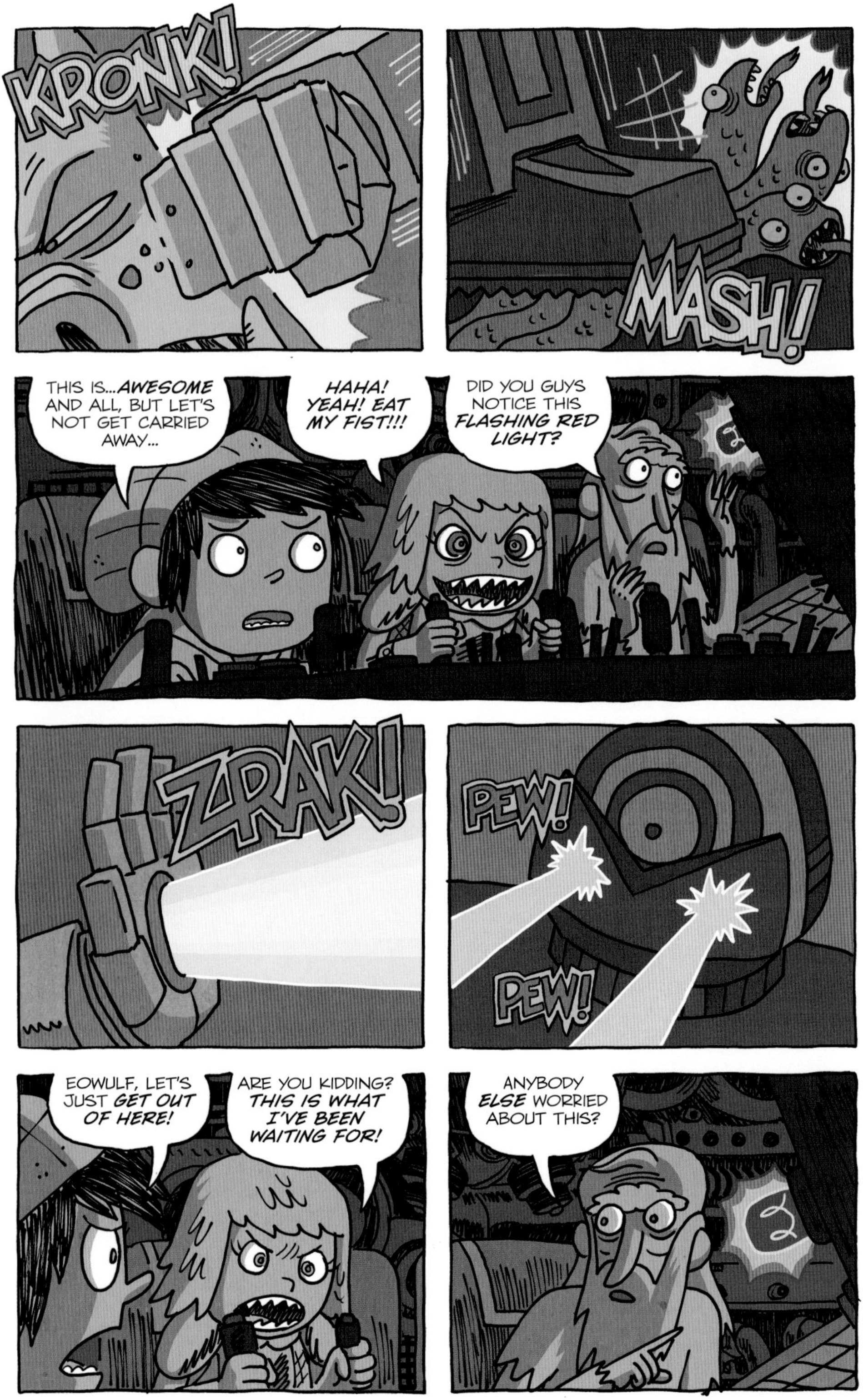
KRONK!
MASH!
THIS IS...AWESOME AND ALL, BUT LET'S NOT GET CARRIED AWAY...
HAHA! YEAH! EAT MY FIST!!!
DID YOU GUYS NOTICE THIS FLASHING RED LIGHT?
ZRAK!
PEW!
PEW!
EOWULF, LET'S JUST GET OUT OF HERE!
ARE YOU KIDDING? THIS IS WHAT I'VE BEEN WAITING FOR!
ANYBODY ELSE WORRIED ABOUT THIS?

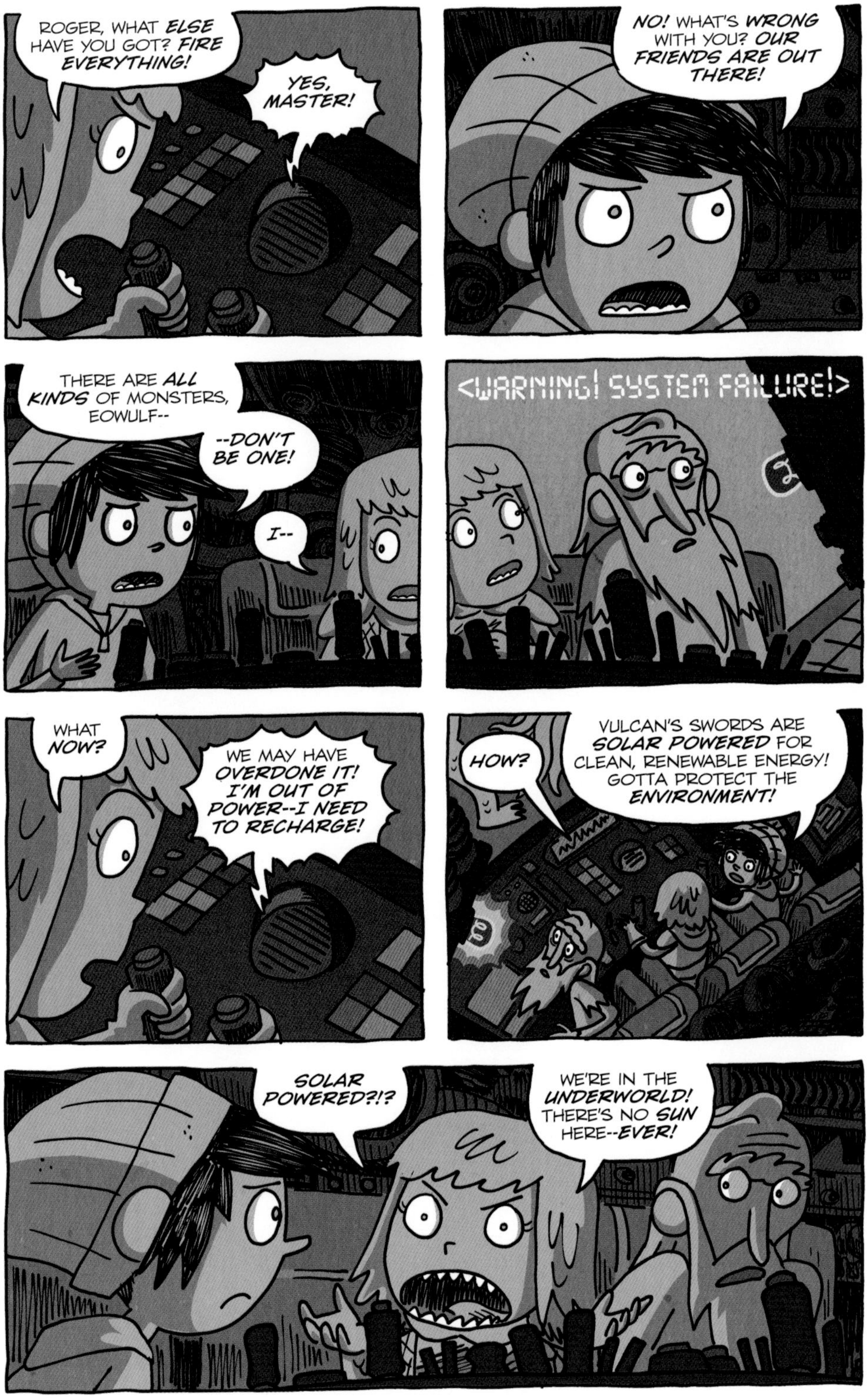
ROGER, WHAT ELSE HAVE YOU GOT? FIRE EVERYTHING!
YES, MASTER!
NO! WHAT'S WRONG WITH YOU? OUR FRIENDS ARE OUT THERE!
THERE ARE ALL KINDS OF MONSTERS, EOWULF--
--DON'T BE ONE!
I--
<WARNING! SYSTEM FAILURE!>
WHAT NOW?
WE MAY HAVE OVERDONE IT! I'M OUT OF POWER--I NEED TO RECHARGE!
HOW?
VULCAN'S SWORDS ARE SOLAR POWERED FOR CLEAN, RENEWABLE ENERGY! GOTTA PROTECT THE ENVIRONMENT!
SOLAR POWERED?!?
WE'RE IN THE UNDERWORLD! THERE'S NO SUN HERE--EVER!

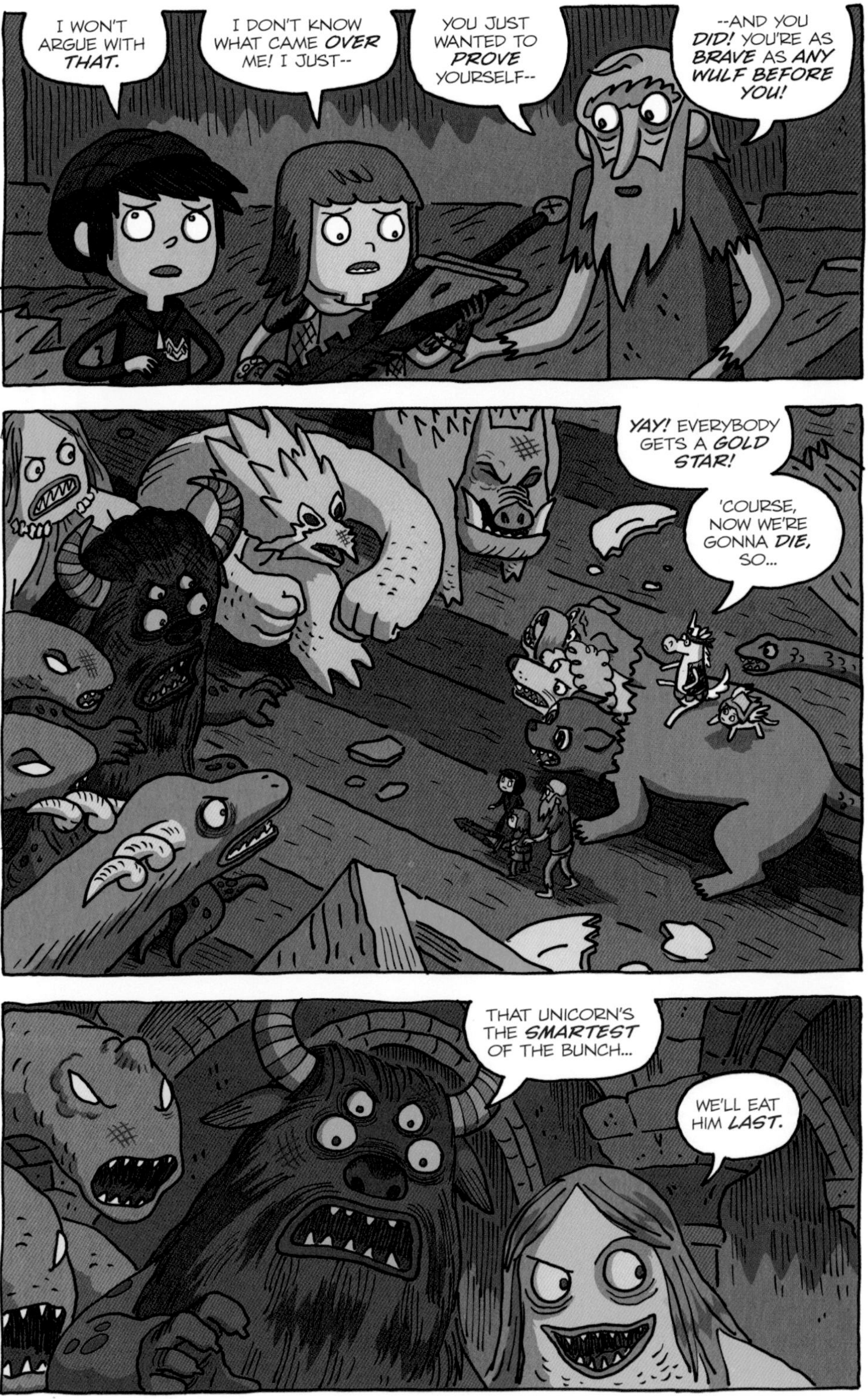
I WON'T ARGUE WITH *THAT.*
I DON'T KNOW WHAT CAME *OVER* ME! I JUST--
YOU JUST WANTED TO *PROVE* YOURSELF--
--AND YOU *DID!* YOU'RE AS *BRAVE* AS *ANY WULF BEFORE YOU!*
*YAY!* EVERYBODY GETS A *GOLD STAR!*
'COURSE, NOW WE'RE GONNA *DIE,* SO...
THAT UNICORN'S THE *SMARTEST* OF THE BUNCH...
WE'LL EAT HIM *LAST.*

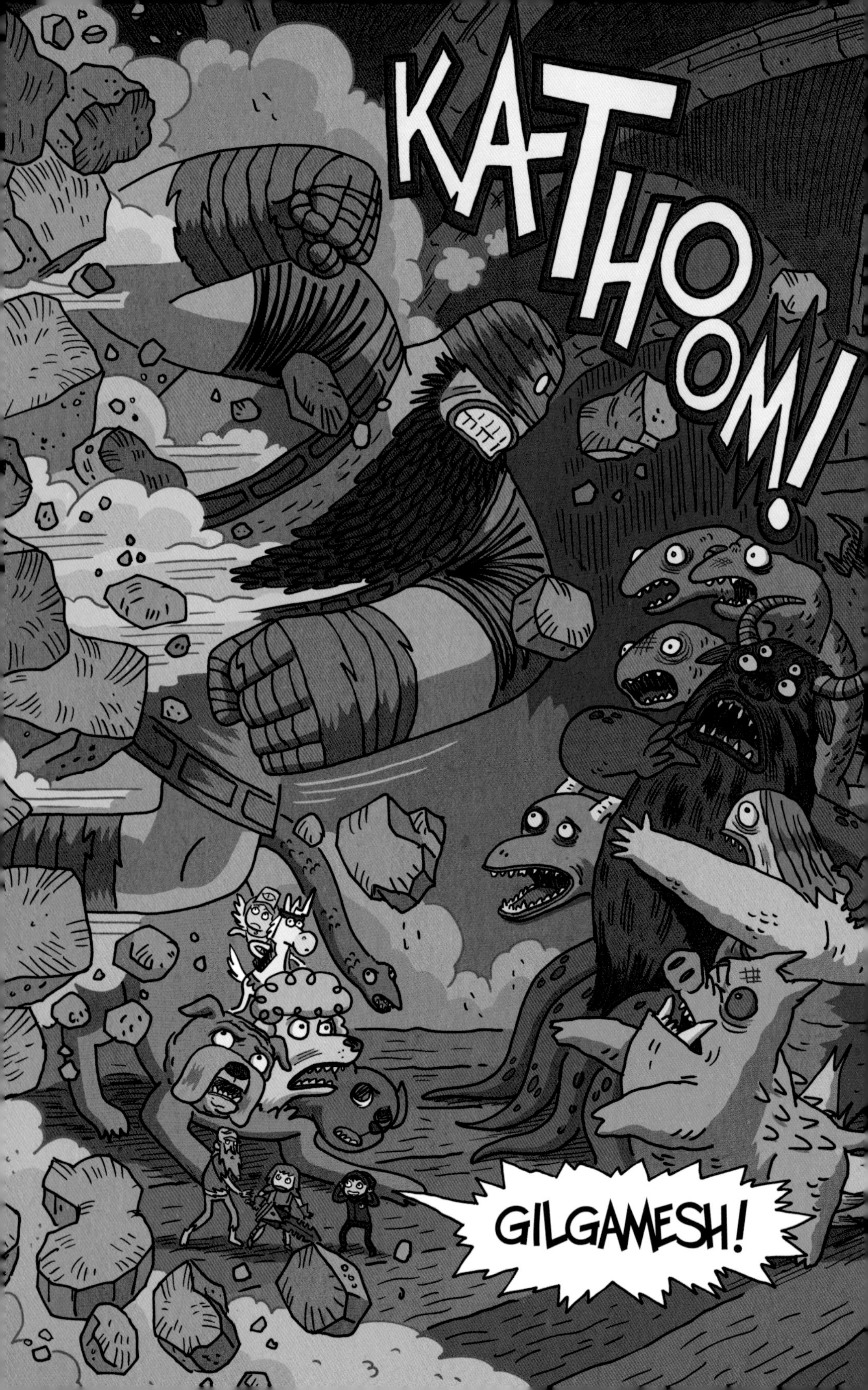
KATHOOM!
GILGAMESH!

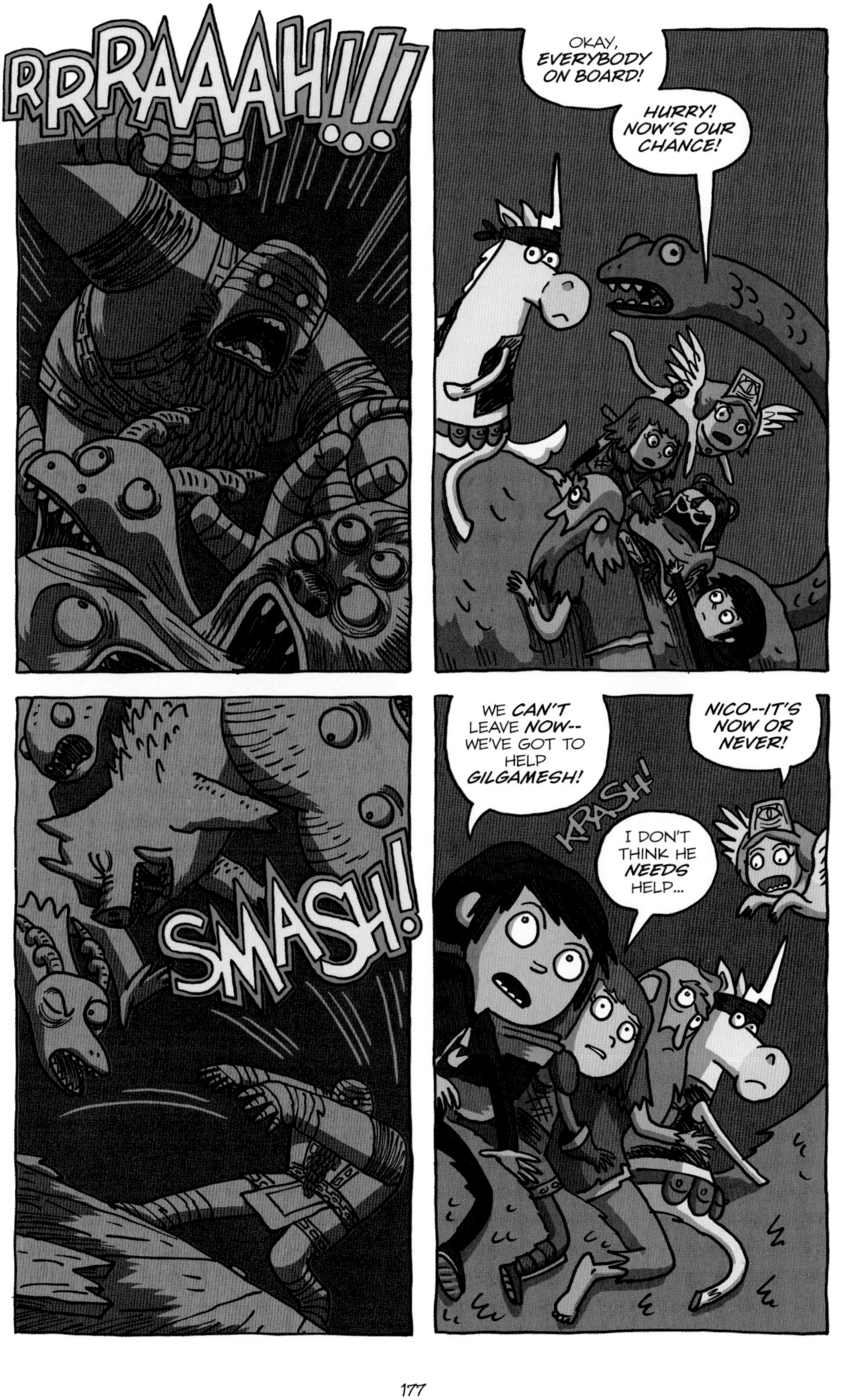
RRRAAAH!!!
OKAY, EVERYBODY ON BOARD!
HURRY! NOW'S OUR CHANCE!
SMASH!
WE CAN'T LEAVE NOW-- WE'VE GOT TO HELP GILGAMESH!
NICO--IT'S NOW OR NEVER!
KRASH!
I DON'T THINK HE NEEDS HELP...

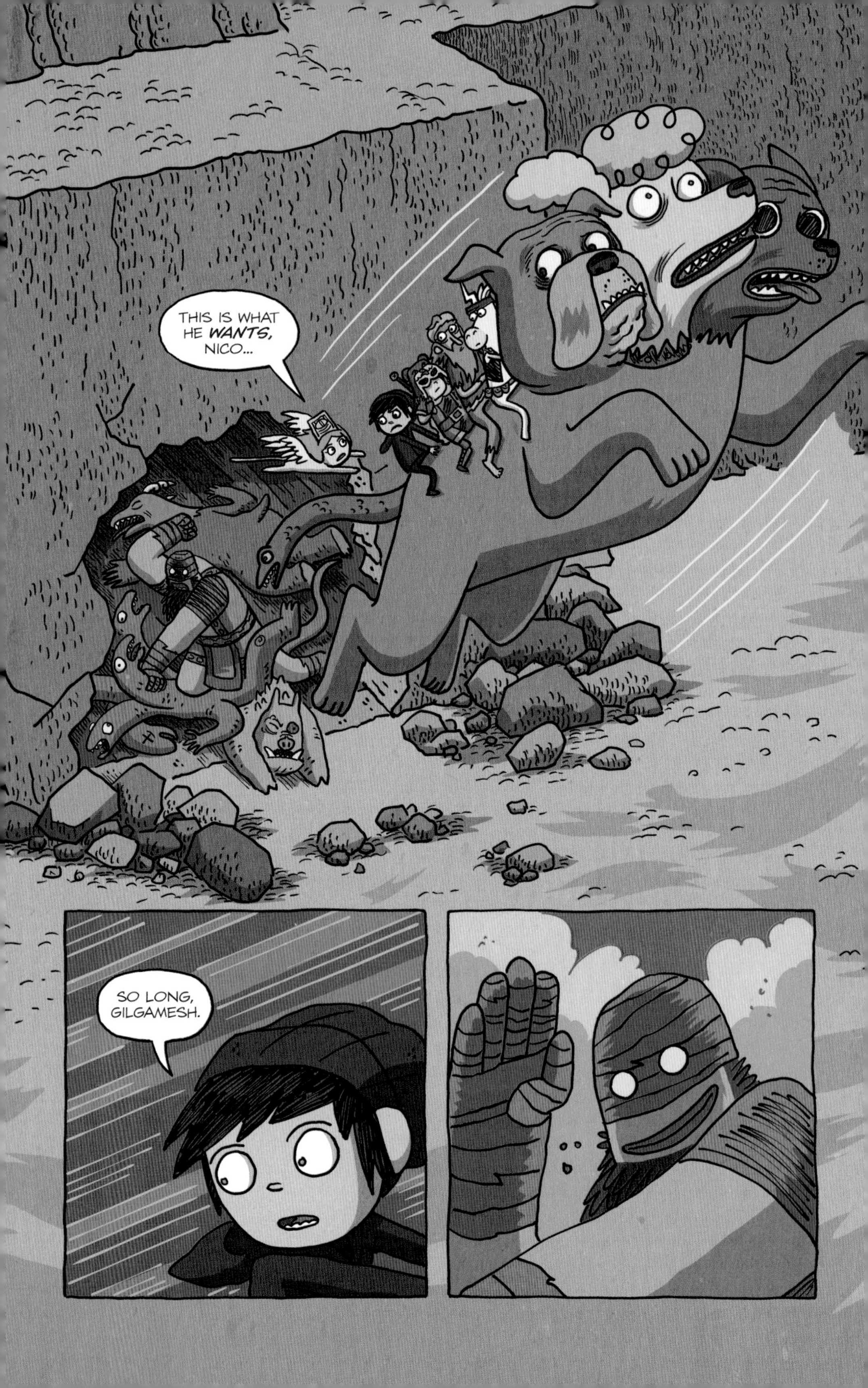
THIS IS WHAT HE WANTS, NICO...
SO LONG, GILGAMESH.

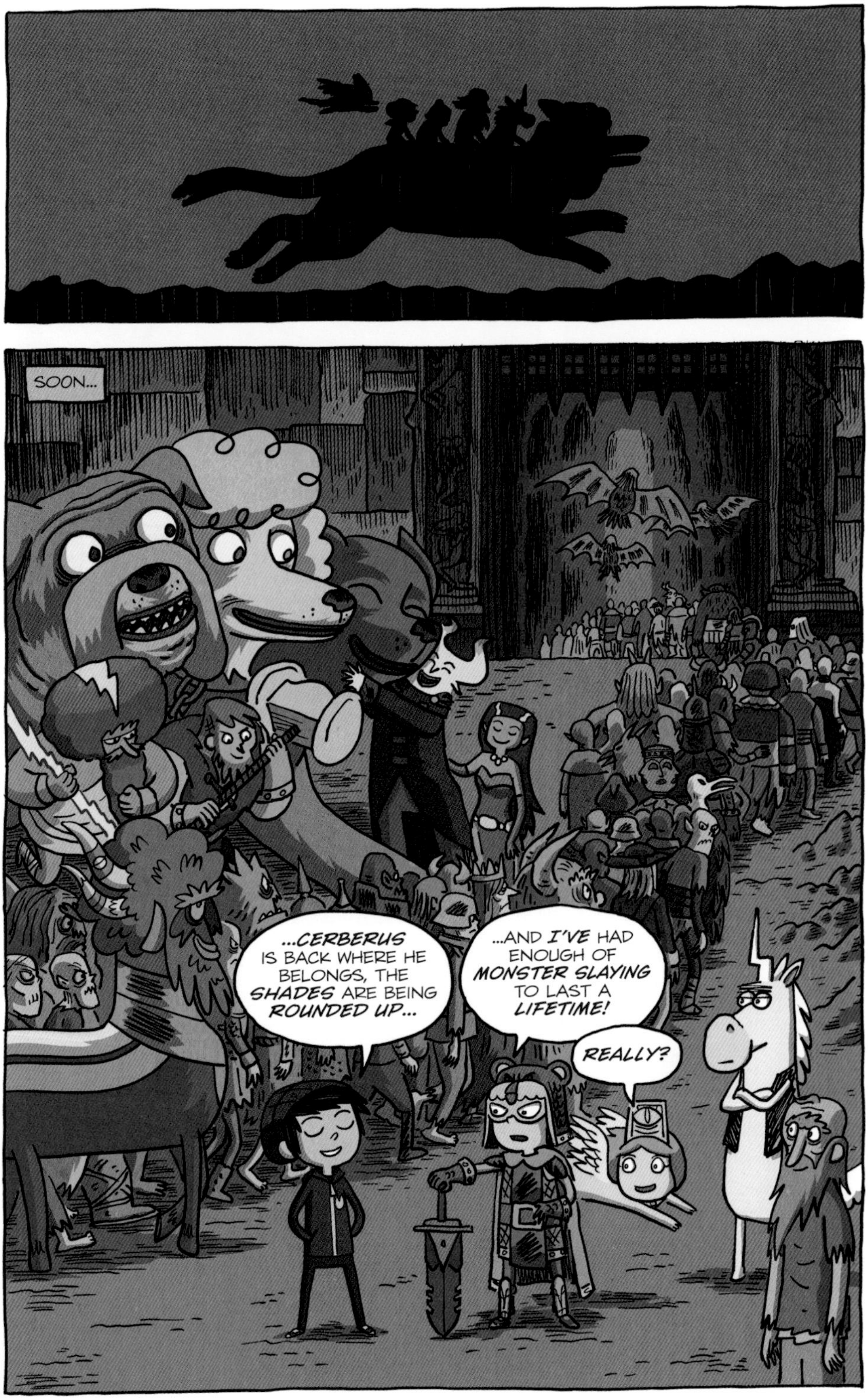
SOON...
...CERBERUS IS BACK WHERE HE BELONGS, THE SHADES ARE BEING ROUNDED UP...
...AND I'VE HAD ENOUGH OF MONSTER SLAYING TO LAST A LIFETIME!
REALLY?

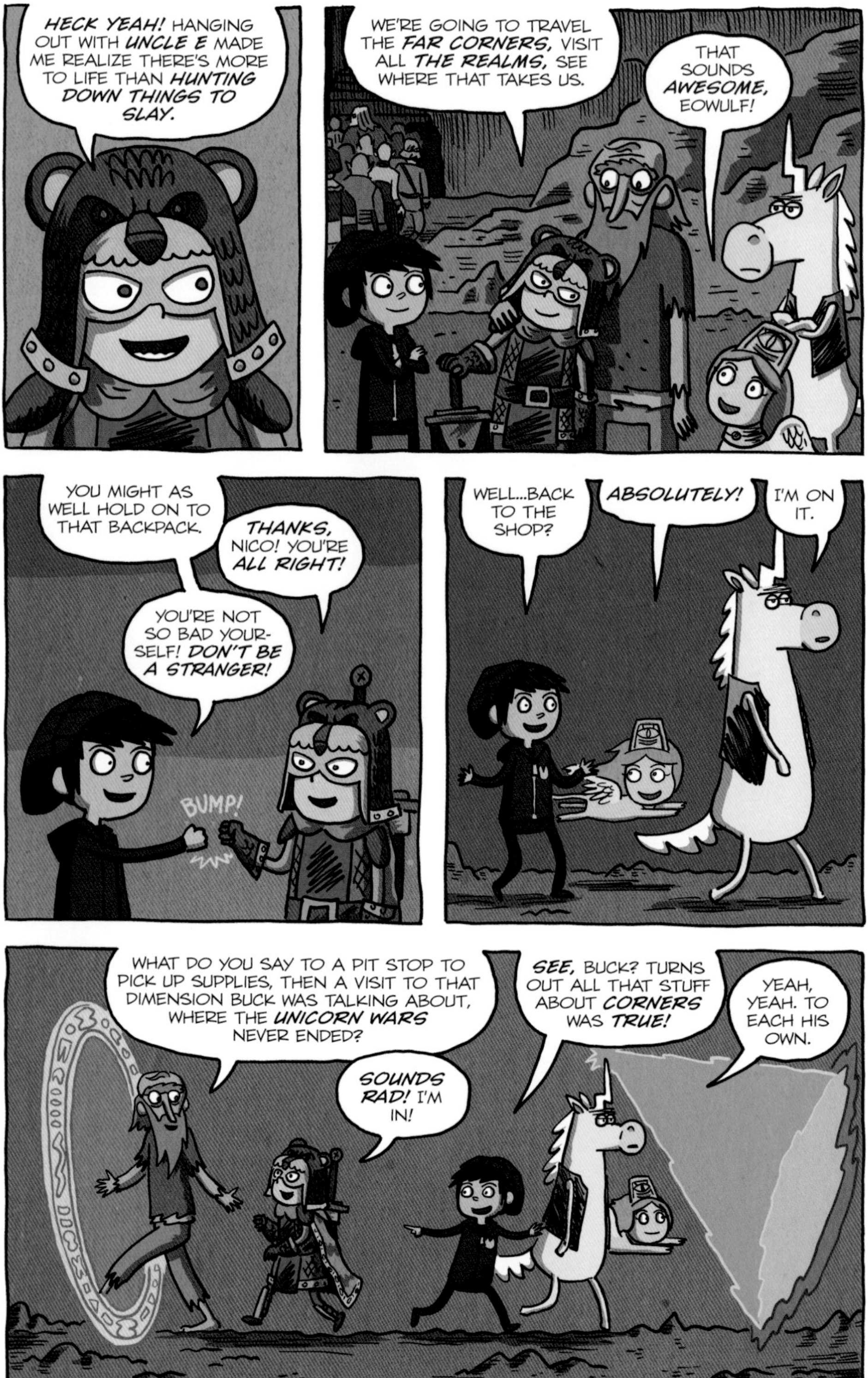
HECK YEAH! HANGING OUT WITH UNCLE E MADE ME REALIZE THERE'S MORE TO LIFE THAN HUNTING DOWN THINGS TO SLAY.
WE'RE GOING TO TRAVEL THE FAR CORNERS, VISIT ALL THE REALMS, SEE WHERE THAT TAKES US.
THAT SOUNDS AWESOME, EOWULF!
YOU MIGHT AS WELL HOLD ON TO THAT BACKPACK.
THANKS, NICO! YOU'RE ALL RIGHT!
YOU'RE NOT SO BAD YOURSELF! DON'T BE A STRANGER!
BUMP!
WELL...BACK TO THE SHOP?
ABSOLUTELY!
I'M ON IT.
WHAT DO YOU SAY TO A PIT STOP TO PICK UP SUPPLIES, THEN A VISIT TO THAT DIMENSION BUCK WAS TALKING ABOUT, WHERE THE UNICORN WARS NEVER ENDED?
SOUNDS RAD! I'M IN!
SEE, BUCK? TURNS OUT ALL THAT STUFF ABOUT CORNERS WAS TRUE!
YEAH, YEAH. TO EACH HIS OWN.

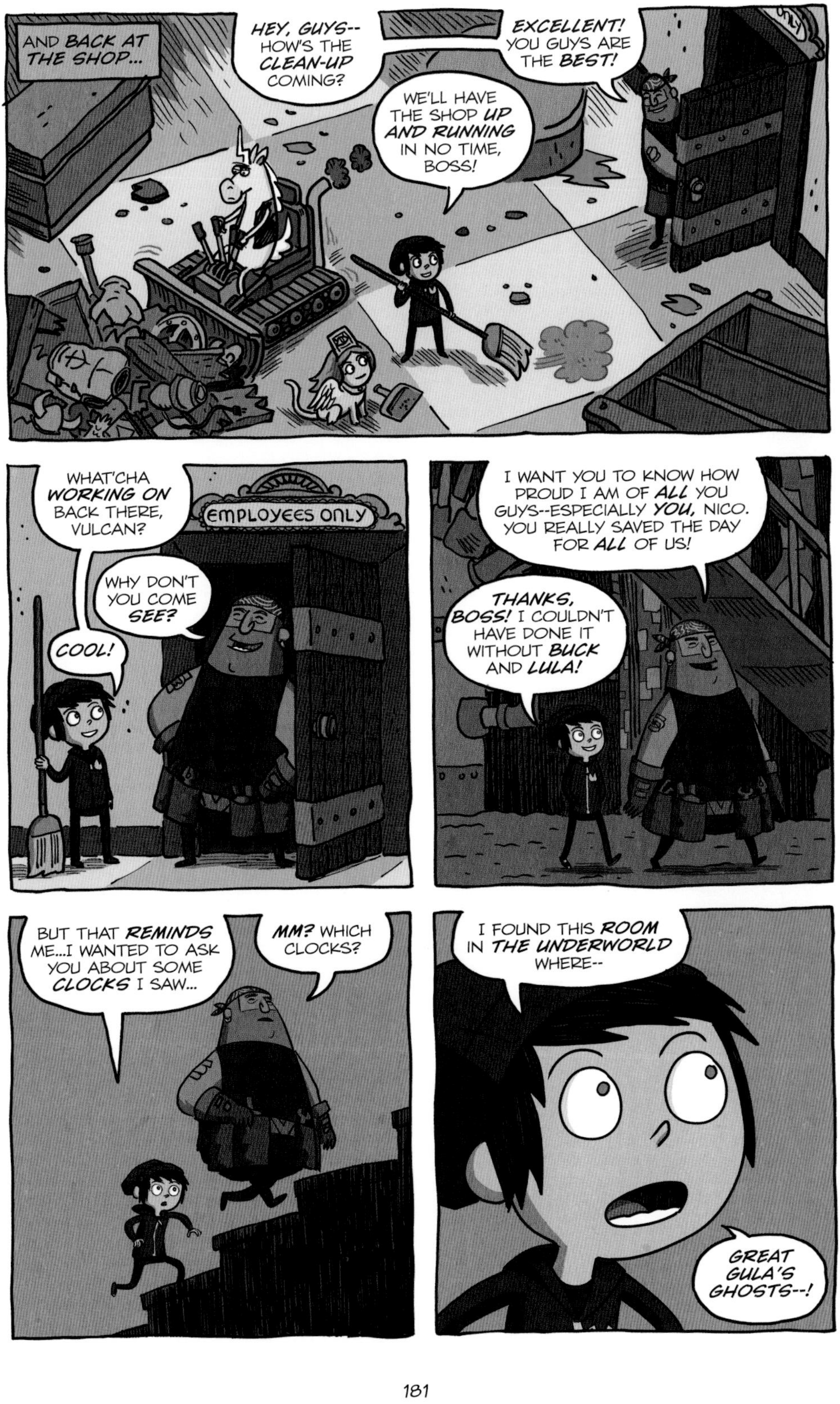
AND BACK AT THE SHOP...
HEY, GUYS-- HOW'S THE CLEAN-UP COMING?
WE'LL HAVE THE SHOP UP AND RUNNING IN NO TIME, BOSS!
EXCELLENT! YOU GUYS ARE THE BEST!
WHAT'CHA WORKING ON BACK THERE, VULCAN?
EMPLOYEES ONLY
WHY DON'T YOU COME SEE?
COOL!
I WANT YOU TO KNOW HOW PROUD I AM OF ALL YOU GUYS--ESPECIALLY YOU, NICO. YOU REALLY SAVED THE DAY FOR ALL OF US!
THANKS, BOSS! I COULDN'T HAVE DONE IT WITHOUT BUCK AND LULA!
BUT THAT REMINDS ME...I WANTED TO ASK YOU ABOUT SOME CLOCKS I SAW...
MM? WHICH CLOCKS?
I FOUND THIS ROOM IN THE UNDERWORLD WHERE--
GREAT GULA'S GHOSTS--!

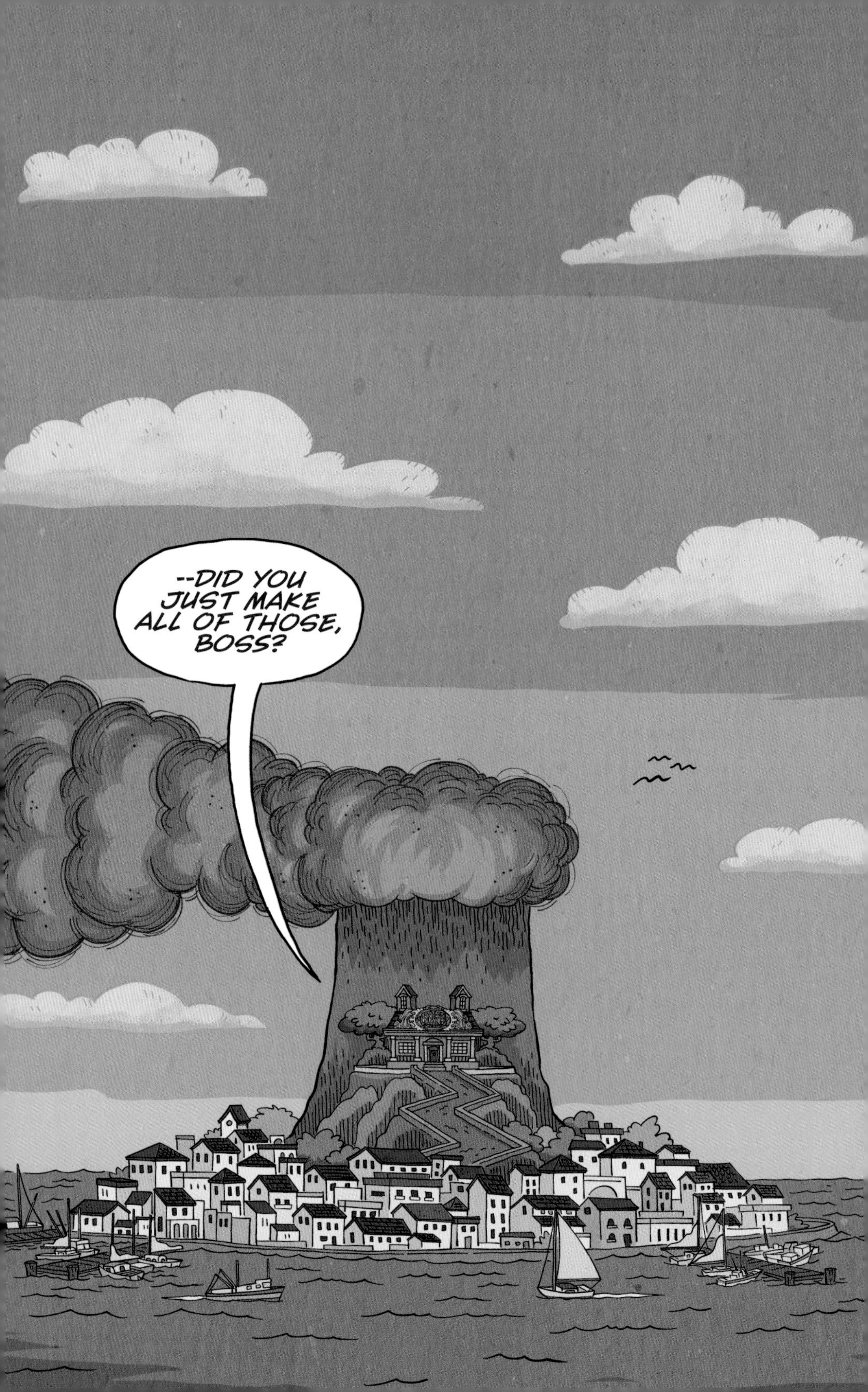
--DID YOU JUST MAKE ALL OF THOSE, BOSS?

# Epilogue

NEW JERSEY.
DEOWULF!
WHERE DOES THAT MAN DISAPPEAR TO?
DEOWULF!
IN HERE, DEAR! ORGANIZING MY CLAW COLLECTION!

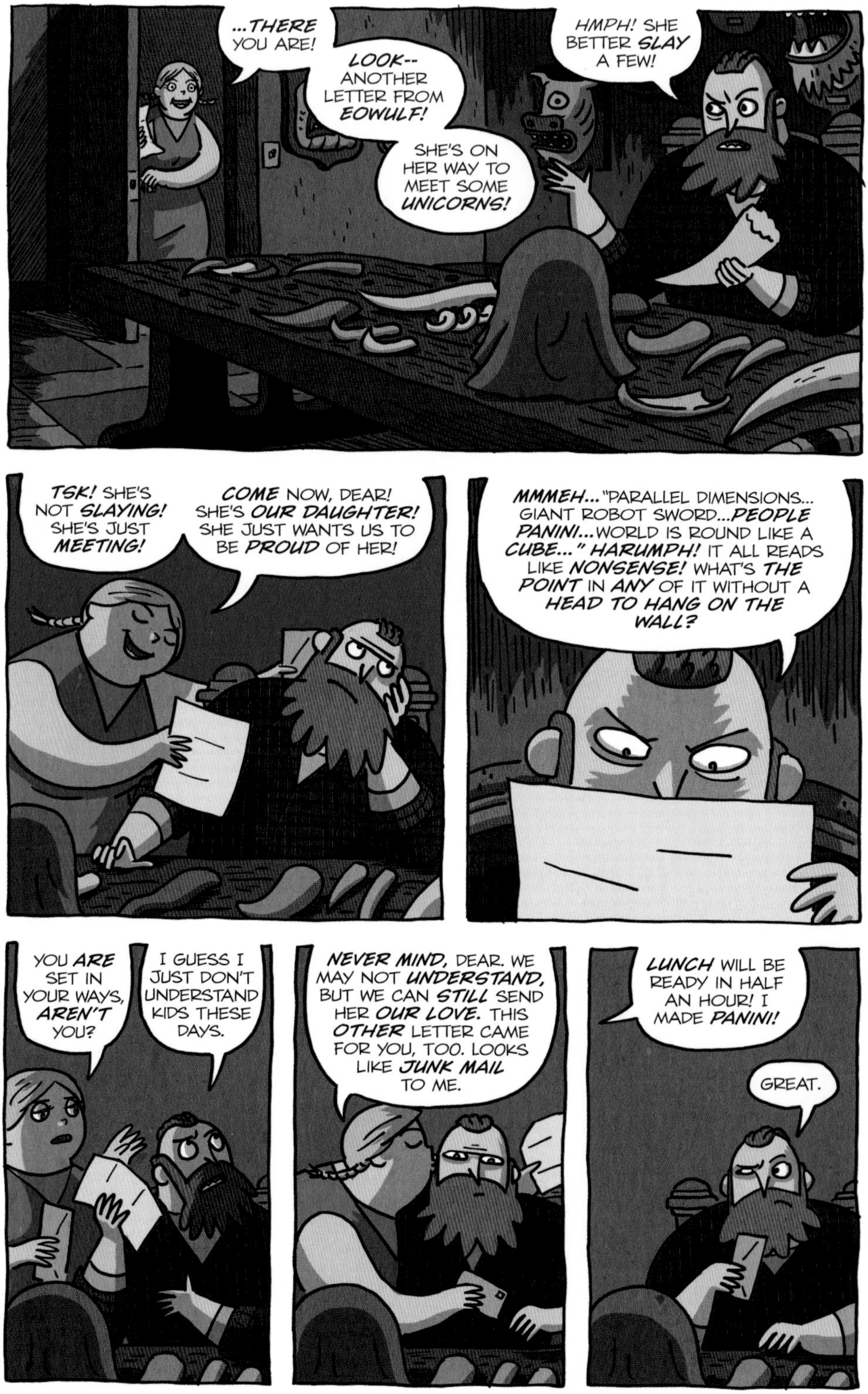
...THERE YOU ARE!
LOOK-- ANOTHER LETTER FROM EOWULF!
SHE'S ON HER WAY TO MEET SOME UNICORNS!
HMPH! SHE BETTER SLAY A FEW!
TSK! SHE'S NOT SLAYING! SHE'S JUST MEETING!
COME NOW, DEAR! SHE'S OUR DAUGHTER! SHE JUST WANTS US TO BE PROUD OF HER!
MMMEH... "PARALLEL DIMENSIONS... GIANT ROBOT SWORD...PEOPLE PANINI...WORLD IS ROUND LIKE A CUBE..." HARUMPH! IT ALL READS LIKE NONSENSE! WHAT'S THE POINT IN ANY OF IT WITHOUT A HEAD TO HANG ON THE WALL?
YOU ARE SET IN YOUR WAYS, AREN'T YOU?
I GUESS I JUST DON'T UNDERSTAND KIDS THESE DAYS.
NEVER MIND, DEAR. WE MAY NOT UNDERSTAND, BUT WE CAN STILL SEND HER OUR LOVE. THIS OTHER LETTER CAME FOR YOU, TOO. LOOKS LIKE JUNK MAIL TO ME.
LUNCH WILL BE READY IN HALF AN HOUR! I MADE PANINI!
GREAT.

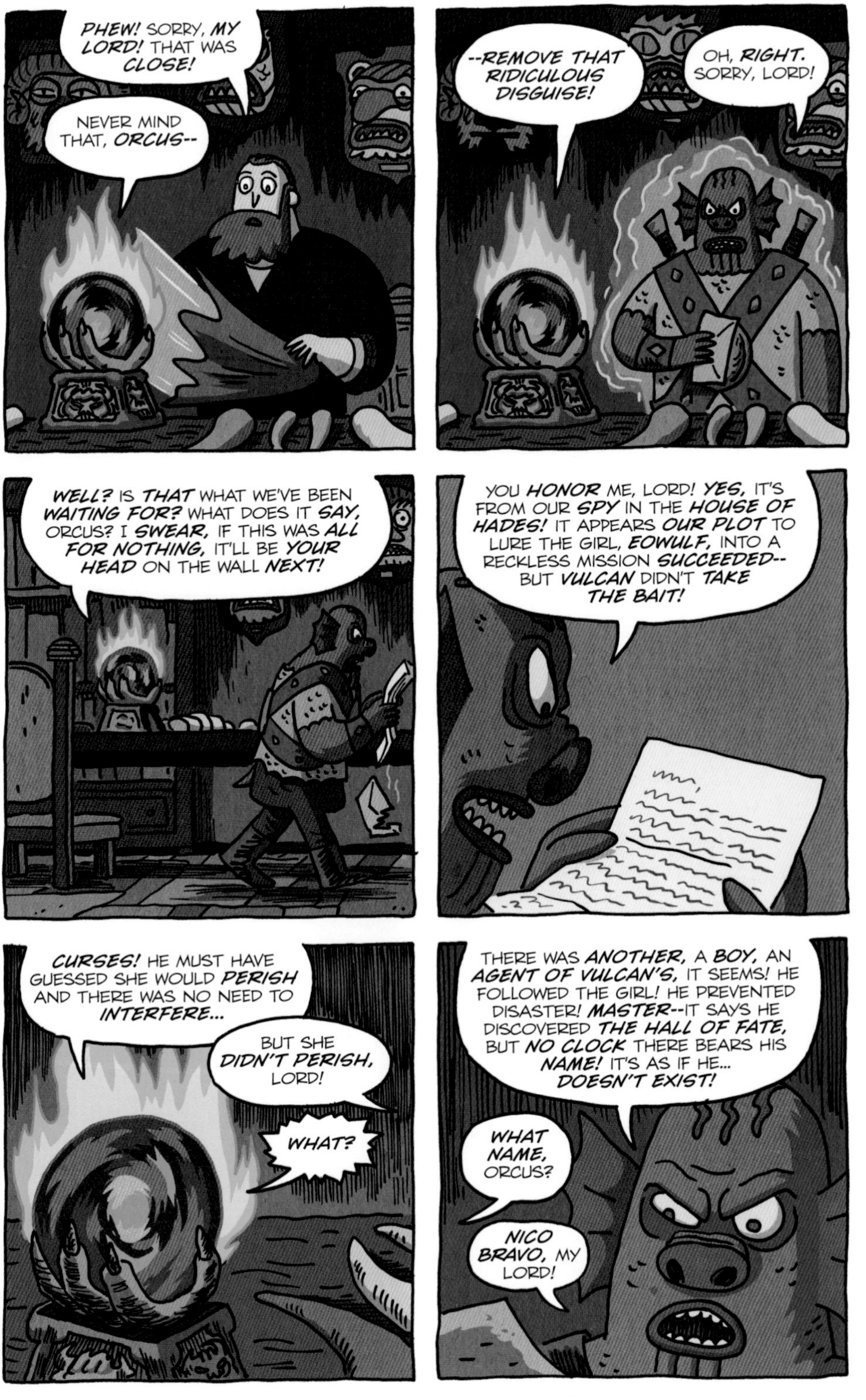
PHEW! SORRY, MY LORD! THAT WAS CLOSE!
NEVER MIND THAT, ORCUS--
--REMOVE THAT RIDICULOUS DISGUISE!
OH, RIGHT. SORRY, LORD!
WELL? IS THAT WHAT WE'VE BEEN WAITING FOR? WHAT DOES IT SAY, ORCUS? I SWEAR, IF THIS WAS ALL FOR NOTHING, IT'LL BE YOUR HEAD ON THE WALL NEXT!
YOU HONOR ME, LORD! YES, IT'S FROM OUR SPY IN THE HOUSE OF HADES! IT APPEARS OUR PLOT TO LURE THE GIRL, EOWULF, INTO A RECKLESS MISSION SUCCEEDED-- BUT VULCAN DIDN'T TAKE THE BAIT!
CURSES! HE MUST HAVE GUESSED SHE WOULD PERISH AND THERE WAS NO NEED TO INTERFERE...
BUT SHE DIDN'T PERISH, LORD!
WHAT?
THERE WAS ANOTHER, A BOY, AN AGENT OF VULCAN'S, IT SEEMS! HE FOLLOWED THE GIRL! HE PREVENTED DISASTER! MASTER--IT SAYS HE DISCOVERED THE HALL OF FATE, BUT NO CLOCK THERE BEARS HIS NAME! IT'S AS IF HE... DOESN'T EXIST!
WHAT NAME, ORCUS?
NICO BRAVO, MY LORD!

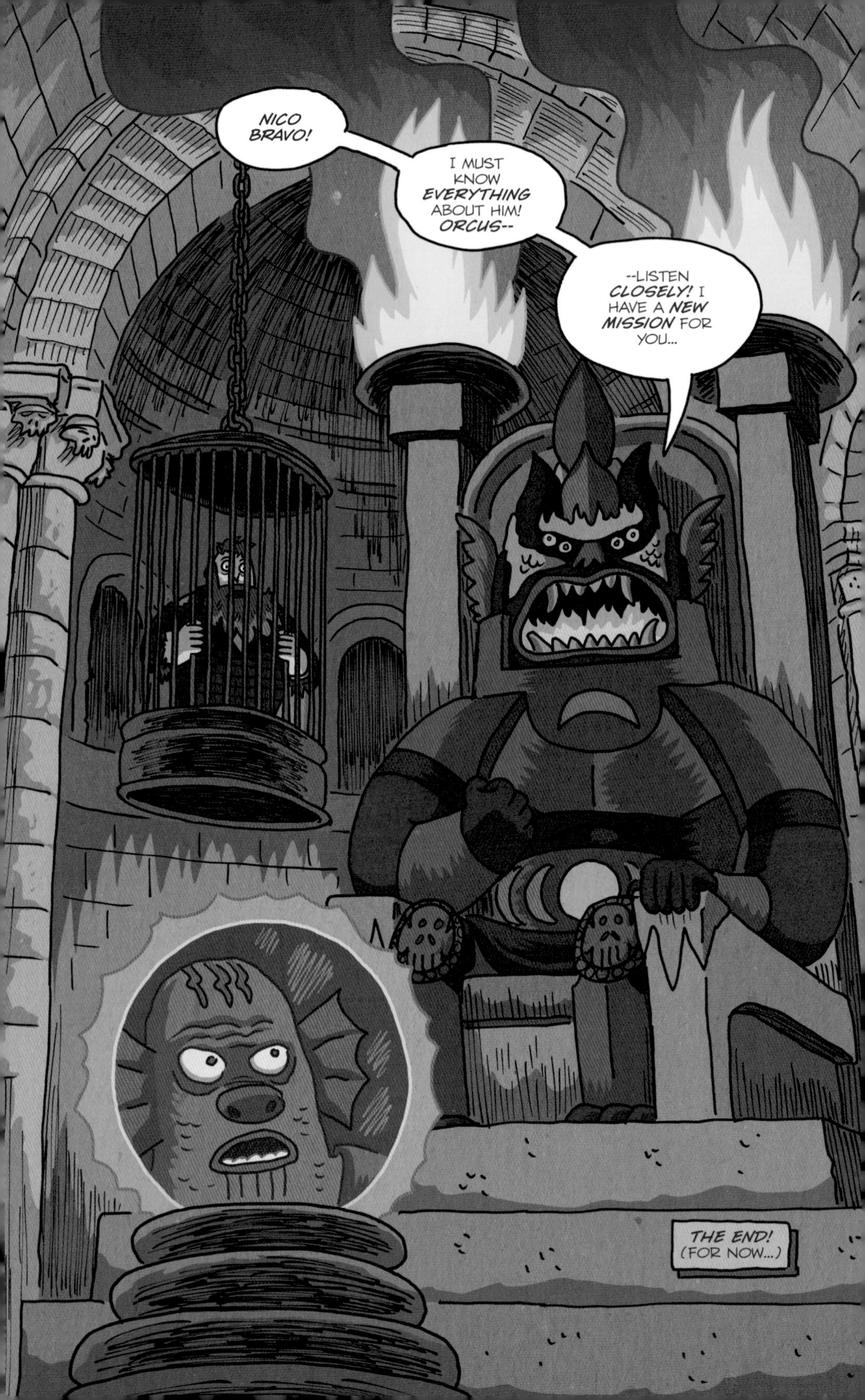
NICO BRAVO!
I MUST KNOW EVERYTHING ABOUT HIM! ORCUS--
--LISTEN CLOSELY! I HAVE A NEW MISSION FOR YOU...
THE END! (FOR NOW...)

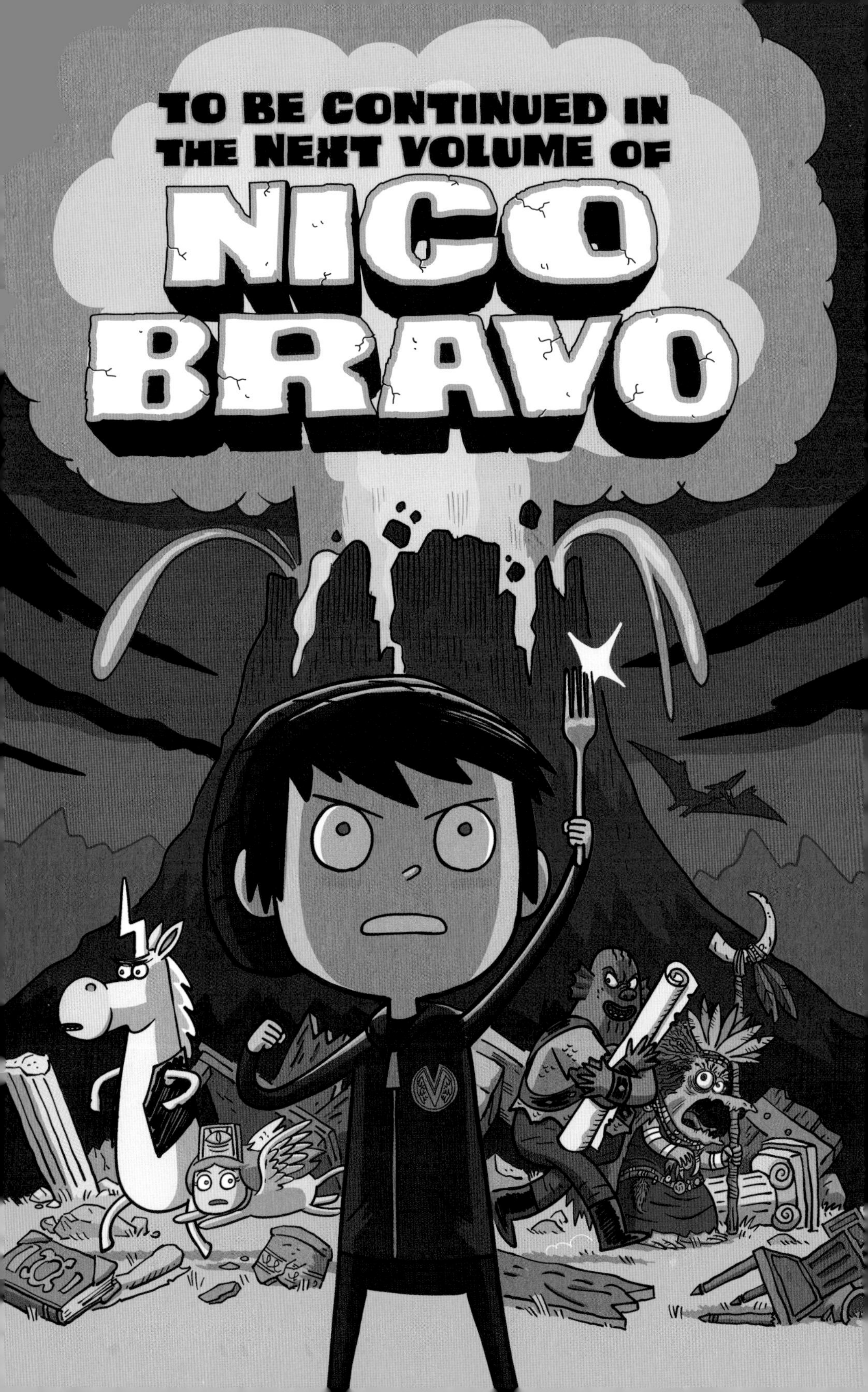
TO BE CONTINUED IN THE NEXT VOLUME OF
NICO BRAVO

# THANK YOU

GIORGIA AND FRANK CAVALLARO; LISA NATOLI;
NICK ABADZIS; ANDREW ARNOLD; ROBYN CHAPMAN;
PETER DE SÈVE; SCOTT FRIEDLANDER; DEAN HASPIEL;
JOE INFURNARI; GEORGE O'CONNOR; JOAN REILLY;
BEN SHARPE; MARK SIEGEL; ED STECKLEY; STEVE BEHLING;
SARA VARON; KIARA VALDEZ; COLLEEN AF VENABLE;
THE BOUNCING SOULS FAMILY: GREG, SHANTI, PETE, BRYAN,
GEORGE, K8, MATTY, JANA, WIG, AND AUDREY;
AND CARYN WISEMAN AT ANDREA BROWN LITERARY AGENCY.